DATE DUE

~~7-23-07~~			
~~6-2~~-14			
9-29-17			

POINT OF HONOR

Douglas De Bono

Writers Club Press
San Jose New York Lincoln Shanghai

Point of Honor

Published by Writers Club Press
an imprint of iUniverse.com, Inc.

For information address:
iUniverse.com, Inc.
620 North 48th Street
Suite 201
Lincoln, NE 68504-3467
www.iuniverse.com

ISBN: 0-595-09724-3

Printed in the United States of America

SERIES

Blood Covenant

This is the very first manuscript,
and it is dedicated to the very best.

For Cathy

Contents

PROLOGUE

Presidential Palace Near Baghdad

Saddam Hussein perused the two pages in his hands. He sat in a high-backed chair at a priceless, antique French desk. The desk and chair were on an elevated platform with gold-laced tapestries hanging behind the Great Leader. The carpeting was a royal red; pillared golden candle stands marked the borders of the room. The trademark black .45 ACP pistols lay casually on the top of the French desk. The muzzles pointed carelessly towards the entry door.

A dour man with thick black hair and scarred hands from his former street fighting days, Hussein now had others to kill for him. It was rumored he still used his guns to murder those who displeased him. His flat black eyes showed no joy or compassion, and the trademark mustache hung heavily over his upper lip. Today he was dressed in khaki fatigues that he found more comfortable than a Western Style suit coat and tie.

Members of his personal bodyguard stood inside and outside the doorway. Each held a machine pistol, and submitted anyone entering the room to a full body search in addition to passing through an airport style metal detector. A trained, bomb-sniffing dog waited outside the doorway under the watchful gaze of its handler. Saddam Hussein protected himself not only from the masses—most of whom were too poor and frightened to attempt anything so bold as assassination—but also from the colonels in his own armed forces.

Generals could be watched easily. They had achieved their rank, and as long as the graft was not terribly expensive, generals understood their place. It was the anxious colonels who always seemed to be plotting grander schemes and greater glory. Saddam went through a lot of colonels.

He looked up to the two people standing twenty paces from his desk. He nodded as he went down the target list: Tel Aviv, Jerusalem, Haifa, Kuwait City, Tehran, Tabriz, Qom, Al-Jawf, Riyadh, and Ankara.

"Add Amman and Damascus to this list. They were cowards who buckled to Bush." It came out BUUUUSH. Every time he considered the former American President, his eyes bulged a little wider and his blood pressure rose a bit higher. "They are not Arab brothers, they are American lackeys." He spat.

Colonel Duri nodded and mentally added the names to the target list. He had no paper or anything to write with. He was painfully aware that at least two rifles were pointed at the center of his back—one of the prices for serving the Great Leader.

The other standing next to Duri was nicknamed *Doctor Germ* by Western weapons experts. Doctor Rihab Rashida al-Awazi was a rather plain woman at age forty-two. It was hard to reconcile this new mother of a baby girl with being Saddam's chief chemical and biological weapons architect. Her black hair pulled back in a loose bun, she stood with hands folded before her. The printed dress hung loosely over her shoulders. She simply did not look like someone who had designed a weapon system capable of killing cities.

"The warheads, Doctor, they will work with this wonder weapon from our Chinese friends?"

She nodded quietly. It was her wonder weapon; the Chinese simply provided the manufacturing facilities. She kept her peace. It was best not to anger the Great Leader.

"We are expecting to receive five casks. They each hold maybe twenty liters of VX-Beta."

"And how much per warhead?" Saddam asked looking back to the target list.

"One liter per warhead. That should have a dispersal radius of five kilometers."

Saddam pulled at his mustache. "The effects?"

She lifted her head proudly, for VX-Beta was primarily her invention. Western analysts called VX-Beta the *City Killer*. Iraq had to mass-produce the chemical in China. Iraq simply did not have the capacity to produce the required amounts without the Americans discovering something. "There is no antidote. There is no degradation in effects. Wherever you aim the missile, they will die. VX-Beta will continue to kill indefinitely. The tests in China indicate they continue to have lethal effects in areas exposed to weather for the past several years. It is no longer a persistent chemical agent, it is a permanent chemical agent," Rashida al-Awazi concluded triumphantly.

"You are certain?" Saddam asked, his eyes dead cold.

Without blinking, Rashida al-Awazi replied boldly, "Yes."

Saddam shifted his focus back to Colonel Duri. "When is the delivery scheduled?"

"Friday night."

Saddam nodded carefully. "We will then stage the incident on Wednesday."

Duri smiled slightly, "Yes, Sir. It doesn't matter where UNSCOM goes, we will deny the weapon inspection teams access to the hotels if need be. It should focus the American satellites and spy planes on those facilities."

"And away from the sea," finished Saddam. United Nations Special Commission (UNSCOM) served as an umbrella organization for America's weapon inspection program. This too changed. At the end of the Gulf War, Iraq held its breath under the threat of the massive Allied Armies. Saddam signed agreements permitting the West to search for banned weapons throughout his country. The alternative had been annihilation, but who would be so stupid as to believe he would live up to the agreements? *The Americans—that's who.*

"Yes, away from the sea," agreed Duri.

"And the missiles?"

"By early next year, twenty Al-Hussein and thirty-five Al-Abbas will be fitted with VX-Beta specific warheads. We probably will be ready to launch sometime in mid February."

Saddam bristled somewhat at the mention of the Al-Abbas missile. It had a range of one hundred fifty kilometers greater than the Al-Hussein named after himself. "Valentine's Day. We will do it when the Americans show their sentimental weakness. You will be able to hit the carriers?" he asked eagerly.

Duri had no idea whether the modified SCUD missiles could even find the *USS George Washington* or *USS Nimitz* carriers. The SCUD was basically an unguided missile that more or less landed within twenty kilometers of where it was sent. Of course, to admit something that might not be as the Great Leader believed could be fatal—especially when they were planning the deaths of thousands of Jews and Arabs. "Yes," he lied.

Saddam held his gaze and looked back to the target list. "You'll be aiming more than one at these targets?"

"The Jews get three each as do the Iranians and Saudis. The rest are distributed among the other targets," he explained.

Saddam rubbed his hands together. "And will they suffer as they die? Will the Jews who bombed my reactor finally be punished?"

Rihab Rashida al-Awazi replied clinically, "First they will have severe convulsions. The spasms will be so violent that even those with biological warfare suits will succumb. Some will lapse into comas; others will simply feel their ability to breathe cease. Death will come eventually. The attacks will come without warning."

"As they deserve," concluded Saddam. He fixed his gaze on Duri and said, "Do it."

Colonel Duri saluted, realizing he had been dismissed.

AP November 12, 1997—Hundreds of Iraqi citizens were ushered into presidential compounds to act as human shields against possible American strikes on suspected weapons depot facilities. UNSCOM inspectors were refused entry to suspected Iraqi weapon facilities.

AP November 14, 1997—Ambassador Richard Butler the head of the UNSCOM weapons inspection teams decided to pull all inspection teams out of Iraq. The turmoil surrounding suspect weapons sites amid rumors of increased activity around the USS George Washington and USS Nimitz battle groups makes it impossible to continue their mission.

PART 1

A Gathering of Warriors

"Should foreign nations...deceived by [an] appearance of division and weakness, render it necessary to vindicate by arms the injuries to our country, I believe...that the spirit of the revolution is unextinguished, and that the cultivators of peace will again, as on that occasion, be transformed at once into a nation of warriors who will leave us nothing to fear for the natural and national rights of our country."

Thomas Jefferson 1809

1

Washington DC, Saturday, November 15, 1997, 10:00 AM EST

Brian Stillwell walked through the metal detectors and retrieved his briefcase from the Marine guard after passing through the security checkpoint to the Pentagon's E ring. While the checkpoint looked like most airport security checkpoints, the difference was the Marine guards actually watched the monitors and checked for weapons. They had 9mm Beretta pistols strapped to their sides and M16 A2 rifles nearby on ready racks.

He followed the signs to the *Tank*. The *Tank* was a secure, windowless room buried beneath ground level that was impervious to all known forms of surveillance technology. Of course, in the current era of peace and goodwill, one only worried about Chinese nukes, the burgeoning Indian Navy, a collection of Arabs, starving Korean madmen, and the occasional Russian weapon of mass destruction gone missing. Oh for the Cold War days, when an enemy could be clearly drawn on the map. You counted their tanks; they counted your fighters. Now you had to worry about Ebola showing up in somebody's shaving kit at JFK.

The National Security Advisor, the Deputy Secretary of State for Middle Eastern Affairs, the Secretary of the Navy, a handful of generals, and other spooks preceded Brian into the *Tank*. All were checked against a retinal scan and a Marine guard checked off each name on clipboard before entering. Something heavy indeed must be going down to pull this many self appointed VIP's away from their Saturday morning play times. Not that it mattered to Stillwell; he was dressed in black jeans, an Annapolis sweatshirt, and new Nikes. He had no reverence for most of those present except the military men who had put it on the line and the Marine guards who might end up in some forsaken no name place fighting for God and country.

Stillwell found a spot reserved for him. He moved his name card out of the way to set his notepad before him and his briefcase next to the chair. He found himself seated at a table next to a collection of spooks and someone from the FBI (probably the counter terrorism unit). These days everything seemed to boil down to countering some sort of threat. Since flight 800 had turned into a fireworks display over Long Island Sound and Oklahoma City had erupted into a morning killing spree, no one seemed to rule out terrorism—domestic or otherwise. It was the *otherwise* that brought Brian to this airless, windowless room on a lovely fall day.

Outside the sun was shining a warm brilliance still possible for mid-November in Washington. The grass remained green with birds chirping in varicolored trees. Lawn tractors were busily scooping leaves into pull-behind carts; kids were chasing basketballs across hardtop and others chased the elusive oblong football. The NFL and NBA were in full swing, and Saturday mornings were a great time for kids to play at being the next Michael Jordan or Joe Montana.

Brian lived in a world populated by grainy satellite photos, dossiers of crazed world leaders, and deadly weapons most people had never heard of. He was an expert, for sale to the highest bidder, as long as the bidder was a government or business friendly to the Uncle Sam. These days friendship was defined by the largest illegal campaign contribution made in the most recent election. Brian sometimes mused whether the crooks in the current administration or the bad guys on the other side of the world represented a greater threat. He suspected it was still the bad guys on the other side of the world.

The normal introductions were made. Surprisingly, the National Security Advisor took control of the meeting. Usually, something in the *Tank* was the purview of the Joint Chiefs. A map of the Persian Gulf snapped up on the digital display screen at the end of the *Tank*. Brian sighed, *another oil mess*. Considering the map was centered on Kuwait, Iraq, and Iran, it didn't take a rocket scientist to figure out Saddam was up to something.

Brian believed the Bush Administration should have let the 24th Mechanized infantry and the 101st Airborne roll into Baghdad when they had the chance. It would have simplified life. Instead, Uncle had parleyed away a battlefield victory for an expensive stalemate. It kept precious resources monitoring Saddam, when the real enemy was across the Persian Gulf working on their own missile platforms, biological weapons and nuclear bombs. Nightmarish artifacts recently procured from the disintegrating Soviet Empire—*All for the glory of Allah.*

A briefing officer stepped to the podium that controlled the screen. He was arrayed in full dress blues, obviously young, and intense. A prominent Adam's apple bobbed as he gulped air waiting for the NSA to finish his introduction. Stillwell had been that briefing officer once. Albeit, not here and not before this many heavies. He had brought the bad news about many nasty problems before Generals, Admirals, and the odd Senator. Thankfully, many of those problems never made it to CNN or the *Washington Post*.

"Approximately twelve hours ago, this series of photos was taken by an unscheduled U2 flight. This particular flight followed the course of the Tigris River from Baghdad to the Shat al Arab." A red dotted border drew a southeastern line from the center of Iraq to the narrow access Saddam had to the Persian Gulf and ultimately to Western ports. It made sense to run unscheduled U2 reconnaissance flights, because Saddam had certainly bought the overflight schedules for American satellites from our steadfast allies in the Russian Federation, or maybe it was the French. Brian mused how long it would be before Tony

Blair—the British Prime Minister—would tire of this expensive game. The screen switched to the hazy, graininess associated with infrared and high altitude night vision photography.

"The U2 continued into the Gulf for approximately one hundred klicks before turning west and landing inside Kuwait." Brian wondered how many of the civilians did not know that klick was slang for kilometer. Regardless of Arab solidarity, Kuwait made sure the United States had whatever facilities it required to keep the nightmare to the north at bay. The Iraqi invasion during the 1990 summer had created an anomaly—pragmatic Arab leadership.

The next photo was a reconnaissance from some other time. It revealed the conning tower of a submarine with the number *404* clearly painted in white on the side. "This is a file photo of a Chinese Han class PLAN naval submarine. It is a nuclear powered boat placed in service in 1988. It is comparable to a Russian Victor class boat, and this particular boat is capable of launching surface-to-surface missiles.

"We know the Chinese do not take kindly to American battle groups paying close attention to their activities. In October 1994, J-7III fighters challenged an S-3B anti-submarine warfare plane from the *Kitty Hawk*. There are five known boats in this class, although, the first boat—the 401—is not believed to be in service due to radiation leaks." He paused as the screen dissolved into another photo from the U2.

"Last night a Han class boat—the *404*—was spotted on the surface fifty klicks from the mouth of the Tigris River." The screen dissolved to the overhead silhouette identified as a *Han* class boat.

Stillwell sat forward in his chair. A Chinese SSN on the surface in the Persian Gulf, as close as possible to Iraq in the middle of the night, was not suppose to happen. A decided rumble emerged across the room. Everyone, except some of the State Department and White House aides, recognized the gravity of the reconnaissance photo on display. Chinese boats did not play outside the South China Sea. Certainly, they were not supposed to be bobbing next to two Carrier

Battle Groups. Since the Gulf War, the Persian Gulf was tacitly acknowledged as an American asset.

"The next series of photos are a composite of over one hundred taken by the U2." He let the imagery speak for itself.

A surface boat appeared. It looked like some sort of light freighter or tugboat. There were four yellowish blobs on deck. Yellow seemed an odd color to use for a clandestine rendezvous. The color screamed like a beacon. Not exactly the effect Saddam or the Chinese were attempting to create.

A greater number of reddish blobs appeared on the deck of the submarine aft of the conning tower and forward of the fin. A black hole materialized on the submarine's deck. Brian remembered the Han as having missile tubes forward of the conning tower. This hole appeared to be square—more like a platform. Could the Chinese have converted one of their boats to be some sort of submerged delivery truck? They were certainly working on a new class that would retire the *Han* boats, but that was scheduled for sometime in the next century. The surface ship pulled along side the submarine. What appeared to be a crane began moving across the deck. It was unclear, however, whether the submarine was delivering or receiving.

The next series of photographs depicted a macabre pantomime. Abruptly, three red blobs from the submarine disappeared into the Gulf. The other red blobs scrambled away towards the conning tower. The black hole in the deck disappeared and the submarine sank beneath the waves. The remaining blobs on deck never reentered the boat. Brian concluded the blobs had to be men. Why were they dressed in yellow and red?

The final series of photos showed flashes from the boat. Had they abandoned their men to the sea? What kind of captain makes a decision like that? Submarine crews are small families trapped inside a steel tube beneath the waves for months at a time. Leaving men behind to fend for themselves was certainly out of character, regardless of the navy.

Stillwell stared at the last image. Already, questions were being fired at the briefing officer.

"Where is the Chinese sub now?"

"Still in the Gulf."

"And the surface vessel?"

"Unknown—most likely port of origin was Basra."

"What happened to the red guys?"

"Unknown—presumed dead."

"Why'd the Chinese leave their own guys?"

"Unknown—maybe they detected the U2."

"What do you know?"

"Nothing for sure."

"What do you think you know?"

Stillwell cleared his throat, "Excuse me, Captain." The idea of civility and politeness from someone as antisocial as Stillwell caused some of the hubbub to subside, and most everyone turned in his direction.

He sat up. "Does anyone have any idea why the Iraqis shot those Chinese sailors?"

"What shots?" demanded the Navy Secretary.

The NSA held up his hand commanding silence and turned back to Stillwell. This was something no one had mentioned up to this point. "Go on, Mister Stillwell."

"The last picture after the submarine disappears. There are flashes from the surface vessel." The photo reappeared on the screen. "Now, something certainly scared the Chinese captain. He dropped back into the Gulf without waiting for his men to get back inside. You know what—the same thing scared the Iraqi sailors. Those flashes look like muzzle blasts from automatic or semi automatic weapons. My money would be on automatic weapons. The Iraqis are shooting the Chinese guys in the water. So something scared them real bad."

He had their attention now. Center stage, all he needed was a white board to draw pictures on. Instead, he asked the briefing officer to back up several photos to the point where the red blobs disappear.

"Up to this point everything looks fine. We've got the Iraqis in day glow yellow suits, and the Chinese in day glow red suits. Kind of strange don't you think? Here they are under cover of darkness, in the middle of the Gulf during a US satellite black out. The sub is obviously black. The surface ship—is probably some sort of gray or mottled brownish green thing. So why do we have a bunch of people bouncing around in reflective clothing?" His eyes locked with the Two Star sitting closer to the front of the room. The General knew the answer, but being a General in this administration brought him under suspicion. That's why Brian had been invited. A civilian expert was needed to tell the political appointees the truth.

"Those look like biohazard suits." He changed gears suddenly on them. "Does anyone remember *The Hunt for Red October*? The Russian captain needs to get his crew off the Red October—so they fake a nuclear accident. They frighten everyone. There is no question but to abandon ship." He tapped his finger at the photo display. "I'll bet the Chinese inside the sub panicked, because whatever they were working with must have been the real thing. Something went wrong or maybe it started to leak. Perhaps, someone panicked on the surface ship. Everyone wanted to run away. Maybe someone thought this was a double cross or they were just plain scared and the shooting started. The easiest thing for the sub to do was to drop out of sight."

The Deputy Secretary of State interrupted, "So what are you saying?"

Brian switched his focus. "Madam Secretary, I am suggesting that something nasty was transferred between the Chinese and Iraqi boats last night. You don't need biohazard suits to hand out lollypops. I am further suggesting that something went wrong and there are some dead bodies floating out there. What I don't know is whether the transfer was from the Chinese to the Iraqis or vice versa. Maybe it's nuclear, or maybe its chemicals—I really don't know. I don't think its something benign like bullets, because there are many ways to procure those items short of using a nuclear submarine as a delivery truck. So something scared them and they started shooting."

"You can't be sure those were NBC suits," countered the Secretary referring to the nuclear, biological, and chemical biohazard suits everyone was wearing in the photos.

"No I can't. However, I know we paint ours day glow orange, and this wasn't a casual visit. It was clandestine—timed to happen when our satellites were looking elsewhere. If they went to all that trouble, why wear something that would catch our eye as being out of place? Saddam plays the odds. He knows we can't watch everything all the time. They know our satellite schedules. That's why we're still flying U2 surveillance, and every so often we find something interesting."

The blood slowly drained from the Secretary's face. However, the NSA saved her before she could utter some inane challenge to Stillwell. "And, Mister Stillwell, faced with a scenario as you describe, what would you recommend to the President?"

A smirk emerged. No one really wanted to hear the answer, but Brian had always worked on the principle that no one hired him to be nice. He glanced at the Two Star before replying. Their eyes locked again for the briefest of moments. "I would suggest that we hunt down the *404* and sink her if necessary. Whatever went wrong, it is obvious that the transfer was not completed. That means whatever it is could still be on the *404*. In addition, I recommend we find the stuff that was on the Iraqi boat."

"Two acts of war," chided Madam Secretary. "Generally, we get the recommendation for only one act of war at a time. May I remind you, the Chinese government is a nuclear power on the Pacific Rim? It is not in our interest to start a shooting war with the Chinese. Furthermore, may I remind you, that no one knows this is an Iraqi boat? Or that anything like the weapons you describe were even present."

"With all due respect Madam Secretary," replied Brian. He had no respect for the woman. She was an idiot manning an important foreign policy position because her politics aligned properly on abortion. "No one is suggesting we start a shooting war, but if nothing is amiss, then why are we all here? To see a picture of the tooth fairy?" He was warmed up and ready for a fight. "Are we to believe nothing happened last night? You have evidence of a Chinese nuclear submarine penetrating the Persian Gulf to meet with a boat most likely based out of Basra. We are here, Madam Secretary, because someone believes Saddam Hussein just got his hands on something nasty enough to make good all the threats he's been issuing since the Gulf War."

"Your suggestions will certainly be considered, Mister Stillwell." With that, the NSA dismissed Brian from the discussion. There were other ideas—ideas less plausible and more palatable to the current administration. Brian did not pay much attention to the discussion. His gut told him he was right. Somewhere in the back of his mind, he prayed he was wrong.

2

Roselle, Illinois, Saturday, November 15, 1997, 10:00 AM CST

Jim Harper turned right into the strip mall at Plum Grove and Nerge. It had a Walgreen's on one end of the mall and a video rental store on the other. It was like a hundred other strip malls popping up in the cornfields of the northern and western Chicago suburbs. In the few years he had lived here, the sprawling growth of Dupage and Kane counties continued outwards. What had once been small farming communities now hosted over 250,000 people in a five-mile radius from where he was standing.

It was starting to get cold. Winter's icy fingers were beginning to gather their grip. Already the sky had changed to battleship gray and a cold breeze rode over the prairie. The occasional snowflake flitted through the air. He could feel the hardness of the coming winter. The places on his body pockmarked with scars; the joints once twisted out of shape and the broken bones, long since healed, reminded him of his mortality.

Only today, as most Saturdays, was not a day for combat, remembrance, or duty. The roar and smoke of battle were days gone by. The blood and sweat endured during peace and war dim memories. Saturdays were those moments when Harper reaped a small reward. A time away from his *day job* when he could pass on a sense of honor to those who would listen. Saturdays were spent teaching kids and adults Tae Kwon Do.

On Saturdays, James Harper instructed lower belts in sparring, kicking, and punching basics. A fourth degree black belt, he was considered a master instructor. After so many years, he still felt the magic of training someone in the martial arts—to take an average person and transform them into a trained fighter. Training someone to fight was only part of the journey. The other half of the journey involved developing a sense of duty and honor. Honor not based on eastern mysticism, rather, he sought to instill a sense of personal integrity. His honor was rooted in the belief that life is precious and God given. Life is not a trivial commodity to be traded lightly. He certainly knew the cost of life. Warriors generally crave peace and shun war.

As far as anyone knew, Jim Harper was a successful businessman. A man happily married with two children, a nice house, and a big dog. Harper had achieved the American dream. Granted, he could obliterate the ten-ring on any target from fifty yards. Yes, he knew how to make a bomb out of household items. Indeed, he could teach the Marine close quarter combat instructors a couple of things. However, those were secrets from a past Harper rarely thought of. He had been a warrior, now he was content to be husband and father; and a karate instructor on Saturdays.

Old habits born out of survival never die. He did notice the pickup truck pulling into the parking lot five slots down from his parking spot. The same truck had picked him up as he left his house—two Caucasian males in a late model Ford F-150. They simply parked and sat in their truck. After so many years, who would be interested in him again?

He opened the rear hatch of his Nissan Pathfinder and grabbed the gym bag containing his uniform, belt, and pads. Leaning into the rear of his truck, he pulled the cased Glock 19 from its compartment. Pretending to examine something in the gym bag, he loaded a fifteen round magazine into the Glock, racked the slide, and slipped the pistol into his coat pocket.

A Glock 19 is certainly close to the perfect weapon for a defensive pistol. Unlike other weapons, a Glock can digest just about any bullet configuration it is fed. Glocks rarely jam. They work in sand, water, heat, and cold. Jim carried 115 grain Gold Dot Hollow Points. A 9mm may not produce a one shot stop, but it does deliver a punch accompanied by an ear ringing bang.

Harper dropped the gym bag on the ground behind his truck, closed the hatch and turned towards the two in the pickup. He did not like people following him. He liked people even less who lurked outside of his home. So, with a wave and a smile, he walked over to the pickup.

The goons inside the pickup were caught off guard. Harper closed the distance before the two had a chance to react. He grabbed the driver's side door and opened it bringing the Glock into view for the first time. Still smiling he said, "You boys have been following me." Stepping in, he jammed the muzzle into the ribs of the driver and pulled a Sig 229 from the driver's shoulder holster. "I don't like to be followed." He continued flipping the safety off the Sig and pointing it at the passenger. "So if I see you around my house, or outside this school or anywhere else—someone could get hurt." He chuckled nodding to the passenger. "I presume you have something similar to your friend here. I'll give you three seconds to drop it in his lap." The Sig turned towards the passenger's kneecap.

The willingness to use necessary force is a barrier everyone must face. These two had read Harper's dossier. The passenger knew that if Harper got to four seconds without results, his knee would be shattered. Harper was hardly a normal suburban businessman. Besides, they were simply here to observe and not to take a tour of the local trauma wards.

A Smith & Wesson .44 Magnum dropped neatly between the driver's legs. "That was right neighborly of you." He frowned at the passenger. "I'm sure you have a good reason to be carrying a fine cannon like that." He dropped the Sig into his other pocket and scooped up the .44. "So let me make sure we understand each other. If I see you again, you'll be spending months in the hospital." The frown vanished and twinkling eyes turned colder than the sky above. "You do something really stupid, they'll be hauling you away in pieces."

The Glock and the Smith vanished into his coat. A smile returned and Harper said gleefully, "Have a nice day." He stepped back and kicked the door shut. To emphasize his point, he thrust kicked the driver's door leaving the heal print of his cowboy boot. The engine turned over and the pickup backed out of the slot. His shadows drove away without looking back. Harper should have been happy with his success, instead, a grim foreboding settled in a cold spot between his shoulder blades. It had been a long time since he had to chase off shadows such as these. Now they were back. Someone was testing the waters again.

3

Washington DC, Saturday, November 15, 1997, 10:45 AM EST

They had been briefed. Obviously, Iraq and Red China were up to mischief. Certainly, those two players were replacing the Soviet Union as the world's chief troublemakers. The briefing was breaking up. A small, select group would meet to make some decision—probably the wrong one—and check in with CNN to see if anything else were amiss. Brian Stillwell had little time for such antics.

He was surprised when the National Security Advisor told him to stay. The meeting after the briefing came down to the Two Star general, a CIA spook, someone from the White House and Lisa Borden, the Deputy Secretary of State.

"Why have you included Mister Stillwell?" asked Lisa.

"Because, we need someone who will tell us the politically incorrect things we need to hear." The NSA smiled. "He has no love for out president. He thinks you folks at State have made disastrous decisions in the Middle East and China. He's against the bail out of Russia, and he supports greater defense spending—kind of a *nuke 'em 'til they glow* attitude. He doesn't really like me. Right now, all we have in this room are people you and I can intimidate. Stillwell doesn't care." He paused.

"In addition to all those flaws, Mister Stillwell is one of the best experts on unconventional weapons systems in the country. We know that something was passed from China to Iraq, or perhaps vice versa," he teased with a knowing look in Brian's direction. "We think it might be a weapon of mass destruction. Something went wrong during the transfer and a Chinese submarine might be experiencing some sort of poisoning. We saw what appeared to be casualties, and we have a big problem if that madman really does get his hands on weapons of mass destruction."

Stillwell coughed and said sarcastically, "In case you folks haven't been following the news, *that madman* already has weapons of mass destruction."

Lisa glared at the NSA, but kept her own council for the moment.

The spook broke his silence for the first time. "I've got the briefing books you requested for this meeting. Louis Edwards is on his way to meet the team leader we discussed this morning."

"Excuse me, but I take it you saw these photos a long time before the rest of us," interrupted Brian.

"Who's Louis Edwards?" demanded Lisa.

The spook looked across the table to the NSA. There was a brief nod before the spook replied, "Louis Edwards is a member of the intelligence community. He has worked on black ops for the past twenty years. These include operations against friendly and hostile governments. From time to time, Mister Edwards has had an opportunity to work with members of the elite services."

"He means Army Rangers, DELTA Force, and that sort of thing," injected Brian.

"Yes, well, the man the computers came up with for Team Leader is no longer employed by the United States Government; however, Mister Edwards has worked with him on several occasions, and it was felt that he should be positioned to talk with our candidate pending the approval of this committee and the strictures of time."

"He means we're really scared this time, and we don't have much time to create the usual bureaucratic disaster you folks at state are so capable of creating," continued Brian. His eyes never left Lisa Borden's perplexed features. He shifted his gaze back to the spook. Suffering fools was not something at which Brian excelled. "Now that we've explained absolutely nothing about Louis Edwards beyond the obvious, could you answer my question? I take it you saw these photos a long time before the rest of us."

"Yes, Sir," explained the spook. He wore no nametag. He had no visible security badge like the rest of them. His posture was something other than the usual bureaucrat encountered at Langley. Perhaps this was something other than an ordinary spook. "We saw these photos nearly seven hours ago. I came to the same conclusions as you did, Mister Stillwell. I think we have a very bad situation on our hands."

"That's why you're still here," explained the NSA. "You passed my test, as much as I don't like you. You made sense this morning. Now, don't get me wrong. I'm not about to authorize military action against a Chinese submarine. I do think, however, that covert action against Iraq is in order. At this moment, a Presidential Finding is being signed to that effect." He turned to Lisa. "Your role here is a courtesy. The President made it quite clear that State be kept in the loop. I think that also means CNN stays out of the loop for the moment. All media control will be run from the White House." He smiled one more time. "Any questions anyone has will be routed through Arthur." The smile faded slightly. "He's our Ollie North. If something goes wrong, or someone needs a Judas goat, Arthur has volunteered to fill the role."

Of course, if anyone believed Arthur volunteered out of the goodness of his patriotic heart, then someone should examine his Bahamian bank account. Arthur would eventually become another of those faceless, nameless bureaucrats that were never hired and never fired, but had complete access to the inner workings of government. Even the cynical Stillwell was somewhat shocked at the NSA's blunt political calculation.

"Who's going to lead this team?" Lisa's eyes were aimed at the NSA, but her question was answered by the spook.

"Our recommendation is to insert a covert team into Southern Iraq and penetrate Iraq's central Data Center. We have no reason to believe we will be able to apply the correct resources in tracking these weapons down now that the Iraqis have had sufficient time to move them in country.

"However, the central Data Center is a major Iraqi installation. It is connected to every major weapon, command, and control center in Iraq. We believe that the Data Center holds the information to tell us exactly who, what, where, and how the Iraqis are preparing banned weapons systems."

"How do you know that?" snapped Lisa Borden.

"The tooth fairy," offered Brian.

He received a collective set of dirty looks from everyone except the spook and the Two Star.

The spook looked over the table to Lisa and replied, "We know this because we've been inside once before. Back in '92."

"Why aren't we still there?" she demanded.

Brian thought of another one liner, but managed to restrain himself.

"We had a presence on their network for almost twelve months. We learned a great deal about how Saddam moves money, how he shuffles his doubles, and the post war condition of his major command bunkers," answered the spook.

"You need to understand the West Germans; they're suppose to be our allies. They built several nuclear bomb proof shelters a hundred meters below the ground on top of big springs," explained Brian. "If we didn't think Saddam was a bleeding maniac, we might think he's a flipping gopher. He has tunnels with electric cars to take him from bunker to bunker. Do you know what we developed during the Gulf War? A bomb that could drill down over a one hundred meters and then blow up. It was really quite ingenious—kind of wish I'd thought of it. Unfortunately, the media folks and State Department schmucks fell in love with the one hundred hour war and we never got a chance to blow Saddam all over the inside of one of his pretty German bunkers."

The spook rolled his eyes and muttered under his breath, "To answer your question about the team leader."

"Yes, my question," snapped Lisa.

"To accomplish our objectives, we need someone with knowledge of the desert, language skills, proven combat experience, and who can not be tied directly to the US government," explained the spook.

Another political calculation was revealed to this select group—a black operation where only someone named Arthur would allegedly have any knowledge or planning. An icy tingling reached down Brian's spine. The administration was scared. This entire scenario had not been concocted this morning. They must have preplanned for something like this. They were following some sort of war plan. As with any plan, it tended to unravel once the shooting started. Brian wondered if anyone besides the Two Star and spook realized this was going to happen. Perhaps Arthur was polishing his sword so he could fall on it at an opportune moment.

"What sort of team? If you don't mind me asking," pressed Brian.

The spook handed them a black covered briefing book. There were no numbers, titles, or logos on the binders. Usually, these things had a bar code in the lower left-hand corner. Brian looked at the spook again. Who was this guy?

"If you'll turn to page two, I'll explain the team composition."

Page one consisted of a map and plot of the U2, the Iraqi boat, and the submarine. Brian fingered the map for a moment before looking up. "Is anyone tracking this sub?"

"You don't have a need to know, Mister Stillwell," replied Arthur.

Stillwell locked eyes with Arthur. Arthur looked away quickly. Well, one thing was certain. Arthur was no Ollie North, and this administration better make sure Arthur never appeared in front of a Senate committee. He would sound more like Janet Reno than Ollie North. Brian turned to the next page.

"The team composition requires a team leader, weapons expert, protective services fire team experienced in chemical, biological and nuclear weapon disposal, and a computer database expert. That's a seven-man team. They will be able to communicate via satellite link to our command post."

Brian's icy tingle frosted over into a full-fledged glacier. His eyes riveted to the words *weapons expert*. Oh, he had passed a test today, but not for being the annoying analyst in the back of the room. The test Brian passed was a database search, and he was still fogging the mirror. His name must have come out on top. This was not going to be handed off to an ineffective UN Weapons Inspection Team. This was going to be Uncle's little party—a party where people usually end up dead, or missing, or both.

"I believe you've found your role in all of this," smiled the NSA. He withdrew an envelope from his suit coat pocket. "You'll find everything very much in order. The only abnormality is that this letter is actually signed by the Secretary of the Army." The smile turned to a prankster's smirk. "We had to get him out of bed this morning to sign it. Arthur took care of all the paper work."

Brian stared at the proffered letter like it was a wiggling, venomous viper. Letters from politicians in meetings like these never came to good ends. Gingerly, Brian accepted the letter.

Brian opened the envelope and stared at the letter.

"It says you've been reactivated as a First Lieutenant, United States Army. I hope you didn't have any plans this evening, because as of now, you're in the army, son."

Brian stared open mouthed at the NSA. Lisa Borden found it all rather amusing. It was comeuppance due for such a rude man.

"You do remember how to fire a gun?" asked the NSA.

Stillwell snapped back to reality. "Oh yes, Sir. Wish I had one right now." Arthur leaned forward and plucked the letter from Brian's fingers.

"I'll keep it safe for you," explained Arthur.

"Just make sure you shred it both ways," suggested Brian.

Arthur nodded as he stole the letter away into his suit coat pocket.

Stillwell realized what was strange about the Two Star General. He had no nametag. All officers were required to wear a nametag. The medals and chevrons looked real enough. He had the bearing of man who had *been there.* Blood and death were no strangers to this warrior. Yet, Brian could not place a name with the face, and this nameless, faceless general sat at a table deciding his future. A future with limited possibilities.

"The protective service fire team is being selected as we speak," the Two Star read from his own notes. "It will be a Force Recon detachment. These men will not have any immediate family and limited ties to extended family. Their service records have been altered to indicate training accidents, discharge, or disqualification for other reasons. Obviously, we can't use the same excuse for everyone. In the event someone decides to look, we need a clean slate for these men." The General looked across the table at a civilian who had just become a soldier again. He found it astounding that a reserve officer would be sent on a covert op into Indian country.

"Their weapons will be standard issue. Their clothing will be authentic to the region and all are Arabic speakers." He paused again and looked at the nameless spook. "All, that is, except Lieutenant Stillwell here. Country infiltration and exit will be accomplished by land vehicle. Air evacuation is only a last resort."

If anyone had bothered to look at a map, they would have realized the supporting details for this mission were bogus. The Iraqi Data Center was deep inside the Southern no-fly zone in fairly rough terrain. The ground was rent with gullies gouged through soft sand and hard rocks. It was uneven and it rained very little. The wind could be fierce, raising deadly sandstorms, and the heat could leach the water out of any man.

They were heading for the edges of the Syrian Desert while Saddam lay to the north along the Tigris and Euphrates Rivers. To the west lay too much desert and hostile Arab territory before arriving in Israel. To the East awaited Kuwait, but if anyone figured out what they were about, an exit back to Kuwait would vanish. Of course, the map indicated a border to the south and refuge in Saudi Arabia. Considering the prize they were after—Saddam's total order of battle for both conventional and unconventional weapons—simple lines drawn on maps would not impede the pursuit. Besides, the great Saudi desert might do the job nicely for Saddam.

Stillwell nodded slightly. The unspoken truth here involved his capture. A weapon expert of his caliber could not fall into Saddam's hands. He wondered who had the chore of killing him to avoid capture. If Brian were designing this mission, all four of the Force Recon Marines would be given the same order either as a group or in private. "Do I get a blindfold or a cigarette, Sir?"

The NSA chuckled, "Brian let's not be so glum. No one is going to get killed, and as soon as you're back, this letter Arthur has disappears. You'll have the personal thanks of the President and the heartfelt gratitude of the country. We find out what Saddam's up to and fix it so it doesn't work anymore."

"All right, so we've got our weapons expert and some marines to shoot bad guys. So who's the computer whiz and team leader?"

"You have such a way with words, Lisa," snapped the NSA. He flipped the page on the briefing folder to a photograph of a soldier in fatigues. "May I present Major James Harper, United States Special Forces Retired. He will serve in both capacities."

Brian found it somewhat curious that nowhere on the dossier or photograph was there an indication of service branch or unit designation. There were no insignia like Navy SEAL or DELTA. This Harper seemed as faceless and nameless as the spook sitting next to him. Special Forces was an ambiguous title.

"He was at the top on both lists of available personnel who fit our mission criteria," continued the spook. "Major Harper is conversant with most information technology likely to be encountered on the mission. He has previously broken into Iraqi computer systems and—"

Lisa Borden looked up from the briefing book. "It says under the psyche profile that he's a born again Christian." She laughed—not a very nice laugh. "You're going to send some fruit cake Jesus freak on a mission into the desert? What are you, nuts?" Her voice rose with passion and volume. "Everyone knows these type of people favor Israel over everything else over there." Brian was unsure whether *these type of people* or *Israel* received more derision from Lisa Borden. But then, she was from the State Department, and American Foreign Policy seemed to be dedicated to a mission designed to deify Yassir Arafat and blame Israeli Prime Minister Benjamin Netanyahu for most Arab terrorism.

"That's all we need at the UN. Saddam gets his hands on a Jew loving, Jesus Freak on a black op to one of his Presidential Palaces. No, gentlemen, I'm afraid State can never approve of this choice. I—"

"Ma'am!" interrupted the Two Star. "I don't care whether State will approve or disapprove of Jim Harper. From 1980 to 1992, he took care of some this country's biggest problems. He's something of a legend in the Spec War community. Most everything we know about the inside of Saddam's computer network came from Jim, and one of the reasons you're here today is because Jim Harper stopped a mess like this once before.

"I've had men under my command. I wish all of them were like Harper." Something seemed to boil out of the Two Star who no longer cared about promotion. He was obviously destroying his chance for career advancement. "We are going to send in a team without support, without backup to find something the Red Chinese gave to a crazy man. Now the only reason we don't go in with all guns blazing is because we want the Red Chinese to like us. So, we'll ignore the problem with a sub running loose in the Gulf, and the transmission of a weapon to the Iraqis because it is politically expedient to do so. We're talking about sending my friend back to hell, and you're upset because he goes to church."

Lisa Borden was as dumb as she was loud. "I don't care if he's King David returned from the dead. You don't send some Bible thumper into Iraq with the possibility of the whole Arab world exploding if he gets caught!"

The NSA closed his eyes. Stillwell watched the hammer drop, and wondered as it fell—what is the agenda? He was sitting in a room with a no name spook, a Spec War Two Star general, a White House hatchet man, the National Security Advisor, and an openly hostile deputy Secretary of State. They were discussing a mission to do what? To capture chemical or nuclear weapons delivered by the Chinese. Perhaps the intention was to lose those weapons. After all, the administration owed its reelection to illegal contributions from the Chinese Government. The politics might dictate certain sensitivities towards Chinese involvement. However, there were other elements equally distressed at the prospect of heavy-duty chemical weapons being made available to Saddam. Evidently, the NSA feared the practical national security issues over a more muddled political agenda.

"Madam Secretary, I am not interested in your proclivities towards or against a person's religion. As you are well aware, our administration is an inclusive administration. The word of the day is diversity. Now, according to Mister Stillwell here, our focus should be on the containment of what we saw this morning. I believe he would like to stomp on everything. It's my job to make national security decisions, and it is my job to determine the best tool to implement those decisions. I'll repeat for the last time. You are here as a courtesy, and we are talking about a very sensitive issue here. Leaks to the press or others will not be permitted. On this point the President has been explicit." Lisa Borden seemed to shrink back into her chair with each statement. Both knew who would prevail today in this room. It was only a battle, not the war.

"Perhaps we can proceed with Mister Harper's credentials," he concluded.

The nameless spook looked up from his report. "I believe some background may be in order. We know Iraq has been able to get its hands on a number of Hewlett Packard (HP) machines. Our best intelligence indicates these machines were diverted from France during a replacement of HP-9000 with IBM RS-6000 systems. The excuse for the replacement is a general market trend towards IBM equipment in Europe. The HP's were supposed to be transshipped back to England. However, the computers returned were about a dozen 386 PC clones and the HP boxes disappeared.

"We believe the HP's shipment arrived in Amman, Jordan. It is a simple matter of trucking the equipment across the border and into the desert. If all software licenses were left in place, the Iraqi's have gotten their hands on about twenty gigabytes of hard disk, five hundred megabytes of memory, and two Oracle 7.1 databases. The software is more than adequate to assist the Iraqi government in managing any secret weapons research.

"One of the things we learned during the Gulf War was the existence of an extensive fiber network. With this equipment, they can connect from a variety of locations to central servers. Such a network enables the Iraqis to continue moving weapon prototypes about in an elaborate shell game. Even with satellite and reconnaissance over flights, we are not completely certain where everything is located. These databases have the precise information we need.

"We know these machines exist. We know approximately where they are located, and we have an electronic backdoor into these systems." He looked around the table. "Jim Harper's last mission, before retiring, compromised this network. We have some hidden user accounts at both the operating system and database level. Unfortunately, the Iraqis do not allow any dial up access at all to their networks. They have hardened their systems to outside attack. We need to get to a terminal and execute an attack from inside the Iraqi network.

"Jim Harper is the logical choice. He knows how the network was put together. It is our assessment that you, Mister Stillwell, working with Mister Harper have the best chance of figuring out where and what weapons systems still exist in Iraq. We believe the data would be in real time. Therefore, we could effectively take out all weapon sites in one stroke."

It sounded so tidy on paper. Brian shook his head, smiling in spite of himself. If they had so many clever facts about Saddam's computers, why not use a couple of stray smart bombs and blast them to bits? Why allow the equipment into Iraq in the first place? Brian had so many questions, and quite a few bad answers. The other nagging fact; it is doubtful that even a massive *Tomahawk* cruise missile and air campaign could completely eliminate the threat.

"You have a comment?" inquired the NSA.

"I don't suppose you've asked the Iraqis if it's okay to raid their database, call up the US Navy on the phone, and bomb their research sites back to the Stone Age. I presume they might be somewhat upset with our presence there. They might even be shooting at us. Besides, it takes time to raid a database and find the right data." He held up his hand. "But I know the answer. We have four Marines to hold off the Republican Guard, that makes all the difference in my mind." He spat out the last.

4

Persian Gulf, Saturday, November 15, 1997, 7:30 PM (GMT + 3.00)

Captain Tze Wong stared across the confines of his stateroom. His gaze fixed on a portrait. It was a color photograph remembering the grand day when the *404* was launched. She proudly flew her colors, slicing through the South China Sea like the shark she was. The 404 was China's challenge to the arrogant Americans. No longer would anyone look upon the People Liberation Army Navy as a toy fleet. The Han Class was a nuclear answer to the surviving superpower. A replacement for the hapless Russians—a people no longer masters of their own destiny. Russia was for sale, and the buyers were American and Japanese bankers.

He was her master. His authority extended to the ninety-two crewmen and the mission he had been given. His responsibility settled heavily on his shoulders. The numbers were overwhelming. In one maddening moment, he had lost a quarter of his crew and damaged his ship. He understood hazardous missions. After all, he was charged with the protection of his nation. He had been chosen to deliver this cargo. His ship had been selected to be the envoy.

Wong kept replaying the disaster as he struggled to come up with a solution. Even now, the American task force might be hunting them. The only escape lay in the *Strait of Hormuz*. If they had been detected, then a *Los Angeles* Class attack boat would be waiting.

Considering the damage to the outer hull, tracking, trapping, and killing them would be child's play.

☆ ☆ ☆

The sea had been somewhat choppy—nothing terribly dangerous. A light overcast and moonless night made it relatively safe for the *404* to surface. Al Faw was to the north-northwest and Bandar-e-Khomeyni due north. They lay in the steady Ocean swells fifty klicks south-southeast of the Tigris River.

The *404* had been specially modified for this mission. A nuclear boat had a better chance of relying on stealth than one of the antiquated diesels. An elevator was cut directly into the top of the hull aft the sail. It lowered into a special storage facility capable of transporting chemical, biological, and nuclear materials. The chamber was sealed off from the rest of the boat. So were the men who served this hazardous duty. Nothing should go wrong with routine material transfers. There was, however, nothing routine about their material.

The elevator dropped like a sinkhole into the back of the *404*. Special infrared lights were rigged to reduce the detection signature from overhead reconnaissance. Wong's men wore night vision goggles to facilitate movement in complete darkness. During these operations, the watch was cancelled. The rest of the boat must be secured from any leakage. Night vision goggles are a marvelous invention, until you combine them with heavy biohazard suits and realize two kilograms of metal are hanging beyond someone's nose. Depth perception, normal movement and balance are all suspect. Add a rolling sea and pitching deck, and accidents can happen.

Wong's masters might understand an accident, but disaster and the possible loss of a nuclear boat was a different matter. Other boats had been lost. Everyone knew about the *Thresher*—another failure by planners who did not realize the need for precision and care when sending boats to sea. All hands were lost off the Atlantic coast because the plumbing failed.

There were five stainless steel double-hulled casks. Each weighed three hundred kilos and required three men to safely manhandle them on the elevator platform. When it came down to it, the People's Liberation Army Navy (PLAN) still relied on its abundant manpower to settle most problems. The platform was large enough to handle eight men. This night it carried four men and a cask up and down three times.

It was the third cask that caused the problems. It rose from the bowels of the submarine. A deadly bottle held by four men. The orange biohazard insignia were visible even in the darkness. Maybe this was where the elaborate preparations failed. Men working in bulky biohazard suits fitted with night vision goggles on a sloping deck. They would probably never know exactly what happened, but Wong would never forget what he witnessed.

The casks were hoisted from the elevator platform to the deck of the Iraqi boat. A crane moved—a phantasm steel arm drifting through the night. Attached to the crane was a heavy hook and cables manipulated by a pulley system. The casks were fitted with a leather harness and chrome carbuncle. The strap enabled swift ship-to-ship transfer. It had been tested several times. Of course, tests performed in calm harbors and research labs never take into account the vagaries of the ocean.

The crane's hook seemed to move faster than the last time. The sea swells may have moved the ships closer together, or the alignment of the decks tilted at the wrong time. Instead of an orderly movement, the hook slammed into the back of one of his men. Cast iron and weighing over one hundred kilos, it smashed him in the back. The audio microphones from the platform recorded a sickening slap. The splintering of bones and the snapping of a spinal column kept pace with the image of a human being suddenly turned into kindling. His man catapulted over the cask. He hit, slid, and disappeared over the side. The sea swallowed him whole and dutifully washed the blood from the deck.

The hook did not end its night's work with the death of one sailor. It turned after its first murder and rammed like a missile into the side of the next cask. Double hulled, stainless steel was no match for the simple physics of mass times velocity. The barrel designed to transport a deadly toxin looked like a crunched pop can. Impaled on a hardened chunk of metal, the breached barrel rose up, smashing the sailor opposite the first casualty. He caught several hundred pounds of metal under the chin. He flipped backward into the sea. They were the first to die. They were the lucky ones.

Another planning disaster—no one was supposed to be hit by container hooks. Men were not supposed to die on a black deck under a moonless sky. The double-hulled casks were supposed to resist small arms fire. No one considered the transfer mechanism to be capable of such mayhem.

A green jet spewed from the ruptured cask. It spun like a child's pinwheel, painting the deck, the men, and the sea. A macabre death dance began with the twirling cask—a deadly pirouette. The green spray slashed a sailor across the middle. In seconds, the yellow biohazard suit parted betraying bare skin to whatever concoction they had been ordered to deliver. It continued to eat right through a third sailor.

The planners never checked the biohazard suit's durability. Or perhaps they had, and this stuff behaved exactly as advertised. The biohazard suits seemed to smoke. Most likely, the chemical agent was fundamentally an air borne acid capable of defeating most safety systems. Wong's men were beyond the safety systems.

Wong hit the biohazard klaxon. Instantly, special biohazard and watertight doors dropped inside the *404*. A seal was created around the storage and elevator rooms, where the casks were stored. Whoever remained in the biohazard area was a walking dead man. Once the biohazard doors dropped inside the *404*, they could not be raised again until they returned to their homeport. Wong was trying to save the rest of his boat. He had no idea how many men he had just condemned.

Incredibly, the Iraqis started shooting. Three Iraqis opened up with automatic weapons—as if steel core bullets could cripple the death spewing from the cask. It was panic fire. The bullets went wide, walking across the deck and ricocheting into the men still standing. Eventually, something important came under fire as well. A submarine has a variety of sensors in the periscopes jutting like misshapen sticks from the sail. The main periscope was shattered by a lucky shot, and all crew on deck that night were cut down.

The Iraqi crane operator yelled for someone to grab an axe. With the clattering of automatic weapons, no one heard him. If there had been enough light, they would have recognized the atomization of the chemical weapon. It began to drift like a cloud over the open elevator shaft slowly settling towards the deck and seeping into the bowels of the submarine. Fright overrode discipline, and no one noticed the coating of death drifting towards the Iraqi boat in the aftermath of the accident.

Realizing no one could hear him, the crane operator found an axe and chopped through the steel cables holding the ruptured cask. The lines snapped like angry snakes hoping for one more kill before sliding away from the Iraqi barge. The cask could not have landed more squarely on the elevator—still leaking its green death. The cables attached to the hook swung around in a vicious tangle, and the elevator platform continued to lower into the hull of the boat. What little chance the men inside the biohazard chamber had for life ended as the cables and cask snagged the machinery necessary to bring the elevator back up and close the hull.

The engines on the barge surged to life. One of the Iraqi sailors had dropped his AK-47. He was clawing at his air mask. Somehow, he ripped it off gagging for air his lungs could no longer process. His lungs were disintegrating with each beat of his heart, and soon it, too, would be nothing more than ruptured tissue. His crewmates delivered the same fate they had rendered to the Chinese. Rifle bullets ripped into his body. The bullets' impact shoved him over the side. Less than ten seconds had transpired since the cask first ruptured.

Wong turned away from the monitor showing the sail camera's perspective. "Override elevator and close the hull." He looked across the control room. The ready board had more red than green showing. “Prepare to dive.” He looked back at the sail monitor. The elevator was not closing. A sick feeling crept into his gut. “Elevator status?”

A moment passed, before a weak voice answered, “Captain, elevator is jammed open.” It came from the intercom. Wong locked eyes with his Number One. Dead men at the bottom of the elevator were piling up, and those that remained had already been poisoned.

Wong turned to his Number One, “Manual override.”

The officer shook his head. “Manual override can only take place from inside the biohazard room.” He flipped the channel switch on the monitor. “The biohazard room, Captain. Those men are dead or close to it. There’s no one left to raise the elevator.”

They could not stay on the surface. The American Navy would find them in daylight, and discover the terrible weapon they had been sent to deliver.

“Take her down.”

“Captain, we’ll have flooding in the hull.”

Wong shook his head. “Secure water tight doors. Rig for shallow dive.” There was another moment’s pause, but the age-old tradition that a captain is lord and master took hold.

“Yes, Sir.” Number One turned and shouted the correct orders.

He turned back to the monitor. The deck canted slightly and the *404* began to disappear beneath the surface of the Gulf. Water rushed in from the open wound in the hull. Waves flung the inert bodies about the biohazard room before the camera failed, and the relentless sea took for its own those men still clinging to life.

That was when they discovered the periscope had been hit by one of the Iraqi bullets. Water began dripping from the eyepiece, and the delicate Japanese electronics did not react well to salt water. The pressure hull integrity was compromised. A vessel that could be tracked by American sonar now made more noise than ever due to the hole in the hull.

★ ★ ★

"Plot a course for open water. Ahead slow." He flipped off the monitor. "I'll be in my cabin. Report when you have a damage assessment."

He had his damage assessment and a casualty list. Tze Wong thought about praying, but who would listen? He had failed in his mission and in his command to safeguard his boat. He had seventeen dead sons and no bodies to return to grieving mothers. He had five severely injured men, and limited facilities to treat them. He had a ship with the handling characteristics of a pregnant whale and a maximum speed of seven knots. He had the American Navy with its aircraft carriers, destroyers, and attack submarines. He wondered when they would start hunting. He could fight, but he could not run.

5

Roselle, Illinois, Saturday, November 15, 1997, 1:30 PM CST

Karate schools are simple places. In the best ones, there are mirrors on one wall, handrails along the other walls, and a fairly good industrial grade carpet. The carpets usually have a different colored square in the middle. It defines a ring without the need for ropes and posts in the conventional sense of a gymnasium. This floor had a red center with a gray border, and it contained two fighters. Each was clad in workout pants and T-shirts. They looked more like aliens than people with their cage masks, rib guards, and hand pads flashing about.

For some, the best part of martial arts is the intricate forms. A form, or *kata,* is simply telling a story of a fight in classical stances and moves. Indeed, classical basics have their place in training and self-discipline, but for others, it is the chase and the fight that holds the allure. Most instructors will explain to new students, "This is a contact sport and you *will* get hit." In the very next breath, they explain that the first rule in sparring is to *not* get hit.

So it was for Jim Harper. He had learned his forms, and worked on his classical basics, but fighting was the chance to test himself against another trained fighter. The most difficult challenge seemed to be against people he fought on a regular basis. They began to recognize the feints and fakes. They understood the tendencies to hook kick towards the head and sidekick towards the stomach. Good fighters made good friends who pointed out things to each other like steel sharpening steel.

Jim Harper was no novice to fighting. A fourth degree black belt represents at least ten years of training as a black belt, and probably another two or three years as a under belt. Today, he was working with an under belt, just as his trainers had worked with him. He was giving back to another generation what he had been given. He surveyed his opponent—a brown belt teenager. Teenage boys were fascinating adversaries. They had magnificent physical capabilities. They could kick and jump higher and faster than Jim could. Youth and speed was rarely a match for age and deviousness.

His opponent came with a double round kick, but Jim was no longer where he had been. The kicking leg dropped. Jim stepped in and back punched—not full power, but enough to remind his student not to make the same mistake again.

"Combinations—kick punch or punch kick," he explained.

The brown belt nodded and turned towards him again. He tried a back fist and punch combination, but Jim slid sideways. He delivered a round kick to his middle and dropped a hammer fist inside the shoulders next to his ear. Again, the brown belt turned.

"Remember to fake next time."

He came with a kicking blitz that looked more like a one legged helicopter than a trained fighter. This time Jim blocked the kicks with his front hand. The brown belt made a common mistake of most young fighters. He was so intent on kicking high and fast that he forgot to cover his stomach. His rear hand was waving behind his hip in an effort to keep balance. Unfortunately, this opens up an enormous target called the body. Jim swung under the leg and struck with a double punch.

"Control your hands."

The fighters danced for another twenty minutes. Jim did little more than counter or jam. Occasionally, when the opportunity was too great to pass up, he landed a sidekick on the brown belt's hip. Sometimes he rolled left and sometimes right. A few times straight in with a hand blitz or a backhand ridge hand. The odd ax kick or turn sidekick. When finished, they stopped, bowed, and clasped hands thanking each other for a good fight.

A good fight usually meant a soaking wet T-shirt and sweaty hair as the cage masks came off. The front windows steamed up from the heated bodies. Jim popped the Velcro tabs holding his rib guard, and started walking towards the locker room at the end of the school.

The slow, ponderous clap from behind the half wall, where parents gather to watch Johnny and Suzy learn how to kick, caused him to turn. A man in his mid fifties stood with a topcoat slung over his arm. The faded blond mustache and bear-like paws belonged to Louis Edwards. The men on either side of him were the same two Jim had chased off earlier that day. His eyes narrowed and his pulse quickened. These people were not supposed to be here. This part of his life was over, and was never to follow him again!

He pulled off his hand and elbow pads, tossing them towards the corner along with the cage mask. Harper never took his eyes off his target and examined his situation. The feral nature of his training kicked into over drive as he started walking across the floor to the trio behind the parent wall.

Louis quit clapping and grinned. “Always a teacher. It’s good to see you haven’t lost your edge.”

“Really?” He shot a hard look at one of Edwards’s flunkeys.

Louis glanced over his shoulder. “Oh, I did hear about your encounter with Mister Smith and Mister Jones this morning. Caught them completely off guard.”

Jim had covered half the distance to the wall. He nodded. “Did they tell you what I’d do to them if they showed their ugly faces again? We don’t allow garbage in this school.”

Louis sniffed the air and wrinkled his nose. “Perhaps it would be best if they waited outside.”

Jim nodded again. "Tell them to get lost, Louis—and while you're at it—you can get lost with them. I don't work for you anymore."

Louis nodded to his men who walked backwards to the door. Jim Harper was not a small man. He carried very little body fat. His posture resembled a cat ready to strike; he projected total menace. "Yes, I suppose you might feel that way, Jimbo."

Harper hated being called Jimbo. He stopped a few paces short of the wall. "What do you want?"

Louis clapped his hands together. "Always one to get right to the point aren't you—no subtle moves—no finesse, just straight to the point. Well, it made you what you are."

Jim folded his arms, waiting. The brown belt he had been fighting came out of the locker room. Louis said nothing and smiled. Jim looked behind him. "Have a nice week, Terry."

"Thanks for working with me, Mister Harper."

Jim smiled and waited until the kid left the through the front door. He turned back to Louis. "You never answered my question. Of course, that's nothing new for you. What will it be this time—lies about North Korea or the perils of Red China? Maybe we need to find what's going on in Bosnia. It's obvious you folks haven't got a clue these days."

"Yes, well, they did warn me you might be less than receptive to a visit." Louis suggested, "Maybe I could buy you lunch?"

Harper shrugged. "Maybe we should go a few rounds Louis. Best two out of three. I promise not to break too many bones. Better yet, why don't I deal with your two flunkies? I'm sure we'll be able to get the blood out of the carpet—eventually." He paused. "I want you out of here Louis. I don't ever want to see you again, and if I do, I'll break something on you."

"Jim, we do have laws against such behavior," he chided.

"Laws never bothered you before, Louis. In fact, nothing moral, or right, or good, or pure, ever bothered you." He spat the last out like bitter peanuts.

Louis nodded again. "We need you, Jim. We need what you, and only you, can give us. We need you."

"The last time you needed me, a whole bunch of people got killed. Good people got killed for very bad reasons." He walked around the parent wall to the door and flipped the lock shut. "What did you ever tell those mothers as to why their sons came home in body bags?"

Louis turned to face Jim. "We told them—"

"*We*!" snapped Jim. "There's no *we* here Louis. What did you tell them? Did you go to their homes and knock on their doors? Did you fold up a flag and hand it to a young wife with a little child? Did you give a medal to a heart broken father with some letter written by our President? Did you do that Louis? Did you make the calls?"

A thought occurred to Louis. Maybe the truth would work with Harper. It was a rare concept for Louis Edwards; he would have to think about it before employing such a bold tactic. "No. I didn't make those calls. A Marine Corp Major and a Chaplain made those calls. I did write the letters, and those boys did die for their country. They followed you, Jim, because they believed in you."

Harper closed his eyes, not wishing to see those men. "They followed me for duty, honor and country. Nevertheless, somebody knew we were coming. Somebody told them where to find us. And they kept shooting."

"You lived and a few others made it out. They lived because you brought them out, Jim," he reminded. "There were some who wanted to nominate you for the Medal of Honor. Of course, it was a black op and everything—big time presidential awards would be somewhat out of step for what never happened. You're a hero." He leaned back against the half wall. "Those boys you brought out alive. They'll always remember you. And this time it'll be different."

Jim snapped his attention back to Louis. "This time? There is no this time. I'm not leading more men into another ambush. I've been there, done that. Louis, I took ten men in and came out with three. One of them will never walk again."

"Yes. One of the three you brought was Jonas. He works for me now. I think he's trying to be like you." He raised his hands in compromise.

"Tell him there are better things to strive for than to be like me. What use is there to have a past that you can't share with you wife and kids because they might think you're a monster once they know."

"Jim, you knew the risks. There aren't any guarantees in this life. You lost some men. You got the job done."

Getting the job done was Edwards's mantra. Jim had always gotten the job done—it's just difficult living with yourself after some of the jobs. "I don't do work like that anymore Louis. So why don't you take whatever it is you're pushing and get out of here. I'm sure the beltway crowd you work for these days will figure something out."

Louis chuckled for the first time. "The beltway crowd I work for would have a hard time finding Florida on the map if it didn't have a lot of rich contributors. This isn't for the beltway crowd. It's for the country. We need you because you've done it before. We can't mess up on this."

Louis had always been quick to wave God and country or honor and duty. Of course, those were just words to Louis. They were more than words to Jim. Throughout his career in the nether world known as Spec War, or black ops, or whatever euphemism was current these days, he had attempted to maintain a balance and a code of honor. Men followed Jim because they believed in his ability to lead them through the hard parts. His ability to lead and his self-confidence in his ability to survive were intangible assets men followed into the hardest battles.

Louis was very good at sending men to die. The part about holding them in your arms as the life left their eyes was something reserved to people like Jim. "Get out of here." He flipped the lock on the door and shoved it open. "Go on. Get out of here."

"It's Iraq, Jim," he said quickly. "Something happened last night. I think it's something real bad and I need you to go back to Iraq. I don't have time to plan a proper penetration. I need a team leader who can think on his feet and improvise a strategy."

Harper paused, a war seemed to rage across his features. Slowly he let the door shut. He closed his eyes trying to forget Iraq—a magic word of sorts—the cradle of civilization where the Tigris and Euphrates ran together, and maybe the location of Eden. Rocks, sand, pain and blood blistered his memory from a ground war that lasted a lot longer than one hundred hours recorded on television. Special Forces had been in country for over six months before Stormin' Norman sent the tanks over the dirt berms. There were subsequent *in country* penetrations required to monitor the Iraqi madman, and the terrible, bitter loss.

"You hunted scuds in the desert. You wrecked communication centers for the Republican Guard. You penetrated their computer systems. You've gone in and out three times since the Gulf War. We may need to get back into their computer systems again. You know them. You coded a backdoor so we could watch what they were doing. Well, they're doing something again."

Jim slowly shook his head. Louis certainly sanitized what he had done. Getting into Iraq's Data Center had been easy. Getting back out had cost him a friend. It's hard to visit a gravesite in the middle of the desert for someone who should have never been there.

"They received something last night. We think it's a chemical or nuclear weapon."

☆ ☆ ☆

Jerry and Jim had just finished planting a series of special user accounts in Iraq military information systems. Jerry looked up from the terminal, sweat streaming down his face. His hands wrapped around the M-16 A2 as he observed the two dead technicians on the floor. Jim hurriedly typed in the last of the commands on the aging HP-3000 systems. They were a two-man penetration team attempting to infiltrate a major installation—madness.

The doors leading into the computer room slid open without warning. Jerry yelled something and charged firing the M-16 from his hip. Jim rolled sideways pulling the black Mossberg up and ready. Rifle shots whistled through the room hitting irreplaceable equipment. The zing of bullets coming too close brought an instant response as the Mossberg roared with its full 12 gauge fury. The firefight was over as quickly as it had started—three more dead men on the floor leading into the computer room.

Jerry had been hit twice in the chest by armor piercing rounds. The Kevlar vest stopped the first at the cost of a broken rib, but the second made it through. The wound made sucking sound each time Jerry took a breath. Jim hefted his friend on one shoulder. They tottered drunkenly down the bunker's long corridor. Thin trails of blood marked their exodus and alarms blared throughout the complex. A distant explosion rumbled through the compound—probably one of the charges they had set up wired into the alarm system.

They came to a corridor intersection and started towards the exit. They collided with an Iraqi fire team. Jim went sideways burying an elbow in the first man's ear. The Iraqi soldier's head smashed against the concrete wall. He collapsed like a broken doll.

Jerry brought his Browning Hi Power to bear. He double tapped the soldier he was hanging on to. The much-maligned 9mm round is extraordinarily effective when jammed against someone's stomach. Jerry jerked the trigger twice. His attacker staggered and pitched backward carrying Jerry into the next soldier.

Jim turned to his next target. He sent a back leg front kick straight to the groin. His target forgot about holding his rifle and concentrated on breathing. Jim latched onto the back of his head and drove his other knee straight into the Iraqi's nose. A bloody explosion erupted as Jim's second target tilted backwards.

Jerry was weakening quickly. His left hand clutched at the rifle of the final fire team member. The Iraqi was kicking violently to free himself from the two men on top of his legs. He never saw Jim's boot reach out and shatter the base of his chin—lights out a fourth time.

Jim lifted Jerry bodily off the two Iraqi soldiers. "How we doing?"

"Never felt better," he wheezed.

"Liar," Jim hissed.

They started their run for the door. Before taking the last half stairway to the outside, Jim slid Jerry back to the floor. Sweat was streaming down his face, and his lips seemed a bit blue. Jim pulled open his combat blouse and pushed back the Kevlar vest. The puckered entry wound continued to leak and wheeze. "We've got to do something about this."

Jerry nodded and smiled, "It ain't pretty, Jim. I've lost a lot of blood."

Jim cut apart the combat blouse into two bandages. Not the cleanest solution, but maybe enough to get them out. From his backpack, he pulled a roll of duct tape and wound his partner's chest until the worst of the sucking sound was gone. They had lost their first aide kit sometime earlier.

"What have you got loaded in that thing?" He nodded to the Mossberg 590 12 gauge on the floor. It was a black, nasty looking weapon with a twenty-inch barrel, ghost ring sites, a pistol, and forend grips. The grips were specially angled to control the considerable recoil of full powered rounds.

"Rifled slug—seven of them." A rifled slug is a chunk of lead weighing one and a half ounces. It has the diameter of a penny and it is a little more than an inch long with a muzzle velocity of 2700 feet per second. A Mossberg 590 is capable of bulls-eye shooting these slugs out to one hundred yards. The close quarter combat situations that Jim found himself in made these things one-shot showstoppers.

The door leading into the bunker began to open. Both men twisted towards the unexpected intrusion. Jim grabbed the Mossberg off the floor. He pushed the safety forward with his thumb revealing the red fire dot, and fired before the door was half way open. The first shot deflected along the angle of the door crunching into and through someone standing to side of the door. It also forced the door open faster than expected for the second man up there.

Pump. Eject. Fire!

The second round caught the next Iraqi full in the chest. He disappeared from the frame of the doorway. The slug pancaked on the trauma plate of his flak jacket and hurtled him backward six yards. The door banged closed followed by a whump! The doorframe seemed to buckle inward.

"Sounds like a grenade, Jimmy."

Harper nodded. "I think we need to leave."

They scrambled to their feet and hobbled up the steps. Jim kicked open the door as they emerged into a rock strewn quarry. Saddam had hidden his most sensitive sites either in the open, behind the façade of palaces, or under the plentiful amounts of sand. Stealth was used to secure locations rather than high security, high profile installations. While this prevented frequent visits from the United States Air Force, it did raise certain security problems when ground teams penetrated installations.

The Republic Guard survived due to resource dispersal. Small four-man fire teams protected these installations. In the case of Saddam's Data Center, they were committed piece meal. Unfortunately, they were still arriving.

They hobbled past two very dead soldiers and two others who looked close to death. Jim folded Jerry into the passenger seat of the jeep before clambering in himself.

"Don't you think I should drive—in case you need to shoot?"

Jim shook his head. He could see his friend was losing consciousness. The best hope he had was to exit them from the battlefield. He pumped another shell into the Mossberg, flipped the safety back on. "I think you should try to sleep." He gunned the jeep and sped into the desert night.

Jerry died two days later in the desert between Saudi Arabia, Jordan, and Iraq. Jim buried him in a small grave under a cairn of stones. He said a prayer and marked the grave with a cross. It took another seven days on foot before Jim found a village in Jordan with a phone.

★ ★ ★

"Look, Jim, I know this is a painful subject for you, but I really do need you. I don't have any time to get someone else prepped for this kind of mission. You know the desert."

Harper focused his eyes on Louis again.

"All right, Louis." He said calmly.

Edwards stopped talking and stared. A smile began to curl under his fading mustache.

"This is what it'll cost you." He flipped the lock on the door shut again. "You'd better get something to write on, Louis, and you'd better have it all taken care of before you come to pick me up."

"What exactly do you want?" He pulled out a notebook.

"One million dollars, tax-free, for Jerry's widow and full scholarships for his kids—you never took care of them after he died, now, we make it right. No strings attached. Jerry already earned it. For anybody going on this mission, same deal—this time the million and scholarships pay off in case of death or serious injury. That's a phone call for you, Louis." He pointed at the office. "Go on, make the calls while I change. I want confirmation faxed back to this number." He started back towards the locker room, then turned back to Louis. "Don't even think of double crossing me on this Louis. You'd never be able to run far enough to save your miserable hide."

"Now Jimbo, I can't exactly—"

"You've got ten minutes." Jim turned and walked towards the end of the school.

6

Fao Peninsula, Iraq, Saturday, November 15, 1997, 8:30 PM (GMT + 3.00)

The Al Faw oil depot sits on triangle shaped strip of land called the Fao Peninsula. It is the southern most Iraqi outpost and serves as the final surface oil depot for the underground pipeline running from the massive Rumaila and Zubair oilfields. The pipeline runs parallel to the Tigris River as it races towards the Persian Gulf. Once out of land, the pipeline continues submerged to the twin oil terminals, Kohr al Amaya and Mina al Bakr.

It is amazing the sand is still gray and not blood red. Across the Fao Peninsula, the Iraq/Iran war extracted a two-year vengeance from the hapless people living there. The Iranians gained the peninsula, and the Iraqis were determined to regain the same piece of land. The cost was horrendous. At one point, the Iraqi army stored tens of thousands of corpses in huge refrigerators. To prevent an uprising against the regime during the Iraq/Iran War, the dead bodies were parceled out as carefully as any other rationed commodity. Saddam believed that if people learned the truth regarding the toll in human life, a revolution might have brought the regime down.

River traffic navigates north on the Tigris moving shallow draft boats from the Persian Gulf to as far north as Al Basra. Traditionally, Al Basra is Iraq's port city serving as the gateway to the Gulf. The Gulf War, and the resulting southern uprising, changed everything. The

Republic Guard crushed the rebellion with murderous rage leaving Iraq's port city barely functioning. The port lies unused, and the city's sewer system has never been repaired.

On the Tigris' eastern bank lies Iran—sometimes ally and sometimes enemy. To the west is the waterway leading to Umm Qasr. It is a natural inlet between Kuwait and Iraq. The Raudhatain oil fields lay along the once contested border. Between Al Faw and Umm Qasr, there is nothing but rugged terrain, burnt out hulls, and craters left from the Gulf War.

During the Gulf War, carrier based aircraft used the same inlet leading to Umm Qasr to navigate towards targets in Kuwait and southern Iraq. The shoreline's angle points like a dagger towards Al Basra, and the Tigris leads straight to the heart of Baghdad. Even when navigation computers failed in the shot up A-6 *Intruders*, pilots still found their way home following the inlet back to the waiting carriers. Had the amphibious landing taken place, as many speculated, part of it would have been against Jazirat Bubiyan—the island forming the eastern Kuwait border.

Tonight Al Faw took on a greater significance. A single lorry drove away from the populous riverbanks and into the desert night. A curious mixture of men rode into the darkness this night. Two sailors huddled in the rear of the lorry. Each was bound with heavy police-restraint handcuffs and leg irons. One was the hapless crane operator, who had killed several Chinese sailors the night before. His inattention with the crane and the ensuing panic left several men to the mercy of the sea. The other sailor was the first officer who had made the mistake of reporting the disaster.

Four members of the Special Republic Guard watched them. None of the soldiers spoke. They knew the price men paid for failure under Saddam's regime. These men had failed on a particularly important mission. They had no need to know the specifics of the mission, and if the truth were known, they had no desire to learn further secrets of their masters. Knowledge could get a person killed. It certainly doomed these sailors. No one doubted the outcome of tonight's activities.

The last two in the rear of the lorry were dressed in neoprene diving suits. In the dim light, they meticulously checked over their SCUBA gear, and the additional gear required for the salvage operation. An inflatable rubber raft, grappling hooks, lines, and underwater lamps lay in the far corner of the lorry. Each checked their weight belts, survival knife, regulator, and tanks. They would be operating underwater at night—something akin to near total blackness. Should the lamps fail, they might never find their back to the surface from inside the ship's hold.

Colonel Taha Duri sat in the passenger side of the lorry. He had no friends. Colonels of the *Al Amn al-Khas*—Iraq's Special Security Service—were supposed to be feared, not liked. He understood better than most the shifting tides within Iraq's security structures. It was like riding a wild horse through the night. He had learned to expect the unexpected. Betrayal and treason were always just beyond the horizon. A sharp knife between the ribs or a bullet in the back of the head often became a remedy for troublesome issues.

During the Gulf War, Duri stood behind hunkered down troops waiting for the Americans. Incredibly, men under his watch began surrendering en masse to the United States Army and Marine battalions as they punched through the berms without slowing. The Iraqi regulars broke under the pressure to fight. They emerged from the holes in the sand throwing away rifles and raising their arms. These men had survived the relentless air war. Day and night without end, the air forces of *Desert Storm* pounded their positions. Incendiary and anti-personnel bombs rained from the sky. They never knew a moment's rest.

Duri attempted to stop the mass desertion. He took his pistol and fired at men until he ran out of bullets. Stupidly, he yelled himself hoarse, his uniform torn and smoke blinded his eyes, an empty Makarov in one hand. Nothing more than a fool overrun by the Americans. They crisscrossed the sky in their *Apache* Gunships, and churned the sand with their *Abram* M1 Tanks. When dawn finally came during that hopeless night, he found himself a prisoner of war. American and British medics were tending his wounds and plastic restraints held his wrists tight. He still limped from the 5.56mm round he took that day in his leg.

Iraq's utter humiliation before the world was complete. For some unknown reason, the Americans stopped after one hundred hours. There was hardly anything left. The road leading from Kuwait to Al-Basra was nothing more than a smoking wreck of armor and men. Nothing survived the horrendous pounding delivered by the A-10 *Thunderbolts*. Death on land and air was complete. Baghdad lay defenseless before the American Armies. Oh, there had been token brigades from other countries, but no one doubted the aggressor. The Americans decided to stop before obliterating Baghdad and the Iraqi government. They left them in place as a gesture, perhaps to serve notice to others as to what they were capable of accomplishing.

Slowly, Iraq emerged from the rubble. Bridges were rebuilt; some equipment restored. The precious secret weapons were dispersed around to special sites. Duri had been repatriated after the war. He was attached to the Data Center security team—another fiasco.

Iraq's strategy for hiding banned weapons became a refined shell game. With oceans of trackless sand deserts and sixty-nine presidential palaces, Saddam had plenty of places to hide things. His chemical weapons labs, two hundred anthrax bombs and eighty SCUD and modified SCUD al-Hussein missiles were dispersed. The existing infrastructure facilities, such as the central Data Center and the nuclear separation labs, remained hidden beneath tons of rock and sand in buried bunkers.

The sites were disguised from the air; there were no surface installations besides the simple blockhouses with security teams within a fifteen to twenty kilometer radius. Of course, there were teams inside the installations, but due to the need for stealth and secrecy those teams were limited in size. Iraq had maintained extensive communications during the Gulf War using fiber optic cables buried in the sand. While the arrogant Americans were searching for conventional copper communication cables, Saddam was calmly prosecuting his war from his German made bombproof bunkers. Unless the air assault obliterated a position, Saddam rarely lost contact with his commanders.

The same fiber optic network remained in place after the war. No one knew for sure whether the Americans could trace the fiber network, but it continued to send data throughout the dispersed weapon centers. The Americans knew there were secret labs, and the Iraqis knew the Americans knew. Saddam relied on the current administration's lack of political will, and his belief in America's naiveté to keep his regime intact.

In 1992, a two-man team penetrated the Iraqi Data Center. Duri had been a captain then. He watched the piecemeal commitment of fire teams to the emergency. In the main computer room, there had been a firefight between one of the internal teams and the intruders. The closed circuit cameras caught most of the action. A great deal of damage resulted from the intrusion. The intruders were obviously from a western power; they wore body armor and fired American made weapons. One man raged with an M-16 A2; the other blasted with a short-barreled shotgun.

The firefight caused the intruders to abort their mission early as self-preservation overrode duty. They fled leaving supplies and weapons behind. A trail of blood marked their passage until they encountered the second internal team. The cameras showed incapacitation within seconds. The cameras also captured the best photographic evidence of the intruders. The faces were now part of a computerized database designed to match a face to existing graphics. Every Israeli, British, and American Special Forces intelligence officer known to the Iraqi SSS had been entered. It also included rogues like the two who penetrated the Data Center.

By the time sufficient security teams converged, the intruders had escaped into the desert. Iraq's computer systems were crippled for nine months. It had cost the General responsible for Data Center security his life. Second chances were not available in the Iraqi security services.

Duri survived the purges and came to Saddam's attention during the spring of 1996. He helped uncover a large-scale embezzlement ring inside the Sixth and Fourteenth Republican Guard divisions. Military weapons and material were being sold off to civilians in exchange for gold, hard currency, and sometimes food. Over one hundred fifty administrative officers were arrested. They took up new residence at Abu Gharib prison.

Abu Gharib had become a holding center for human guinea pigs. As with so many other things, the arrest and punishment of the Republican Guard officers became an object lesson. This lesson was directed both to those who might consider similar actions against Saddam's regime as well as to those who were the regime's defenders. Duri was charged with the transportation of the entire group from Abu Gharib—where they might have simply starved to death or received a merciful bullet—to Al Salman.

Al Salman had become a place cloaked in mystery. It was one of the secret special warfare sites where people entered and never came out. It had started out as an agricultural facility. There were even studies published regarding strains of wheat and corn. Most of this information was culled from the Internet and regurgitated for international consumption. Al Salman's true purpose was to test chemical and biological agents, first on animal, then on human subjects. The stench of urine, feces, and vomit lingered throughout the facility. It was protected by Special Republican Guard troops wearing biohazard uniforms and respirators. Visitors were not issued respirators or earplugs in order that the sites, smells, and sounds from Al Salman would have a lasting impression. Failure could cost much more than death. The lesson was not lost on Duri.

This night found Colonel Duri rushing towards the waters between Al Faw and Jazirat Bubiyan. He had risen through the ranks to become a responsible and trusted member of the security forces. Responsibility and success now raised the twin specters of failure and disappointment. Duri had no desire to join those he had sent to the chemical and biological warfare labs as test subjects. Even a man who had cut himself off from the pleasures of family and devoted his energies to survival could not vanish the sights and sounds he witnessed at Al Salman.

His particular charge was a delivery from the Red Chinese, and his specific problem were the two idiots riding chained together behind him. While those two would find their deaths this night, Duri intended to see the sun rise many more times. To do that he had to recover what he could of the shipment. Saddam's precious target list and his goal for revenge would probably cost more lives before it was over.

The lorry came to a halt on the shoreline of the Gulf. The sound of the surf rolling against the rocks and sand replaced the engine noise. Nothing but stars served as a faint light over the sand. Duri got out of the cab and walked around the end of the truck. He pounded on the side of the vehicle. The flap covering the interior flipped open.

"Bring them," he commanded and walked towards the surf casually unsnapping his holster.

His driver remained seated inside the truck. He, too, had learned the object lessons of Al Salman.

The two sailors were prodded forward at bayonet point. Chains jingled with their shuffling steps. The divers hung back by the truck waiting for instructions.

Once the shuffling stopped, Duri turned from the surf to the prisoners. He looked at both of them. Even in the cool autumn night, these two were sweating. He shrugged. "I will ask these questions one time."

Both nodded quickly.

Fear induced such compliance in people. Certainly, these fools knew what was coming. Their cooperation simply bought them the mercy of a quick death versus a prolonged torture at Al Salman. Duri enjoyed the fear he induced. He understood the nature of accelerated heart rates and adrenaline pumping like a raging river into their blood streams. It would change nothing.

"Where did you come ashore?"

Both sets of eyes leaped from his face to shoreline. A manacled hand rose and pointed down the shoreline. "I think I see the raft we landed in."

Duri followed the raised hands to where they were pointing. A crumpled yellow shape lay some two hundred meters down the beach. Duri started walking towards the spot. The others followed him in the jingling shuffle through the sand. No one spoke over the shuffle, jingle, and surf. Their fear spilled forth like a spreading oil slick on a calm sea. Both were praying to whatever gods they might know that it was the survival raft.

The divers and truck followed at a distance. Eventually, they arrived at a punctured raft pulled up on the beach. Two life preservers lay in the bottom of the raft. "This is it?"

"Yes." They nearly fell over answering him.

Duri turned to the pair. He considered shooting one of them. His hand fingered the leathered flap on his holster. Perhaps these two could still be useful. After all, no one would want to handle the casks anymore than required. Dead men should have no qualms about cleaning up the mess that they had created. The guards tensed expecting the Makarov to emerge in Duri's hand.

The moment passed.

Duri motioned the divers forward. They were special troops from his SSS command.

"Where's the ship?"

"Out about one hundred meters," explained the first officer. "It's about twenty meters below the surface."

Duri pursed his lips. He waved the truck and divers forward. He looked back to the two sailors. "Sit." They dropped to the beach like pair of highly trained dogs.

Now the wait began. Duri lit a cigarette and paced down the beach towards the surf. He took several deep drags before flipping it into the sea. An entire crew poisoned by the Chinese gift. If the story was to be believed, the entire crew succumbed to the chemical agent—men clawing at their respirator masks while their eyes dissolved at the same time. A toxin so deadly, the Captain made the decision to scuttle his ship rather than risk moving through the *Shatt Al Arab* waterway.

Instead of a few sailors lying dead at the bottom of the Gulf an epidemic could have spread on both sides. The Captain could have killed both Iraqi and Iranian citizens. Duri doubted the Mullahs would understand such a mistake. The Captain pulled his ship away from the densely populated banks of the *Tigris* River towards the waters between Iraq and Kuwait. He managed to scuttle the boat before they all died, and more importantly, before dawn.

Duri wondered about the American satellites and the spy planes. Did they know what had happened? Did they have pictures popping out of their computers and analysts examining the evidence? No one doubted their ability to search for things, but Iraq had developed an even greater ability to hide things.

A buoy broke the surface. Its tiny red lamp flickered advertising its position. Duri leaned forward. Perhaps he would survive this set back. His own heart rate accelerated as he began to believe his life would continue after tonight.

A second buoy sprang up two meters closer. Both casks had been found. Duri turned back to his prisoners.

"You have a chance to redeem yourselves. I want you to get those casks into the truck and make sure they are secure." He lit another cigarette. "Release them."

Incredulous, they lifted their hands to the guards. A key appeared and the manacles dropped to the sand. They galloped towards the surf.

Duri walked back to the truck and pulled out a map from his tunic. He opened the map for the driver and pointed to a red X. "Do you know how to get here?"

"Yes, Sir."

"Good. We leave immediately after the casks are secured in the rear. I don't care how fast you drive, but no accidents. That would be the least of our problems." He turned back to the surf. His prisoners were gleefully pulling the casks back towards the shore. If they dropped dead from anything other than bullet holes Duri had another problem. They were his canaries in the coalmine. The miners knew enough to leave when the canaries died.

He walked back to the guards. "I intend to leave you here to clean up the mess. When they have finished with the casks, shoot them. I'll send another vehicle for you in the morning."

Duri turned back to the truck. He climbed into the cab and lit another cigarette. He closed his eyes wondering how much longer he could continue in this present life. Sometime soon, it would be time to get out. He dare not ascend to the rank of General Officer.

The truck engine turned over. A noisy putter overpowered the surf outside. The gentle rumble working its way through the frame and a drowsy Duri barely heard the stutter of two automatic rifles. Another failure buried in the sand.

7

USS Springfield, Persian Gulf, Saturday, November 15, 1997, 8:30 PM (GMT + 3.00)

The *USS Springfield* slid through the dark waters beneath the Persian Gulf—a black hull on a black night in black water. She was a phantom cruising the sea on patrol. A constant vigil against enemies emanating from Iranian ports or interlopers emerging from lands further away. The United States had made it abundantly clear; they would tolerate no interference to keep oil flowing from the Arab spigots. This was a policy of national survival overriding the leadership vagaries residing at 1600 Pennsylvania Avenue.

Designated 761, she was one of the improved *Los Angeles* Class fast attack boats. This meant there were more options available in terms of armament coupled with a stealthier sound signature. The *Springfield* was a hole in the ocean constantly searching, listening, tracking—and if called upon—killing. She was a long way from Groton, Connecticut, the homeport of Submarine Group Two, Submarine Squadron Two. Her sister ships escorted carrier surface action groups like unseen terriers, watching and waiting. The *Pittsburgh* and the *Toledo* were Improved 688 fast attack boats as herself—the rest were first generation boats.

She wore her colors proudly. Her crew of one hundred forty ventured out on six-month patrols, and sometimes longer. This time they were attached to the *USS George Washington* task force. The *George Washington* was one of the newest Nimitz Class aircraft carriers. The aircraft carrier was a symbol of American power. Two carriers working in tandem provided air power totaling one hundred sixty aircraft. They were the forward presence of American authority and might.

The *Springfield's* task was to ensure troublesome underwater predators did not come close enough to endanger the 80,800 ton behemoth. She was one of the silent killers that roamed the seas beneath 6000 man boats. If the National Command Authority gave the order, the small one hundred forty man crews in deadly boats would ensure the *George Washington* could deliver the 4,600,000 pounds of ammunition she carried. While some may question America's leadership resolve, no one should ever doubt the ability of the American Navy to deliver.

Considering the *Springfield's* mission, the FLASH message traffic she received tonight disturbed Executive Officer Rob Bremmer. He carried the message folder to the Captain's quarters. Somehow, a Chinese *Han* class boat had penetrated the protective barriers surrounding the carriers. Certainly, the Chinese Boat must have come close to the *Nimitz or George Washington*. He knocked on the Captain's cabin door.

"Come," summoned Captain Jeff Andrews.

Rob entered and closed the door behind him.

Andrews looked up. "Robbie, what've you got?"

Rob set the folder on the Captain's table and took a chair across from him. "FLASH message traffic from COMSUBGRP2. It seems we have a visitor."

Andrews examined the photograph taken by the U2. He looked at the map plot and let out a long, low whistle. "What's a *Han* doing here?"

"It doesn't look they were enforcing the UN embargo," suggested Rob.

He pulled the photo from the papers and stared at it. "Any idea what they were giving the Iraqi's?"

Robbie shook his head.

"Okay. It's too small to be a missile, and no one in their right mind would try a nuclear transfer in the middle of the night on a choppy sea." He reached behind him and pulled an Intel folder from its rack.

"According to this, we've found most of the nuclear sites. What does that leave?" He stared at his XO.

Robbie followed his boss's thinking, "Chemical or biological."

Andrews nodded.

"It says here they think this boat might be hurt."

"Yeah, I saw that too, but I don't know what they're talking about. All this photo shows is the sub and the surface ship." He paused, "You have any idea what this is?" He pointed at the black square barely visible at the top of the *Han's* hull.

"Looks like a hole to me."

"Square?"

"Isn't this where their missile hatches should be?"

Robbie traced the square shape backward along the spine of the boat. There were no missile hatches. "Yeah, you're right. I don't see anything like what should be there."

Andrews picked up the photo again. He tilted his reading glasses forward to get a better look. "If I wasn't looking at a sub, I'd say this was a cargo hold."

"Maybe they know something we don't."

One thing submarine drivers despised were cute little intelligence boys sitting in their nice Virginia office buildings deciding what could and could not be shared with ships at sea. Andrews had a nasty feeling about this one. "Maybe they do."

He flipped to the orders page. "Did you take care of this already?"

Rob nodded. "Yes. I've plotted a course to the southern gulf about fifty to seventy-five klicks inside the Strait." There was only one Strait as far as the Persian Gulf was concerned. The *Strait of Hormuz* is a narrow choke point where an inordinate amount of the world's supply of oil flowed in huge supertankers. It was another duty of the US Navy to ensure no one took it into their fancy to block the Strait. The only way for the Chinese boat to exit the Gulf was through the Strait, and it simply was not possible to do without being noticed.

"It says here we're supposed to be goal keepers," Andrews scowled. "I wonder what they think that means. Deny sea passage to a Chinese sub. Does that give me authority to sink him?" He shook his head. An Admiral had not written this order. This order was issued by some flunky in Washington—or worse yet—Langley. Why would Langley write orders to submarines on carrier protection patrol concerning specific tactics in regard to a Chinese sub? He flicked his finger at the photo.

"I wonder how they got into the Gulf."

"The Russians used to have a trick with the SOSUS line where they would try and get their boomers through by riding the wake of one of their surface freighters. A really dangerous game in case someone stopped too soon." Andrews laughed. "It never worked really. The boys with the big ears at the NSA always heard them. We always knew when they were going to sortie a boomer and simply waited until they left their freighter before picking them up. I'd guess the Chinese followed a tanker through the Strait and we plain missed it."

He shook his head and snapped a finger at the map. "Fifty klicks south of Al Faw." He shook his head gravely. "That means they snuck up as close as possible to the coast without showing themselves." His mind started to churn with the possibilities—the same possibilities that had surfaced half a world away earlier the same day. The inescapable conclusion surfaced for Andrews. China was working with Iraq. Nothing good could come from such an alliance. He remembered the rumors from back home about campaign contributions, the Chinese manipulation of the elections, and Iraq's continued intransigence over UN weapons inspectors. Now, he had to find a Chinese sub. It all began to smell.

Sometimes it's better to ask forgiveness, rather than permission. Andrews could ask for clarification from COMSUBGRP2, or he could use his latitude regarding the orders. He sighed.

"Robbie, make sure we have fish in tubes one, two, three, and four. Tubes flooded, doors closed." He looked back to the photograph. "If we find this guy, he doesn't get to open water. If he twitches, we send him to the bottom."

Robbie looked across the table. Those were war fighting orders. "You think that's wise?"

"According to this message there is a suspicion that the *Han* might be damaged."

Robbie nodded slowly. "Damage can cut two ways. He may be slow or noisy or both."

"Yeah. Put yourself in his shoes. Say you've got a damaged boat and some casualties. First thing you've got to assess is whether you can fix the problems at sea." Andrews shrugged. "Maybe—maybe not. It would take some time to figure those things out and come up with a plan. I would rig for ultra quiet and go slow hoping to avoid detection."

"So you think a sub driver with a damaged boat is more dangerous?"

Andrews shook his head. "More desperate. And desperate men tend to gamble closer to the edge of their performance envelope. Until we know otherwise, we treat this one like a hostile."

8

Bartlett, Illinois, Saturday, November 15, 1997, 7:00 PM CST

Lynn Harper walked down the basement steps. From her vantage point, where the half wall of the staircase ended, she could see the back of her husband. He was sitting at his workbench. The gun safe was open in the corner, a canvas bag sat at the foot of his stool, and the computer screen flickered on the far corner of the bench. The Culpeper Minuteman Flag hung from the ceiling above him. Its motto read *Liberty or Death/ Don't Tread On Me*. That (and a few karate tournament trophies) was all that he kept as a reminder of a secret life and a secret past.

Metal ammunition cans were open and he was working bullets into several magazines. His stereo was playing Fernando Ortega's *Meditations*. The haunting piano melodies lilted throughout the basement. She knew it was one his favorites. It was the same album that he had played over and over during those dark days when his father lay dying in a nursing home. Cancer is such a devastating disease for it not only wastes the body, as in the case of Jim's Father, it kills the spirit too. Taped to the monitor edges was a picture of Jim when he was ten. He stood in the garage with his father and a Black Labrador Retriever named Josh. Another photo was propped on the keyboard. It was very recent with his father, mother, and their children clustered next to the fireplace during Christmas—photographs and memories without pain and suffering.

Behind him on the concrete floor rested a massive Black Labrador Retriever named *Indiana Jones*. The sad eyes looked across the basement to where Lynn was standing. Both wife and dog knew something was up. Jim had cleaned some of his guns. The pungent odor of Shooters Choice and Hoppes Number 9 permeated the basement air. Spent patches and lint free swabs were tossed in his garbage can. Jim always kept his guns cleaned and oiled, so any additional work meant he was preparing himself for action.

Action was one of those words Lynn could live without. Throughout the early years of their marriage, he had disappeared sometime for months at a time, sometimes for a few brief days. It was a part of his life about which she never quite knew the specific details. There were the times he had returned beaten and bruised. The broken arm, dislocated shoulder and bullet holes were not unusual injuries. Nor was it unusual for him to spend long hours brooding about what had happened.

There were the holidays, birthdays, and anniversaries he missed. The nightmares accompanied him home. He trained harder with a quiet intensity. He gave his entire being to becoming the best shot and smartest fighter. His trainers never questioned his bravery or his ability to hit hard and fast. They chided him about taking a hit to give one. His attention to detail and near photographic memory gave him an ability to work through complex problems.

His passions ran deep, and his commitment to his family ran deeper. She never questioned his commitment or his love. He was truly her best friend, and now this very dear man was preparing for *action* again. She did not need much imagination to understand that her husband would probably face danger and possible death, nor did she have any illusions that he would dispense the same. It had been years since someone had brought the past back. She thought this part of his life was over, but maybe it would never truly end.

Lynn had exploded angrily at him when he explained he was going back to Iraq. He had tried to explain about honor and duty. He had mentioned he was the best man for the job, something about unfinished business, and he had broken a promise about going back to the field. He had stood before the sweeping fury of her tirade, and made no effort to defend himself against her pointing fingers and angry scowls. He could only nod and agree with her.

She regretted her anger now. She also knew the name of the man calling her husband away from her and the girls again—Louis Edwards! She knew the lever used to pry Jim from his decision never to go back—Jerry. Jerry had been the best man at their wedding. Jerry and Jim had been on so many missions together. A Batman and Robin duo who, according to the rumor and gossip, could accomplish anything, go anywhere, and do anything a Langley mole or Beltway bandit concocted.

Then the unthinkable happened. Jerry did not come back from a mission. Jim came back a sunburned and dehydrated wreck. He spent two weeks in a NATO military hospital in Germany. When he arrived home, he was silent. He established a fund for Jerry's family, but not much got contributed. Today, they needed him again, and Jim extracted a steep penalty from Louis. A million dollar trust fund had been established this afternoon. The final cost might be very high, for Jim was leaving tonight.

Lynn knew his heart sometimes led his head, and she knew his sense of honor. Duty, honor, and fidelity summed up the man she had married twenty years ago. Over time she had learned to trust Jim's heart. He had an instinct to know the right thing to do without always being able to explain why it was right.

She closed her eyes again. She had spent the past half hour alone in their bedroom praying. Of the two of them, Lynn was the prayer warrior. Jim had learned to fight with his hands and mind. She learned to fight from her knees conversing with the Lord of creation. She prayed for her children and her husband everyday. There were tearstains on her Bible. Lynn Harper knew the meaning of sacrifice, and, once again, she was being asked to sit tight, put on a stiff upper lip, and wave good-bye.

She took the final steps down the staircase into the basement. She knew very little about the guns he kept. She never liked them, and asked why he wanted another one. As far as she was concerned, they all did the same basic thing—pull the trigger and go bang. Jim would talk about his guns like they were old friends, and she patiently listened to his descriptions. Eventually, he figured out she was humoring his exuberance.

She recognized the dull, black Glock and the Mossberg shotgun laid out on the bench before him. The third weapon was a Browning Hi Power. It was field stripped for cleaning and oiling. Lynn recognized the Browning from the distinctive hardwood grips and the stainless steel barrel. It was the gun he had brought back from Iraq. It was Jerry's gun. He had kept it after Jerry had died.

It occurred to Lynn—Jerry had died in Iraq. There was one reason for Jim to go back. He intended to right a wrong or fix a misdeed. He had come to some decision deep in his heart, and perhaps, even he did not know what that decision was.

Indiana Jones lifted his massive head and slowly his tail thumped hard on the floor. He revealed two other things Lynn had missed from the staircase: a combat dagger—favored by the British Special Air Service, and a combat knife favored by the United States Marine Corps. They had also been recently sharpened and oiled. No wonder the dog was worried; her husband was preparing for war.

She rested her hand on his shoulder and squeezed him assuredly. He looked up and patted her fingers. His touch lingered for a several moments. She leaned forward and whispered, "I'm sorry."

He nodded. "So am I."

"You have to go don't you?' she continued. There was no use fighting. She needed to send him to whatever fate he faced knowing she loved him—even if she did not completely understand.

"Yes."

She pointed to the disassembled Browning. "It has something to do with Jerry?"

His bottom lip quivered, "Something."

"And its something only you can do?" She needed to hear him say it was so. She needed to understand that he believed he was the only one capable. Even it were untrue, she needed to hear his conviction.

"Yes. Only me—I know how to get in and out." He replied knowing she had forgiven him again. How many times he had failed her he could not count. Yet, she continued to forgive him. "I'm simply going to diddle a computer system or two."

"You need guns to do this?"

"Well, the client might not agree with my approach to data management." He paused and said aloud what he had kept to himself when talking to Louis Edwards. "I don't intend to leave it in one piece this time. I'm going to destroy it all—completely."

"That's what I don't understand," she said shaking her head. "You have your guns, and your karate, and your shooting and sparring buddies. Why do you have to go and try to get yourself killed?" The terror she had calmed threatened to rise up and overwhelm her again.

"It's a point of honor. I never finished a task, because someone thought it better to leave the Iraqis with certain capabilities in place." He paused grinding his teeth. "That decision cost Jerry his life." He shook his head and muttered, "For what?" Had anyone watched Jim's face, they would have seen the warrior's mask descend on his features.

"Honor," she said hollowly. "What about the honor of a husband and father? What about the needs I have as a wife or those of your daughters? Where is the honor in getting killed? Jim, there are other people who can do this. There have to be," she said desperately.

He turned for the workbench and held her hands. He saw the tears held back and nodded. "Lynn, listen to me. I've been there. I went in and I went out. I know the technology better than any commando team they can drop in there. I know how to fight and I know how to survive. This is the last time. I promise you it's the last time." Even as he said those words, he wondered if it was truly the last time.

Lynn felt the conviction and the icy fear of her husband's intentions. "When do you leave?"

"Tonight—they'll be here in less than an hour."

She looked at the shotgun shells. They were a mixture of rifled shotgun slugs and various sizes of buckshot loads. Next to shotgun shells were the 115 grain full metal jacketed 9mm shells, and a collection of .45 ACP Gold Dot hollow points. They all weighed in at 230 grains. He had pulled them out of the ammo cans. Jim loaded them on the Dillon 650 XL reloader bolted into the bench's other corner.

He decided to take the Glock 21 because he trusted the gun to perform in the harshest conditions with virtually all types of ammo. Regardless of bullet configuration, sand, water, grit and congealing grease, the Glock had always performed. He had ten magazines for the 21, and decided to take a complete reload for each magazine.

The Mossberg was an obvious choice for close quarter combat. The last time they had penetrated the Data Center, the M16 A2 had proven to be a liability. There were too many angles and corners for the light 5.56mm round to deflect. The shotgun provided compact devastation without the fear of ricochet. Besides, the sound of a 12 gauge chambering a round has an incredible intimidation factor. People tend to run for cover.

The Browning was for luck. Jerry had carried the gun through several missions. The gun was considerably thinner than the Glock, and he had ten magazines loaded with hardball. He intended to use it as his backup gun stuck in a holster located on the small of his back. Since he was headed back to the place where Jerry had been killed, perhaps there would be a chance for pay back.

"Why are you bringing your stuff?" she asked, "Can't they supply what you need?"

He closed his eyes and breathed out. He dare not panic his beloved. "I know what I need, I have what I need." He was the doctor again. He waved his hand at the weapons. "These are my tools. I know how they act; I know what they do. I shoot them all at least once or twice a month. I trust them, and I am betting my survival on things I trust. Should I take a weapon that I know nothing about? Somebody else's gun?" He shook his head. "Trust me Lynn, I know what I'm doing."

He did not voice the other concern—his distrust of Louis Edwards and those who were sending him. He lived in a land ruled by people who had no honor, no integrity, and no allegiance to duty. He did not know yet what shape it would take, but a Judas would be along. Someone to ensure he did not get out of hand.

The most important weapon Jim would take with him was between his ears. But, it helped to know that when you squeeze the trigger and the firing pin punched forward, something went bang.

He squirted oil on the rails and behind the hammer down where the sear lived. He slid the barrel into the Browning slide, then attached the spring to the underside of the barrel. He slid the slide and barrel on the receiver's rails and punched in the retaining pin before working the slide back and forth a couple of times. Finally, he slid an empty magazine into the well of the Browning and pulled the trigger. The hammer snapped forward on the empty chamber. He removed the empty magazine, and slid a loaded magazine into the gun. He racked the slide again, and pushed up the manual safety. It was now cocked and locked.

He holstered the Browning. Carefully he placed the shotgun shells, magazines and reloads for the Glock into the canvas bag. He slid the Glock into a black nylon holster. He would secure on his belt and around his upper leg. The Mossberg was a modified from the factory original. Tacstar pistol and forend grips had replaced the normal stock grips, and a combat sling to carry it over his shoulder. He pushed six buckshot rounds into the sidesaddle carrier on the left side of the receiver.

The combat dagger was attached to his right leg above the boot. It never hurt to have things ready before Louis showed up. The combat knife was placed in the canvas bag. He felt the weight and was satisfied. It would be heavy, but not unmanageable. Finally, he loaded seven rifled slugs into the Mossberg's magazine.

"Come on, let's go talk to the kids before I leave."

Lynn stood with folded arms watching the man she loved change into a weapon. "You will be careful?" The cold ran its fingers down her spine.

He smiled and held her gaze, "I'm always careful."

"I have something for you. I know you'll be busy, but you'll need this somewhere along the way." She handed him her small pocket Bible, the one she carried in her purse. The gold leaf name at the bottom right corner said Lynn Harper.

"This is the one I gave you?"

She nodded. "It's small, and I know you don't have much room, but I would feel so much better if you took it with you."

He took it from her and placed it in the canvas bag next to the shells and magazines. "Thank you. I'll be sure to bring it back in good shape."

She closed her eyes and grabbed him as a sob racked her frame. "Just bring yourself back."

He patted her back and replied softly, "Always, love—always."

9

Washington DC, Saturday, November 15, 1997, 8:00 PM EST

Harvey Randall peered into the telescopic lens to stare at lump of rock next to a park bench. Staring at rocks on a Saturday night is not the stuff of recruiting posters. It is the fundamental action of a cop chasing bad guys. This particular rock was a dead letter drop.

A dead letter drop is like a night deposit box at a bank. Only in this case the bad guys used it to pass secrets from inside the government to a not so friendly foreign power. This particular dead letter had been dormant for six months. Tonight someone had used it.

Two hours ago the motion sensor, managed by non-visible laser light, detected someone moving the rock. This caused the PC connected to the laser via serial cable to activate a dialer program. The dialer flipped on the computer modem and dialed a series of special phone numbers. The software then waited for an answer and the triple chirp of the pager PBX to respond to the call. The computer responded with a preset number and disconnected.

A little less than two hours ago Harvey's pager went off. He read the number off his pager display and realized something big was happening. The robotic sentinels were calling. Someone had just put something under the rock.

Simultaneous with the motion detector alarm, three low light sensitive video cameras activated. They were positioned to triangulate on the same spot. The high-speed film recorded a man bending down behind the park bench, lifting the rock up and depositing a plastic wrapped bundle into the hole beneath the rock. The hole was lined with a PVC pipe four inches across and a foot deep. If needed, one could hide a full size automatic pistol and still have space left over.

Ever since the eruption of Chinese campaign irregularities, the Federal Bureau of Investigation had been tasked with surveillance of all Red Chinese intelligence operations. Perhaps the public had forgotten, but bagmen for the Red Chinese government influencing federal elections is a national security threat. The implicit payment for the contribution was to place several people into sensitive positions inside the administration.

The FBI is a member of the intelligence community like the Central Intelligence Agency. The FBI is the primary federal agency tasked with security issues related to domestic terrorism such as Oklahoma City and countering foreign intelligence services like the former Soviet KGB. When the Berlin Wall came tumbling down, America's enemies became a far more diverse lot. The number of hostile foreign services attempting to penetrate and steal secrets from the American Government and industry had multiplied like a terrible cancer.

Larry Wheeler, Harvey's partner, ran the videotapes again. "Any idea who he is?"

Even with three cameras triangulated to capture the drop from multiple positions, the only tangible evidence was the back of a head and gray raincoat. The face and hands were obscured. For all the modern technology, a cop on the spot would have been a much better witness. Due to budgets being what they were in a cost conscious Washington, and the unpopular nature of chasing Chinese moles, a cop on the spot was a fantasy that Harvey would never be realized.

Harvey shrugged and looked away from the telescope. "No, but something must be up. They haven't used this drop in six months. I thought they knew it was being watched."

Larry nodded. It bothered him. He suspected the Chinese knew they were under intense surveillance. He speculated that there was someone in the White House passing information over to the Chinese Embassy. They were not very far from 2300 Connecticut Avenue Northwest—the home of the Chinese Embassy. It was a brisk evening's walk. The question before them was who would be servicing the drop. Was it a junior level flunky or someone higher up the food chain? The answer to that question would indicate the quality and urgency attached to the drop.

"I wonder how they make contact," mused Larry. This was a point that bothered both men. The sophistication of their quarry suggested they were past the days of using chalk marks on sidewalks or changing the position of bricks in a walk. Maybe it was as simple as the position of the drapes on somebody's windows, but the problem was that most everyone who might be the security leak lived outside the District's boundaries. The Chinese had been strictly confined to a very narrow and manageable boundary.

Harvey shrugged as he poured some tepid coffee from his thermos. "Do we have authority to grab anyone?"

"Only *Goldenrod*," replied Larry. *Goldenrod* was the suspected chief of station for the *Guoanbu*, China's State Security Ministry. Of course, *Goldenrod* was rarely seen doing anything but promoting Chinese culture. The only victory the FBI had been able to manage with the State Department was to restrict *Goldenrod's* activities to the Washington—New York corridor.

"I say we start with the White House on this one. I think the leak is there," explained Harvey.

Larry nodded. He popped the top on a Diet Coke. He never got use to the taste of coffee, especially coffee on a stake out. "I know what you're driving at, but I don't think we'll get to start there. They're still upset over congressional testimony on campaign finance irregularities, at least, I think they're suppose to be upset."

Harvey flipped the video monitors back to real time. The gray-green shadows of the night vision scopes reflected the nether world in the park. A shadow flicked in the background across the screen. Harvey took a sip of his coffee. A second and third shadow emerged flanking the first shadow. They moved like bodyguards. Their heads kept moving back and forth searching for any anomaly.

Harvey tapped Larry's shoulder. "I think we've got company."

Larry looked at the monitor over Harvey's shoulder. He turned to a manila file folder and flipped it open. *Goldenrod*'s fish dead eyes stared back at him—a face without a trace of humor. Certainly not the sort you would pick for a cultural attaché. However, if the Chinese had multiple assets in the American administration, then they would need a pro to manage those types of resources.

Goldenrod was the prize—a man with no known identity. He appeared across the world at several postings: Moscow, Berlin, London, Bonn, Tel Aviv, and now, Washington. The name was inconsequential and the embassy position usually benign. Each time he appeared the face had changed. What had not changed were the eyes. The British had developed a long-range retinal scan. They managed to match *Goldenrod* to three other legends around the world, and the powerful computer databases at Langley made the other connections. Each time a different legend meticulously developed, and the common thread was always a highly placed mole inside the host government's elite power structure. *Goldenrod* was given a free reign because he produced intelligence product unlike anyone else.

He had another trait of usually disappearing like the fog on a bright day just before the scam collapsed. Now, *Goldenrod* was operating inside the United States. Harvey and Larry knew the pattern. They had read extensively the information shared with them by the British and American intelligence communities. They were dealing with an artist.

The face on the screen slowly swam into focus as he approached the dead letter drop. The bodyguards fanned out to form a box around the central figure. Two more were visible in the background, and they were doing very little to disguise the weapons in their hands. "You taping this?" Larry asked excitedly.

"Every second," said Harvey.

He picked up the phone and punched the speed dial. The phone connected to a tactical response team on duty at the Hoover Building.

Larry looked at the green face blurring in and out of focus and back to the photo he had in his hand. "Do you know what we got here?"

"Pay dirt?"

"We got the man!" The face in the photo matched the face on the screen.

Harvey looked over his shoulder at Larry. A big grin was emerging across his features. They had *Goldenrod* in the act. "This is Harvey Randall." He spoke into the phone. "I need an intercept on the Chinese Embassy. That's at 2300 Connecticut Avenue Northwest. We've got hostile action by Chinese nationals." Well, it was not hostile quite yet, but four bodyguards visibly brandishing firearms did not make for a nighttime picnic.

He dropped the phone back into the cradle. The figures on the screen had formed a protective circle around *Goldenrod*. He was bending over the rock like an uncertain cat—curious yet cautious. One last time he looked up and scanned the surrounding area. He sensed the eyes watching, but could not see them. The hand hovered over the stone as he weighed the risk of discovery against the value inside. Risk lost out.

Several blocks to the southeast a squad of black-clad marines clambered into a helicopter. Two squad cars from the DC Police Department diverted from their normal patrol routes and headed for the entrance to the Chinese Embassy. A phone call was made to the office of the FBI Director. Any action against the Red Chinese drew the interest of the highest levels of the American Government. Sometimes the interest was not devoted to protecting and preserving the Constitution.

Harvey flipped the tape system to full automatic. He grabbed his coat and followed Larry down the hall and out the back door of the house. Both had pulled their badges and guns. Neither wanted a shoot out, but sometimes you did what you had to do.

"You got your vest on?" Harvey asked.

Larry shrugged. "I didn't think I needed it for tonight." These things always went down when you thought it was over for the day.

They raced around the front of the house and darted across 15th Street Southwest into the park. Harvey held up his badge in one hand and flipped the safety down on the Smith & Wesson 1066. Harvey liked the 10mm round, and did not mind the wrist twisting recoil it delivered. Larry, like many others in the Bureau, had opted for the tamer recoil of the .40 SW round.

Both men spread at diagonals once they crossed the street. Harvey waved the badge once before pulling his hand down and yelled, "Stop, FBI!"

Having seen the guns on the night scopes, and recognizing they were attempting catch a Chinese spymaster in the act, Larry found the nearest shrubbery with a diving roll. Harvey came to a rolling stop next to a tree bringing the hefty Smith & Wesson 1066 to bear. The Novak LoMount sites had been augmented with tritium inserts. A perfect three-dot site picture emerged on the chest of the nearest bodyguard.

Time seemed to slow down as the startled Chinese spun towards the voice and started to raise his gun hand. It was obvious these boys did not intend to come away peacefully.

Before the bodyguard had raised his gun hand half way, Harvey squeezed off the first shot. He felt the kick and barely noticed the solid crack of the gun. His ears were already ringing from the blast. He reacquired his target and fired a second round. He dropped the weapon to his hip and rolled his body around the other side of the tree.

The 10mm slugs punched two convincing smacks on the trauma plate of the Chinese bodyguard's Kevlar vest. He flipped backwards coming down hard on his seat, before rolling over on his hands and knees to crawl away from where he had been shot. Harvey reacquired his target and grunted, "Figures—body armor."

Goldenrod snatched the packet from the drop box and scurried back into the gloom of the trees and playground. The other forward flanking guard sent two rounds of return fire. They thunked into the tree trunk inches from Harvey's head. Wood splinters punched out from the tree and threw dust into Harvey's eyes.

Larry, having witnessed the resistance of the first guard, aimed for the kneecap of the second shooter. He was not the marksman that Harvey had become so he opted for a *pray and spray* strategy. He pumped out six rounds before scuttling across the ground to end up behind one of those garbage cans chained to a post. He went prone since the thin sheet metal of the garbage can would hardly stop anything above a .177 pellet gun.

The rear two bodyguards had physically grabbed *Goldenrod* and were actively hustling him through the park towards the Euclid Street Northwest park border. If they got to a car, it would be far more difficult to capture and convict the Chinese of any wrongdoing.

Harvey rolled out from cover and headed in a sprint after the three retreating Chinese. A flash and zing greeted him from the second shooter. Larry's *pray and spray* had missed. Harvey bent double into a crouch and held out the Smith with his weaker left hand. He fired two more rounds in the general vicinity of the second shooter.

Boom! Flash! Boom! Flash!

Harvey never saw the first shooter rise out of the bushes and rush him like the Green Bay Packer's Gilbert Brown. It must have taken whatever was left of the bodyguard to make the hit, but he expertly buried his right shoulder into Harvey's middle. The collision sent Harvey sideways and down a short hill. His gun spun away into the dark, and he might have gotten up again had it not been for the steel handrail on the steps. He slammed headfirst into railing, and the lights went out.

The second shooter retreated towards the thickening gloom. He squared his shoulders and presented a larger target to Larry. Larry pulled himself up to a picnic table and settled himself into a crouch that extended his arms over the table. He locked both arms and steadied the butt of the gun on the table's surface. The bouncing target was becoming increasingly difficult to see. Spots danced in Larry's vision from the first volley of shots.

He figured he had half a magazine left, but at best, he would get off two shots before his target changed direction and disappeared forever. He let out his breath, steadied his body, and started shooting. He continued until the slide locked back on an empty magazine.

He left the picnic table in a loping run hoping to miss whatever obstacles remained. Night had fallen completely, and the few lights in the park provided little help in tracking down the second shooter. He pressed the magazine release catching the empty magazine in his hand and depositing it in his side jacket. Hollywood always let their heroes throw magazines away, but at thirty dollars each, Larry would just as soon hold on to his. He slammed a fresh magazine home and thumbed the slide release.

Larry never saw the second shooter laying face down in a blossoming puddle of blood. He was heading for Euclid Street, already knowing he was too late. The slam of car doors and the squeal of tires told him he had missed his chance to catch *Goldenrod.* He came to a stop in the brighter lights of the street lamps, his gun held at his side, his chest heaving from the run, and a foul taste in his mouth.

He pulled the portable Motorola radio from his inner coat pocket. "Harvey—you there, buddy?" He clicked the receive switch and listened—nothing but the radio hiss. "Harvey!" he repeated anxiously.

Larry turned back to the park and cursed. He started running back towards where he had last seen his partner. They were out of the fight for now. It was up to the District Police and the Marines. Larry doubted *Goldenrod* would head for the Embassy tonight. They probably had a safe house somewhere in the city. There would be no protest from the Chinese because this never happened. It was one of those silent battles sometimes fought in exotic places, but more often in the mundane and everyday locales of picnic tables and playgrounds.

Larry never saw the first shooter slither through the shadows to the body of the second shooter. He was intent on finding Harvey alive and in one piece. The last two Chinese agents disappeared into the night as well. The explosion of gunfire in the nation's capitol did not even elicit a 911 call. Drug dealers and gang lords had long since made this a common occurrence.

Harvey blinked his eyes open, then closed them again. His forehead felt like it had been used for batting practice in the World Series. His radio squawked. He found he was lying on a slope with his head pointing down. It was awkward to reach his radio, but he managed it on the second try. "Yeah, Larry," he said.

"Hey, buddy—you're still alive!" He laughed with relief and happiness that comes from finding out everyone was still breathing after a firefight. "Eh, Harvey, where are you?"

Harvey looked around and swung his feet down. "At the bottom of some steps," he answered. "Larry, did we get them?"

A longer pause—a less exuberant reply, "No, they got away."

Harvey nodded to himself in the dark and spat some blood from a cut cheek. "Okay, we start on the White House in the morning. This guy had some important stuff. Otherwise *Goldenrod* wouldn't have come out tonight."

Larry came puffing over the slope and spotted Harvey on the ground. He dropped the radio back into his pocket and said, "I know, but let's go get a beer first. It's been a long night." He helped Harvey to his feet and found his gun. They limped towards the house where the surveillance system was still running.

"I wonder what was in that packet," muttered Harvey.

Larry chuckled, “When we find out who, then we’ll know what. You got his picture, all it’ll take is some time.”

Harvey nodded. Their investigation had entered a new phase. It came down to knocking on doors and showing photographs. Usually this was an easy thing to accomplish for the FBI. The intimidation factor alone caused most people to tell all. Not so when the address was 1600 Pennsylvania Avenue.

10

Andrews Air Force Base, Saturday, November 15, 1997, 11:00 PM EST

The massive C-5B *Galaxy* lay waiting under the watchful glare of the hanger lights. Vehicles were still packing gear aboard the huge craft. Technicians were checking data read-outs on hand held terminals, and fuel trucks were quietly moving away from side of the aircraft. The pilot was taking a final walk around the plane looking for anything that might be amiss.

It was parked at a hanger away from the normal traffic in an area reserved for high security aircraft like *Air Force One* and *Two*. The anxious air surrounding the men and women running through the final checklists was palpable. While they might not know what was going down, the last minute arrival of two AH-64 *Apache* gunships armed with the best weaponry Hughes Aerospace could deliver, and a pair of HMMWV's packed with .50 machineguns and hand held stinger missiles spoke of men going hunting.

The desert battle dress uniforms worn by the Force Recon Marines identified the general location; the only question was whether this mission would ultimately land in Iraq or Iran. The visibility of hard plastic ammunition boxes, a Barrett .50 sniper rifle, and plentiful amount of C4 plastic explosives for demolition suggested the rules regarding security would once again be reiterated. In addition to those toys there were several canisters of non-lethal nerve gas, gas masks with regulators, and a dozen M-181A Claymore Antipersonnel Mines. This was being carefully packed into the HMMWV's rolling aboard the C-5B *Galaxy*.

The nose of the *Galaxy* was still flipped up and over the flight deck that sits above the cargo deck. The mottled gray and green coloring suggested a deployment designed for Northern Europe rather than the deserts in Iraq. It was one of the newer planes built since 1989 with improved engines, structural support, fuel economy, and state of the art avionics.

Jim Harper stood next to Louis Edwards. He had changed into desert BDU's during his flight from Chicago to Washington. The Glock 21 was strapped to his leg in a drop down holster secured to his web belt. The nylon straps were pulled snug, and an extra magazine rested in the built in pouch secured by a Velcro strap.

The Browning Hi Power rested beneath his clothing at the small of his back. Its holster hung on his belt as the straps slid through the built in belt loops. The gun butt pointed to the right making it a natural motion to grab and draw the weapon should the need arise.

His combat knife was opposite the Glock on his left leg. It was held in a black leather sheath. The six and half inch blade had a curved tip and serrated edge opposite the cutting blade.

The distinctive Mossberg rested in the grip bag between his feet. He became the soldier he had been for fifteen years. His bag held the extra ammunition and magazines for his guns, a change of clothes, and Lynn's small Bible that she had pressed into his hands as he left the house. As with many black ops, there were no dog tags, clothing labels, or wallets. He had left his wedding ring on his nightstand, and held secret the Bible and pictures inside.

"It's almost time Jimbo," he smiled.

Harper grunted. He had been briefed on the plane ride about the mission. It was 1992 all over again. This time they wanted him to waltz into the buried bunker guarded by an unknown number of soldiers, raid a database, and peruse the data with a Lieutenant Stillwell—a weapons expert from the civilian sector. Somehow, the six of them were suppose to neutralize the Iraqi security detachment.

Jim turned to Louis and asked, "Do they know we're coming?"

Edwards paused, "No. How could they know?"

Jim looked down at the ground then back to Edward's eyes. "They knew when Jerry and I went into their Data Center back in '92. They knew. They were waiting for us."

"You think we have a leak." Edwards smiled. "No way. The only people who know about this are Jonas, George Carnady and myself. Which one of us would want you to fail?"

Jim rested his hand on the butt of the Glock. "Louis, I don't think you have leak. I *know* you have a leak. What I want to know is whether or not it has had a chance to leak yet."

Louis chuckled nervously. "It didn't come from me, Jim. I—"

"Louis, if it did come from you, remember something. I'll be back. I'm not going to die in the desert this week. If they know we're coming, you won't be able to run far enough or fast enough." His eyes never left Edward's face. The dull blue gray hue showed no mercy. The warning had been made—betrayal would not be tolerated. This time someone would pay.

Louis shifted his weight uncomfortably. Jim Harper could become a ghost capable of passing through security systems and international borders as easily as most people change clothes. Louis had been one of his trainers. They had made a human weapon, and tonight the weapon was being pointed and fired at Saddam's war machine. In a few days, the weapon could boomerang. Jim's certainty and passion suggested Louis spend some time investigating the possibility of a leak elsewhere in the intelligence community.

Louis nodded. "I understand. I'll look into it."

"Okay. Let's go meet the team." He reached down and hefted his grip. They walked towards the ramp where five men were standing. None of them wore insignia designating rank. The marines were obvious by their young looks and excellent condition. The fifth man standing at the end of the line was pale and somewhat chubby. He looked as though the prospect of a mile hike might be more than he was capable.

Louis smiled at Harper then turned to the team, "Gentlemen, may I present Major James Harper—your team leader."

The five turned their attention towards Jim. He felt like a horse at auction. Men roving over his features attempting to evaluate what sort of major they had been saddled with this time. No one wants to take a baby-sitting mission into Indian country. They already had one over the hill Lieutenant in their midst, but Lieutenants can be ignored. Majors with command rank were a different matter. Men who had been civilians for five years represented a more ominous factor—the loss of drive and the keen edge a warrior needs in order to survive.

"May I present Captains Anderson, Burns, and Kincaid, Master Sergeant Hayes and Lieutenant Stillwell." Stillwell looked up from his position at the end of the line. He definitely wanted to be somewhere else. Harper did not detect fear, rather resignation to his fate. The other four dissected their new leader.

"Gentlemen," continued Louis, "This is Major Jim Harper. Any questions?"

Burns looked at the civilian spook. "Yes, Sir." He was looking at Edwards, not at Jim.

Harper knew what was coming. He probably would have had the same objections. However, age tempered youthful folly. "Captain."

His voice carried the command authority learned in the field. If he was going to bring these men home, they needed to trust him now. They had to believe he could do the deed. *There must be no doubt.* Burns snapped his head around to examine Harper, the loathing evident on his features quickly dissolved to respectful neutrality.

"Sir?" The response was automatic.

"Speak your mind, but be quick about it." He nodded to plane they were standing next to. "We've got a plane to catch."

Burns shrugged. "Yes, Sir. I think I speak for the rest of us—"

"Really?" Harper surveyed the group. Burns might speak for the Marines; no one spoke for the pudgy man standing by himself.

Burns followed Harper's gaze. "Yes, Sir."

Harper became immobile. He was the fighter in the match now waiting on his opponent. When he moved, the counter strike would be swift and certain. His stature seemed to grow like a cat suddenly cornered by a large dog.

"Sir, with due respect, you have been retired for five years. For some reason, you've been placed in command over us. I don't think it's good idea to have a civilian running soldiers in a military operation."

Edwards held his breath and waited.

Harper moved a step forward sucking the air and light from amongst the group. "Captain, let me put it correctly. You tell me when I get this wrong—okay?" He never waited for a reply.

"You've pulled duty to spend time in Indian country. It's what you've trained for—all those simulations and drills. There were nights when they dumped you upside down in a swamp and told you to phone home. Now, when the big dance arrives, you've got to follow a forty-year-old Major you never heard of.

"I've been told you are Force Recon Marines. The best of the best this country has to offer. I know you have trained, sacrificed, and believe you are better than anyone else around. Who knows—maybe you are. The most important thing you bring with you is not your weapons or your training or your fine knowledge. The most important thing is your honor to do the right thing at the right time—the ability to use your head and your heart, instead of just your fists and gun.

"You've been lined up for a black op by a fat old spook, and you look around to find you got an out of shape Lieutenant hanging around the end of the line. You don't like what you see. You think you're smart enough, keen enough to pull this off yourself and you resent the idea of somebody coming out of retirement to steal your thunder. IS THAT ABOUT IT CAPTAIN?"

Burns looked straight ahead. He had crossed a line to find steel.

"No answer, huh?" Harper walked down the line towards Stillwell. "I didn't think so." He turned back to the Marines ignoring Stillwell. Stillwell was a different problem. "Let's all understand something. Yes, we are going to Indian country. Yes, they have guns and they know how use them. It is my fervent hope and intention to bring each and every one of you back in one piece." He came to a stop before Burns. "That can only happen if you jump when I say jump. I've been there, Captain. It's not as simple as you might think, and these things always look easier from a distance. I buried a good friend in the desert, and I had to go see his wife. I had to explain that I failed to bring her husband, her best friend, home again.

"I don't know what will happen this time. I'm not sure where Murphy will pop up. However, I give you one promise; I will do my best. Let's get one thing straight—I lead, you follow. If you can't live with that, then stay here on the tarmac. Otherwise, cross me in combat and the Iraqis may not get a chance to shoot you."

He looked at his four Marines. "Any other questions?" he snarled.

They were all standing crisply at attention—except for Stillwell. He ignored Stillwell for a moment longer, "Good. Then get your gear and get aboard—or get out of the way."

The four Marines saluted and headed towards their gear. No one spoke. No one braved eye contact. Stillwell stared at their retreating backs and shrugged. He hefted his grip.

"A moment Lieutenant," said Harper.

"Jimbo, you really know how to endear yourself to your men." The gray eyes were not smiling and the ruddy complexion was a couple of shades redder.

Harper turned to Edwards. "Louis, those men have every right to be suspect of my abilities. They're the ones under service right now, and if our positions were reversed I wouldn't think too much of the idea myself. Now, run along and make sure the Iraqis aren't waiting for me." He spun on his heal back to Stillwell.

Stillwell spread his hands. "Look—ah, Major I didn't have anything to do with this. I sort of—"

Harper clapped him on the back saying, "I know that Lieutenant, but why don't you tell me what you are suppose to be doing. Forgive me, but you don't look like someone ready to hike through Southern Iraq. By the way, what's your first name?"

The animal on display seconds ago was now caged. Stillwell wondered briefly if they were headed to Iraq with a psychopath.

"Brian—Brian Stillwell, and until this morning I was honorably discharged for twelve years."

"This morning?" Harper shook his head. They had certainly been busy today. It was as if they had a checklist they were following. "What happened this morning?" He picked up his grip and the two started walking up the ramp towards the main cargo deck.

"I was called to a briefing over at the Pentagon. They showed us the photographs of the Chinese sub and the Iraqi boat. They had lots of pictures. Anyway, there was a meeting after the meeting and, pretty as you please, the National Security Advisor handed me a letter personally signed by the Secretary of the Army. It basically says I am on active duty."

"Just like that?"

Brian nodded, "Just like that. Next thing I know they are fitting me out in BDU's finding me some boots, and going through the basics of the M-16. I end up with a doctor and get half a dozen shots before meeting the Marines." He shrugged again. "Needless to say, they were less than thrilled to see me."

The last thing loaded into the *Galaxy* was a trailer. It resembled a small, mobile command post. The festoon of antennae and satellite dishes carefully tied down to prevent damage during transport.

Stillwell and Harper found a pair of seats on the flight deck above the cargo hold.

"Why don't we strap in and you can explain to me what you do."

Brian laughed for the first time in several hours. "You know, my boy asks me the same question." It sounded familiar to Jim as well. "Roughly, I am a specialist in unconventional weaponry. Not the simple stuff like homemade napalm or C4, but the more damaging stuff like VX, your basic suitcase sized nuclear bomb, fuel air explosives, and the like.

"I write books on the subjects, albeit, most of what I write is classified and has to be shared between governments. I worked with Teller's team when Reagan announced he was going to build High Frontier. Of course, no one calls it that anymore; we all refer to it as Star Wars. Anyway, that's where I learned about *Brilliant Pebbles*." *Brilliant Pebbles* was the anti ballistic missile system of orbiting platforms designed to seek out MIRV (Multiple Independently targeted Reentry Vehicles) platforms and explode a barrage of ball bearings into the warheads. It acted as a huge shotgun blasting at nuclear clay pigeons.

"They worked too. If we put enough of them in orbit and timed the trajectories correctly the Russians could have launched as many warheads as they wished. It's hard to land on target or in tact with thousands of holes in your warheads. It didn't even have to be explosive. When an ounce of metal hits something at five six thousand miles an hour it leaves a noticeable hole in it."

"Like a shotgun spread?' offered Jim.

"Exactly!" His enthusiasm faltered slightly. "Of course, we never deployed anything. The Berlin Wall crumbled. You know, Reagan was right. He knew it was going to collapse. We met with him a couple of times. He never cared what they were saying about him. He just plowed ahead. His vision of the world was a world without the Soviet Empire. Teller and the rest of us were a convenient club to threaten the Russian bear. It worked. They had no doubt we could achieve a space-based defense against missile attack.

"Reagan was too successful. We never got it deployed before the Russian economy collapsed, and with it the Soviet military threat shrunk overnight."

Jim nodded. "We still have enemies."

Brian warmed to his subject. "That's exactly right. We have a lot of them too. The Red Chinese, North Korea, Iraq, Iran, perhaps India and Pakistan—they all want to be top dog. They all are attempting to become the bully on the block.

"Of course, once you develop the kind of expertise we engendered when we were working for Teller, no one was willing to throw it all away. The new administration shut down SDI, but they kept most of the brains on retainer. They set me up in Crystal City in my own little office. They gave me direct access to several top-secret labs and told me to imagine new weapons systems and evaluate old weapon systems. I was discharged from government payroll, so they could pay me more as a contractor, and that's what I have been doing through the nineties. I think about the unthinkable. I figure out ways to bring bombs, biological, and chemical agents into this country. I read most of the classified intelligence abstracts on all the bad boys.

"We even try and keep track of all the Russian scientists loose around the world. Some of them are working for us. Of course, the current administration would never want to admit that they are just as interested in creating doomsday weapons as the rest of them. They just don't want to build or deploy the weapon systems. If we come across anything really nasty, we work out countermeasures and then track the technologies necessary to build those systems. That's why we watch Iran and Iraq so closely. They've got the money to build some bad stuff."

Jim nodded. "So you're my unconventional weapons expert. Louis said you could figure just about anything out."

"Yeah, that's me. You've seen the photographs of the submarine transfer?"

"They showed me a couple of them. I assumed there had to be more."

"I spent the afternoon looking into those photos. They managed to get me the computer-enhanced stuff from the National Reconnaissance Office. It really is rather ingenious what the Chinese did. I think the Chinese built an elevator shaft into the hull of their submarine. They probably traded some hull integrity to build a delivery truck—so to speak. It makes a certain kind of sense. They certainly couldn't fly the stuff into Baghdad through the no-fly zones, embargoes, and the US Fifth fleet on patrol."

"So they tried to sneak it in under water."

"Exactly! Pretty slick adaptation of the technology. After all, the *Han* class sub isn't that their first line boat anyway. They never were that much of a threat—too noisy for one thing, limited payload for another. They kind of copied what we do with our old missile boats. They find a new application and use the hull.

"Anyway, they bring whatever they're passing to the Iraqis under the cover of darkness, and we just happen to capture it on film. It's dumb luck really. If they hadn't started shooting at each other, we would have never paid any notice to the files. But there aren't supposed to be rifle shots in the ocean fifty klicks south of Al Faw.

"The NRO boys find this stuff and run the image enhancement software over the digital images returned from the U2. They find themselves a Red Chinese submarine where no Red Chinese submarine is supposed to be. Now it makes an awful kind of logic.

"China wants to control the Pacific Rim. There are all those Asian economies booming out there. You've got a couple of problems though. Japan, which is an economic superpower, a fragile superpower, but still the eight hundred pound gorilla. The other problem is South Korea. They are pumping out computer peripherals, VCR's and TV sets like there's no tomorrow, out doing Japan at its own game.

"China and the Pacific Rim countries are like Russia andWestern Europe. The Soviets never wanted to incinerate Western Europe. Their goal was always to capture it intact, otherwise, why bother to attack.

The Russian's problem was always the United States and its nuclear shield. Okay, so we cross out the Russians. We got the same problem on the other side of the world. The Red Chinese want to control the Pacific Rim, and maybe they want Taiwan back too. Personally, I think that's lip service."

"So they start handing out weapons of mass destruction to Middle Eastern madmen?" suggested Jim.

"Yeah. That's what's going on. Only it's bigger than that. They need to neutralize America. They obviously can't beat America in a head to head fight. They are basically a land-based power. Any confrontation at sea might be costly to us but we would win. There is no more potent weapon system than a carrier based task force. We'd sink them just like we would have sunk the Russians.

"The Chinese have a problem. First, they have to create a threat outside of the sphere of influence. There are a lot of candidates, but certainly, Saddam is the craziest of the bunch. That's not to say the Iranian Mullahs aren't bonkers, but we need a proven bogeyman, so we use what's already been created. None of the Iranian Mullahs have name recognition like Saddam, and George Bush never finished Saddam off. They were too busy working on the one hundred hour war speech and playing silly geopolitical games.

"Next, they start funding presidential elections through illegal campaign contributions. A little hoopla in the South China Sea with war games, and pump up Saddam's war machine with a few nukes and chemical weapons. Not enough to make the fellow dangerous to the homeland, but enough to threaten American interests like the Saudi oil fields and Israel.

"Finally, the Chinese sit on the UN Security Council and refuse to agree to reasonable American demands about weapon inspections in Iraq. Keep thc pot boiling and eventually it'll blow. That's what they are counting on. Force the US to act unilaterally against Saddam, pick your target, and move. They couldn't care less about Saddam or the oil. They want America distracted and committed to the wrong threat."

It made a sick kind of sense. "You figured this all out this afternoon looking at some pictures?"

Brian shook his head chuckling, "No, no. I wrote this scenario up this past summer. The Russians always used the chess paradigm. The Chinese prefer indirection. You know, martial arts and that sort of thing."

"I'm vaguely familiar with the martial arts kind of thing, but I'm not following you exactly," replied Jim.

"Well the martial arts thing is split into two basic systems. Use your attacker's force and power against him—that's basically Aikido. Or, you cause your opponent to believe the fake move just before you punch their lights out—that's Tae Kwon Do. I think the Chinese have merged both concepts into their current strategy."

Stillwell might not be in fighting trim, but he was a great talker, and Jim could appreciate the thought behind his words.

"Besides, you're the data expert right?" asked Stillwell.

"Amongst other things," replied Jim.

"Do you think we're simply going after a couple of barrels the Chinese delivered?"

Another scenario brewing? Jim had his own reasons for going back to Iraq. In part, it was revenge and closure. He intended to wreck their database and cripple the Iraqi weapons program as effectively as he could. Knowledge was power in any complex data model, and weapons research was a complex data model. Destroy the model and the backup tapes and he could destroy the program. It was pay back for Jerry's death. This time he could come back home knowing he did his best.

Harper chose, for the moment, to ignore what he knew to be the truth. *Vengeance is Mine, I will repay.* He had no illusions as to feeling better about Jerry's death after this was over. He simply wanted to make the price for his blood cost the Iraqis more than it had. Jim had considered what he intended to do. Stillwell was not the internal threat, and probably Captain Burns had not been given any dirty assignments either. That left the other three.

"Well do you?" repeated Brian.

Jim returned from his musings and shook his head. "No, we're not going to find the barrels. We're going to find where the barrels were sent."

"We need a copy of their database," continued Brian. "If the Chinese and Russians have been feeding them weapons material and research we could learn a lot about Chinese advances."

"I don't think we'll have time to make a tape backup. I suspect the Iraqis will be on top of us pretty fast." Especially if the Iraqis knew, they were on their way. The nagging doubts regarding the last mission continued to haunt him.

"No, I thought we could just steal one." Jim appraised his seatmate again. "Look, I don't want to get shot up either. They told me we are going in to open up their database and transmit back to Uncle where everything is. I think that's a pipe dream."

"Really?"

"Sure. *Tomahawk* Cruise missiles are wonderful things, but mountains can absorb a great deal of damage. The only reason Saddam still has a weapons program is due to camouflage. He hid everything under rock and sand in the desert. We aren't going to get this stuff with air strikes and missile attacks."

The old adage came to Brian. "What you're saying is very expensive. The only way to secure these systems is with a soldier and a rifle on the ground."

"That's right. We need the ground pounders again."

Duty, honor, country was a soldier's call. The seeds of the second Gulf War had been sown by the failures of the first. How many would die this time to satisfy political rather than military objectives. Jim closed his eyes.

"You've been to this Data Center," stated Brian. His mind seemed to zip from subject to subject like Nintendo games flipped from screen to screen.

Jim nodded. "Once."

"They've probably upgraded computer systems since then. How do you propose to get inside?"

"I built some backdoors the last time. Those back doors should still be there. I never really got to test what I had done. You see, the bad guys showed up and started shooting."

"You have an account on the UNIX system?"

"Uh-huh. We also had a satellite modem. It was powered by a solar battery and connected into their fiber network. They must have found the modem or unhooked that segment of their network. It went dead six months later. From what I understand, we got a pretty good idea where things were in late 1992.

"That was five years ago. They've shuffled things around since then, moved to new holes—so to speak."

Stillwell glanced back at the Marines who were catching up on their sleep. Not a bad idea since he doubted they would get much once they hit the ground. "So why are you along for this joy ride? I mean, I don't get the idea they could simply hand you a piece of paper and reenlist you."

Harper's game face fell back into place. He pulled away to the icy cold core inside and back to a time he thought had ended. "Unfinished business." The eyes were flat and the voice cold.

"Huh? You're along because you want to be here?"

"I'm not sure anyone would understand why I decided to come back." He paused wondering why he decided to try and explain this to a stranger. He might need this stranger to watch his back in less than twelve hours. "I left a friend in the desert five years ago. He was with me when we went in the last time. I don't think the Iraqis have paid enough for his blood.

"The other reason might sound self serving and prideful, but I'm the best man for the job. I know where the Data Center is. I know the layout and I know the technology."

Stillwell calculated his response. "Besides, you want a shot at the guy who killed your buddy."

Jim simply nodded.

PART 2

Blood and Honor

"There is need of a sound body, and even more need of a sound mind. But above mind and above body stands character—the sum of those qualities which we mean when we speak of a man's force and courage, of his good faith and sense of honor."

Theodore Roosevelt 1913

11

Persian Gulf, Sunday, November 16, 1997,
6:00 AM (GMT + 3.00)

The ninety-seven thousand ton carrier sliced through the turquoise gulf waters—the block white letters CVN-73 prominent on her bow. She was better known as the *USS George Washington*. Her four and half acre flight deck was relatively calm as two F-14 *Tomcats* lifted off for combat air patrol. The snarling snake insignia of the VF-102 *Diamondbacks* glittered in the morning sun off the twin tailed fighters—members of Carrier Air Wing One were taking up flanking position around the carrier.

Each *Tomcat* is capable of tracking twenty-four targets simultaneously. The potent AIM-54 Phoenix system has a published range of ninety nautical miles. With fire-and-forget-me capability, the *Tomcats* could easily repel an attacking force several times their size. Standing orders were to protect the carriers in a three hundred sixty degree configuration; for the forces hostile to the carrier task force could come from any side of the Gulf.

A third aircraft followed the *Tomcats* into the crystal blue skies over the Gulf. A *Seahawk* SH-60F helicopter lifted to the north towards Al Faw. Once airborne, a second flight of Tomcats would be launched to follow the *Seahawk* on its journey towards the Iraqi coastline. *Desert Storm* had devastated the Iraqi Air Force, but it still existed and the potential for mischief could never be underestimated. The *Tomcats* ensured the Iraqis would never get within a hundred miles of the *Seahawk*.

The twin General Electric T700-GE-700 engines sent them towards the coastline at one hundred fifty knots. A four-man crew, three Navy divers and Jonas Benjamin, hurtled towards the inevitable discovery waiting for them in the waters south of Iraq.

The crew had been outfitted with flak vests, and the window mounted 7.62 machine guns were fully loaded. The only one aboard who had any idea as to why such precautions were being taken was the civilian sitting ramrod straight in the rear compartment. He had conferred with the divers before leaving the carrier, and he had provided a map with the approximate destination. They would be within half a klick of the spot they were looking for.

As to what they were actually going to find, no one really knew. The body bags stacked in the rear of the *Seahawk* suggested something unpleasant. The additional oxygen masks and special breathing gear suggested something considerably worse than a couple of floating corpses.

Jonas Benjamin held a brief case tight to his flight suit. Inside were the entire series of U2 photographs, plus additional enhancements of the area since the encounter from the National Reconnaissance Office. Every attempt had been made to track the Iraqi vessel as it pulled away from the *Han* class submarine. It apparently had disappeared into the gloom.

He had had little sleep since the briefing yesterday morning with the National Security Advisor and the Deputy Secretary of State. He had left the Pentagon directly for Andrews, and found himself strapped into the rear seat of an F-15 *Eagle*. From Andrews to Kuwait City, it had been a rocket ride at speeds approaching Mach two. Now he was the forward edge of an intelligence operation that could lead him just about anywhere.

A command post had been established on the *George Washington* and a second post was inside a hanger at Al Jabar. The Navy was not unfamiliar with accommodating the intelligence community. Since *Desert Storm*, several black ops had been staged from the floating American armada. The Kuwaitis were very happy to do whatever the Americans asked for, and they rarely asked any questions. Liberating one's homeland has a way of focusing one's attention on reality. The people of Eastern Europe honored Ronald Reagan by putting his photograph on their fireplace mantles for defeating the Soviet Empire. George Bush was equally honored in the homes of Kuwait. Ten months and several thousand lives had driven a hefty stake through the heart of Arab unity.

Jonas Benjamin checked his watch. By now the infiltration team assembled by Louis Edwards would be leaving Andrews Air Force Base for the Gulf Region. They were scheduled to land in Kuwait City late this afternoon. Hopefully, Jonas would have some answers for them.

The pilot looked back into the cabin and keyed his microphone. "Mister Benjamin, we're coming up on target."

Jonas looked through the open side door of the *Seahawk*. "Okay, we're looking for debris and anything that shouldn't be here. That includes funny looking water, dead fish and so forth. Depending on what we find, we'll figure out how to safely retrieve it."

The pilot glanced at his copilot and both turned to stare at their passenger. They had done some strange things for the spooks before, but never had anyone bothered with dead fish before.

"Yes, Sir."

The *Seahawk* slowed to ten knots and began a slow scan over the surface of the ocean. The brightening day found a solitary helicopter bobbing across the surface of the Gulf looking for bodies. The radar detectors indicated land based signals from Al Faw, Kuwait City, Abadan, and Bandar-Khomeyni were tracking them. The Iranians were smart enough not to light up American aircraft with attack radars. They had learned the lesson clearly in observing the response elicited from the Americans each time the Iraqis were foolhardy enough to try.

It was one of the gunners who spotted the yellow suited corpse rolling in the waves below. Jonas moved quickly through the cabin to stare through binoculars at the body. It rolled on the surface, kept buoyant by the containment capacity of his suit and the gases released as the body decomposed.

Success is generally greeted with a pat on the back. Jonas could only feel the bile gurgling at the back of his throat. Their worst fears were being confirmed, and Stillwell's scenario seemed to be playing itself out. Jonas had a copy of it in his brief case. He dare not think of the connections between Chinese mischief, campaign contributions, submarines delivering deadly product, and Iraqi madmen. He lowered the binoculars and turned to his divers.

He pointed through the open side door at the bobbing yellow mass. "That corpse is possibly contaminated. It is very important that none of you touch the body or the material. While it is reasonable to believe the sea water has washed the surface contamination away, we can't be sure." He paused. "If anyone of you wishes not to go, that's alright. No one—I repeat—no one will count that against you."

Jonas had given the same speech aboard the *George Washington.* It was the second time he had offered the divers a chance to avoid deadly contact. He had explained that they were dealing with a chemical or biological warfare product, and that the hazards were unknown. It was the first time for the helicopter crew.

A second time the pilots looked across to each other. "Excuse me, Sir, did you say chemical warfare?"

Jonas turned to the pilot and nodded. "Yes. I have every reason to believe that man down there was exposed to something thirty-six hours ago."

The lead diver interrupted to exchange, "Sir, we know the risks. We were trained to do this job, and I appreciate your concern. Not everyone cares like you do, Sir. But we've got a job to do." He turned to the pilot. "We'll double bag the corpse and load it into one of the skiff canisters for transport. If you can get about ten to fifteen feet off the deck, we shouldn't have too much trouble."

The pilot nodded and keyed his microphone. “All right, you heard Mister Benjamin’s explanation. We’ve got a job to do, let’s get to it.”

Jonas had a character defect for his chosen profession. It was called a conscience, and he detested sending men into situations they were ill prepared to face.

The *Seahawk* swept in low towards the target. It came to a steady hover about a hundred yards from the floater. The pilot did not want to risk disturbing the body with the down wash from the rotor blades. He brought the *Seahawk* low as the three black suited divers slid from the side door into the sea flippers first.

Jonas watched them disappear beneath the waves and turned his attention to the floater in the distance. He lifted the binoculars back to his eyes and pressed the telephoto zoom key. The image snapped towards him in a blur, before the glasses had a chance to recalibrate the focus. Enemy or not, no one deserved the ignoble dumping into the sea.

A wave slapped the floater’s faceplate rolling him to reveal the dissolved remains of a face. Jonas gasped as the haunted eyes stared back. The neoprene faceplate had shredded corrosively and the floater’s face had suffered great damage. It had the appearance of being torn by an angry beast. The eyes bulged as if they were struggling to escape the skull, and the lips were pulled back in a startled, strangled rictus. The skin was scarred with green and black stripes.

No stray bullet had killed this man. Something far more sinister had invaded his body and ripped the life from his very being. The savageness of the expression and obvious pain inflicted suggested their worst-case scenario was beginning to unravel. Should Saddam mount this terror into warheads and launch them toward Israel, the Jewish State would retaliate with a nuclear firestorm that would level Baghdad and engulf the world in a dangerous confrontation.

“Mister Benjamin, I have FLASH message traffic coming in for you.”

Jonas dropped the binoculars and turned his unfocused gaze towards the pilot.

"You can take it on the monitor in the passenger compartment, Sir."

Jonas nodded dumbly. He cleared his throat. "Could you make sure the cameras are turned on to record the body's recovery, and indicate the date, time, and global positioning coordinates? Thank you." He turned towards the rear monitor. The world would need evidence, and the evidence must be unimpeachable.

He flipped the monitor on. The screen warmed up and scrolled the first twenty-four lines of the message.

FLASH MESSAGE VIA USS GEORGE WASHINGTON
EYES ONLY JONAS BENJAMIN
FROM NATIONAL COMMAND AUTHORITY
NATIONAL SECURITY ADVISOR OFFICE

SATELLITE RECONNAISSANCE SUGGESTS RECEIVING IRAQI VESSEL DID NOT ATTEMPT TO NAVIGATE THE SHATT AL ARAB WATERWAY RIVER TOWARDS AL BASRA FOR PACKAGE DEPOSIT. BELIEVE VESSEL WAS SCUTTLED BY CREW TWENTY (20) TO TWENTY-FIVE (25) KILOMETERS SOUTHWEST OF AL FAW BETWEEN THE JAZIRAT BUBIYAN AND THE IRAQI COASTLINE. YOU HAVE COMPLETE NATIONAL COMMAND AUTHORITY TO PURSUE THIS TO CONCLUSION. CINCFIFTHFLEET HAS BEEN APPRISED OF YOUR STATUS.

Jonas pressed the print key and a thermal printer produced an image copy of the message for his briefcase. He pulled a chart from his briefcase and flipped it to southern Iraq. He looked at the message and drew a circle in red ink around where they thought the boat had vanished.

The *Seahawk* is tasked with close quarters anti submarine capabilities. The detection gear should work equally well on a scuttled boat as well as a submarine trying to hide.

He tapped the pilot on the shoulder and pointed to the chart. "Can you get us here?"

The pilot checked fuel gauge on his instrumentation panel. "Not without refueling first, besides that's Iraq proper and we don't have sufficient force to ensure your security. That was something the flight boss made real clear to us. Your security is top priority."

Jonas pulled out the flash message and said, "This is my authorization, tell me what we can do?"

The copilot looked over their shoulder and said, "You know they could get a company of marines from the *Peleliu* pretty fast."

Jonas seemed puzzled. "What's the *Peleliu*?"

"Amphibious assault ship—part of the carrier task force. They got something like thirteen hundred marines on board. I'm sure they could spare a company or two for you."

"How long?"

"Don't know, Sir. But we can sure dial up the *George Washington* and get it started," suggested the pilot. "Just love telling Admirals what they're going to do next." He chuckled his best evil laugh. "Makes it worth getting up in the morning if you know what I mean, Sir."

"Do it. We have to go back to the carrier anyway once we get the floater," replied Jonas.

Twenty minutes later a CH-53 *Sea Stallion* lifted off the deck the *USS Peleliu* with thirty marines, two fresh divers, and a course heading straight for the *George Washington*.

The *Seahawk* and its divers retrieved the floater. The badly bloated corpse already was rotting in the elevated temperatures of the Gulf. Besides the violence done to the floater by nature, the brutal assault of the nerve toxin had ruptured most of the blood vessels in the man's face. His death had been particularly violent.

The lead diver pulled off his hood taking the proffered towel to dry his hair. He looked up at Jonas asking, "Why's this guy Chinese Navy?"

Jonas stared at the man. "You sure?"

"Yeah. He's got the flag on his arm patch. The bio suit he's wearing kept him afloat, but it sure didn't stop whatever it was that killed him. It looks as if the stuff ate right through the suit."

"We think something went wrong, but we really don't know what."

The diver dropped the towel between his feet and spat. "From everything we have seen in the training films they send us, it looks like there was a weapons release. His torso is almost cut in half like it was a kind of acid or something."

"Could it have been an accident?" asked Jonas.

"Pretty strange way to have an accident. Unless this stuff was under pressure, it certainly didn't get there by simply opening the top."

"You double bagged him?"

The diver laughed, "We triple bagged him once we saw what we were dealing with. Don't worry, none of us were too keen to touch the bugger once we saw what happened."

The pilot keyed his microphone, "The *Washington's* coming up. Best strap in for landing."

They roared towards the massive carrier seemingly alone on the blue sea. Only she was not alone; over the horizon standing picket duty were the frigate *Reuben James* and the destroyers *John Young* and *Ingersoll.* In addition, the powerful AWACS battle management aircraft, owned by the Saudi Air Force and flown by the United States Air Force, maintained a constant watch on all aircraft. The Saudi's had purchased twelve AWACS systems.

The AWACS was basically a Boeing 707 with a rotating radar dome mounted like a huge knob on the back of the plane. It was packed with avionics, electronic counter measures, and constantly escorted by fighters. It could literally track hundreds of aircraft and direct counter force aircraft in a defensive posture, or prosecute a massive air campaign in an offensive posture.

The *George Washington* remained safe under its protective umbrella. Should the order be given to punish Saddam, the *George Washington* could deliver more precision guided munitions—what the public called *smart bombs*—than had been launched in all of *Desert Storm* with two thirds the available air wing that had been present on the carriers during the Gulf War.

The *Seahawk* came to rest on the rear deck of the carrier. Jonas clambered out of the chopper and found a smartly dressed commander waiting for him. The General Electric motors were winding down, and the commander leaned close to Jonas, "The Admiral would like to see you, Sir."

Jonas turned to the skiff canister and the commander waved to detail standing to one side. "They've been briefed on your requirements, Sir."

Jonas nodded, "Lead on."

The commander headed into decks of the *George Washington.* Jonas was relieved no one expected him to find the admiral on his own. A *Nimitz* class carrier is basically a floating city hosting between five and six thousand men. There are flight decks, hanger decks, and two nuclear reactors. The carrier has 450 computer workstations networked using Novell. The information systems department processes over 1200 messages per day during peacetime, and the eight ATM machines disperse $320,500 in an average month. The various messes provide upwards of 18,000 meals everyday. Into this, Jonas plunged after his escort certain he would be lost if left to his own devices.

Jonas was totally turned around by the time he found himself face to face with Admiral Trevor Barnes. He waved Jonas into his stateroom and closed the door. Barnes was the task force commander responsible for the lives of several thousand men, billions of dollars in ships, and aircraft and directly answerable to the Fifth Fleet Commander.

"Coffee?" he asked pouring into his mug.

"Yes, thank you," replied Jonas unsure of what was coming next.

Barnes turned with two steaming mugs proffering one with a drawing of the Naval Academy. "Sugar is on the table over there."

Jonas accepted the mug and settled into a chair.

"I suppose you're wondering why I asked to see you." He settled himself in a chair across from Jonas. Barnes did not wait for a reply. "I understand you're the analyst who first saw these photos." He dropped a spread of photos on the table. They were copies of the ones in Jonas's briefcase.

Jonas cocked his head to be sure, then replied, "Yes, Sir."

"I see a Chinese sub with a hole in its pressure hull. I see another boat, presumably Iraqi in nature, along side. And I am getting nonsense from Washington which brings me to you." His eyes bore down on his visitor.

Jonas looked right back at the Admiral. He kept his silence. Jonas had met men like Barnes before—tough, honest men trying to the right thing and uncertain that they were being told the entire story.

Barnes let the pause linger a moment longer. "I have received orders to give you all possible assistance. The Chief of Naval Operations signed it. Now, the CNO doesn't sign my orders unless he is directed by National Command Authority, namely someone in the White House." He spun in his chair and pointed to the choke point in the Gulf. "I've got an attack boat sitting twenty knots inside the *Strait* playing goal keeper on this Chinese sub. Her skipper hasn't asked for clarification of his orders which means he's ready to sink the Chinese boat if he has to.

"So tell me, Mister Benjamin, is that the right decision?" He turned back to his visitor.

Jonas thought back to Stillwell's analysis in the initial briefing yesterday. He recommended sinking the Chinese boat because he was unsure whether the transfer had been from the Chinese to the Iraqis or the other way around. "I don't know."

Barnes smiled for the first time. "An honest answer. I like honesty, son. Nevertheless, let me tell you a reality that is going take place sometime in the next twenty hours. I've got a very good sub driver by the name of Jeff Andrews, and he has an improved *Los Angeles* Class attack boat called the *Springfield*. He got a photo of this little transaction as well. If I were in his shoes, I'd say he has a wounded animal coming towards him. What do you think he'll do if the *Han* opens her outer doors on her torpedo tubes?"

"Fire first," replied Jonas without blinking.

Barnes nodded. "All right." They had sent him a sharp one. "Besides dumping a reactor core into relatively shallow water and killing some fish, what else are we sending to the bottom?"

Stillwell had been so certain the transfer was incomplete. He had written an Official Naval White Paper on Chinese global strategies related to the Middle East. Some had dismissed it as fantasy, but what if the National Security Advisor believed Stillwell? What if Brian Stillwell was right?

Jonas leaned back in his chair and closed his eyes. "I think you might be sinking components for a first strike chemical or biological weapon."

"Anthrax?"

Jonas realized Barnes had read the same intelligence briefs suggesting Saddam had a thousand-year supply of dried anthrax. "No. Something much worse."

"And its targets?"

Jonas had worked through this scenario several times. Saddam had some conventional forces, but nothing capable of challenging the Turks to the north or the Americans to the south. "We were basically unsuccessful in targeting SCUD launchers in the last war. We believe we can account for up to eighty missiles. Now, what we don't know is what he is capable of loading onto those missiles. But he certainly would target Israel, the Saudis, and you."

Barnes turned back to the map.

"The SCUD doesn't have to hit you, it only has to be close. An air burst on the wrong side of the carrier could kill half your men and take you out of any conflict. A coordinated strike against all his targets could kill millions and provoke a nuclear response from Israel. Then you have a major conflict on your hands. Indeed, we have stated publicly that any use of chemical or biological weapons against our troops would result in an American nuclear strike."

"You don't paint a pretty picture Mister Benjamin," Barnes said slowly.

"My job's to prevent that from happening. If I fail, and I pray I don't, you may have to do your job."

Barnes nodded and set the mug down on the side table. "I understand you've requested a company of marines."

"Yes, Sir. We believe the Iraqis did not attempt to navigate the Tigris River up to Al Basra. It looks like they scuttled her southwest of Al Faw."

Admiral Barnes stood. "Good hunting, then."

"Thank you, Sir."

"I hope you can stop this, because I have no desire to be in the chain of command that launches nuclear weapons against civilian targets," he said sadly.

"But you would if you had to?"

Barnes imagined what the *George Washington* would be with three thousand casualties. He remembered the private moments between husbands and wives, boyfriends and girl friends before a deployment into harms way. It was quiet, personal time before a long separation. He thought of the moms and dads, wives and children who turned up at Norfolk to receive them back from the sea. They were his people, and his people were his responsibility.

"Oh yes, Mister Benjamin," he said solemnly. "I would send fire from heaven. May God forgive me."

12

White House, Saturday, November 15, 1997,
11:30 PM EST

Arthur clicked the PRINT icon on his word processor. A happy faced Window's character shaped like a paper clip winked back and started a print pantomime on the screen. The document spooling to the laser printer next to the screen was more serious than the smiling paper clip. A Presidential Finding is a legal document indicating that the President is convinced, for reasons of national security, a clandestine action against a foreign power is required. A Finding provides the president with the latitude to take unilateral action on behalf of the country without the immediate knowledge of the various Senate and House oversight committees.

The Executive Branch directs American foreign policy, but there is a tension between the Secretary of State and the National Security Officer. Modern Secretaries of State tend to fly around the world meeting with foreign leaders and acting as mouthpieces for administration foreign policy. They preside over a large bureaucratic organization and attend cabinet meetings, however, space and time limit their access to the President. The State Department is located at Foggy Bottom, inside the District, not 1600 Pennsylvania Avenue.

National Security Advisors operate with a much smaller staff out of the White House West Wing. Their offices are the largest, second only to the White House Chief of Staff. They have the opportunity to see the

President every morning and craft foreign policy presentations that, more often than not, circumvent a Secretary of State. Best of all, the NSA is not a cabinet member and thus avoids the lengthy and sometimes embarrassing Senate confirmation process.

It is a strange irony that the people who become the most powerful figures in the world's greatest democracy never stand for election or submit to congressional inquiry. National Security Advisors have been called before various congressional committees, but not for the purposes of advise and consent. They appear to report and explain, sometimes behind closed doors away from the prying eyes of the fourth estate. NSA staff members become virtually invisible to the American people, even though they daily enter through the White House gates and have FBI security clearance. Staff members become the true architects of American foreign policy, each specializing in their own niche of expertise.

Arthur plucked the pages from the printer's tray and made his way down the hall to the NSA's office. He knocked once on the half open door before entering. At this time of night very little was happening in the White House.

The NSA looked up and smiled, "Arthur, have a seat. You've got everything typed up the way we talked about it?"

"Yes, Sir." He handed the proposed finding across the desk.

The NSA cocked his glasses further down his nose. He carefully went through each paragraph trying to assess it the way a lawyer would. After a few minutes he smiled, "Good work, very good work."

"Thank you," replied Arthur. "We really should get it signed immediately. The *Galaxy* left Andrews about and hour ago."

"Yes, well—eh, the President is currently in conference. The Secret Service has promised to notify me as soon as he is available."

A flash of anger rippled across Arthur's features only to be replaced by the same happy-faced nonchalance they expected. Conferences in the Oval Office at midnight on a Saturday meant the President was pursuing another dalliance. Arthur supposed every leader had their foibles, but this one seemed to have so many of them. This administration claimed the ethical high ground, and found itself hounded by special prosecutors and right wing media critics. So far, nothing had stuck to this President, but the behavior and arrogance seemed to increase with each passing day.

"You don't approve, do you?" asked the NSA.

"It doesn't matter what I think," responded Arthur. "I'm here to do a job, and I perform those duties very well. What the President chooses to do on his own time is up to him."

The NSA chuckled, "You know, I might make a politician out of you yet."

"I doubt we could be that unlucky. Leave me to the details we would both rather not talk about."

"Yes, yes. The housecleaning always has to be taken care of. So did we get everyone we wanted on the team?"

Arthur nodded. "Harper made a bargain about insurance policies for everyone on the team. I believe the CIA man took care of it. Of course, you can cancel those at anytime. We are certainly under no obligation to honor something forced on us by a steroid driven Spec War nobody."

"You don't have a great deal of respect for this team."

Arthur shook his head. "What do we hope to accomplish? By the time anyone gets on the ground, the Chinese contraband will have disappeared into the desert again. We've accomplished nothing except the exposure created by a Presidential Finding."

The NSA raised an eyebrow. "You think I should shred this document and not bother the President? Seems to me there was a predecessor of mine who failed to tell his commander and chief about secret mission. He ended up with a passel of lawyers and a special prosecutor." He shrugged his shoulders and shook his head. "I have no desire to spend the rest of my days in Washington defending a covert action and make another group of lawyers rich. No, we play this by the book."

"All right, we play it by the book. Let's suppose they get in and get out. Let's suppose they come back with enough information to pinpoint every weapons facility in the country. What are we going to do? Start a war?"

"Maybe." The NSA spread his hands. "You see, Arthur, we need to look beyond the scope of the current mission. It's obvious to a number of people that a female Secretary of State is fundamentally ineffective when dealing with the Arab and Asian states. Their cultures simply do not accept the idea, and in fact, they look at this as a sign of weakness.

"That's where we come in. The National Security Advisor runs foreign policy in this government, not the State Department. We make the policy decisions and maintain a low profile. Maybe this team will strike it big, and maybe there's nothing left at this data site. I don't know. Nobody does until it's over. However, consider the possibility that tensions between America and Iraq continue to escalate.

"Eventually, someone is going to ask for a target list and we all know who will be running that meeting. The Pentagon will have some ideas, but State is filled with people who remember the Tuesday afternoon luncheons during the Johnson administration. Do you know what they did?"

Arthur stifled a yawn wondering how much longer he would have to endure the NSA and wait on a cavorting President. "Must have missed this during high school history?"

"It's all quite fascinating. They sat around during their luncheon and picked out the target list for the next week's bombing raids against North Vietnam. You could hit this airfield, but not this SAM site. You can bomb this bridge, but not this road. It drove the Air Force and Navy guys nuts. It also got a lot more people shot down. Now think about this place." He waved his hand towards the corridor.

Arthur followed his lead and muttered, "They don't do anything around here without a poll or focus group."

The NSA clasped his hands together. Once again, Arthur recognized the direction of their conversation without having to be told. "Precisely! Everything in this White House is driven by polls. They stick a finger in the wind and figure out how to screw the loyal opposition, and how to frighten old people—threaten to throw grandma out on the street. They tell people the Republicans want to starve kids by cutting the school lunch dollars. Oh, it's positively brilliant. Except for one thing, you can't run foreign policy the same way."

Arthur nodded, wondering what this had to do with the mission to Iraq.

"So what happens if we find ourselves in a shooting war with Iraq?" He paused for effect. "Do you think they'll be smart enough to turn over target selection and management to the Joint Chiefs?" He chuckled cleverly and rubbed his hands together. "Of course not! There's no way this group would want to share limelight with a Stormin' Norman. No, these are liberals who think they can remake Kennedy's Camelot. They'll want to pick the targets."

Understanding blossomed across Arthur's features, "You mean they'll have a target selection committee."

The NSA nodded gleefully. "Of course! The second Gulf War will be handled straight out of the West Wing. No one is going to share the thrashing of Saddam with generals and admirals. As long as they keep the casualty counts low and have those spectacular TV pictures, everyone will be happy.

"So wouldn't it be nice if we happened to have the right targets?" he suddenly finished.

Arthur nodded. "Sure. You let them have some near misses or a few spectacular blunders, then you spring the list on them." Arthur enjoyed the thought of most of the cabinet caught flat-footed.

"Now you understand why this mission is so important. We'll be the heroes, and State will be the goats. We make the right moves and save some navy pilots from being shot down over the wrong targets. Best of all we actually nail Saddam, and the spin masters have a field day. Time it right and we might even get the House back in the mid-term elections next year.

"Remember how popular Bush was after the Gulf War? If he could have stood for election in '91 instead of '92, you and I wouldn't even be sitting here. That's how we sell this to President. We tell him his legacy will be the elimination of one of the worst dictators in history. Oh, we don't have to go overboard, but we can play the Jewish card. After all, we'll tell the world Saddam had his missiles full of bio germs aimed at Tel Aviv and Jerusalem. The Israelis won't contradict us. They'll be glad the bastard's dead."

Arthur rolled his eyes towards the corridor and the Oval Office beyond. "What about his penchant for chasing skirts? I mean we see this happening increasingly often these days."

The NSA dismissed it with a wave of his hand. "It's been going on for a long time. The media isn't interested in what he does. The public had their chance to trounce him and elected him President instead. It's a non-factor."

Arthur kept his peace about the rumors. The money was good and it was building up to a tidy sum in the Cayman Island bank. The scandals and dead people seemed to follow this President around, but never had he suffered for his foolishness. Quite the contrary, his critics were always considered off the wall, right-wing nutcases.

A Secret Service Agent stuck his head in the office and indicated the President was free. The two men got to their feet and followed the agent to the Oval Office. They walked passed the American Western statues and presidential portraits towards the very seat of power. A Marine Captain sat on a chair outside the Oval Office. The briefcase with the nuclear launch codes handcuffed to his wrist. The nuclear *football* was never beyond the immediate reach of the President.

A second agent opened the door to the Oval Office and they passed from the outer sanctum to the President's quarters. It reminded Arthur of a throne room with the royal blue carpeting emblazoned with the presidential seal, and the massive gold drapes hanging behind the President's desk.

The President was dressed casually in short sleeved polo shirt and khaki colored slacks. The presidency had changed since Ronald Reagan who always appeared for work in the Oval Office in a suit and tie out of respect for the institution and honor for the men who came before him. He got up from behind his desk towering over the other two men and welcomed them to sit down. His effusive charm disarmed both men as the NSA handed him the Finding explaining, "This justifies the mission we started in response to the Chinese submarine this morning."

The President read quickly through the document asking, "Anything new on the Chinese sub?"

"No, sir. We've repositioned our attack boats to make sure it can't leave the Gulf, and we are actively looking for it with carrier based anti-submarine warfare planes," explained the NSA.

He nodded, and fixed his NSA with an earnest gaze, "And if we find this submarine, what do you think we should do about it?"

Arthur was wondering the same thing himself. What good did it do to hunt them down, if the final solution meant nothing?

The NSA met his President's gaze and explained, "We give them the chance to surface and be boarded. Failing that we force them to the surface and check her out."

"Failing that?"

Without blinking an eye he explained, "We should let her escape the Gulf and sink her in deep water. Claim it was tragic accident, and send our condolences when the news leaks out."

The President turned to Arthur, "Do you agree with that?"

This was no time for independent thought. "Mister President, I think we have evidence that some sort of chemical or biological weapon was transferred to the Iraqi government. We believe something went wrong, but we aren't completely sure what it was. And we have a Chinese sub that may or may not be in trouble. I don't think they'll let us board her, so I think we end up with letting her go or sinking her. When the pressure hull explodes, there won't be any survivors."

He walked over to his desk to sign the Finding and asked, "Does this document cover that eventuality?"

"You mean sinking the Chinese sub?" asked the NSA.

"Uh huh."

The NSA looked at Arthur who shrugged. "I believe it could be construed to mean that."

The President handed the finding back to the NSA and explained, "You make sure whatever sub driver gets picked to sink this Chinese sub understands we don't want any survivors. I don't want to have to explain something like this to Beijing. Maybe you could create a story like they have cruise missiles with Anthrax or something."

The NSA furrowed his brow, "Mister President are you suggesting—"

"I think you understand exactly what I'm saying." He smiled and yawned, "But I need to get some sleep, church tomorrow. Have a good night." He left them standing in the center of the Oval Office and sauntered through another exit towards the White House family quarters.

They looked at each other and made their way back out the door they had entered. Arthur noticed a portrait of Abraham Lincoln as they headed back to the NSA's office.

The contrast between Lincoln and his successor could not have been greater. Lincoln was remembered for a two-hundred word speech called the Gettysburg Address, and this man would be remembered for not inhaling. It was hard to imagine the current president using the Capitol as a 2000 bed hospital for the sick and wounded—and finally seeking God in the darkest hours of the Civil War. Lincoln's reward for saving the Union had been a bullet in the back of the head at the Ford Theater.

Arthur closed his eyes as he followed the NSA. They had been given a tacit order to commit an act of war, but were to make sure they did not get caught. The NSA closed the door and said, "Find out which sub is patrolling the Strait. Write up an order to seek and destroy the Chinese sub."

"But what about boarding her?" protested Arthur.

The NSA shook his head. "We can't risk any communication between the sub and Beijing. The consequences would be too great. Draft the order over my signature and find the Chief of Naval Operations. We'll make sure she goes down."

Arthur nodded and tried to ignore the foul taste in his mouth. He went back to his office to draft another order, and decided it was time to consider retirement.

13

Odricks Corner, Virginia, Saturday, November 15, 1997, 11:30 PM

Goldenrod set the documents on the table before him. He closed his eyes and folded his hands. He considered what he had read, and the cost he would ultimately pay for the information—one man dead, another injured. The FBI was alerted to his presence and possibly his own agent—*NightHawk*—inside the administration.

There were possibilities to fathom. Had the FBI compromised *NightHawk*? Had they compromised the means of identification and verification? Had they planned an elaborate trap? Had he been lucky or stupid?

He opened the other file available to him. The one he kept at the safe house where his protectors had hustled him. Access to the Embassy had been cut off. District squad cars augmented by a Marine Emergency Response Team convinced his guardians to move him directly to the safe house. Diplomatic license plates on the Embassy vehicle would not prevent the American counterintelligence services from apprehending him in the act of espionage with the pilfered goods on his person.

The second file listed the surveillance maintained on *NightHawk*. There were no sudden absences or anomalies over the past twelve months. *NightHawk* had accompanied the President's Party on several foreign tours. The national security product delivered was astonishing in its detail and analysis. The corresponding payments to the Cayman bank account continued. *NightHawk* continued in his position of trust seemingly disinterested in the accumulated 1.5 million dollars.

The Defense Intelligence Agency routinely swept *NightHawk's* apartment for surveillance devices. *Goldenrod* performed a counter sweep to ensure the checkers did not implant their own surveillance devices. None had ever been found. For appearances, *NightHawk* retained the trust and respect of his government. Yet, the FBI had been waiting.

Perhaps, they had learned of the dead drop. Considering the incredible array of technology available to American intelligence, it was not inconceivable that some sort of electronic minder had been set up. The Americans tended to deploy high technology in ever changing configurations. With their cell phones, pagers, and fax machines, they seemed to accomplish more with one man than he could with ten trained field officers.

Goldenrod considered the facts:

1) The American FBI had compromised the dead drop.
2) *NightHawk's* current intelligence product contained the proper identifications and countersigns to verify authenticity.
3) There was no evidence to support the notion that American counterintelligence had compromised *NightHawk.*
4) *NightHawk's* previous intelligence product had provided an accuracy level close to ninety percent. The inaccuracies were mostly minor details subject to change or simply wrong, but no agent ever produced error free product.
5) *NightHawk's* current product needed to be acted on tonight.

Goldenrod folded his fingers into a steeple. How odd that an avowed atheist should assume a position of prayer. He smiled, closed the second folder, and returned to the first one.

He considered the report before him. What possible benefit could American counterintelligence derive by describing a clandestine meeting between the Iraqi and Chinese, the description of an entry team, and the mission objectives? Did they suspect the relationship between their respective intelligence services? Had they surmised some sort of link? Nothing to date suggested they had pierced the veil of indirection so carefully erected. Could the clumsiness surrounding the American elections and their Byzantine campaign finance laws have produced some information nugget?

Perhaps the FBI had simply been lucky—a coincidence? He dismissed the notion. In his line of work, people who believed in coincidences ended up dead, or worse. The FBI must have known of the dead letter drop prior to tonight's activities. Again, he found himself confronted with the plentiful supply of American technology arrayed against him. What was another motion sensor or computer system to these extravagant barbarians? Did they stumble upon the dead letter drop and did that lead them to himself and his agent?

Certainly, there were some intelligence agencies one could dismiss. Many were bureaucratic mazes, but he could not say the same for the FBI. Once aroused, the Bureau would continue to gather evidence and hound witnesses until something simply fell into place. Their forensic labs were legendary. Something had aroused the notice of the Bureau, and nothing good would come from such knowledge.

No, he concluded, they had not found *NightHawk* yet. The Bureau suspected something was amiss. Despite their best efforts, something had aggravated the persistent counterintelligence efforts. The information before him was accurate, he decided. This being the case he must act on it immediately.

He perused the Q files regarding the action team sent to Iraq. These were incredibly detailed documents listing the biographies and legends used by the men sent into the country. Five of them were one-page summaries, but the team leader—he was something exceptional. He examined the face photograph printed in the upper left-hand corner. His summary ran four pages of covert actions against several nations including North Korea. If this could be believed, the Americans had infiltrated the North Korean nuclear program. Someone still understood the value of human intelligence gathering.

The greatest problem facing any western government was the proliferation of technology at a personal level. The computers, fax machines, and cell phones created an atmosphere of instant communication. The success of Microsoft, Intel, IBM, Hewlett Packard, and Oracle created a world of fingertip information. The efficient, secure transmission of voice, data, and video to any similarly equipped node in the world made the transmission of industrial, military, and technological secrets trivial.

Incredibly, the American government had permitted its own citizens to create data encryption software second to none. A software programmer named Phil Zimmerman wrote a program he called *Pretty Good Privacy* (PGP). The National Security Agency quietly approached Mister Zimmerman suggesting that he was a threat to national security. They demanded, in the delicate manner ascribed to heavy-handed, knuckle-dragging Washington bureaucrats, that Phil insert a backdoor into his code so they could read all the messages. The reason being that a single programmer had written an encryption program on his personal computer that essentially defeated the extraordinarily expensive mainframes buried in the Maryland countryside.

America was founded in part on personal freedom. PGP provided the very real promise that individuals could secure their email from Uncle Sam's prying eyes. Next, the 1991 omnibus crime bill threatened to make all software manufacturers insert special *trap doors* in their products the government could read encrypted messages. PGP was released as freeware and became the domain of the hackers roaming through cyberspace. The result was one of the most robust and secure encryption packages available to anyone.

Goldenrod gathered *NightHawk's* report together. He went across the room to his personal computer. "Shu," he called.

Shu entered from the outer room. He was totally bald without an ounce of visible fat. He had the appearance of a man mountain—chiseled features, slate gray eyes, and a thin, humorless mouth. He bowed to his master. *Goldenrod's* personal security was Shu's responsibility. The fact that he had lost a man tonight did not bother Shu. The fact that the FBI was waiting did.

"Please scan these documents for me while I prepare my report."

Shu took the documents and walked to the scanner—the latest Hewlett Packard model. *Goldenrod* insisted that no expense be spared to keep his safe house current with the latest American technology. Everything purchased had been acquired using cash at any number of computer super stores in the surrounding counties.

What *Goldenrod* failed to understand was the very technology he chided the Americans for releasing had helped bring the Soviet Empire to its knees. The free flow of information, goods, and services actually caused the American economy to expand exponentially. *Goldenrod* believed himself quite clever to use American technology against itself; the same technology could just as easily spark a peasant revolt.

"It is as you commanded," murmured Shu.

"Good, good." He clicked the mouse pointer on the Netscape Icon. The modem clicked on and started dialing up a local Internet service provider. Why pay for long distance, when the Internet provided a simple, albeit circuitous route, to his recipients.

While Netscape went through its startup and verification routines, *Goldenrod* encrypted the scanned pages and his report for his superiors in Beijing and a second for his colleagues in Baghdad.

He clicked back to Netscape and brought up the Messenger mailbox then clicked the New Msg Icon. He looked up two addresses, attached the file to both emails, and clicked Send twice. Within a minute, the very sensitive contents were racing in opposite directions through cyberspace.

Goldenrod had not required the services of the Embassy's signals room, or the immunity of a diplomatic pouch. He operated from a secret location connected to an Internet Service Provider (ISP) located in Virginia. For twenty dollars a month, *Goldenrod* operated an espionage operation totally separate from the Embassy compound.

He disconnected from the Internet and shut the machine off. Turning to the waiting giant he said, "Now, what have you done in the past few hours?"

Shu's eyes brightened. "The car and body have been disposed of as you requested." The car had been abandoned in one of Washington's many ghettos. By the morning, it would lucky to still have fenders. The corpse had been stripped of clothing. The hands and head were chopped off and fed into separate trash bins miles apart. The rest of the corpse, weighed down with several diving belts, was dropped unceremoniously into the Potomac River.

"Good."

"I have arranged for additional lodging and transportation tonight," he announced. "Come, we must leave now. I have kept you here for too long already."

"Yes, I suppose you are correct." He turned back to the dead screen. "The machine?"

"It will be taken care of," promised Shu. He turned and snapped his fingers quickly. The keepers of the safe house scurried in like frightened children. Shu spoke quickly in their native dialect. His were short, sharp orders demanding instant obedience.

The man and woman immediately began unscrewing the computer's case. Within a few minutes, the hard disk would be removed and replaced with another. There were now only games and the couple's modest checking account. They used *Quicken* to keep their affairs in order. The hard drive used by *Goldenrod* would be bubble wrapped and lowered into a false furnace duct.

Goldenrod looked at the scanner. "The papers must be burned and flushed. There must be no trace."

Shu nodded. This was a duty he left to no one else. He disappeared into the bathroom with his Bic lighter and made sure no trace of their mission remained.

Goldenrod found the remaining two men who had accompanied him on this mission. "You will drive to New York, enter the UN mission there, and leave the country. You must be very careful to obey all traffic laws, and not get caught. It would be best if you waited until Monday morning so that you can leave in heavy traffic. Until then, you will be invisible. You are not to go outside or appear next to the windows. Do not answer the telephone or make phone calls. You will be traveling on false papers. They are fine for a cursory examination; however, any proscribed scrutiny could cause problems. We are at a sensitive point, and you must avoid problems."

Both men scrambled to their feet and bowed to *Goldenrod.* He simply acknowledged their obsequiousness with a curt nod and dismissed them. He walked back to where Shu waited with his coat in hand. *Goldenrod* turned to fit his arms into his topcoat. He took one last look at the safe house before darting into the crisp Washington night.

A white Ford waited on the curb. It had been borrowed from another group of illegals—Chinese agents posing as American citizens. It was safer to use a car they totally controlled rather than risk using a credit card that could later be traced to the car—the fewer electronic signs left, the less chance of being tracked.

Shu drove them South on the Memorial Parkway past the entrance to Arlington National Cemetery and across the bridge behind the Lincoln Memorial. They turned north and detoured around the Embassy. It was hard to miss the continuously flashing lights of the District Squad Cars or the constant throb of two helicopters crisscrossing the skies.

By now, it had become a pure show. The FBI knew they would never catch their man with anything incriminating. Although, it never hurt to make their night as sleepless as possible either.

Shu delivered them to the Days Inn, Uptown. Just beyond the parking lot the Burger King sign had turned off. The car rolled up under the teal green canopy that proudly announced the hotel's name. Shu left the motor running and emerged from behind the car carrying two suitcases. They were empty suitcases, but only Shu knew that. To the hotel staff, it was two weary Oriental travelers running late. The tall one was kind of ugly—he reminded the girl behind the counter of Lurch on the *Adamm's Family.*

14

Al Jabar Air Base, Kuwait, Sunday, November 16, 1997, 6:00 PM (+3.00 GMT)

The huge *Galaxy* C-5B dropped from the sky towards the ten thousand foot runway. A pair of F-15 *Eagles* flew by the transport having ferried it across the dangerous Iraqi airspace. The *Eagles* circled Kuwait City and headed north back towards Incirlik, Turkey. Incirlik was the massive NATO airbase home to British, French, and American aircraft responsible for the enforcement of the northern Iraqi no-fly zone. The *Eagles* waggled their wings before kicking in the afterburners and disappearing across the desert.

The *Eagles* ensured the *Galaxy* arrived in Kuwait unmolested by the errant MiG Fighter, or the attack radar of a SAM-6, or *Roland* antiaircraft battery. The laden *Galaxy* was no match for either threat, but the *Eagles* changed the equation. The Air Force had always claimed the F-15 was the dominant air superiority fighter. *Desert Storm* removed all doubt. Those Iraqi pilots who had attempted to challenge the *Eagles* during the war either bailed out (if they were lucky) or became intermixed with the debris that had once been their aircraft. The domination of the aerial battlefield enabled the British *Tornado*, the carrier based *Intruders* and *Hornets*, and *Big Ugly Fat* Fellows to deliver the bombing campaign's massive ordinance load.

Jonas Benjamin watched the *Eagles* vanish over the horizon and felt, rather than heard, the sonic boom *pop* as they left. Al Jabar Air Base was the home of the 8th Air Expeditionary Fighter Squadron consisting of six F-117 *Nighthawk* stealth fighters. The *Nighthawks* flew through the dizzying flak storm surrounding Baghdad during the opening Gulf War salvos.

The *Galaxy* rolled off the main runway and towards a far hanger. A platoon of Marines already surrounded the hanger, and two Bradley Fighting Vehicles held vigil as the huge plane rolled towards its final stop. Jonas tapped his driver's shoulder and pointed towards the hanger. Night was coming and he had a briefing to give before Harper hopped off into the growing darkness. Fleetingly, Jonas wondered if war was somewhere over the horizon as well. They should have killed Saddam when they had the chance.

The HMMWV rolled passed the Bradleys and inside the hanger. Jonas figured they had two hours before Harper's vehicles and gear were ready. The *Apache* gunships would take an Army crew the better part of a night to get ready. They were for the extraction phase of the operation. Jim Harper could probably penetrate the Data Center without detection, but getting out in one piece might require a little more firepower than they could haul in on their backs.

Jonas stepped out of the HMMWV and towards the satellite communication center. He settled down in one of the chairs between technicians and brought up Louis Edwards's profile. Two mouse clicks later, a real time connection was created between Kuwait City and an office inside the Central Intelligence Agency's headquarters in Langley, Virginia.

Louis Edwards's visage swam into focus on the monitor. An automatic encryption cipher became active. "Jonas, a busy day I see from the reports sitting on my desk."

Jonas nodded his head. "Yes, Sir. Harper's team just arrived. I'd guess jump off will be in about two hours."

Louis glanced at something off screen and nodded. "All right. Give him my best, and all that."

"I will."

"Anything new on the barrels?"

"Nothing new since this afternoon and my findings on the Fao Peninsula. I think we have to assume everything is gone by now." The trip to the Fao Peninsula after his talk with Barnes had turned up little more than a scuttled boat, a pair of bullet-ridden bodies, and a deflated life raft. The barrels were gone. The Iraqis had beaten them to the prize. After three hours of walking around a beach surrounded by a platoon of very twitchy Marines, Jonas decided there was nothing there to pursue and left.

"Yes, I'm afraid you're right. Let's hope Jim can get us the information on where it went." Louis paused, "one last thing, make sure Stillwell's body armor fits. He's an irritating fellow, but basically, I think he's on the money about what might be going down."

"You mean the China angle?"

"Yes. I'd rather have him back than dead."

Jonas made a note to mention the concern to Harper. "I'll give you a call after mission jump off."

"Very good." The image went black.

Jonas rubbed his eyes. Except for some bad sleep on a supersonic flight from Washington, he had been working on this problem since midnight on Friday. He turned to the Air Force Staff Sergeant managing the center, "Which way to the conference room?"

"Through those doors," he said pointing.

Jonas followed the extended finger. "Sweep it one more time. Our guests are here."

"Yes, Sir," replied Sergeant Ralph Hanson. He snapped his fingers to two men examining one of the monitors. He gave quick instructions and turned back to his charge. Jonas Benjamin was already walking towards the *Galaxy*.

Jim Harper bounded down the ramp. A less exuberant group followed him with less energy. Harper came to a halt several feet from the ramp and looked about the sky. He seemed to be taking in the desert, the feel of the air against his skin and the smell of the earth. The trademark Mossberg shotgun was slung over his shoulder and the customary baseball cap pulled down over his eyes.

Harper started a slow walk towards the hanger. The sun was fading fast now. Night was coming and the day's heat dissipated quickly. A nervous energy gripped him. The excitement of the chase was beginning to consume his conscious mind. The very qualities that gave so many handlers difficulties in managing Harper made him the consummate operative for covert ops. He was sniffing the air like a Springer Spaniel—ready to run, ready to fight. Harper turned suddenly to see Jonas slowly walking towards him from the hanger.

A puzzled look transformed to one of recognition and then a grin emerged. Harper broke into a run towards Benjamin. "Jonas! You running this op?" They slapped each other on the hand.

Benjamin smiled, "Yeah, me and little help from my friends here. Welcome to Al Jabar."

Harper looked around him again. "Yes, Al Jabar. It has been a while since I was last here." He laughed, "They've fixed the place up some since then." Saddam started oil fires as a scorched earth policy that had poured thick plumes into the sky. The shattered remains of Saddam's mostly Soviet and somewhat West European military machine had been dragged away for target practice. The horrors of war and the torture inflicted during Iraq's invasion was cleaned up but not forgotten.

"I see you've brought your toys." Jonas nodded to the shotgun.

"Yes. I made a couple of promises. You're here to make sure I keep them."

Jonas nodded and hoped the *Apache* Gunships did not break down under the harsh desert conditions. He clapped Harper on the back as they headed towards the lighted interior of the hanger. "I managed to get you some additional help."

"Really?"

"I talked with the Admiral running the *George Washington* task force. The long and short of it is that I have a couple of Marine companies for a week. They're going to list it on the books as desert training."

"It could get to be little more than that," cautioned Jim.

"Yes, I know that. The Marines know they are going into a hot zone situation. Full gear, full rations and I can have two *Eagles* over you within half an hour, tops." Jonas tensed. "This is for your ears only, Jim."

Harper hardly missed a beat as they stepped into the hanger. "You think we've got the same problems as before."

Jonas shook his head. "Something—I don't know—I just can't put my finger on it." But he could. The image of Arthur sitting so prim in his chair during the Pentagon briefing yesterday continued to haunt him—a man who seemed to have all the answers, but none of the risk.

"What's the story on Stillwell?" Harper shifted gears suddenly.

They stepped through the monitors, receiver stations, and JSTARS and AWACS computer links into the conference room. Jonas kicked the door shut and settled into a chair. "When we saw the reconnaissance photos on Saturday morning, the national security advisor executed a preplanned response to the crisis. They had an entire script ready to go. Kind of like a checklist of things you do before leaving on vacation."

"Espionage in a box?" quipped Harper.

Jonas shrugged. "Your name popped out and Stillwell's came up as the weapon expert. The others are a security team, so you can work."

"They don't seem to like that idea very much."

Jonas perked up slightly, "Really?"

"Not terribly happy about some old guy who's been retired coming in to steal the show."

Jonas waved it off. "They've got their orders. They make sure you have the time to do what you need to do."

"Four men? Somehow, I think you've underestimated the Iraqi sensitivity towards their data. If this is truly the same nerve center it was before, we're going to have company."

"Yes. That's why you have Stillwell. If you can't effect a rip-off of their database, then he needs time to look at the data and assess where it is most likely they are producing the junk."

Harper shook his head not believing his ears. "Jonas. If I don't have time to rip off the database, I doubt I'll have time to take Stillwell on a guided tour. Don't you guys remember the last time we went in there? The Iraqis got very upset and they have guns. Big, black, loud guns and they like to shoot them."

"That's the mission brief," explained Jonas.

"But that doesn't make any sense. Look, the best we can do is rip off the database and bring it home with us. Hopefully with ten fingers and toes."

Jonas did not want to argue the point. Those were the mission orders from the White House. Indeed, the problem could stem from the White House's attempt to control intelligence operations. He had already stretched the mission parameters by getting the two Marine companies. The sense that something was terribly wrong flitted through Jonas's thoughts again. He dismissed it.

He pushed a black metal box across the briefing table to Harper. "Those are your 'call home to mama' signals."

Harper opened the box. Inside were two cylinders about the size of a cigarette. A chain was threaded through the rings on each of them. "They will send a continuous signal to one of the satellites we have permanently placed over the region. The green one is for normal pickup. The red one means you need the cavalry *now*."

Harper slipped the chain over his head and around his neck. The signal devices slipped beneath his shirt and behind his body armor. "The cavalry includes the Marines, at least two—maybe four F-15 or F-16 fighters, and the *Apache* gunships. Everything and everyone I can throw at your position. The fighters will probably get there first. Once you're on your way into Indian country the Marines and the gunships will be moved into Iraq as well."

Harper nodded. "I notice you haven't brought the rest of the my team into this briefing."

Jonas pursed his lips. "You can tell your team whatever you wish to tell them. They don't have a need to know. The only one who knows about the submarine and the intended target site is Stillwell. The others—like I said, they are along to make sure you have time to do whatever you believe you need to do to satisfy the mission parameters. Nothing more."

"Then they don't know about the signaling devices, the Marines, the aircraft, the databases, or much of anything else?"

Jonas shook his head. "They know about nothing. Jim, the less they know, the better. They've got a job. If it comes to it, they'll kill Iraqi soldiers. You've got to have enough time to finish your job. Stillwell can look over your shoulder if need be. He knows what the data looks like. He probably can tell you about the major players inside Saddam's chemical warfare apparatus better than we can. He really knows his stuff. If you run into something that doesn't make sense, ask him. He's the absolute best when it comes to figuring out the data."

Jonas pulled out a remote control and pointed it towards the television propped on the end of the table. "I have reconnaissance photography of the Data Center site." The television snapped on revealing an infrared depiction of the rugged hills surrounding the underground bunker. Five white circles appeared on the screen and Jonas hit the FREEZE FRAME button. "These are air shafts leading down into the facility. We count five from the air, but I suspect there are probably more. The sixth spot in bright red appears to be the heat exchanger. They have to keep those machines cool, that creates a heat bloom."

"How wide are the shafts?"

Jonas pressed PLAY. "Big enough for a man." Harper had transformed again. He was staring at the screen drinking in the details. The mind was churning with possibilities—formulating, rejecting, then reformulating plans.

The video shifted around to a sideways view showing the quarry and the harsh metal door framed by hewn bedrock. The Navy could send air strike after air strike and no bomb damage assessment officer would ever be able to identify whether the target had been destroyed. It was literally built into the side of a mountain.

"As you can see, there are no overt security features. The Iraqis are relying on stealth to hide their treasures. We guess their best response time is fifteen minutes. That's with two four-man fire teams. Another five minutes and they can have three companies of Republic Guard. The problem for them is ingress and egress. There is one door in and one door out." Getting in and out was the same problem Harper and his team faced. His mind wandered back to the airshafts.

The infrared picture faded showing a normal terrain shot from the air. It looked like nothing but rock and sand. "Unless they are already camped out inside."

"No. Any sizable security attachment needs to have more air ducts. They would have a supply problem. None of which exists here. We estimate ten people inside. The bulk of them have to be technicians."

"A self contained facility?"

"Completely. They repaired the holes you left and pulled the desert inside with them."

"We go in tomorrow night."

"The sooner the better." Jonas paused debating the wisdom of his next decision. He shrugged and went with his instinct. "Jim, you need to understand I have the cavalry, but we're dealing with some pretty desperate folks here."

Jerry's ashen face visited Harper. "I know." Payback was coming and it was coming soon.

"We found what was left of the crew from the Iraqi boat—the one that hooked up with the Chinese sub. They were shot dead. We found them on the Fao Peninsula. The boat had been scuttled and whatever they were bringing back has vanished."

"Dead men tell no tales. That's standard for this part of the world," replied Jim.

"It looked like they had been brought back to where they scuttled the boat. You're dealing with Saddam's top security people here. They'll do whatever they wish if they capture you. We've had reports. Nothing we can substantiate—probably because we don't have survivors. They've got gas chambers. They've been using this stuff on prisoners, then dissecting the corpses. It's like something out of Hitler's Germany."

Harper nodded. The horrors of the past were coming back towards final days of the twentieth century. The concept of ethics vanished in the relentless pursuit of a higher goal. Right and wrong blurred under the need to produce deadly weapons. Weapons designed to be used against Tel Aviv, Teheran, or New York? The delivery system could be something as benign as a shaving kit.

"I understand. Look, Jonas, why don't you go talk to the rest of the troops. We step off at twenty-hundred hours local time."

Jonas got up from the briefing table and left Harper alone. He waited until the door shut before opening his grip. There amidst the ammunition, magazines, and night vision goggles was the small red-bound Bible. He picked it out of the grip and thumbed the snap open. Two photographs slid into his hands. One showed his girls dressed up for Easter. They stood in their finery on the deck on a sunny spring day. The other, from when they were first married, was a picture of Lynn with longer hair and younger skin.

Had they ever been that young? Where had all the years gone? Now he had two girls half a world away. He was sitting in a makeshift briefing room about to step off into the desert night and chase the bogeyman.

He opened to the Ninety First Psalm. He read the following:

You will not be afraid of the terror by night,
Or of the arrow that flies by day;
Of the pestilence that stalks in darkness,
Or of the destruction that lays waste at noon.
A thousand may fall at your side
And ten thousand at your right hand,
But it shall not approach you.

There are no atheists in foxholes. Combat has a way of bringing a man to stark acknowledgement in his mortality and the immortality of his Creator. Harper closed his eyes and breathed out. More than anything, he wanted to hug his girls tight to his chest and stroll on a warm beach with Lynn. For some reason, he had ventured back to this barren place close to the Promised Land to chase a phantom.

It had seemed so clear back in Bartlett. Now, the certainty ebbed with the nearness at hand. He bent his head to his chest and whispered, "Forgive me." Jim closed the small Bible and slipped it back into his grip. He never read the last lines of the Psalm, and never claimed their promise.

He will call upon Me, and I will answer him;
I will be with him in trouble;
I will rescue him and honor him.
With a long life I will satisfy him
And let him see My Salvation.

Jim stood and gathered himself. It was time for battle. He fixed his game face and checked his weapons. There were no illusions about where he was going or the chances he was taking. Life is an extraordinary precious gift, and families are an extension of that gift. For Jim Harper, it was a sacred trust.

15

Baghdad, Iraq, Sunday, November 16, 1997, 6:00 PM (GMT +3.00)

Colonel Taha Duri settled himself in his office. Unlike his Western equivalents where status was measured by the number of windows and highly stylized office furnishings, status in Iraq's Special Security Services was measured by how far below street level and how bombproof one's office was. The threat of American *Tomahawk* cruise missiles and precision guided munitions launched from F-117 *Nighthawk* stealth strike aircraft caused the intelligence services to burrow deep below Baghdad's busy streets.

Duri's office had its own safe built into the concrete subwall, a bombproof door, and a special ventilation system not dependent on the visible surface vents. The laughter evoked from the assembled press corps as an American Air Force General commented on the destruction of his counterpart's headquarters during *Desert Storm* had caused Iraq's top defense and intelligence ministries to leave the visible targets in place while the real work was sheltered under tons of concrete. Saddam's own generals never knew when he might provoke the American's to strike again.

The surroundings were dreary, and the paint on the walls was a pale green. Duri had some assurance that his officc would still be there the next day. Certainly, the current tension over UN Weapon inspectors and the increasingly belligerent attitude of the American administration could be a predictor of future attacks. The *USS Nimitz* and *George Washington* carrier battle groups had the firepower to prosecute any orders delivered.

Duri's job was not to defeat the US Navy, but merely to protect the secret weapon programs from detection and exposure. He managed a complicated shell game of moving truckloads of important looking equipment from one Presidential Palace to another. Half the time the trucks were filled with empty boxes and shiny metal canisters. American satellites and U2 spy planes dutifully recorded the transfer. The lack of American human intelligence on the ground in Iraq was used mercilessly against the robotic watchers. Indeed, the Americans could count tanks and guns or boxes and canisters as the need arose, but they lacked the ability to know what was inside. The most technically advanced nation had lost its soul to machines made of melted sand and copper filaments.

The UN inspection teams attempted to gain entrance to the identified Palace sites, and the Iraqi foreign ministry pointedly denied access. The ping-pong game would continue for a week, maybe two, before the rage and stammering on the international stage mounted. Then, without any resistance, permission would be granted to the inspection teams. Remote cameras and listening devices would be uncovered, and Iraq would allow the inspection teams access again.

It was the beginning of another crisis largely over nothing. The UNSCOM teams placed cameras next to suspected chemical, biological, or nuclear sites. Duri had already ordered for two sets of cameras to be sprayed with black paint—effectively blinding the electronic surveillance. Over the next few months, the pressure would be stepped up by denying access to additional sites and leaking the stories that chemical and biological labs could be taken down and set up overnight.

The true chemical and biological warfare labs had been dispersed to desert and mountain sites. Some of the smaller labs were left in Baghdad and Tikrit for the UNSCOM teams to find. After all, their charter was to find weapons of mass destruction. As long as they found some test tubes, Anthrax vaccine, and the potential for basic botulinum toxin, they would have plenty to report. Duri supplied something for the UN teams to find, and this seemed to keep the Americans happy—confident in their fantasy that they were punishing Saddam.

Duri managed a game of cat and mouse. The truly important weapon systems were gone. However, the file sitting before him posed a real threat to Duri's entire subterfuge. The weakest link in Iraq's special weapons program was information management. The problem was rapid development of complex weapon systems without sufficient computer systems. The computer systems they stole and bartered for came through third parties largely barred from advanced technology by American import/export laws.

Computer technology did not reside in the former Soviet Empire or the burgeoning Chinese Empire. Computer technology was dominated by America and, to a lesser extent, Europe. But European technology was eighteen to thirty months behind America, and anything Iraq was able to steal from its silent allies was close to five or six years out of date. The tempo of American technological expansion continued to increase, and the gap between American computer technology and the rest of the world widened daily. In some ways, American computers were more valuable than Plutonium. After all, there were enough Soviet warheads floating around to maintain a healthy supply of Plutonium.

The other problem was finding people to support the technology Iraq was able to acquire. The graphical user interface was merely a paradigm to interact with a much vaster and complex technology ocean hidden from the casual user. Maintaining complex database servers, local area and wide area networks, and supplying the unending programming responses for those laboring in the weapon labs was a constant strain. Iraq simply did not have the people available to support the information infrastructure required for modern weapon research and development.

Today, an American team had been dispatched to raid Iraq's single information processing asset. The black and white photographs stared back at Duri from his desk. Their names, service records, and areas of expertise were written in precise script below each face. The mission plan, timetable, and immediate assets were listed on a separate sheet.

Duri glanced at the wall clock and realized the Americans could already be on the ground in Kuwait. Infiltration through the border would probably take place tonight.

He pulled the photograph of Major James Harper. According to the attached service record, Harper had been inside the Data Center once before. A thin smile emerged on Duri's lips. Harper had caused a great deal of trouble by linking into the fiber network connecting Iraq's military and weapon sites. He had seemingly walked into the Data Center, initiated a firefight and walked back out.

This time it would be different, and Duri would have an interesting prisoner to dangle before his superiors. It was the second photo, though, that piqued Duri's interest. It seemed odd that an expert of this caliber would be given the lowly rank of Lieutenant. He was an expert in unconventional warfare and a member of one of Washington's prestigious think tanks devoted to studying the unthinkable.

Somehow, Brian Stillwell had been attached to a covert mission deep into Iraq. He was a talented analyst, but no warrior. Soon he would be within Duri's grasp. An expert such as Stillwell could very easily tip the balance of Iraq's weapons program from experimental novelties to practical wartime applications. The Americans expected problems, and they were sending Stillwell to do some sort of analysis based on the information obtained from the Data Center.

Duri's phone rang.

His call to the Special Republic Guard Company garrisoned near the Data Center had been completed. The captain in command listened as Duri explained his new mission. When Duri dropped the phone receiver back into its cradle, he tapped Harper's photograph. "This time, Major, it won't be so simple."

Duri stood and walked across the room to his fax machine. At least this level of technology could be acquired from friends in Jordan. He placed the six photographs and his own instructions face down on the document feeder. He punched in the numbers for the Data Center fax and fleetingly considered the possibility of getting out of Iraq. The Alps were lovely this time of year. Who knows, perhaps he could even sell Stillwell back to the Americans.

16

Strait of Hormuz, Sunday, November 16, 1997, 8:00 PM (+3.00 GMT)

The S-3B *Viking* rolled west, away from the *Strait of Hormuz*, and parallel to the southern Iranian coastline. In the darkening skies, the red and green lights from off shore oil platforms twinkled brightly. The running lights from freighters and oil tankers moved ponderously into the Gulf. The myriad of small islands dotting the boundary between the Persian Gulf and the Gulf of Oman quietly vanished with the setting sun.

The lights from Bandar-e Moghüyen and Bandar-e Lengeh reminded the pilot of home and family. Mothers were still getting children ready for bed, and fathers were coming home from work. They may have thought America was the Great Satan, but life was pretty much the same for families in both countries.

The *Viking* was heading back to the *George Washington.* They had spent a long day hunting for a Chinese sub that might only be a phantom. The S-3B *Viking* is fundamentally a flying video game capable of launching torpedoes, mines, rockets, bombs, and missiles. However, before it could destroy a target, it had to find one.

To do this, the *Viking* dropped acoustic and non-acoustic sensors—much like a giant game of battleship. The entire ocean was the enemy's board and the little white pegs were sensors, special radar and sonar systems. Somewhere below and to the east the *USS Springfield* also searched for the same elusive prey.

Computer monitors, sonar screens, and flight controls illuminated the Viking's flight deck. The Inverse Synthetic Aperture Radar (ISAR) took another reading from the sensors bobbing in the sea below. The computers gathered a blizzard of information from the sensors as long as the batteries lasted, and blended it into a hunt for man-made sound.

Tommy Hargroves was popping the top of his last Diet Coke when ISAR started chirping. The other crewmembers turned to stare at the alarm board. Tommy pulled his headset back over his ears and fiddled with a couple of dials. "I've got some sort of submerged signature—making one weird racket," he announced.

Tyrone Masters flipped the satellite up-link toggles on and directed the data feed back to the battle management command center aboard the *George Washington*. He looked over his shoulder at Tommy and asked, "What's ISAR think it is?"

Tommy shrugged and flipped the cabin speaker on. A combination of a buzz saw and snapping filled the rear of the flight deck. "I don't know. You can hear the screws turning, at least I think they're screws, but something is really wrong down there."

"It's not one of ours?" asked Bernie Mueller.

Tommy looked towards the pilot, "No. It's definitely something else."

Bernie toggled his microphone and said, "*Washington*, this is *Eyepiece 3*. We have unknown contact. Repeat, *Washington*, this is *Eyepiece 3*. We have unknown contact. Approximate position is thirty klicks south of Bandar-e Lengeh—that is three-zero klicks south of Bandar-e Lengeh, and approximately one hundred ten klicks due west of Al-Khasab—that is one-one-zero klicks due west of Al-Khasab. We are uploading data to you and are turning south into a figure eight formation. Oh, and *Washington*, if we have to stay up here much longer, we'll get kind of thirsty."

"Roger, *Eyepiece 3*. We confirm your data link. Ah, we have a tanker from *Nimitz* closest to your position. About twenty minutes."

Bernie toggled his microphone again, "Thank you, *Washington*." He clicked off.

Martin Hansen checked their position on the global positioning satellite feed and joked, "Tommy, you'd better nurse that Coke, I think we're going to be here awhile."

Tommy grunted as he tuned ISAR. "We're moving away from contact."

Bernie looked at the onboard navigational map and pulled the *Viking* towards the north. "You just guide me in over the top of him."

★ ★ ★

Captain Jeff Andrews moved through the *Springfield's* crowded control room asking, "What've we got Robbie?"

Rob Bremer looked up from the chart table. "It looks like a *Viking* found something right here." He circled a spot about ten klicks south-southeast of marshes between Bandar-e Moghüyen and Bandar-e Lengeh. "We're getting data link from the *Washington* right now."

"How long before sonar has the sound signature loaded?"

Chief of the Boat, Ernie Watson, poked a thumb over his shoulder and said, "Ten seconds. I just got Henderson out of the rack. He's the best we got."

Jeff nodded, "Good work, Chief." He glanced back to Robbie, "Did we get any clarification on our orders?"

Robbie shook his head.

Jeff scowled. "Henderson, you got that fancy boom box working yet?"

A curly haired, pimply looking kid with thick glasses looked back. "Yes, Sir. We're playing the *Stones* on channel two."

Jeff nodded, "Carry on." He glanced at the chief. "You say he's our best."

The Chief, closing on the far side of forty, who nursed, cursed and cajoled his men, replied, "Total computer geek, Sir. Trust me on this, Sir. He's the best I've seen in ten years."

"Robbie, distance to target."

Robbie drew a line on the plot chart. “Seventy two knots, Sir.”

“Are we shallow enough to get real time feed from the *Viking*?”

“Towed array is deployed. Satellite links are stable,” replied Chief Watson.

“Set course, three-three-five—speed seven knots,” he told Robbie.

Robbie turned to the helmsmen and repeated the order. Three hundred sixty foot metal tube guarding men against the sea outside turned towards the southern Iranian coast. The *Springfield* made a hole in the ocean and slid into it. The BQQ-5E sonar suite consisting of over 1000 hydrophones was located in the very forward end of the boat. It began to probe the shallow depths. Henderson ran the digital image captured by Tommy Hargroves's sensors, and sought to match that image with something he could hear.

Andrews turned to the weapons board. If this was a damaged Chinese boat on a covert mission, they could be getting desperate. He turned to Robbie and ordered, “Spin up the ADCAP's in tubes one and two.”

Robbie nodded and gave the order.

★ ★ ★

The active *ping* hammered the *404's* double hull like an ancient gong being rung. Captain Tze Wong looked up from his plot table and sighed. The second ping seemed even louder. He found the anxious eyes of his remaining crew watching him for strength and courage. Strength and courage were important, but honor meant more.

“Number One, source and distance to threat?” He looked down at the chart facing him on the plot table. They were very close to the *Strait of Hormuz*, but it appeared the American's were waiting to trap him.

Ping!

It was obvious they could not continue on their present course. Somewhere between his present position and the Gulf of Oman an American submarine would soon be alerted to their position.

“Sonar source appears to be a surface sensor.”

Wong nodded. With their computers, aircraft, and satellites, they would be able to plot his course for him. Since they already knew where he was, he had to lose them fast.

"Helm turn to heading one-seven-five, ahead two thirds." His new course would take them towards the island of Jazireh-Ye Sirri. Perhaps, they could lose them among the shoals, shallows, and dark.

"Prepare counter measures."

Ping!

★ ★ ★

Tommy Hargroves pulled the headsets off his ears howling, "Oww!" He dialed the volume down to a more reasonable level and took a sip of his Coke.

"You okay?" asked Tyrone

Tommy nodded. "Bernie, you'd better tell the *Washington*, he's making a run for it."

Martin pulled up the navigational charts. "Which way do you think he's going?"

Tommy held up a hand for a second and checked a read out on his computer monitor. "ISAR thinks he's heading straight south."

Bernie looked over at the chart, "What's south?"

"Islands. He's heading towards some rocks in the water. Maybe he thinks he can get lost in the funny acoustics."

Tyrone checked the plot map. "We didn't drop anything around those islands."

"So we could lose him?" asked Bernie.

Tyrone bobbed his head, "It's possible."

Bernie keyed his microphone, "*Washington*, this is *Eyepiece 3*."

"We copy you *Eyepiece 3*."

"It looks like we've got a runner. He's headed towards some islands south of Bandar-e Moghüyen. We don't have anything dropped in that location. My people tell me we could lose him."

"Roger, *Eyepiece 3*. Continue pursuit."

The radio went dead once again.

Tommy swallowed the last of his Coke—so much for saving it. "He's picking up speed, and making a lot more noise."

☆ ☆ ☆

Henderson peered at the high-resolution color monitor. He glanced at a second set of monitors that showed matching sound signatures using a waveform. He dialed through a series of frequencies, listening carefully. He flipped a series of toggle switches that imposed different types of amplification filters.

He knew it was unlikely that he would find the *Han* immediately. They were seventy knots away. He continued to dial through the sound spectrum. His fingers tapped commands into the computer system before him. The personal computer had made it into the mainstream of the American military. It was revolutionizing the manner by which technical specialists performed their jobs. Henderson had been playing Nintendo games for over ten years before his posting to the *Springfield*. His new duties were nothing more than an expanded form of Mario 64.

The waveforms on the two monitors tilting towards him suddenly matched. Henderson glanced up and a satisfied grin emerged on his features. He had just made it to the boss and it was time to win. He clicked one of the icons on his main screen and heard the same buzz-saw snapping sound Tommy Hargroves heard several minutes ago.

"Got him!" Henderson said more loudly than necessary. The headset pressed to his ears muffled his sense of volume.

Chief Watson looked across to the sonar man's cave. He turned to Captain Andrews, "You see, he's a little weird, but the best I've seen in a long time."

Andrews nodded. On the plot table, the image of the *Han* class boat emerged. The vector indicating speed and course popped up next to the image.

"Twenty knots?" asked Rob Bremer.

"He's running," announced Chief Watson.

"Robbie, plot an interception course. If we're hearing him this far away, then he's got to have hull damage," Andrews speculated.

Robbie gave the appropriate orders.

Andrews rubbed his chin before saying, "Make sure we keep the wires attached to the ADCAPS. I want full control over these fish. If the *Han* is running, he doesn't care if we can hear him. He's panicked and that makes him dangerous."

Chief Watson turned back to the Captain. "We're getting satellite data from the *Washington*. They think he's running towards some islands."

"Robbie, retrieve the towed array. We know where he is and we may have to make some quick moves."

★ ★ ★

The *Han* continued its beeline run. Wong resigned himself to the inevitable. The Americans had found him damaged and alone. He was far from home, and the prospect of seeing home again seemed like a distant dream. Perhaps the delivering of the toxins was a dishonorable act, and now they were being asked to pay for it. The twin demons of duty and honor were demanding penance for his deeds.

Wong shrugged. He looked at the plot table measuring the distance before he dropped to dead slow and attempted to slide out of the Gulf. Maybe they would get lucky, but the evidence of hull damage and the racket it produced had alerted the Americans.

He lifted the stopwatch that hung around his neck. His thumb flipped it on and he stared into the control room now illuminated with red lamps. A frenetic forty-five seconds had been spent to rig the damaged boat for ultra silent running. He eased into the captain's chair and said, "Number One, on my mark turn zero-nine-zero and reduce speed to two knots."

He glanced down at the chart and back to the stopwatch. The bottom was coming up fast on his boat. If the charts were wrong, or he misjudged the timing, the Americans would overhear the *404's* keel being ripped apart on the rocky bottom.

Five more seconds.

"Number One, fire tube one."

The *Han* shuddered as a vintage Russian torpedo left the ship.

Two seconds.

"Mark."

His Number One tapped the helmsman on the shoulder and dialed the speed down himself. The *Han* glided sideways on a perpendicular course from the torpedo. Hopefully with all the noise being generated by the hull damage, the Americans would miss the torpedo noise.

The stopwatch ticked passed the mark two more times, and Wong quietly said, "Detonate." The ship's blade revolutions were already spinning down as he pointed the *404* in a shallow dive towards the *Strait*.

Two thousand yards away the warhead ignited barely two fathoms above the bottom. Wong had indeed cut his margins very close. The water in the immediate vicinity of the warhead superheated into steam and the rocky bottom was pulverized by the pressure wave. The sudden creation of water vapor sent a surge of bubbles racing to the surface

★ ★ ★

The *Viking* pulled away from the tanker and rotated back over the islands where they expected the *Han* to emerge. The first sign of something wrong came as Hargroves pulled his headset down and stared with decided puzzlement at the ISAR computer system.

"Something's not right," he declared.

Tyrone turned away from his communication board, "What're you talking about?"

Hargroves scratched his head and checked the sound signature. It had vanished from his monitors. "It sounds like he piled into the bottom, but that doesn't make sense."

He looked at the trace screens, and rewound a backup digital recording tape. "Here, listen to this."

The buzz-saw sound thundered through the speakers and abruptly changed to heavy static and faded out to nothing.

"He's gone."

Bernie leaned back, "You saying we lost him?"

"No, I'm saying he's gone."

Bernie dialed up the *Washington.*

★ ★ ★

Henderson was listening from a different perspective. His hands were tapping on the chrome sides of the sonar monitor. He had his prize. It was the high-speed propeller noise that stopped his hands from tapping. His training had been on Russian torpedo noises. The US Navy had an extensive library of such noises, and Henderson had learned them all.

"Torpedo! Torpedo in the water!"

Chief Watson's jaw dropped open. Robbie cocked his chicken neck and glanced at the chart table. They were still some forty thousand yards distant from the *Han*. No other boats—friend or foe—appeared on the chart table.

Andrews swung around to the weapon's officer. "Do we have a solution?"

"Extreme range, Sir. We might or might not get him?"

Robbie asked the other question, "What's he shooting at?"

Henderson had dropped back to his hunched over gamer crouch. His eyes rattled across the threat boards, because he heard the next sound as well. "Detonation!"

Robbie leaned over the chart. He did a quick calculation based on worst case, and calculated the largest possible target area for the torpedo. Andrews glanced over his shoulder and said. "Dead slow."

Watson walked over to the sonar cave and laid a fatherly hand on Henderson's shoulder. "You still got him?"

Henderson held up a hand. He fiddled with some dials, within half a minute his shoulders started to relax. "Yes." He sighed, "Yes, I've still got him." He punched a couple more buttons on the keyboard, and the new position of the *Han* appeared on the chart table.

Chief Watson squeezed the younger man's shoulder. "Good work."

Robbie examined the new vector. He drew two lines that were virtually parallel. He glanced at the large red LED numbers on the ship's clock and did some quick math. "In about at hour, we'll be within twenty-five thousand yards. We'll continue to close in until we're about three thousand yards apart. That'll be a little more than three hours from now. "

Andrews nodded. The *Han's* captain had gambled. He ran for the rocky shallows, fired a torpedo, and changed course. He wanted them to think he was stupid enough to drive his boat into the bottom.

"Captain, the *Washington* wants to know if we still have him."

Andrews met his XO's eyes and said, "Yes! Tell them yes, and ask them, Robbie, what they want us to do. This guy just fired a torpedo and he's got at least five more ready to go."

"Yes, Sir."

Andrews walked across the control room to Henderson's domain. "Can you keep him pegged?"

Henderson, forgetting it was the captain, simply said, "He's mine—all mine."

"Good." Andrews had learned a long time ago not to argue with success, especially when that success might mean the difference between life and death. Henderson might be quirky, but he heard the torpedo. He heard the explosion and now he heard the *Han*. Something the flyboys had lost.

"Robbie, I guess we're about thirty minutes from a decent solution?"

Robbie nodded.

"Spin up tubes three and four as well."

★ ★ ★

Admiral Trevor Barnes was sitting in the command chair of the *Washington's* Battle Management Center. The threat boards listing all ships near the *Han* were painted on the blue screen that held the central view. From this room, Barnes had computer images with speed and course vectors of everything floating or flying in the Persian Gulf. He could direct any offensive or defensive action for his task force from this chair.

He took a sip from his coffee mug realizing his *Vikings* had lost the target, and perhaps this target was stupid enough to rip the bottom of his keel apart. Barnes did not believe in stupidity on the battlefield. There were good commanders and bad commanders, but most everyone out there had the welfare of their troops and the mission in mind. He kept a plaque on his wall that read: NEVER UNDERESTIMATE YOUR ENEMY. Barnes had stared at the plaque before coming down to the battle management center tonight.

The men playing cat and mouse out there were professionals with wives and families. Barnes had a duty to ensure they were given adequate opportunities to defend themselves, and the strange orders he had received from the Chief of Naval Operations continued to haunt his waking thoughts.

Something about this *Han* boat scared the very powerful people to whom he reported. They wanted it to disappear but not in the Gulf. He glanced back to the threat board, and the icon designated for the *Han* materialized on the screen. It was heading East out of the Gulf and straight towards the *Springfield.*

"Where did that come from?"

"The *Springfield* still has him," replied the watch officer.

Barnes leaned forward to get a better look at the situation. From his chair, he could dial up any part of the threat board to a monitor in front of him. He hit the appropriate keys and stared at the image. He turned to the watch officer. "What happened? The *Vikings* lost him and *the Springfield* still has a lock?"

"According to this, they claim he fired a torpedo, detonated it, and drifted east," explained the watch officer. "And they want to know what their orders are."

The two boats were heading straight at each other. He knew Jeff Andrews. The man would never fire unless an attack was imminent. He was asking for orders regarding the security of his boat. Command is never an easy position. It always appears simple for those who view from their own perspectives, but now a life or death decision was required. Barnes knew what Washington wanted, and he saw the threat to one of his attack boats.

He chewed his inner cheek and sighed, "Tell the *Springfield* to sink the *Han*."

★ ★ ★

Andrews stared at the message signed by Barnes. Before him in black and white, he had his orders. Sink the Chinese boat. His emotions were a rancid mixture of relief and regret. Relief that he had authority to protect his boat, and regret that his actions would cause grief in some Chinese homes.

Robbie stood studiously at his side. Jeff pushed the transmission across the chart table. "Enter it into the log."

"Yes, Sir."

He turned to Chief Watson. "Make sure your wonder kid understands we aren't playing a game anymore. I want to be sure he's listening for any counter strike from the *Han*."

Watson nodded and retreated to the sonar cave.

"Weapons!"

"Sir."

"Do we have a solution for fish one and two?" He already knew the answer, but when firing a warshot you have to be sure.

"Solution plotted and programmed into fish one and two. Current range to target is twenty-eight-thousand-four-hundred yards."

"Set the ADCAPS to short range attack mode and cut wires after two thousand yards." He turned back to the plot table.

"Open outer doors."

Like a lizard's eyes opening, the doors on tubes one and two opened to the outer sea. The glossy black cover of the acoustic hood pointed out of the tubes, ready to fire. A Mark 48 Advance Capability torpedo is one of the most efficient weapons in the world. It is smart enough to beat most countermeasures. It can swing around for multiple attacks until it runs out of fuel, and it carries a six-hundred-fifty pound warhead of PBXN-103 explosive. It can *see* a one-hundred-eighty degree angle. The *Han* was following a heading straight towards the *Springfield.* There was very little to miss. The seeker heads were smart enough to feed data back to the BSY-1 fire control system. If anything, the second pair of fish in tubes three and four would be more accurate.

"Fire one. Fire Two."

The piston engine, pump jet swirled out of tubes one and two into the dark sea. Quickly, the ADCAPS accelerated to attack speed of over sixty knots, and they began to descend on the damaged *Han*. The torpedo men played out the wire guidance to ensure they had an even spread towards the port side of the Han. At slightly past two thousand yards the wires were cut, and the ADCAPS shot toward destiny.

Andrews looked at the fire control panel. "Ahead ten knots. Weapons, do you have a solution for fish three and four?"

"Yes, Sir."

"No wires this time. Do we have sufficient data from the first two fish to target the *Han*?"

"Yes, Sir."

Andrews looked across to Robbie and said quietly, "Fire three and four."

The slight shudder from the second pair of ADCAPS rumbled up to deck. Andrews checked his position on the chart table. "Close outer doors. Helm ahead flank speed, steer course three-five-five, and bring us down to four-five-zero feet."

The *Springfield* turned away from her prey, turning north and away from the doomed Chinese boat. It was only a matter of time. Less than twelve minutes before the first pair arrived.

"Load counter measures."

Andrews stared hard at Henderson's back. Chief Watson was hovering close by, but far enough away to make sure Henderson had room to do his job. Four of the smartest torpedoes in the Navy's arsenal streaked through the midnight water. They were beyond recall.

★ ★ ★

"Torpedoes! I have one, no, two incoming!" shouted the *Han's* sonar operator.

Wong looked at the chart table. "Course and speed?"

"I have them at sixty-five knots, course one-nine-five, range ten thousand meters." The young sonar operator turned and stared in horror at his captain.

There was no time to fire a salvo at the American submarine, if indeed there was an American submarine. He had to run and possibly pray.

"Steer course one-seven-five, ahead flank speed." He picked up the microphone and toggled the reactor room. "I need everything you have got and more. No limits." He dropped the microphone and wondered what the *404* was capable of producing.

"Launch countermeasures." Perhaps these were not American ADCAP torpedoes, and perhaps he would see the sun rise tomorrow. Both seemed unlikely. He picked up his stopwatch and started the timer.

The *Han* rolled towards the south again—kicking away from its course—towards open water. She barely made it past twenty-five knots at flank speed. The hole in her hull simply caused too much cavitation to permit her to reach the thirty knots she was supposed to have.

Six minutes passed before the active seeker heads on the first pair of ADCAPS came to life. They began to pound the *Han* with active sonar pings. The *Han* limped further south like a wounded deer running from a wolf pack. It was only a matter of time before the wolves cornered and killed their prey.

The sonar operator held his head in his hands. He found two more incoming torpedoes. The countermeasures had done nothing to confuse the incoming weapons.

Wong stared at the interior of his control room. There was little left to try. He had jinxed his course. He launched the last of his countermeasures. His reactor was redlined and overheating, and the American torpedoes were fifteen hundred meters away.

He found that his legs were not turning to water. He picked up the ship wide microphone and said, "This is the Captain speaking." He paused and stared back down at the stopwatch. "In a few minutes, the first of several torpedoes will impact our hull. There is nothing left to do. I want to apologize to you, the members of my crew, for bringing us to this point. However, you have served with honor and pride. I thank you and bid you farewell." He clicked off the microphone.

The first two torpedoes were spiraling towards the *Han*. Impact would take place in less than forty seconds. Wong looked up and said, "Chief of the Boat, prepare for emergency blow on my mark."

The ping frequency reverberating throughout the boat was increasing. The warhead was nestled behind a sonar seeker and guidance control. When the ADCAP ultimately impacted, the warhead would smash through the fragile electronic parts and pancake against the titanium outer hull.

At five seconds, Wong gave the order to execute the emergency blow. High-pressure air flooded into the main ballast tanks of the *Han* in an effort to give it positive buoyancy. The bow nosed up and pulled the *Han* forward at thirty-degree angle. The turboelectric drive continued to push the boat forward so that the screw was much closer to the ADCAP than the bow.

The first torpedo detonated twenty yards beneath the keel. A violent tremor slammed into the entire boat, causing lights to flicker and pipes to burst. Water sprayed over the top of the radio gear. The deck was lurching too violently for anyone to find the valves and stop the water flow.

The second torpedo had a few seconds to adjust its targeting. It impacted at an oblique angle to the hull above the main ballast tanks. The explosion shattered the integrity of the ballast tanks and broke the propeller shaft into three pieces. The *Han* continued a momentary lurch towards the surface, before stopping short and drifting sideways. The blast tilted the deck almost vertical.

Wong slammed against the periscope housing and rolled off coming to rest on one of the bulkheads. The emergency battery lights flipped on. He levered himself up with one hand before realizing his other arm was hopelessly broken. Amazingly, they were still breathing after two explosions. He looked down at his stopwatch, but the crystal had shattered.

The deck canted in a strange direction as the forward ballast tanks attempted to pull the wounded ship towards the surface. They hung like a fly caught in amber at seventy-five meters below the surface. They did not stay there long.

The third and forth torpedoes slammed simultaneously amidships. The *Han* broke into two pieces and began its final death spiral to the bottom of the Persian Gulf. The cold seawater flowed through the ruptured watertight doors as the pressure-water reactor disintegrated under the blast. It had taken a little over eighteen minutes to kill the *Han*, and she never saw her attacker.

☆ ☆ ☆

Andrews stared glumly at the chart table. The *Han* was dead. He looked around the crew in his control room, and gave them a brittle smile. They had gone to battle and they had won. He should feel good about his accomplishment, instead, he felt rather empty.

"Robbie, stand down from general quarters and resume normal patrol. I'll be in my cabin," he paused and looked at his XO, "and tell the *Washington* the *Han* is dead."

17

Al Jabar Air Base, Kuwait, Sunday, November 16, 1997,
8:00 PM (+3.00 GMT)

A few minutes before Tommy Hargroves got his first reading on the *Han*, Harper and his team rolled away from Al Jabar Air Base and into the coming night. Kuwait consists of one city, a couple of air bases, a rudimentary road net, and oil fields. George Bush talked of the savagery committed by Iraq's Republic Guard, and the unprovoked invasion into Kuwait, but the high ideals of democracy and freedom did not bring five hundred thousand American troops in the fall of 1990. Oil did.

Once beyond the bright lights of Kuwait City and her attendant airfields, the desert begins to gather itself like a dark cloud. It is not a classic desert of drifting sand and broiling sunlight, rather, it is a treacherous desert of hard gravel, mountainous terrain, and wadis where the infrequent water has cut an uncertain course through sand and rock.

Police posts and towers act like a connect-the-dots picture defining the vague border between Kuwait and Iraq, a border now insured by the American force of arms. The few roads that pierce the border are matched with token forces on both sides. A night sky illuminated only by stars, and the occasional flames burning off excess gases on an oil well, served as impenetrable cloak for Harper's excursion.

The HMMVW's veered north heading towards a police post just below the thirtieth parallel. They would take to the hard packed sand before reaching the border and cross just above the thirtieth parallel. It was a spot where the road net on the Iraqi side did not exist, and the corresponding Kuwaiti army barracks were set several miles back from the border. Using night vision goggles the two vehicles slipped through the darkness without any visible lights and vanished into the Wadi al-Batin, which acts as an informal barrier between the two countries.

They skirted the western edge of Iraq's massive Rumaila oil field. The oil towers flashed red, green, and white navigation lights towards the night sky. The separation plant, pumping substation, and storage tanks continued their incessant thumping as the machinery that fed Saddam's military monster continued to produce oil in defiance of the export ban.

They rumbled across the road leading from Al Basrah to Ash Shabakah. The plan was to drive along side the road always tending towards the northwest. Five hundred meters north of the road two lone vehicles were running with special mufflers and no lights. No one saw or heard them navigate the rough sand, strewn boulders, and occasional wadi.

They crossed the Al-Muthanná and An-Najaf Provinces steadily angling towards Baghdad. Next they crossed the main road leading back to the capitol just north of Ash Shabakah. The road was the last manmade thing they saw as they turned north-northwest.

The Tigris and Euphrates Rivers form the western and eastern boundaries that enclose most of Iraq's population. It is bordered on the south by a huge lake called Bahr al-Milh. It is virtually a single city from Baghdad to Karbalá. Saddam, always the coward, made certain he had a human shield composed of women doing their wash and children playing in the streets, surrounding his major nuclear, chemical, and biological warfare factories. He created a human shield with his own people, and dared the Americans to attack with their smart bombs.

Bombs capable of finding the third window on the second floor could obliterate the chemical plants and shatter the vials containing viruses. Those same bombs could not prevent a fallout pattern that would leave thousands gasping for air as their lungs shut down. Saddam knew the effect of his weapons on the human nervous system. His experiments at Salman Pak demonstrated the effectiveness of his arsenal. He did not believe American political leaders had the stomach for such a spectacle.

The obvious attraction for so many people in a country containing little more than rock, sand, and oil is water—plentiful supplies to meet the needs of those citizen hostages. Not only did they hug death to their breasts, but they effectively buried the strategic web of Iraq's communication and data infrastructure. Saddam remained confident the Allied Air Force would not bomb civilian homes to destroy his precious command and control network.

Beyond the western edge of Bahr al-Milh, the population drops off to nothing. Some two hundred kilometers southwest of Baghdad on the Wadi al-Ubayyid and thirty kilometers east of Nukhayb, the Iraqi Data Center lay buried in the side of an abandoned quarry. All data links were run using fiber optic cable and not conventional copper.

One of the major frustrations during the Gulf War was knocking out Iraq's communications net. If they had used conventional copper wire, Allied pilots could have followed the network to every major commander and control center in the country. Saddam had gone to the enormous expense of replacing his conventional network with fiber optic cable prior to the war—a development that slipped past the vigilance of American Intelligence. The American Air Force adopted a policy of obliterating every identified command and control van. Saddam might have state of the art communications, but by the end of the war there was no one left to talk to.

After the war, what remained was hardened and expanded. The Achilles heel remained the need for centralized processing. Saddam had plenty of desert and oil. He had his share of brilliant scientists who left their ethics at the border. He could manipulate his people to act as human shields before the American armada gathering in the Gulf.

However, he had very few computers capable of processing his data and maintaining his databases.

It was just after four in the morning when Harper stopped their advance. They emerged from the HMMWVs looking like a group of distended beetles with their night vision goggles, throat microphones, and headphones built into their helmets. Weapons bristled in the darkness. All communication was encrypted using a frequency-switch algorithm based on a twenty-four bit encryption system. Harper jogged down the wadi and scrambled up the crest of a ridge. Stillwell tagged along with his own set of night vision binoculars.

Harper leaned across the crest of the ridge and focused down on the quarry. The heavy, metal door he and Jerry had struggled out of snapped into a gray-green image. He flipped the range finder to active and found that they were 1200 meters away. Besides the single door leading into the ground and strewn rocks, Harper could find nothing else.

He slid back behind the ridge.

"You sure this is the right place?"

Harper nodded. They had pinpointed the location by satellite and triangulated the global positioning system coordinates. He flipped the GPS system back on and stared at the numbers. "Yeah, that's the place." He glanced at Stillwell. "You'd best carry your rifle from here on out. If someone sees you, shoot them. The weapon is silenced so it won't make much noise."

Harper walked towards the two HMMWV's sitting at the end of a wadi. A camouflage net had already been strung across the top of the vehicles and the marines were unloading gear.

"Sergeant!"

Darby Hayes looked up from behind the nearest HMMWV. He set two canisters of non-lethal nerve gas down. He rose slowly eyeing Harper and Stillwell. He had seen many men come and go in special ops. Conventional wisdom dictated that a man who had been out of the game for over five years was not fit to lead. Yet Harper did not seem like someone who had grown soft during civilian life. He seemed like a bomb waiting to explode.

"Sir?"

"About thirty klicks west of here is a town called Nukhayb. Fill up both vehicles and take the empty jerry cans. We'll need some gas and we won't have anytime to stop on our way out of here." He looked up at the sky. "You've got an hour and half. If we don't see you in two, I'll assume you've been blown." He slapped Stillwell on shoulder. "Help him with the gas cans."

Harper took his other three marines. They each held various pieces of gear. Ronald Anderson was holding the drag bag for the Barrett. "Anderson? You're the sniper?"

"Yes, Sir."

Harper reached down and grabbed two .50 caliber ammunition cans. They were the old metal kind with a latch that pulled the lid tight to the frame. He hefted them feeling the weight in both. "My—my, what'd you bring along?"

Anderson smiled as he pulled the rifle over his shoulder. "A hundred rounds, Sir—armor piercing, frangible anti-personnel, high explosive, and incendiary. They weren't very specific as to what we might need."

Harper nodded. "The scope—is it day/night capable?"

"Uh-huh."

Harper grinned. Ronald Anderson was big old farm boy from Nebraska. The rifle in his hands was a Barrett M82A1A .50 Caliber sniper rifle, capable of taking out small trucks and four-man fire teams. It fires a round slightly shorter than four inches in length, with a muzzle velocity of two-thousand-eight-hundred feet per second, from a mile away. Measuring fifty-seven inches from stock to flash deflector, the Barrett is the state of the art sniper weapon. Depending on the munitions selected, the Barrett could become a long-range hand held cannon.

They stopped below the crest of the ridge. "Okay, Captain, this is the deal." He jerked his thumb at the ridge. "Just over there is a quarry.

According to my range finder, we're about twelve-hundred meters away. When you set up your toy here, you'll find a door and rough track leading into a quarry.

"I want to know two things from you. First, I want to know if anyone shows up. If there is someone that looks like they're in charge, take 'em out. If it's just supplies, hold your fire. The second thing I want to know is if anyone comes out the door. If that happens, we're most likely in big trouble. Make sure nobody leaves."

Anderson nodded. "I can handle that."

"Thought you could, I hope you slept on the way here, because you'll be watching until we go in sometime after eight tonight. I don't care what time it is. If you have to shoot, call me."

"Yes, Sir," answered Anderson.

Harper smiled and turned away. Anderson set the drag bag down and opened the catches. Carefully, he pulled the thirty-three pound rifle from its padded case and began assembling his toy.

Darby Hayes rolled away from the camp and headed for Nukhayb. Kincaid, Stillwell, and Burns stood next to a stack of gear. Harper flipped on a hooded torch and knelt down. "Kincaid and Burns."

They squatted next to him.

"How many Claymores we got?"

"Ten, Sir," replied Kincaid.

Harper looked at the hooded faces surrounding him in the night desert. Neither betrayed any emotion, but neither revealed any confidence. Harper sighed. These two would be difficult.

"Okay. We've got ninety minutes before the sun comes up around here." He drew a circle in the dirt and marked the door with a X. "This is the quarry. From the sky, it looks like all the rest of the rocks down here." He drew the track leading into the quarry. "This is a track leading into the quarry. Now, when the alarm goes up a whole bunch of angry people are going to come down this track. Most likely, they'll be riding trucks or jeeps. There may be an APC, but I doubt it."

He checked his audience. They were listening. They might not care for an old man leading them, but they were paying attention. "I need a killing field inside the quarry, and I need kill zones down this track. The bad guys will come running real hard."

"Sir."

Harper looked at Kincaid. "Yes?"

"We've got a couple of anti-vehicle mines. Darby put them aboard just before we left the weapons depot."

"What kind of mines?" Harper was beginning to like Sergeant Hayes.

"We can set them up to blow on different types of circumstances. For instance, maybe on the third vehicle that passes over the mine. They key on metal content." He drew two circles on the track boxing the length of the track. "If we placed mines at both ends, we could rig to blow this one closest to the quarry on the first vehicle detected, and this one on the end to the fourth vehicle. Then we trigger the Claymores off infrared and motion sensors."

"It makes for a lot of dead ragheads," explained Burns.

Harper liked what he heard. "Don't let me keep you gentlemen. Take Stillwell to help you haul everything."

"No need, Sir. Tom and I can handle it."

Harper snapped off the light. "Let Anderson know what you're doing." He tapped his microphone. "Everybody got one of these things on?"

They both nodded.

He looked over to Stillwell who was sitting next to the HMMWV. "Lieutenant, grab those canisters sitting next to you. We got seventy minutes to take care of a few things."

Harper leaned into the back to the HMMVW and grabbed the case of C4, detonators, and a small bag with his name. He adjusted the Mossberg across his back. "All right, Stillwell, here's something they probably don't write down in any of the manuals. We're going to make sure that whoever is inside this hole goes to sleep at the right time."

Stillwell pointed at the silvery canisters. "What's in there?"

"Non-lethal nerve gas. It should keep everyone inside tucked away for twelve hours." Harper grunted. "They'll wake up with a bad headache, but hopefully we won't have to shoot anyone if this goes according to plan."

"Does it ever go according to plan?"

Harper shook his head, "Never."

He handed the canisters to Stillwell and motioned him to follow. Without the night vision goggles, Stillwell would have lost Harper within ten paces. Instead, Harper became a gray-green ghost dancing across the desert floor.

They started across the desert towards the air vents above the quarry. They picked their way through gravel, small boulders, and around holes. Harper stopped about two hundred meters from the air vents. He pulled Stillwell next to him and whispered, "From here on, no talking."

Stillwell nodded. He produced garbage bags and a roll of duct tape from his pack. "There are four roof vents set in a quadrangle on the summit ahead. They are spaced about fifty feet apart from each other. They look like clumps of dirt. You need to clean them off and wrap them with the duct tape, then wrap the garbage bag around the vent." Harper tapped the nerve gas, "When we put them to sleep tomorrow night, I don't want them waking up because they have a good exhaust system."

The thick black night blanket was already starting to fade in the east when they arrived in the quadrangle of air vents. Stillwell found the first vent and settled down methodically making sure it no longer worked very well.

Harper slid down a gully to find two large grated air intakes. He shined an infrared torch around the edge of the intakes. There were sensors on each of the bolts holding the grate tight against the rim of the intake. Harper checked the other intake. It looked as though a heavy gauge wire traveled down the shaft and out of site.

He set down the nerve gas canisters and unslung the bag carrying the C4 plastic explosive blocks. Harper flipped the plastic plate covering the timers on both canisters. He punched the power switch and the red LED display panel blazed to life. The timer was part of the regulator gas valve. Any attempt to fiddle with the timer was an attempt to fiddle with the regulator. He set the timer to activate at 1800 hours before switching it on. It started counting towards detonation showing 0534. It blinked to NOT ARMED then back to the time. Harper pressed the arming button and held it down for fifteen seconds. The display blinked to ARMED.

He leaned both canisters against the edge of rock holding both intake vents. Fishing out some duct tape, two blocks of C4, and a pair of detonators, he wound the tape over the timer display panel, then sandwiched the C4 tight against the panel. He slid a mercury detonator into the block and wound some more tape. Finally, he took a three-inch shotgun shell labeled 00 BUCKSHOT. Fundamentally, he had created an anti- personnel explosive to ensure that any tampering would result in killing those foolish enough to try.

He slid a pair of bolt cutters off his belt and snipped an opening in the center of the grate. The bolts holding the grate to the rim of the intake vent were electrified, but the rest of the grate was cold. He tied a thin nylon cord around the neck of the regulator and pushed the canister through the grate's center hole. The canister travelled down the side of the shaft, and disappeared over the edge. Harper figured the intake fans were probably several feet below the edge. He guessed at ten feet and stopped.

He tied the ring of a phosphorus grenade between the grate, the grate centerpiece, and the line holding the canister. A sharp tug would pull the pin on the grenade and send it cascading down the shaft. A phosphorus grenade would incinerate an unlikely hero. He rigged the other canister in the same way.

Stillwell nervously looked around from his perch. He had failed to follow Harper, so when Harper emerged over the side again he breathed easier. He could see without the night vision goggles. The day was coming quickly.

Harper signaled they should head back to their base. They scrambled quickly towards the HMMWVs. Running before daylight and detection, they dropped back over the rim of the wadi where the HMMWVs were parked. Darby Hayes looked up and poured some hot coffee in to a mug. "Thought you might be thirsty, Sir."

Harper nodded and took the mug. "You found some gas?"

Hayes chuckled. "Indeed, gas, an RPG-7, one dead Arab, and some groceries." He looked at the brightening light, "Drink up, we'll need to get under cover soon." He tossed Harper half a loaf of bread.

Stillwell looked at Darby and whispered, "You killed someone?"

Darby flashed him a grin. "Yes, Sir. Don't be so shocked." He waved a hand at the weapons leaning against the side of the HMMWV. "We'll probably kill some more people before we're done here tonight. My job is to keep you and the Major in one piece long enough to get the job done."

Stillwell looked at the bread in his hands, it did not seem very appetizing. "Lieutenant, you need to eat up," chided the Sergeant. "You may not like the idea of killing somebody, but you need to understand, we're the good guys and everyone else we meet out here are the bad guys. Once you understand that, the rest gets easier."

Stillwell nodded and lifted the bread to his mouth.

Harper noted the exchange, saying nothing. It was good his men could pull the trigger when necessary. There was no glory in killing people, and he would like to believe no one would die on this mission whether they were good guys or bad guys. He knew better. He turned his attention to Burns and took another sip of his coffee.

Burns settled down beside Harper. "I worked up a watch schedule between the two of us. Kincaid and Hayes drove, so they should get some sleep. I'll take first watch and wake you around noon."

Harper nodded. "And your handy work?"

"It should make a really big mess." He smiled. "The Claymores are set up in a open box formation. Four on each long side and two on the closed end tied to a motion sensor and a Clacker override." The Clacker was a hand held detonator for a string of Claymore mines. A simple ten-pound squeeze and seven thousand .38 ball bearings would explode in a blinding steel maelstrom.

"The anti-vehicle mines are set here, and here." He marked the ends of the road. "They'll simply explode on automatic sensors. Kind of a present for the reaction force when it shows up here."

"Good work." Harper finished off the coffee. "We jump off at 2000 hours. The gas goes off at 1800 hours. If something goes boom, we move out immediately. Burns and Hayes, you'll come in with Stillwell and me. Kincaid mans the road and Anderson gets to play sniper. If the alarm goes off, we get out in ten minutes. Oh, and Sergeant—"

"Sir?"

"You bring one of those gas cans with you when we go in tonight." He turned to Stillwell. "Do you know how to work a 40 mm grenade launcher?"

Stillwell shook his head.

"Sergeant, before you get some shut eye show the Lieutenant how to use one of those and fix him up with a dozen fletchett rounds."

Burns looked at Harper. "You're not planning on taking any prisoners?"

Harper shook his head. "Somewhere out in that desert between here and Jordan, I buried a friend." He gazed at the dirt. "We tried to minimize casualties. After all, it was supposed to be an easy in/out kind of thing. Jerry took a bullet for me, and he kept fighting. I don't know what's waiting for us inside, but I do know we taught them a lesson about Special Forces and what we are capable of doing."

He turned towards Burns. "I made you a promise before we left Andrews. I don't want to bring anyone home in a body bag, and regardless of what we were told at Al Jubar, we're deep inside Indian country on our own. I wouldn't even be surprised if they already knew we were on our way."

"Major, we're the only ones who know we're here."

Harper shook his head and said sadly, "Captain, it's never that simple."

18

Washington DC, Sunday, November 16, 1997,
10:00 AM EST

Harvey slumped down in the front seat of the car. He looked across the top of the steering wheel watching faces move along the sidewalk in front of the Chinese Embassy. Two District Police cruisers were parked blocking the vehicle entrance and exit. He tapped the wheel nervously wondering if hc had pushed the issue too hard. No, he decided for the umpteenth time, a Chinese National had tried very hard to spread his brains across the park lawn last night. That made it *personal.*

Twice someone from the Embassy had emerged from the security kiosk and demanded the meaning of the roadblock. A thin, reedy looking man named Brook Hamilton had been sent down from the State Department. He quietly explained that they were dealing with a threat made against the Chinese Embassy. As the host country, the police and additional security measures were simply being proactive in response to a terrorist threat.

It was a good lie. Who could doubt the very essence of violence in a society where a fertilizer bomb could obliterate the Federal Building in Oklahoma City, or the botched World Trade Center bombing? Spectacular headlines made it easy to suggest equally spectacular fabrications. There were plenty of people inside and outside China who would make threats. The Taiwanese even had the capability to carry out some of their threats.

Larry Wheeler flipped through the Sunday *Washington Post*. "Do you think the State Department weenie is on our side or their side?"

Harvey sighed, "Their side. I mean he wouldn't cooperate if we told him the truth about waiting for one of their precious diplomats."

"He seemed real upset to see the Police cruisers," Larry observed.

"He'll be a lot more upset if we grab *Goldenrod* and cuff him within shouting distance of the Embassy entrance," grumbled Harvey. He was sick of politicians and administration officials. He would take a good old-fashioned criminal any day.

"How long you think this is going to last?"

Harvey swallowed the last of his coffee. "About as long as the Secretary of State remains unavailable." He shrugged. "Maybe another two hours."

Larry nodded, reading the furniture ads. "Yeah, but do you think he's stupid enough to show up now?"

"We might get lucky. He won't have anything on him, but we'll bring him in and shake him down. He knows we can't hold him. He's got one of the diplomatic passports the folks at Foggy Bottom pass out like candy," scowled Harvey.

Harvey was tired. They had spent most of the night monitoring the police band for news of *Goldenrod*. It never came. They had walked through the park with forensic and ballistic experts reviewing the gun battle and examining the dead letter drop. Portable arc lamps had been erected so that the slugs could be drilled out of the trees, and bloodhounds had been brought in to search the park.

Sometime after four this morning it had settled down again. The tapes had been retrieved from the monitoring VCR's. Copies of the tapes had been sent directly to the FBI's photo enhancement lab. The image enhancement software and the speed of desktop systems now made it possible to produce decent photographs of each Chinese agent. Harvey needed hard evidence to prosecute his espionage claim.

Goldenrod managed to vanish. He never attempted to return to the Embassy, which meant he had some other hole to crawl into. A safe house was somewhere in or around the District. Embassy personnel may have their diplomatic passports, diplomatic protections, and state department doublespeak, but agents operating in deep cover were vulnerable to prosecution and imprisonment.

Safe houses, dead letter drops, and agents of influence suggested a network. The very mention of Chinese agents raised red flags through out the Bureau's hierarchy. The presidential campaign seemed to have accepted a great deal of money from Chinese front men. No one in his or her right mind chose to provoke the White House on the China question—certainly not FBI field agents.

Those in the top floor of the J. Edgar Hoover Building had become sensitive to the China subject. Every time something began to emerge related to China, the White House spin machine gathered force like a swirling hurricane. Administration officials from the Department of Justice and the White House Counsel's office began calling the Deputy Directors. The Secretaries of State and Commerce once again explained the significance of China to America's foreign policy and economic security.

The special agents in charge discovered the true potency of presidential displeasure. More than one agent had been shuffled off to Billings, Montana or Gillette, Wyoming. Others were hounded from their positions and simply turned in their resignations rather than deal with the harassment. Careers ended once the White House determined an agent became too much of an irritant. Both Harvey and Larry knew they were skirting the edges themselves.

Since last night, Harvey had twenty agents working for him on this case. He was not interested in the niceties of statecraft. These people had stolen from his country. They had tried to kill him last night. Harvey wanted his pound of flesh, and he was not terribly concerned on how he got it. His concern did stretch to Larry. He wanted to punish the Chinese Agent, but spare his partner the risks associated with the pursuit of Chinese wrongdoing.

The radio clicked, "Harvey, this is the north team. We've got your suspects getting out a of a taxi about two blocks north of the Embassy."

Larry leaned forward to grab the street map. He picked up a second radio and said, "Pursuit team north, stop the cab and find out where they were picked up."

A mistake! Harvey knew it had to be a mistake. He did not have a clear idea what kind of mistake it was, his gut simply told him something critical had occurred. "Pick them up." He banged the steering wheel with the heel of his hand. "Pick 'em up. Don't even let them close to the embassy."

"You got it."

The north team erupted from two cars, four agents holding their identification in one hand and brandishing their weapons in the other. Their excited shouts lingered over the din of the traffic. Their targets began to protest, only to be propelled and shoved against the stone wall of another embassy compound. Handcuffs emerged and were snapped on with practiced precision.

The District cruisers charged towards the commotion, and the diminutive Brook Hamilton craned his neck to discern the problems down the street. His brow furrowed as he began to understand the FBI's deception. He started running down Connecticut Avenue towards the area where the FBI and District police were bundling their charges into cars. A cell phone was in his hand as his thumb flipped the speed dial to find his boss.

☆ ☆ ☆

Goldenrod found himself seated in a gray room with a single table. A heavy metal door was the only way in or out. It had no knob on the inside, and a single wire-meshed window for someone to check on his condition from the outside. The fluorescent lights above bathed the room in a neutral white light, and the mirror to side of the room was obviously two-way glass.

He had been on the other side of the glass before watching the videotape cameras roll and listening to each word spoken. They had fingerprinted and photographed him. The ink still stained his fingertips. He examined the faint ink stains and considered the need to surgically change his identity again. His protests regarding diplomatic immunity were ignored. So now, they let him wait. He closed his eyes and calmed his mind. The rules might be bent, but no one would seriously breach the etiquette governing international relations.

The door opened and two men entered. One carried a manila file folder under his arm and a pistol holster inside his suit coat. The other was smaller in a gray pinstripe suit. He flipped open his credentials and explained. "My name is Brook Hamilton. I represent the US State Department in this matter."

"What matter might that be?" he asked ignoring the small State Department man and focusing his attention on the larger man—the policeman.

"Espionage, attempted murder, assault of a federal officer. I'm sure we could come up with more charges," Harvey explained. "It really doesn't matter. You'll be leaving our country within the next twelve hours." He produced *Goldenrod's* diplomatic passport and tossed it on the table. "I suggest you come up with a new name. The one printed here won't really work anymore."

"I wish to speak—"

Harvey leaned forward and landed the file folder on the table with a loud *plop*. "You'll speak when you're spoken to."

"Agent Randall, this man is a guest in our—"

Harvey gave Brook Hamilton a venomous glare, and said evenly, "This man is a criminal."

Goldenrod looked from the file folder to Harvey. "I don't think you—"

"I understand completely. You are in our country under a false name with a diplomatic passport. The people Mister Hamilton works for say I have to respect the nature of that protection," snarled Harvey. "So I made a deal with them. I get you for a while before they pack your sorry butt on a airplane bound for home sweet home."

Harvey settled into one of the chairs opposite *Goldenrod.* "I don't know your real name—yet. But I know a few things."

"Really, detective?" *Goldenrod* responded in clipped British accented English. "What could you possibly know about what I do?"

"Last night your goons tried to blow my head off. I don't like that very much."

Open hostility is sometimes very refreshing. "Yes, well, next time they'll have to do a better job. I'll have them train harder." Brook Hamilton opened his mouth to speak, but it simply flapped shut. *Goldenrod* examined the State Department man and wondered why the policeman tolerated this excuse for a man. "The policeman is correct. My men did try to kill him last night. They failed—the next time they shall succeed."

He looked over at the mirror and laughed. "I hope you got that down correctly in there. Now, is that all detective?"

Harvey opened the file folder displaying enhanced photographs of *Goldenrod*, Shu, and the others. He spread the photographs across the table. He pointed to Shu explaining, "We have the tall geek in one of the other rooms. He's going home with you."

He pushed the other three photographs forward. "I think one of these boys is dead. We found a great deal of blood last night. Maybe you'd like to tell me where you dumped the body."

"I really don't know what you're talking about. However, I do know one thing, detective. You won't be—how do they say in your country—ah, dogcatcher. You won't be dogcatcher after treating a diplomat like this."

Harvey nodded, "Yeah, you just keep on thinking that way. You need to understand something. Last night you made this personal. I don't like people shooting at me. It makes me real angry. I'm real angry now. So I may be a dogcatcher by noon tomorrow, but your pack of dogs are the ones I'm going to catch."

He pulled another photograph showing the original drop. "This must be a big deal for you to risk picking up the intelligence yourself. I don't know who he is yet, but I'm going to find out. In fact, I'm going to find your entire network of safe houses and illegals working in my country."

Goldenrod's eyes mocked him. "And do what? Arrest them," he laughed.

Harvey nodded.

Goldenrod shook his head and laughed. "Detective, you're country is for sale. All that is needed to run your country is enough money, and leaders dance for whom ever pays enough. You think you are the protector of a great power, but you don't realize your time has passed you by."

He nodded to the last photograph. "The man in that picture. There are more where he came from. I don't make people betray a trust. I don't have to. It is so simple detective, so incredibly simple to purchase your most precious secrets. And even if you should find this man, the damage is already done." *Goldenrod* locked eyes with Harvey. "There is nothing you can do to prevent the damage. It's already done." He laughed.

"I spit on your threats detective. I laugh in your face, because you live in a land where people are slowly killing their culture. It's like riding the subway—if you have enough tokens—you can go anywhere. Well I have enough money, and I can buy anybody." He snarled again with a derisive laugh. "You need only look at your own White House. We bought them, we bought them both for silly campaign contributions." He shook his head.

Harvey leaned forward planting his nose inches from *Goldenrod*. "Some of us can't be bought."

"Ah, I see. You are an honest man amongst thieves. The protector of your once great democracy and open society." He paused. "Then you are a fool detective. There is nothing worth protecting. You shoot women at Ruby Ridge, and incinerate whole families in Waco. This is how you protect this mighty country." The eyes went dead. "I chop up babies before their mother's eyes. You see, we're not so different."

"I didn't—"

"Your Hostage Rescue Team shot a woman holding a baby in her arms, and then tried to make people believe your sniper with a forty power scope thought it was a rifle." He shook his head dismissively. "In my country, we would have simply leveled that shack. Randy Weaver would never have come to the attention of anyone. You and I are the same side of the coin."

Harvey gathered up his papers. He balled his fists resisting the urge to smash the mocking stare. He knocked on the door and turned as the US Marshall unlocked the door. "Another time, then," said Harvey.

"Indeed, detective, another time. One thing though, in my country I would never let you get on an airplane. I'd simply make you disappear." He tipped his head. "Perhaps we will get a chance to test that theory someday."

Harvey stood rooted to the ground. "I'm the exception to your rule, and I'm your worst nightmare. Sometime in the last eighteen hours, you made a mistake. I'm going to find that mistake."

Goldenrod shook his head. "You're a very dumb detective. The damage is already done. No matter what you do, people are going to die today or tomorrow. And they're not even going to know why, or who, or where, they are dieing. They are simply going to die." He sighed, "A pity, even I regret the death of a great warrior, but what has to be will be." He refocused on Harvey. "Good hunting, detective. Nothing you do matters."

Brooke Hamilton trailed Harvey out the door, and Harvey turned to the Marshall in charge of prisoner transport. "They stay handcuffed all the way to Hong Kong."

Brook Hamilton opened his mouth to protest and found Harvey's penetrating glare. He simply said, "Seems like a reasonable precaution."

Larry Wheeler was waiting at the end of the corridor. He was tapping a file folder between his fingers. He could sense Harvey's gloomy countenance, and said brightly, "I think I found his mistake."

Harvey nodded. What did a warrior and the damage already done mean? Why was *Goldenrod* so confident that there was nothing he could do? *Goldenrod* was daring him to find the network. Harvey looked at Larry and asked, "What do we have?"

19

Washington DC, Sunday, November 16, 1997,
Noon EST

The Chinese ambassador was a squat man measuring slightly more than five foot four inches. His short-cropped black hair matched a perpetual dour expression. He had a pair of perfectly round spectacles that only seemed to emphasize his melon shaped head. With a shadowy mustache and little black pools for eycs, he waited quietly outside the National Security Advisor's office. Resting both hands on his black serpent-headed cane, he managed to control the rage he felt welling up inside.

The National Security Advisor sat ensconced behind his heavy oak door glaring at the videoconference phone built into the walls behind his desk. The defiant FBI director glared back through the digitally enhanced signal.

"No, Sir. I am not going to debate last night. When the safety of my people is involved, I don't care to discuss your geopolitical concerns. I have more than enough forensic evidence to satisfy me. These two men will be deported today by US Marshals." He fired the words much like a range master did to raw recruits on a Quantico gunnery range. "They were engaged in espionage activities and they attempted to kill two of my men last night."

The FBI director had been carefully chosen after the President had fired his successor over several very public and damaging confrontations. Many of the President's inner circle felt it safer to have a tame

FBI director. Unfortunately, a cop is a cop, and the allegations of Chinese connections to illegal campaign contributions and the transfer of American missile technology brought the administration to loggerheads with the FBI once again.

"Are you refusing to tell me what this investigation entails?" snarled the NSA.

Targeted and embattled by the White House spin machine, the Director sighed. "I think it's obvious why we are concerned regarding this investigation. The White House has been a constant source of security leaks with regard to any issues related to Red China."

The NSA rolled his eyes visibly upset with the other man sitting at his desk at the JEH building. "We continue to hear about all these leaks from inside the White House. You've yet to supply us with one name or one clear incident that implicates anyone in this administration."

"When we have a name and evidence I'll personally arrive with the warrant," snapped the cop.

"Those are tough words. I hope you can back them up. Otherwise, I'll have your scalp someday."

"Go ahead and try. We'll sit down with the Senator Judiciary Committee and ask all those former prosecutors what they would think of political tampering with a crime scene where we are still picking bullets out of the trees," he replied. He was feeling very old and tired and wondering what purpose, he served.

The NSA scowled. This was degenerating into another pissing contest. He considered the headlines and news stories. It might be best to let this China story slide quietly to the back pages of the *Washington Post*. "I have the Chinese Ambassador sitting outside my door right now. What exactly do I tell him?"

A smirk and slight shake of the head responded over the videophone. They never stopped trying to get you in this town he mused. "Tell him the truth—a new idea I realize." He also realized he needed to keep his sarcasm under control. Missing church with his family so he could joust with the NSA on a Sunday morning did not seem to make much sense. "We caught them red handed and we're shipping them out today. They can pick them up in Hong Kong.

"But understand something very clearly. *No one shoots at my people and walks free*. They chose to play rough last night. They chose to violate our laws and steal our secrets." He held up a file folder containing photographic evidence and waved it at the fish eye lens. "I have their faces. I have a time plot. I have ballistics. And I have two men with diplomatic passports."

The NSA decided to cut his losses as he eyed his side of the door. The next conversation might not have the same acerbic tone, but it would be fraught with similar peril. "All right—all right, we'll let this one slide. But please, in the future consider the politics before you let your cowboys loose again."

The Director set his lips and his teeth ground uncomfortably. "I'll consider the law. That's my job. Now if you'll excuse me, Sir. I have a Bureau to run." He reached forth and clicked the line off. Any FBI investigation would require careful scrutiny to ensure it did not lead any closer to the Administration.

The image blanked out on the NSA's screen. He quietly chewed the inside of his cheek wondering what Arthur had managed to drag up. He tapped a cigarette from a pack of Winstons. Technically, the White House was smoke free according to the First Lady's edict. The First Lady merely had political adversaries; he had several very real enemies to deal with. Switching the White House's internal system on, he dialed up Arthur's office. His aide's face came into focus.

"I'm afraid we don't have good news."

The NSA's stomach sank further into his high-backed office chair. What else could have gone wrong? "How bad?"

"As far as I can make out, the Chinese boat fired on one of the 688 boats." He said referring to the *Los Angeles* Class attack boats.

The NSA half rose out of his chair as he remembered last night's conversation with the President. Could the Chinese know about a naval engagement inside the Gulf? "What!" He glanced at the oak door once again. Which crisis was the dour little man with his black serpent's head cane here about? He pulled a folder from across his desk and glanced at the current information on the Chinese Ambassador. Looking back to Arthur, he said quietly, "All right, what exactly happened?"

"The Chinese were still inside the Gulf when it happened. Seems one of the *Vikings* found the Chinese boat and they vectored a 688 boat," explained Arthur.

"Casualties?" He already knew the answer, but hearing Arthur's reply did not lessen the impact.

Arthur shrugged. "The *Han* was a complete loss. We've been training for underwater combat since the twenties. I guess it paid off last night."

"I wonder what they know about this?" mused the NSA aloud. He looked towards the door again.

"If they know we sunk one of their boats. I think they'll be pretty mad," offered Arthur.

"An understatement," muttered the NSA. "Look, I'm going to shut down your video feeds into this office, but I want you listening to this on your end. We might have to come up with something fast." There were other implications to the attack on the Chinese naval vessel. Implications the NSA did not care to contemplate.

Arthur nodded. He glanced at the document emerging on his PC screen. He leaned forward to start keying in the words necessary to transform a policy recommendation into orders. "I think we'll need to limit our visibility with regard to the Iraqi actions and the *Han* boat."

"What are you getting at?"

Arthur glanced back to the camera eye and clasped his hands carefully. "Sir, we sent a team into the Gulf in direct response to a transfer of material from the *Han* to a Iraqi boat. That suggests knowledge that we knew the *Han* was in the Gulf. We will have certain proof before the end of today that some form of advanced nerve agent was delivered. They planned the transfer when our satellites were not looking, and when our spy planes were not airborne over the area. It's an accident that we found this transfer."

The NSA nodded. "Okay."

"So what happened in the Gulf between our forces and their forces was a result of American knowledge. We saw the transfer on Friday. We have U2 photos, and we formed a preplanned response to the issue. What if the U2 photographic evidence never happened?"

The NSA wrinkled his brow. "I'm not following you."

"If the U2 never flew over that part of the Gulf and the camera never took the pictures, we would know nothing concerning any transactions between the Iraqis and the Chinese. You would never have called a meeting on Saturday, and Louis Edwards wouldn't have been dispatched to put an infiltration team together. If we never *saw* a Chinese submarine, then we'd never start hunting it and ultimately if it sank it's a Chinese *maintenance* problem."

"And what do we do about the infiltration team?"

Arthur smiled coyly. "*What infiltration team*?"

"You mean cut them loose?" completed the NSA.

"Exactly!"

The NSA looked across the room and back to the camera eye. "Six men Arthur. We're talking about six men who might not come home." Others had died during this administration, and no one seemed to care. Perhaps a right-wing weekly would pick up the story, but no one at the *New York Times* or *Washington Post* would give credence to right wing ravings.

"It would be best if they didn't come home." He sighed. "Sir, it would be best if this operation never appeared on the books. Part of the plan involves forces from the *George Washington* and Air Force assets. That can easily be cancelled—six men versus repercussions with the Chinese government. It's a cheap price to pay. We've already sunk their submarine, and who is going to believe it was in self-defense?

"We sent over a hundred men to the bottom of the Gulf. We hunted and hounded them into a mistake, and our commanders acted within their orders. Granted there is a log of those orders, but if we bury this deep. If it ever did emerge, we'd both be long gone." He paused. It was important to paint the spin properly. "The people who know about the Chinese submarine are manageable. It's not the sort of thing we want to advertise after all. Besides, these men are all naval officers. We slap a high security label on the incident and forget it."

"We're the only ones who know where the *Han* sunk. *So, what we don't know can't hurt us*. As for the infiltration team, it is a direct result of the same action." Arthur shrugged. "Six men inside Iraq with no exit strategy. If they survive the inevitable firefight, how are they going to get out?

"A handful of men sent into the region." He prattled on, "They were specifically chosen for their deniability. We control the intelligence assets and we control the information. If anyone has a sudden attack of conscience, we'll ship them out to the Aleutians to count baby seals."

"Certainly, we can bury this long enough to handle the Chinese outrage. And the President need never know what exactly happened."

The NSA smiled and shook his head. "I have to tell him about the Chinese boat. That's sure to come up in conversation somewhere along the way."

Arthur nodded knowing they had pressed beyond the barrier of betrayal. It was now simply the positioning of stories and pieces on the geopolitical stage. "Of course, of course," he said hurriedly. "The President does need to know about the Chinese boat, but he need never know anything more about this mission. We simply tell him its been cancelled and we allow the Iraqi's to do the right thing with our team."

The NSA nodded. He pressed his lips together and nodded a final time. "Okay. Get it done. Make sure no one comes back."

"I've got an order drafted over your signature."

The NSA nodded tightly and removed himself from the scene of actual carnage. Here in the safe confines of the West Wing behind several barriers of security, the lonely Iraqi desert was little more than a mind game. Outside there were gardeners tending the White House grounds, and people were settling down for a NFL afternoon. The President was returning from church, and the weather was cooperating to be a fine autumn afternoon. The NSA could imagine that Iraq did not even exist. There would be no cameras or reporters, just words transmitted digitally via satellite—a push button decision—simple, clean, and remote. "Send it." It felt tidy.

He switched off the video and audio feeds from Arthur's office. His stomach growled as he rose to open the door. He opened the door and stuck out his hand smiling, "Welcome Mister Ambassador."

Li Zhaoxing nodded and shook the NSA's hand. A seasoned diplomat with numerous postings in the Chinese Foreign Ministry, the most recent being Vice Minister of Foreign Affairs, and before that, Ambassador Extraordinary to the United Nations. He was not simply an ambassador for show. He had contacts in with the People's Liberation Army and the intelligence services.

The coded faxes from Beijing had arrived early this morning. Li Zhaoxing read the summary of American actions against Iraq and China. Li Zhaoxing could appreciate the former Soviet Union's reluctance to directly attack the United States. After all, it still was the technological goose laying the golden eggs.

The Soviets had chosen to steal technology in an effort to stay within sight of the Americans. Ronald Reagan changed the Cold War marathon into a sprint and destroyed the Soviet economy in less than eight years. China dare not make the same mistake as the old Soviet Union. For now, the American administration could be held at bay and manipulated. However, should someone emerge on the scene in the 2000 elections with a Reagan-like instinct, then all might be lost by 2010.

Zhaoxing came to sit across a coffee table from the NSA. A White House Steward entered with tea and short bread cookies. The Chinese Ambassador smiled broadly as he took a few cookies and the proffered cup.

"Now, Mister Ambassador, what brings you here on a fine Sunday morning?"

Zhaoxing looked across the table to the smiling NSA as he sipped his tea and set it down before him. "I do not wish to give offence to your fine hospitality, but there have been some disturbing developments," he began.

The NSA's smile faded slightly. A crinkled brow and a sudden look of concern rippled across his features. "Developments?"

The Ambassador bobbed his head. "It appears one of out submarines is missing."

The NSA settled back in his chair. "Really? Tell me more."

"Yes, well, we have information that elements of your Navy are actively tracking one of our submarine boats." He stared directly over his cup.

The sentence hung between them like a black cloud on a summer day. "Mister Ambassador, we have naval forces around the world. There is contact everyday between forces of different countries. Our forces, as your forces, must maintain a vigilance towards local aggression—"

"Are you suggesting that there has been some sort of incident?" snapped Zhaoxing.

The truth fluttered hopelessly in the air, before the NSA replied. "If there has been an incident, nothing has crossed my desk officially. Perhaps, you could give me some idea where this might have happened."

Zhaoxing considered the matter. It he acknowledged the existence of a Chinese submarine in the Persian Gulf, and the Americans did not know of its existence, then he had damaged his own security. Yet the coded fax had been marked *NightHawk*. *NightHawk* was a primary intelligence inside the White House. Zhaoxing had been briefed on the existence of the agent only last week. It was one of China's most closely guarded secrets, and *NightHawk* had never been wrong.

Zhaoxing focused back on the NSA and said, "Our information indicates the submarine is in the Indian Ocean," he replied shading the truth.

The NSA examined his guest. What little truth existed evaporated like the morning mists. "Maybe we have identified the wrong navy. The United States seeks no fight with your great nation. Maybe your submarine has run afoul of the Indian Navy."

NightHawk was never wrong, and it appeared that *NightHawk* was accurate again. Zhaoxing sipped his tea hiding his conclusions. "The Indian Navy, you say."

The NSA nodded. "They do maintain a sizable naval presence. Perhaps, they detected your *Han* boat there."

"I never mentioned the class of submarine."

The NSA paused perturbed with his own stupidity. "Mister Ambassador, I don't wish to be argumentative, but I'm sure you told me the submarine class." He spread his hands palm open and upward.

Zhaoxing pressed the point home, "I'm certain I never mentioned the submarinc class, so where would you get the idea it is a *Han* boat?"

"Is it one of your *Han* boats?" stressed the NSA.

Zhaoxing nodded curtly. "Yes."

"Maybe I just assumed it was that type of boat. I doubt I even know of another Chinese class submarine. You know, my kids have a new Tom Clancy game based on your *Han* boat and one of our *Los Angeles* fast attack boats. I'd guess that's where I heard of it," explained the NSA.

Zhaoxing relented. "And I may have misspoken as well. There is another matter."

"Regarding what?" smiled the NSA.

"You are holding two of my diplomats and I demand their immediate release."

The NSA nodded understandingly. "I am aware of the situation. Unfortunately, they have run into some problems with our FBI. This afternoon, US Marshals will escort them back to Hong Kong."

"Your federal police force?"

"Yes. Gunshots were exchanged not far from where we are sitting. The two diplomats, as you put it, were identified as being involved in the shootings. Needless to say, this is unacceptable behavior. Of course, we will observe the international rules regarding Foreign Service diplomats."

"You seem much better informed on this matter than the submarine," observed Zhaoxing.

The NSA chuckled. "Mister Ambassador, I can assure you this matter got me out of bed this morning. I hope we can move beyond this issue and recognize it for what it is." He spread his hands. "We each have intelligence services. Sometimes operations get out of hand. It is best to quietly deal with the matter and remove the irritant. I hope we can put this matter behind us."

Zhaoxing considered the NSA's words. "I shall report back to my government, but I must warn you there will be repercussions regarding any US diplomatic status in my own country."

"Yes, Mister Ambassador, I understand your warning. Understand, too, that the United States is not in the habit of deporting diplomats without cause. There is cause in this matter, and reciprocating with a round of expulsions from our Embassy in Beijing will not be greeted kindly by the Administration. I would not think this is a matter requiring escalation and retaliation." The collegial atmosphere between them disintegrated.

Zhaoxing nodded curtly and set his tea down on the coffee table. Reaching for his cane he said, "I thank you for your time today." He stood and turned towards the door without further acknowledgement.

The NSA watched the retreating back of the Chinese Ambassador before flipping the video and audio feeds back on to Arthur's office.

"Assessment?"

"They seem to know a great deal," observed Arthur.

"Indeed they do," muttered the NSA. "Indeed, they do. You've taken care of the orders regarding the team going into Iraq?"

"They were transmitted during your meeting. All military support for the operation has been scrubbed. The orders went out over your signature. I doubt we will be hearing from those people again."

The NSA grunted. "We'd better not. Anything else?"

Arthur looked down at his note pad and crossed off another item. "As a matter of fact, there is."

"Okay, what is it now?"

Arthur clicked his mouse on another screen and checked the deployment status. "I think we'd better find out what's on the *Han* boat for sure. After all, if this turns nasty and the Chinese Ambassador suddenly remembers it was the Persian Gulf and not the Indian Ocean where they last heard from their boat, then we might need some justification."

"If our analysis is correct, and there are weapons of mass destruction being transported, then we could justify our actions like JFK did during the Cuban Missile Crisis."

"You mean a picture show at the UN and a couple of well placed editorials," he murmured.

"We did the same thing when the Soviets shot down the Korean 747 over Sakhalin Island. George Schultz played the tapes of the Soviet pilots. We nailed the Russians hard, and we could do the same with the Chinese if they start to get out of line."

The NSA nodded. Nailing the Chinese hard could become a major policy issue. "Okay, I'll bite. What have you come up with?"

"According to the regional deployment roster, we have the DSRV-1 sitting on stand-by in Diego Garcia," Arthur explained hurriedly.

The NSA held up his hands. "You're spouting jargon again."

"Yes, Sir. The *Mystic* is a deep submergence rescue vehicle. We've got two of these on active duty. They are there to rescue downed submarines. You know, like the things they used to go and find the *Titanic*."

The NSA nodded. "What has this got to do with anything?"

"We've prepositioned one at Diego Garcia. The Naval Support Facility has one on stand-by alert. This is probably to handle anything that might go wrong in the Gulf."

The NSA continued to nod as if he had any clue as to where Diego Garcia was located. "Still not tracking, where is this Diego place?"

"In the middle of the Indian Ocean. We can scramble the *Springfield* to rendezvous with the *Mystic's* transport and bring her into the site of the *Han.* The capabilities of the DSRV will let us find out exactly what was on the boat. Plus, we can record the entire session and uplink it directly to the Pentagon."

"You mean we'd have photographic evidence of the rescue attempt."

"Yes, Sir."

The NSA considered the possibilities. They already knew the *Han* was dead in the water, and they knew its location. "If the Chinese discover our involvement, we could claim we were using our resources to perform a humanitarian mission." He paused. "You believe that something might still be on board."

"It seems reasonable. We know the transfer did not complete and that the Iraqi's started shooting. The acoustic evidence of the sonar tracks indicates there was significant structural damage to the boat. I think they never got the hatch closed they were using to transfer barrels. It stands to reason that they had a significant loss of life and were simply trying to run away."

"All right, get those orders going as well."

20

Washington DC, Sunday, November 16, 1997, 1:00 PM EST

Larry Wheeler tapped the file folder in his hand with a staccato urgency. He waited for Harvey to get rid of the State Department geek. They had enough problems with this investigation without tipping the State Department and subsequently the White House to their next target. He waited while tapping the folder knowing it held some answers.

Harvey looked down the corridor towards his partner. The stress and shock of the past twenty hours was beginning to tell. He had achieved a long-standing goal of getting his man. The victory seemed somewhat hollow, because the real problem was still walking around free and they were no closer to identifying Goldenrod's agent today.

The problem was that *Goldenrod* really did not care. He had been compromised. He had been trussed up like a criminal. He was about to be deported in handcuffs and he did not care. Harvey was missing something. That *something* seemed rather important, but he could not seem to visualize the problem. If the State Department knew about *Goldenrod*, then his target would know, too.

The damage is already done. There is nothing you can do to prevent the damage. It's already done. The words were spoken with the confidence of an intelligence officer who has already achieved the end game. Could they have possibly transmitted and acted on the intelligence already? What could possibly be damaged? How could *Goldenrod* know? They had to be extremely confident in their source, but over confidence is always a weakness.

Brook Hamilton, the smaller State Department man, had to hop step to keep pace. He was explaining something about the niceties of diplomatic relations and the importance of China in the world. "After all, Agent Randall, you have to understand the special relationship between the United States and China. China and India together represent over two billion people, and they are the keys to the modern Asian economy.

"We are a Pacific Rim power. We must maintain a level of influence with all the major players. You can't simply threaten diplomats and bundle them back to Hong Kong because of certain animosities you may hold personally. These are delicate relations which must be nurtured between countries, and—"

Harvey paused his stride and turned to the smaller man, "Mister Hamilton."

Brook Hamilton stopped.

"That man in there tried to kill me last night. Forgive me if I don't quite grasp the subtleties of why he is more important than my own hide. Secondly, let me point out that I have him on film retrieving something from a dead letter drop. We know it was high-grade information, and considering that he dealt with it personally, it indicates he was summoned or sent.

"In case that was too technical, let me put it bluntly. We've got another Chinese agent inside the White House—and I mean inside. Not at the Commerce Department or running little fundraisers with Buddhist Monks in California. No, I mean we have security problem compromising American interests. And you know what happens when something like this is allowed to fester. People get killed. Good people who trusted us to keep their names secret. They get killed.

"It's my job to stop those sorts of things. Maybe you don't like the way I do my job, and maybe I don't like the way you do your job, but those two are going back to China in chains with Federal Marshals. Now, if you'll excuse me, I have some spies to catch."

Harvey turned away from an opened-mouthed Brook Hamilton and heard, rather than saw, Louis Edwards award a slow *clap—clap—clap.* Hamilton quit his incessant hopping up and down as if Harvey were somehow unaware of the State Department man. Larry Wheeler turned towards Edwards recognizing the face, but failing to place a name to the sardonic look. He stood half in shadows in the corridor where the track lighting did not fully illuminate his features.

Both Harvey and Larry found the disconcerting bodyguards flanking him. Edwards acknowledging their looks and smiled, "Permit me to introduce Mister Smith and Mister Jones."

Harvey recognized them for what they were—freelancers. He had little doubt they had all the necessary permits to carry the obvious artillery. "Charmed, I'm sure," he replied.

"Agent Randall, I understand you've apprehended a Red Chinese agent known as *Goldenrod*," he smiled.

"I really wish you people would quit using such inflammatory language," whined Hamilton.

Harvey focused on Edwards and ignored the State Department man saying, "I may have. But I'm not in the habit of volunteering information to just anyone."

Louis glanced disdainfully at Brook Hamilton, then suggested, "Mister Hamilton, could you excuse us? Perhaps we could have a private chat. The three of us." He nodded to Larry Wheeler.

Harvey looked back to Brook, "Is there anything else?"

Brook shrugged, "You must understand the seriousness we take with regard to China's special relationship."

Harvey nodded, "Yeah, yeah. I understand we don't want to do anything to upset the Chinese. The cost of tennis shoes might go up. And I explained to you, I don't like people who shoot guns at me."

Hamilton gave up and walked away towards the elevators. Edwards waited until the elevator doors slid shut behind Brook Hamilton.

"You don't trust the State Department?" queried Larry.

"Agent Wheeler, do you?"

Harvey turned from the elevator doors to Louis. "You have some credentials, Mister..."

"Edwards, Louis Edwards." He flipped open a small wallet displaying his CIA identification card. "Maybe you remember me from the Henderson case a couple of years ago."

Harvey frowned, "Can't say that I do." He opened a door into a conference room, and three of them shuffled in leaving Smith and Jones outside.

"Well then, how about Jim Harper? He was the key to that whole affair."

Larry snapped his fingers, "And you're the guy who showed up and explained it would be best not to arrest Harper." He turned to Harvey saying, "Remember, Harper was some sort of special combat spook. The kind they keep tucked away for really nasty missions."

Harvey nodded. "Yeah, and the Henderson thing was pretty messy. Harper did most of the work for us, but he slipped his leash and made a big mess of Henderson."

Larry shrugged. "Henderson was a pretty foul character as I remember. Once we got inside the shack, well, I'll never forget it."

Harvey glanced from Larry back to Edwards. "Your man Harper saved the government a trial. Not that I condone his methods."

Edwards smiled briefly, "Jim does have a habit of doing his own thing. It's kind of his own code of honor, and Henderson broke that code."

"You can say that again," echoed Wheeler.

"Yeah, that's real nice. Now what can I do for you, Mister Edwards?" asked Harvey flatly.

"You did apprehend *Goldenrod?"*

Harvey let himself smile, "We got him. We got him good. He's on tape servicing a dead letter drop himself and firing on Federal agents. Diplomatic immunity—he goes home today."

Louis nodded. "Fine, fine. I'm not here to ask for his custody or interrogation. In fact, it would be better if we did not meet. However, a Red Chinese agent poses certain curiosities."

"Such as?" asked Larry.

"Gentlemen, I'm going to tell you something that is highly sensitive and it involves the lives of six men right now. I realize you are cleared for classified information, but—" he sighed, "How can I put this…but I'm afraid there may a mole somewhere inside the intelligence community. I am concerned because I have men in the field prosecuting a hostile action against Iraq and China. I'd prefer you didn't share this with your superiors." Louis had considered the coincidence of a China/Iraq transaction, and the fireworks surrounding one of China's premier spymasters. The correspondence of events bothered him the more he considered the possibilities—none of which were healthy for Harper and his team.

Harvey stared at Edwards. "What do you know about last night?"

"Merely that you were fired on, and this morning you took two Chinese nationals into custody."

Harvey looked to Larry, who nodded. Harvey nodded back. "Okay, Mister Edwards, same rules with what we tell you."

"I'll go first as a gesture of good will," continued Edwards. "Jim Harper is one of the men in the field. Considering past dealings, you understand that he is not an asset we activate frivolously.

"Friday night a U2 spy plane observed, quite by accident, the transfer of several barrels from the deck of a Chinese nuclear submarine to an Iraqi trawler in the Persian Gulf. We have reason to believe the barrels contain some sort of chemical or biological weapon system. We also think something went very wrong.

"Last night I sent Jim Harper and team into Iraq to find out about those barrels and a few other things. Before they left Andrews, Harper told me he thinks there's a leak somewhere in my organization. Now, I find it hard to believe the Iraqis have the skill or resources to mount a major and sustained intelligence operation inside the United States, but China is a totally different story.

"We joked earlier about Harper's code of honor. I think he might take it very personally if something were to happen this time inside Iraq that smells of a leak from Washington."

"But you have Smith and Jones out there," replied Larry cocking a thumb towards the door. He was referring the Louis's body guards hovering in the corridor.

Edwards permitted himself a slight smile. "Let's be very clear as to who and what Jim Harper is. He's a weapon created by this country designed to seek and destroy those people and/or assets that pose a national security threat."

"You make him sound like a machine," protested Larry.

"No, he's no machine. He's a man of extraordinary moral character, and believe me, I do not say those words lightly in the current climate. Make no mistake, if this mission is compromised by something taking place in Washington, Harper told me he would hold me personally responsible." Edwards nodded to the door. "Mister Smith and Mister Jones would never even know what hit them.

"Jim Harper is part of an elite corps trained to fight anybody, anywhere, anytime, with anything. We trained fifty teams in the early eighties. We sent them into Cuba, Iran, Iraq, China, Russia, Central America, and several other hellholes you've never heard of. Most of them are dead. Even those who died accomplished their missions.

"Its all history now, but the purpose of this elite corps was to nudge the Soviet Union towards collapse. It'll never get written into the history books. We prosecuted a very real war against the Soviets during the Reagan years. Harper and others like him were key elements in making that war happen.

"Those who survived their missions are watched. These are men and women who have performed exemplary service to their country. So they've been released back into the civilian population where they came from. It's kind of like releasing wolves back into a sheep herd. One of my jobs is to make sure they stay out of trouble and do not come to the attention of various law enforcement agencies. Of those survivors, Harper ranks close to or even at the top of his class."

"Like the Henderson deal," interjected Harvey.

"Like the Henderson deal," echoed Louis. "Jim got involved in something he should have left for real cops. He's not trained as a cop; he's trained like a soldier. The rules soldiers operate under during wartime are somewhat less restrictive than the Constitution puts forth in terms of due process. Jim viewed Henderson as something extraordinarily evil, and he set out to destroy it.

"If Jim believes something went wrong and I have no answers for him, then I'm a dead man." He paused and examined his audience. "Yes, gentlemen, he's that good. I've come to you without a great deal of leverage or official sanction. I think the mission was compromised last night, and it's too late to recall them.

"You see, in Harper's mind I am guilty of violating his code of honor, just like that fellow Henderson was guilty of violating Harper's code of human conduct."

No wonder Edwards had two bodyguards, mused Larry. He probably was riding around in a bombproof limousine and wearing Kevlar body armor. "Why would Harper think there's a problem inside Washington?" asked Larry.

"A fair question," replied Louis.

"Harper never struck me as the type who would blindly condemn somebody for being a jerk," continued Harvey. "If he thinks there's a leak, then he must know something."

Edwards pursed his lips. "Know something." He shook his head. "Harper is an instinctive fighter. He *senses* rather than knows what's wrong in a situation. Six years ago, he went into Iraq. Two men went in and one came out. Harper has maintained that the Iraqi intelligence services knew they were coming. He buried a friend in the desert. He blames me for that. A man like Harper does not make friends very easily. Losing a friend or men under his command, both being the same thing in his mind, requires payment." Edwards looked at a spot between his hands. It occurred to Edwards that Harper had decided to take the mission for the very reason of making someone pay for Jerry's life. He closed his eyes considering the perilous track of Harper prosecuting his own agenda inside Iraq.

"Which brings us to last night," suggested Larry.

"Precisely. Last night the two of you observed something."

"We observed a Caucasian male servicing a dead letter drop that had not been used in six months. We then observed the highest ranking intelligence officer at the Chinese Embassy service the drop," explained Harvey.

"That suggests to us, that we are dealing with high level information," continued Larry.

"We think the source of this information comes from inside the White House," explained Harvey. "Now, you see the obvious problems. Look, there have been security issues ever since the President was elected to his first term. The number of people that could not be vetted for security passes was incredible. You had dope smokers, shop lifters—you name it. But a Red Chinese agent?" Harvey spread his hands.

Edwards sat back in his chair thoughtfully. "When you say White House, do you mean a steward, uniformed officer, maid, cook?"

Harvey shook his head. "No."

Wheeler was paging through his day calendar. "You sent Harper into Iraq six years ago?"

Edwards nodded.

Harvey stared blankly.

"That would be during the previous administration?"

Edwards nodded again.

"Harper thinks he was sold out."

"I doubt you could convince him otherwise. Naturally, I asked him for proof. He kept saying the Iraqis knew they were coming. He had nothing but his gut." Edwards shrugged, then added quickly, "Harper's gut has kept him alive in some very bad situations."

"What are you driving at?" asked Harvey.

"Don't you see?" asked Larry.

Harvey shook his head.

"The leak can't be a Presidential appointee, at least, not one new to the job when the President took office," explained Larry.

Understanding spread across Harvey's face. "A holdover." He nodded his head slightly. "Sure, that makes a lot of sense. They couldn't fill all the spots, and we couldn't clear half the people they sent us. They kept people on. Particularly in Iraq, because the last thing they wanted was a debacle in the Gulf."

Harvey stopped and looked back to Edwards. "You're here because you think it has happened again."

"I'm here because I don't believe in coincidence. We detect a Chinese transfer by accident, because it took place when our satellites were over the horizon. The U2 strayed off course and kept right on taking pictures. We got lucky, because someone in the first tier of intel recognized that Chinese sub shouldn't be in those pictures.

"You folks have a major arrest against a Chinese national. Now maybe those two events aren't related, but the time frame suggests to me the contents of that drop box was, at a minimum, evidence of the weapons transfer and at a maximum the entire operational plan."

"Which means?" asked Larry.

"Which means, Agent Wheeler, I've sent six people into a hornet's nest. It means the Iraqis know who, what, when, and where we plan to penetrate their security."

Harvey leaned forward. "But you don't know that."

"No, I don't. It's a hunch."

"So help me out. Let's say you're right. Where do we look?"

"National Security Council staff. If there's a leak, it's there."

Larry Wheeler let out a long whistle.

"Let's be honest," continued Edwards. "China snuck up on us. Ronald Reagan was busy defeating the evil empire. George Bush waged the Gulf War—more or less successfully. China is our rival for the near future. They've been running a major operation against our country for several years now. From a foreign operations perspective the Soviets and Iraqis are non-factors, but I keep coming back to China. We'd be foolish to ignore the security issues."

"Yeah, but the NSC leads directly to the Oval Office," whispered Harvey.

"Agent Randall, the entire Chinese mess is going to end up there sooner or later," Edwards sighed. "You can't have money pouring into one political party from foreign sources and not expect it to culminate in a national security crisis. I know you folks have been reluctant to share intelligence product with the White House for fear it would be compromised in some manner.

"I must say we have similar concerns. Let it suffice to say we have an agency within an agency over at Langley. Certain aspects of the national intelligence product are kept from the eyes and ears of the Director."

"But that's against the law," offered Larry.

Edwards merely nodded. "What would you have me do?"

Harvey shrugged. "Okay so you think the NSC is either dirty or compromised."

Edwards nodded again.

"You're concerned that whatever passed last night to *Goldenrod* is related to your mission."

"The preponderance of coincidence," murmured Edwards.

"So how do we find out?"

"Could we agree to put aside the rivalry between our respective agencies and work on this one item together?"

Harvey grinned. "I won't tell if you won't." He turned to Larry who nodded.

"Good." Edwards waved a hand towards Larry. "I believe Agent Wheeler has found something. He appeared anxious to talk with you."

Larry looked down at the file folder in his hands and opened it. "We discovered some interesting things at the Day's Inn where *Goldenrod* spent the night." He ran his finger down the middle of the second page and stopped three quarters of the way. "We found a car registered to a couple from Virginia. One problem—they were not registered at the hotel. In fact, it was the only car that couldn't be accounted for from the hotel's registration list. It gets much better. Someone came to pick up the car this morning."

"Someone of Asian ancestry?" asked Harvey.

Larry nodded. "The short version is simple. The car is registered to a couple in Virginia. But the car was returned to a different residence in Virginia."

Harvey allowed a big grin to ripple across his features. "Two addresses in Virginia."

"Yeah."

Larry flipped to another page. "Both addresses are owned by Chinese Americans."

"So we seem to have found one, maybe two, safe houses," concluded Edwards.

"That's how I read it."

"The question remains as to why these people have decided to help someone like *Goldenrod*," continued Edwards.

"It doesn't matter," snarled Harvey.

Louis frowned. "On the contrary, it matters a great deal, Agent Randall. We may be dealing with people who are true believers. They will spare no effort to protect their secrets. They may be extremely violent or prone to placing nasty surprises throughout their homes.

"Or they may be caught in some web. Consider the possibilities. Illegal aliens that could be turned over to the INS, or perhaps they have relatives inside China itself. A dissident parent or someone involved in one of the many home churches. A child trapped under a bureaucratic boundary. There are several possibilities, and before your elite teams shatter the quiet countryside, I'd suggest surveillance and background checks."

"That could take days to run down," complained Larry.

Edwards permitted himself a slight smile, "I'm sure certain databases, generally off limits to the FBI, could be accessed for this particular search."

"In return for what?"

"Knowledge," replied Louis as if it were obvious to everyone. "China represents the biggest threat to our survival. We need to understand how they work. How have they infiltrated our country? Where are they loose inside our networks? These are questions we need to answer. Whether our collective masters understand the threat yet is irrelevant. When they panic and demand answers, we'd better have some to give them."

"How much time do you need?"

"A few hours," replied Louis. "Whatever's been done, a few more hours won't matter."

21

Baghdad, Iraq, Sunday, November 16, 1997,
10:00 PM (GMT +3.00)

Colonel Taha Duri walked the length of the underground hanger. Above him lay tons of reinforced concrete and a small park dedicated to the war dead of the Gulf War. It was one of many hidden airfields, armor barracks, and weapon depots scattered throughout Baghdad and Tikrit. The shell game of Presidential Palaces continued for the consumption of Western news teams and UN weapon Inspection Teams. The real strength of Iraq's power lay in the hidden warrens hundreds of feet below school grounds, parks, and baby formula factories.

From Israel to Iran, no one knew exactly what Saddam still clung to in his lair. Israel pointed her nuclear missiles at Baghdad, Tehran, and Damascus. Then she made sure a flight of F-16 *Falcons* was always fueled and ready in the Negev. The *Falcons* waited against hope with their deadly payload to rain fire on whatever Arab neighbor chose to break the peace. So went the peace of the one hundred hour war.

His hands were clasped behind his back as he surveyed the three Sikorsky S-61 helicopters. They squatted in the harshness of the artificial light like sleeping locusts. Known in Vietnam as the Jolly Green Giants, they took on a more ominous role. They were repainted in desert camouflage identical to those used by the US Army and adopted by the RAF. The side doors were pulled wide revealing twin .50 machineguns resting of swivel mounts—the dark steel barrels strapped downwards in a stored and locked position. Slung beneath the fuselage, with deadly intent, were twin rocket pods. It was not the most accurate weapon, but when facing villagers with little more than 1927 VZ24 Mausers and Enfield .303's, they were quite effective.

A small ground crew was going over machines now. They were a specially trained crew with exclusive equipment. The transponders for the aircraft were being removed and replaced with NATO transponders stolen from similar aircraft in Bosnia. Iraq traded heroin for the transponders with Kurdish tribesmen in return for peace.

The southern no-fly zone extends from the international border, with Saudi Arabia and Kuwait northward, to the outer Baghdad suburbs. The Data Center is hidden inside the no-fly zone. The only way to rapidly move troops as a reaction force is by helicopter. Thus, the need for the RAF markings and the stolen Bosnia transponders to fool the ever-present AWAC planes.

The Royal Air Force markings were stenciled on the fuselage of each Sikorsky. The tail numbers matched the markings on the original RAF aircraft. The pilots and crew were dressed in the fatigues of RAF crewmen and each flight crew spoke perfect British accented English. It was an expensive ruse, but it had worked before to ferry banned weapons throughout the no-fly zones.

Duri had few illusions as to how well these aircraft would stand up to close inspection. From a distance, it appeared to be NATO aircraft performing a maneuver over restricted airspace. The crews could respond to challenge, and generally they had a fairly good idea as to what the current counter signs were for the day.

Duri made ready for his encounter with Major James Harper and an elite team of Force Recon Marines. Duri slid his tongue over his teeth contemplating Harper. The entire file had been delivered complete with photographs of his children and wife. In it was an address in a safe Chicago suburb and a service record indicating the many missions this man had performed on behalf of the Stars and Stripes.

By the end of the night, forty-five additional troops would bolster the inner defenses of the Data Center. Not elite troops like those who would ride the helicopters, but battle hardened veterans from the Iran/Iraq and Gulf Wars. Duri gave them one chance in five of surviving Harper's initial assault. There was no doubt, he had planned for some sort of ground attack relying on the illusion that there were few Iraqi aircraft left, and the protective barrier of American air power would be there to protect him.

Three Special Republican Guard platoons, localized air superiority, and overwhelming firepower, relative to what six men could bring over land, should tip the scales in Duri's favor. They would come like Jews to Jerusalem unaware of the waiting car bomb. The hunters would be snared in their own trap, and Iraq's secret weapon projects would remain secret.

He smiled inwardly at the Israeli team he had caught several months ago. Tough Jews, never willing another holocaust to embrace them again, had screamed and begged for mercy. They all do eventually. The combination of drugs, sleep deprivation, beatings, and non-lethal doses of nerve gas did most of the work. When Duri had learned all he thought they could possibly know, he left them staked, spread eagle, and naked in the desert—food for the vultures and jackals.

There would be great pleasure in first hobbling, then humbling James Harper. He would remember to take a video of the moment when Harper broke, so he could send it to his eventual widow.

Duri checked his watch. According to the schedule provided by the Chinese, the American spy satellites would disappear over the horizon in a few minutes. It was time to move the Sikorsky's to their hanger at the Karbala Water Treatment Plant.

22

Odricks Corner, Virginia, Sunday, November 16, 1997, 4:00 PM EST

Three pale green Fords with government car-pool license plates gathered in the side streets off Spring Hill Road and Lewinsville Road. Each had an angled view of a neatly trimmed white Cape Cod styled home. A picket fence adorned the front, and a gravel drive led to the garage that lay behind and to the left of the house. There were a few apple trees in the front yard and older more imposing pine trees looming behind.

Next door two boys between three and five years old chased each other on a scooter. An older man trimmed a hedge on the other side. The play by play of the Washington Redskins could be heard on a radio located in somebody's garage. Leaf blowers and lawn mowers could be heard droning over the quiet. A couple of bicycles rode down the street past three Fords with bad paint jobs. A couple of dogs noticed more than one obnoxious squirrel and ran barking and leaping at a tree without effect.

Inside the cars, a collection of Federal officers representing FBI, INS, and CIA traded donuts and stale coffee. They, too, were listening to the Redskins and focusing a high-powered lens on the doors and windows of the well kept home. In the trunks were a collection of shotguns, tear gas and body armor.

Beyond them, a black van was sweeping north from Tyson's Corner on the Leesburg Pike. It was filled with a FBI High-Risk entry team.

They were clothed in black fatigues, facemasks, and ballistic body armor. The ceramic trauma plates seemed heavier in the warm weather. Each man was festooned with flash bang concussion grenades, tear gas, telescoping batons, and handcuffs.

Most of them were armed with Heckler & Koch MP-5 sub machine guns. The others had Mossberg 590 12 gauge shotguns with specialized loads designed to shatter door hinges. On the floor between them lay a battering ram designed to bring down anything else that might prove stubborn. A specialized military encryption system was wired into the Kevlar helmets, and shatterproof goggles would finish their gear when the time came for entry.

Silence gathered about them as they neared their destination. The lighthearted jokes and quips common when they started their journey were replaced with a somber and reflective tension. Some performed final checks on weapon loads, spare magazines, and positioning body armor. Others went through entry scenarios.

Behind the van rode Harvey, Larry, and Louis. Each anticipating the rush that accompanies bringing bad guys down. Louis had seen it before. He checked his own weapons and felt the discomfort of a heavier vest. He doubted whether he would even draw his Sig Sauer today. The high-risk entry team should handle any opposition they might encounter.

Mister Smith and Mister Jones followed in a third car. Their job was simply security, but the main threat to their charge was off running about the desert. Jim Harper needed to survive the desert and return in order to be a threat. At present, they concerned themselves with the normal level of risk—muggings, kidnappings, and petty street crime.

The background checks run against the CIA database turned up nothing. These people appeared to be deep cover resident agents planted—maybe years ago—by the Red Chinese. The homes had been purchased in the late seventies and early eighties. Both families were established in their communities, paying taxes, mowing the grass, and buying a new car every five years. They had credit cards and monthly

VISA bills. They seemed to be ideal American citizens, except for the fact that no trace of their lives existed prior to 1975.

Both families popped into existence and began developing a paper trail. The social security numbers were duplicated in the Health Care Finance Administration database. While this was not impossible or even rare, the fact that all four people involved had duplicate numbers for people deceased between 1960 and 1966 pushed the coincident envelope to the breaking point.

The college records appeared to be real until names of those issued the diploma were checked against a special death and birth database maintained at Langley. The four people had either died in college or after high school. It was a sophisticated, deep cover operation capable of creating the forgeries and the paper and data processing trails necessary to make four people look real enough to the IRS and the SSA. They even got letters from their congressman asking them how they felt regarding the important issues of the day. The most recent voter registration listed them as active voters and two had served on jury duty in the past five years.

According to the AAA databanks, they had taken separate trips to Disneyland, the Grand Canyon, and the Wisconsin Dells. There was even a Tommy Bartlett water show bumper sticker on one of the cars. However, never had they ventured beyond the confines of the United States where scrutiny regarding passports and visas could take place. Not even day trips to Canada. Nor had either attempted to purchase a firearm. Obviously, they had acquired a sufficient amount of firepower from other sources.

They blended into the American landscape and vanished from the counter intelligence consciousness—perfect spies until today. The unsettling item that Louis Edwards mulled was where there were two, there would be more. He figured neither family knew the other. They simply followed the same sort of path towards American success, and in a country of two hundred fifty million, it was impossible to analyze all the patterns related to a false identity.

The surveillance team reported the station wagon was leaving the house with two Asian males. Harvey looked to the back seat at Edwards and said, “What do you think?”

“Could be your friends from last night,” he suggested.

“Take them or leave them?”

Edwards drummed his fingers on the back of the front seat. “Have one of the cars follow them. The other two are still inside. They own the place. They’re the ones we really need right now.”

Harvey nodded and picked up the radio microphone. “Car one, stay with the wagon, everyone else sit tight.”

They turned off the Leesburg Pike and angled into the maze of winding suburban roads called Odricks Corner. It was a disconcerting site as a black van with its blinking blue and red strobe lights coursed down the quiet heart of suburbia. People poked their heads out from under raised car hoods, and an impromptu football game took pause to watch the three vehicles wind through the twists and turns until they emerged on the street where the white Cape Cod style home lay.

Harvey clicked the microphone and said, “Right through the fence.”

Edwards eyed the two kids playing with the scooter as the car skidded to a halt. The FBI van smashed through the picket fence splintering the wood planking. The van gouged an ugly divot through the green grass coming to a halt inside the tulip bed and churning the magnolias.

The rear and side doors exploded with an eight man team boiling out like an oversize army of black ants. No warning or shout as the two men with shotguns rushed the front door. They fired together on both sides of the door *top—middle—bottom*. Then stood back as the other six hefted the battering ram and ran towards the door. They hardly noticed the welcome mat.

Harvey emerged from the car holding his gun down at his side and hanging his FBI shield around his neck. Mister Smith and Mister Jones came to flanking positions around Louis Edwards. The members from the two surveillance cars had hopped over a couple of back fences to ensure no one tried a quick exit out the back door.

The front door snapped in two as the ram drove home into the living room. As quickly as it had been hefted it was dropped. Two flash bang grenades sailed through the opening and the black clad men instinctively tensed and flattened themselves to cushion the shock. The interior windows flashed momentarily and the thunder of battle rolled through the quiet neighborhood.

One of the boys on the scooter grinned widely and said, "Cool." His suddenly attentive mother grabbed both boys off their feet and ran for the protection of her own home, uncertain as to what was happening.

The shotgun toting team members rolled around the yawning door jam and moved quickly into the house. The smoking hole swallowed the rest of the team six seconds later.

Harvey said into a hand held radio, "Find the basement first."

The man trimming his hedge stopped clipping when the van shattered the picket fence. He stood to one side craning to see what all the fuss was about. After the shotgun blasts, it occurred to him to grab his camcorder and start recording the event. He would get his name on the evening news.

Louis walked down the driveway towards the garage. The door was shut tight. He eyed the distance between the corner of the house and the garage. He waved Smith and Jones forward drawing his own side arm. It seemed there was a reasonable distance for a tunnel to be constructed. A tunnel could conceal a number of curious items.

The roar of a heavy caliber weapon broke the queasy din. It was met with the sharper and faster bursts from the MP-5's. Another roar responded. Edwards glanced up at the dormer windows where the muzzle flashes bounced off the glass. One of the windows starred as a stray bullet punched through. The drapes swayed as a second roar thundered from the upstairs.

He dismissed the action as a diversion. No one would seriously hide something on the second floor. Escape routes were non-existent. Obviously, they had sufficient firepower available and they were not timid about using it. Tactically, it drew the FBI team away from the basement and bought precious seconds. He idly wondered whether it was the husband or wife making the ultimate sacrifice. He quickened his pace towards the garage.

From inside he heard the muffled scream, "Grenade!"

The windows on the rear of the house exploded with thick and furious tongues of fire. Glass splinters rocketed across the carefully groomed yard and caught some of the plain clothes Federal Agents. They dropped back bleeding and cursing. The heat roiled upwards just as quickly, and the double hung window frames cart wheeled drunkenly across the back yard coming to land next to a swing set.

Jones tried the garage side door finding it locked. He glanced back to Edwards who nodded. Jones stepped back and double tapped the doorknob only to find the door still firmly sealed against his entry.

Edwards lifted his hand held radio and said, "Harvey, are they in the basement yet?"

"Not sure. This isn't going too well."

A second concussion grenade exploded towards the front of the house knocking one black clad agent backward onto the front lawn. Nasty gray smoke billowed from the blast.

Edwards sighed. It probably always went according to plan when they ran the drill at Quantico. He motioned Smith yelling, "Get the car."

The twelve gauge shotgun broke the neighborhood's lethargy next. Someone decided to charge up the steps towards the dormer.

Pump!

Blast!

Pump!

Blast!

Pump!

Blast!

The window facing the driveway broke outwards as a body smashed through the frame. A final crack from a .44 Magnum revolver flamed from the falling figure. Only to be met by a fourth and final shotgun blast. The bloody and broken remains of a young woman in her late twenties or early thirties—it was hard to tell—slammed like a broken doll to the driveway below.

Edwards stepped across the blood-spattered body and kicked the heavy Smith & Wesson from her hand. He crouched down and felt for a pulse on her neck. The accusing eyes glared defiantly at him and the lips moved awkwardly as the life glow faded and the body stilled in its final seconds.

The home's interior resembled something from a bad World War II movie. One of the entry team members was propped against the wall. His leg was broken in three places. Another was winding a self-made tourniquet around his arm. Bullet holes from the H&K's 9mm rounds, bigger holes from thc Mossberg's and ragged holes from the fragmentation grenade were grim reminders of the battle.

Harvey moved through the blasted furniture and blistered walls to the door leading to the basement. It appeared to be a solid piece of steel half an inch thick. The entire staircase seemed to be lined with some sort of steel plate from the basement, making it impossible for the small arms fire to penetrate the walls much less breech the most vital section of the house.

Harvey scowled. He had one dead agent, a stalled entry, and another foreign loose inside the basement probably destroying everything in sight. This was quickly turning into a disaster. He looked from the steel door to the floor in the living room and brought the hand held radio to his lips, "Larry?"

"Yeah."

"We need chain saws, skill saws—whatever. We need to cut through the floor of this house. Go get one of these rubbernecking neighbors and get something to chop through to the basement."

Outside, Mister Smith gunned the engine of his government Ford. He twisted the wheel and dropped the hammer. Stray rocks and dirt spurted from behind the rear wheels as he accelerated towards the garage door. He passed Edwards in a blur before smashing head on into the double door and coming to an abrupt stop.

The top of the garage buckled and snapped downwards banging over the top of the car. The air bag exploded into Mister Smith slamming him against the back of the driver's seat and effectively taking him out of the action for the moment. A geyser of steam spewed from the broken radiator grill creating a blue-green cloud of sickly sweet smelling antifreeze.

Edwards saw the car only peripherally. His attention focused on the man standing in the rear of the garage. Time seemed to come to a standstill. There was movement around the man's shoulder. The kind of movement it takes to bring a pistol upwards and to present a weapon. Louis was much quicker. Sometime between the start of Mister Smith's run and the shattering of the garage door, Louis had jacked a round into the Sig-Sauer P220.

He stood with a two-handed grip, one foot ahead of the other, in a modified Weaver stance. The gun slightly lowered so he could see effectively into the garage. Once he processed the man's arm motion, it was a much easier movement to bring the front site to cover the head of the man and double tap the aggressor. The .45's roar seemed muted in the netherworld of personal confrontation.

Louis paused, lowered the Sig-Sauer to a ready position, and assessed the effectiveness of his shots. The arm seemed to hover for a moment. The deadly appendage of a weapon rolled over in the man's hand before vanishing from site. The Chinese agent took a drunken step towards the left, before his legs quivered and gave out underneath. His central nervous system shut down the rest of his body as blood and brains dribbled down the side of his shattered face. He pitched forward against some shelves, and then he lay very still.

Mister Jones rolled around the side of the garage door opening. He vaulted the broken door and skidded next to the fallen man. He kicked the gun away before dropping to one knee and checking for a pulse.

Louis stepped behind Mister Jones and looked at the dead man on the cold concrete garage floor. A thickening pool of blood was forming near his skull, another ghost to join Louis on the coming cold winter nights. He shuddered at the thoughts and idly replaced his Sig-Sauer in his shoulder holster.

He flipped the corpse over and stared at the dead fish like eyes. Truly, his adversary had been surprised to meet death this afternoon. He was wearing a Tommy Hilfinger pullover, and in his frenzied death, his golf clubs had scattered in the vacant spot where the other car should have been.

The boxy dry cells and the coiled electrical wires colored red and blue brought Louis back to the present. A trap door leading down into a tunnel and the uneasy feeling that their Chinese comrade had been busy preparing to launch his house, the FBI High Risk Entry team, and whatever other secrets he kept, towards the moon. Visible from where Louis stood, there were thick red cylinders with blasting caps lining the walls.

He pulled the hand held radio from his coat pocket, "Harvey?"

"Yeah."

"I think we need a bomb squad, but I found the bolt hole for our Chinese friends."

"Tunnel?"

"Yeah. Oh, and I have another corpse in the garage. And Harvey, do you think we could take down the other safe house with a few less dramatics?" He clicked off.

Harvey came back, "By the way, we lost the other car. Any ideas?"

Louis stared at his radio and shook his head, "No, but I would assume they're going to try to get out of the country." Add two missing agents to the two dead ones. It was not going well.

It was about then he recognized the distinctive heart beat of a helicopter's rotor blades. He stepped through the garage debris to see an *Eye Witness News Team* helicopter surveying the damage wrought this afternoon in a quiet Virginia suburb.

Louis wondered what else could go wrong. It was still early.

23

East Of Nukhayb, Iraqi Data Center,
Monday, November 17, 1997, 2:00 PM (+3.00 GMT)

One of the problems with all military plans is they tend to come apart in unanticipated ways once human beings get involved. What appeared to work on paper, or drawn in the dirt with a stick, suddenly collapses when the Murphy comes calling. Ask any soldier, they know Murphy quite well, and so it went with Harper's war plan.

It happened a little after two o'clock that afternoon. Anderson was hunkered down under camouflage netting and thermo blankets. Stillwell, Hayes, and Burns were catching a nap before the shooting started. Kincaid was checking his weapons for the evening's festivities and Harper had pulled his Bible from his pack. He found another picture from another time and place.

It was a photograph of Jerry and Jim taken ten years ago. They both had rather large Cuban cigars and a gurgling bottle of champagne between them. They had big smiles and hearty laughter, the kind warriors exchange after surviving something particularly harrowing. He could see an F-14 *Tomcat* resting on a steam catapult behind them. They were on the flight deck of the *USS John F. Kennedy*, having just exited from inside Iran.

Harper shrugged. They had brought everyone back that time. No casualties, a couple scrapes, one bullet hole and some blood, but there was always blood and sweat. So full of life and laughter, they had brought out a family. Sometimes they did things that avoided blowing up things, and brought out people. Harper never learned what was so important about these people to Uncle Sam. They were people who wanted to be free of a theocratic regime bent on killing everyone who failed to agree. The God of Abraham may reserve vengeance, but He also reserved forgiveness and grace.

Lynn had slipped this one in behind the back flap. How did she always know what to do? Even if she disagreed with what he was doing, she understood the why. He tried to believe he had not failed, but he did not have the strength to bring Jerry's body out. Too many people chasing him, too far to run to the border, and too beaten up to do thc honorable thing.

He still didn't know how he was going to pay for Jerry's kid's college education. He only knew it would happen, and that Edwards better come through. Somewhere beyond them Jerry was buried, no marker besides the cairn of rocks and a wooden cross. He considered a dying friend's last words and request. He was so pale and so cold. The desert night was closing in and they both knew only one would see the dawn.

Good men always seemed to die in the dark hours after midnight. It is a still time where the deceiver creeps into your thoughts and the harsh reality of Adam's sin once again raises its ugly head. The grand mocker proclaims, "You weren't meant to die, but you will die today."

Jerry had two requests, the spittle dry on his lips and the light already leaving his eyes. His grip was surprisingly strong for a man almost beyond the reach of this world.

"Jim."

Harper touched his hand. "You'll look after my family—my kids."

Harper nodded and remembered dumbly that his friend was probably blind by then. "Yeah, I'll take care of everything."

His head nodded frailly, but the mind, the most incredible creation next to the soul, was still working. Jerry said deliberately, "I know you Jim Harper. I know your stubborn sense of right and wrong, black and white." He paused and gathered himself for some final statement.

"If you're going to keep your word, you've got to leave me here." He coughed and blood dribbled from his nose and mouth. "I know all the stuff about your warrior code and soldier's honor, but I want you to keep your word about my family, and maybe I can't see too well, but I know. I know you're running on empty. I want you to bury me."

Harper said something stupid like they were both getting out. Tears dribbled down his dust stained cheeks and transformed the dust to mud. He held his friend tighter on a nameless patch of sand.

Jerry laughed the ragged laughter dead men seem to develop. "I can't feel my feet anymore and my hands seem to be disappearing. I think its night, but I'm not sure. One of us, Jimmy, has to leave this desert alive. That's you. You promised. You gave your word. I hold you to your word." Jerry knew about Jim and his word. There were many things men can take from you in this world, but Jim would never let his word and his bond be something tossed away frivolously.

His head sank back and Harper replied quietly, "I promised."

No one could see the tears, but Harper knew someday that he'd be back. There was a score to settle. *Vengeance is mine saith the Lord.* Harper chose to ignore those wise words. Harper chose to go his own way. Now on the verge of settling part of the score, things began to unravel. Of course, they unraveled on both sides of the equation, Duri's trap sprung Harper's surprise.

A tongue of flame licked up and away from one of the side vents. A plume of black smoke replaced the orange flame hanging like the angel of death whispering in the still desert air. A *whump* traveled across the desert floor to be swallowed up in its vastness.

Jim was vaguely aware of the blast, however, Anderson clicked on the FM radio link they all wore. "Major, I think we've got problems."

Jim stirred from the painful ashes memories can bring. He snapped the Bible closed and replied, "What's up?"

He took one last glance at Lynn and the girls. Quietly, he slipped the photo into his breast pocket beneath his flack vest. Closing his eyes, he heard the answer.

"One of your surprise packages just went off. If there was an alarm rigged, I'm sure we just told everyone we're here."

Harper nodded. He pulled the Glock 21 and racked the slide. A 230 grain Speer Gold Dot rode into the barrel's throat. He dropped the dull black automatic back into his holster not bothering to pull the Velcro strap over the back of the gun.

He walked over and kicked the feet of Stillwell, Hayes, and Burns. He pulled the Browning Hi Power from the small of his back holster and racked the slide sending a 115 Winchester Silvertip from magazine to barrel.

"Show time, gentlemen," he said without much fanfare.

Hayes and Burns were up immediately checking their weapons. Stillwell yawned trying to figure out what Harper had just said. The burning yellow ball above certainly did not look like the cover of darkness.

Harper reached over and grabbed his Mossberg. He shucked the three slugs from the magazine and alternately loaded number 4 buckshot and rifled deer slug. Seven rounds later he asked, "Any activity?"

"Negative," replied Anderson.

"Kincaid, we may have company sooner than we thought."

"Understood, Major."

Stillwell focused on Harper who was busily checked spare magazines, shotgun shells, and grenades on an Alice vest with an impossible number of pockets.

Harper kicked the bottom of Stillwell's foot again, and turned to Burns. "Take the RPG-7 and blow the front door when I give you the signal. Take whatever else you need to raise holy hell, and keep yourself hidden from everybody."

"Good guys too?"

Harper fixed him with a look. "Everybody. We're inside Indian country now. There are no other good guys but us."

Stillwell sat up and checked his watch. "It's not time yet."

Harper nodded as he slung the shotgun over his shoulder and slid a pair of Silenco twenty-nine decimal noise reduction earplugs into his ears.

"Yeah, I know. That's the trouble with battle plans, they never seem to know about those nagging little details." He looked over at Hayes.

"You're with us Sergeant."

Hayes nodded and continued gathering grenades, spare magazines, and ugly round magnetic bombs to his person.

"You mean we're going in," snapped Stillwell.

Harper nodded and spoke into the throat mike. "Okay, listen up. Something went boom inside. We have to assume the bad guys have figured out there's a problem. They'll be coming.

"We are working on plan Bravo. Assume everyone and everything is hostile. Unless you hear the cavalry call sign."

Burns slung the RPG-7 over his shoulder and started jogging down the wadi. A web belt of procured rockets slapped at his back and hips.

They had not even fired a shot in anger and plan Bravo was in effect. There was no plan Charlie.

Harper tossed a pair of earplugs to Stillwell. "Put those on. It'll be noisy inside."

Stillwell caught the earplugs and pealed open the pack.

"Hayes you got some extra cans of gas?"

Hayes nodded and produced two five-gallon jugs.

"Give one to Stillwell here and kick him in the butt, before he gets himself killed."

Hayes dropped to one knee and said quietly, "What the Major means, Sir, if you don't get your stuff together, he may shoot you himself."

Stillwell peered at Hayes not believing what was going to happen. "What happened to waiting for night?"

"Murphy!" snapped Hayes.

Harper slid to the top of the wadi and said, “How long since she blew?”

“Two minutes,” replied Anderson.

Harper scanned the surface of the desert. The air quivered with heat, and a painful bite from overhead sunlight gnawed at him already. The old enemy, a waterless ocean, rose to meet them. It seemed like he had been crawling through sand, scorpions, and snakes for more than half his life. In mere seconds, he would be dropping down a hole doing his level best to kill someone’s child, or brother, or husband, or father. He closed his eyes wishing it was not so.

“Kincaid?”

“Ready when you are.”

“Burns.”

“Another half minute.”

“Anderson.”

“Primary targets are antennae and epaulets.”

“Secondary?”

“People with the biggest guns.”

“Hayes.”

“Just finishing up on the Lieutenant, sir.”

“Stillwell.”

“Here.” What else did one say at a time like this?

“Anderson make sure you’re dug in deep.”

“I am, sir.”

He looked over at Stillwell and Hayes. “Move out.”

Hayes bounded up over the lip of the wadi and started a loping run with both five-gallon gasoline jugs. Stillwell slid a helmet up over his eyes and realized what the chinstrap was for. He managed to buckle it and not shoot himself as he hopped behind Harper and Hayes.

The grillwork on the air vents was crinkled from the blast. Hot air seemed to spill out in jittery heat waves causing the terrain behind them to jiggle uncertainly. The huge fans used to draw air in and out had failed. The blast concussion probably broke something important.

Harper dropped to one knee and pulled a gas mask over his face. He pulled heavy four ply rubber gloves over his hands and sealed himself into his uniform. No one knew if the nerve gas had erupted yet. He spoke softly, "Stillwell, get your mask on." He tapped his own mask.

Hayes came to a stop and tossed two of the round magnetic mines to Harper. Harper planted one on either side of the shaft and punched the ten-second-countdown timer. He rolled back under cover and clamped his hands over his ears.

Stillwell had barely looked up when the blast tore the grillwork apart spitting shrapnel across the desert. The blast knocked him backward onto his rump. He shook his head and concentrated on getting the mask over his face.

Hayes lobbed a brick of C4 plastic explosive with a pencil fuse into the gaping hole. A third gout of flame belched from the side of the Data Center.

"Stick with the Lieutenant," muttered Harper as he dropped feet first down the shaft. The Mossberg was cocked and ready as he smashed through the broken fan blades to the floor of the machine room. The smoke from the three explosions hung heavily on the air.

A door leading into the center was missing. The doorframe was mangled and shattered by the successive shocks. He dropped to one knee and flipped the infrared goggles over the top of his gas mask.

Several hot heaps shimmered into view. Either they came to see what all the noise was about or the nerve gas was active. "Moving," he whispered.

Harper slid out of the machine room to verify seven men, most of them Iraqi regulars, laying in fetal positions. Gas.

Hayes handed both five-gallon jugs to Stillwell and sent him down the shaft. Stillwell landed more or less on his feet. Hayes came down next to him and said, "You carry and I'll shoot, okay, Lieutenant?"

Stillwell nodded.

Harper moved further down the corridor. The smoke was clearing, but the gas had penetrated the interior corridors outside the actual computer room. He looked around two corners and found several more men, a mix of technicians, and soldiers gasping for air and clawing their faces.

There seemed to be a lot of Iraqi regulars roaming around the corridors. At least, they had been roaming until the gas took them down. Harper leaned away from the corner and thought about what he was seeing. The center was too small to successfully house a great many soldiers and technicians, so why were so many regular army types?

The cold feeling in the bottom of his gut rumbled nastily.

He looked at the color coded "You are Here" map on the wall. He was on the top level. Below them was the computer center. Behind him was the machine room and next-door was the electrical room.

"Hayes, the power mains are next to where we came in."

Hayes tapped Stillwell on the shoulder and sent him towards Harper. He turned back and moved to the power mains. He tried the door finding it locked. He stood back and shot the lock off with his Berreta.

The door leaned out towards him revealing three breaker panels. He took a magnetic bomb and attached it to the center panel, pressed the countdown timer. Slamming the door shut and diving back into the machine room. The blast ripped the door in half burying the top half in the side of the corridor wall.

The lights failed immediately, and the huge Uninterruptible Power Supplies switched over below them. The computers trembled and some of the dust that had accumulated on top of the cabinets shook loose, but the disks continued to spin. At least, until the diesel generator could be started.

The battery lights switched on and the internal camera system failed. Harper figured whoever was manning the command center had been blinded by the attack so far.

"Anderson?"

"Nothing so far, Major."

He leaned over to Stillwell and said, "We're going down the steps and into the Data Center. I figure we'll find some live people. If they move shoot them."

"What about these?"

Harper looked at the gasoline jugs and produced a short rope from one of the inner pockets. "Tie it around the handles and sling it over your neck." He motioned to Hayes that they were going to the left and down.

Hayes nodded and brought his M-16 A2 to ready. The trio slid from the corner to the stair well. Harper glanced through the safety goggles integrated into the gas mask, and found no one. He pulled a grenade and tossed it into the stairwell. Another *whump* slammed the door towards Harper.

He moved very quickly, taking the steps in quick jumps. Already the door leading into the Data Center level was opening, and someone found out how potent rifled deer slug can be at ten feet. Harper caught the door with his shoulder sliding to the floor and sending a blast of number 4 buckshot into a crowd. He rolled sideways and fired a third time. This time a slug ripped through two people before leaving a hole the diameter of a two-pound coffee can in the ceiling.

Hayes arrived with a measured *tap-tap* from the M-16. Brass spit sideways out of the receiver as the Marine pushed himself forward and down. Stillwell joined in with a set of three round bursts. It ended with a violent silence. A single empty brass case spun harmlessly against the wall and the thin smoke generated by the attack hung between the attackers and defenders.

A heap of broken bodies lay before them. Obviously, the nerve gas had not penetrated the lower level. Perhaps there was a different air system, or the complex failed to circulate air further since the blast that loosed the nerve gas probably burned some of it up.

Harper leaned on the shotgun and levered himself to a standing position. Sweat ran down his face as he pulled the gas mask down below his chin. The air seemed stale. The emergency lights bathed the corridor in an eerie yellow glow. He wondered idly how long the batteries would last.

He turned to the end of the corridor, and said quickly. "Sergeant, how we doing on your little bombs?"

Hayes hefted the ruff sack holding his invention. "Maybe half dozen left."

Harper pointed to the telephone exchange boxes at the end of the corridor. "Get rid of that."

Hayes nodded and loped towards the far end of the corridor.

Harper pulled out some double 00 buckshot, three inch shells, and calmly recharged the tubular magazine for the Mossberg. He said without checking Stillwell, "Change your magazine with a fresh one. This ain't the movies. You only got thirty rounds per mag."

Stillwell nodded dumbly. It was largely due to the earplugs that they could hear anything at all. The back of his neck ached from the explosions. However, the noise reduction had been enough to prevent the terrible drumming that would have resulted had they attacked without ear protection.

Harper pushed the last shell into the magazine and checked the thumb safety. His owner's manual strongly suggested that you should not mix regular and magnum shells together. But Harper doubted whether the writer had ever been thirty feet below an Iraqi desert.

"Anderson?" he whispered.

"Nothing Major."

"Let me know when it changes." There would be a reaction force.

Harper nodded towards the other end of the corridor. "Data Center's that way, Lieutenant."

Stillwell worked the bolt on his M-16 and checked the grenade launcher slung uncomfortably around his middle. He felt very tired as they stepped around the dead soldiers and technicians. His stomach churned as the dead eyes and open mouths convicted him and his actions. If Harper had given him time, he might have been sick. There simply wasn't time.

"Eh, Lieutenant, we might need one or two of these fellows alive." Harper glanced at the carnage behind them and continued. "Let's try to leave someone in a white smock alive."

Hayes was running towards them waving his hand frantically.

"Party time." Harper started running to the corridor's end where it took a sharp turn towards the Data Center entrance. Stillwell scrambled after him and Hayes slid around the corner to clamp his hands over his ears and bury his face against the side of the wall.

Stillwell thought about doing the same thing. Unfortunately, the clatter of an AK-47 distracted him. The heavier and fatter 7.62mm bullets *thunked* into the wall beside him. He lifted his M-16 when Hayes's bombs let loose.

Harper dropped to a prone position and pumped out three blasts—filling the narrow corridor with a lethal barrage of ball bearings each capable of making a hole the size of .38 special. The air seemed to brighten with flame and then disappear with a frightening blast. The shock wave rippled over the top of them and knocked the next line of defenders backwards. The roar thundered like a giant locomotive drowning all thoughts except fervent prayers that they live through this horror.

Hayes recovered first and pulled his grenade launcher to a ready position. He fired two 40mm fragmentation grenades towards the end of this shorter corridor and ducked again. If anyone had survived the buckshot, they were torn apart by the grenades. The heavy glass doors marking the entrance to the Data Center imploded through two layers of security doors. They sent a deadly shower of razor sharp shards into the final three soldiers positioned inside the Data Center.

Harper lifted his head once the air seemed to return. A thicker haze hung ominously in the corridor. Nothing moved. The number of conscious defenders had been reduced to a handful. The entire top level had succumbed to the nerve gas. Only those within the final security layer of the Data Center survived, and they were no longer paying attention to an orderly shutdown of the systems.

They froze like a deer in the headlights as the three predators emerged from the dust and smoke. Harper leveled the still smoking Mossberg at the glass door and nodded towards the entrance. Stillwell stared at the dead men laying about their feet. The white floor and clear glass of the third inner wall was pock marked and blood spattered. No one ever explained in the sparkling briefing rooms over polished wooden tables this part of the operation. They talked about casualties and acceptable losses, force multipliers and power projection. Blood splattered walls and broken, lifeless bodies never came up in polite discussion. The old adage regarding a man with a rifle doing the work no satellite or airplane could ever accomplish ran through Stillwell's thoughts.

Hayes let the grenade launcher drop and pulled the M-16 to ready. He spat on the floor and said quietly, "Major, I might have had my doubts about you, but you know your stuff."

One of the white smocked technicians raised his hands over his head and moved slowly to the door release.

Harper shrugged, "Sergeant, getting in was the easy part."

★ ★ ★

Colonel Duri looked up from his cot. The corpsman handed him a signal. He looked up and checked the clock. "You're sure that we have lost all contact with the Data Center."

"Yes, Sir. No radio or land line contact."

"The database?"

"All lines are dead, Sir."

Duri scratched his chin. It was not unusual for Iraq's communication systems to fail due to the quirkiness of the equipment. He looked at the file folders on the table next to the cot. He assumed Harper would have waited for night. Why attack in the heat of the day and in daylight?

To move through the air in the no-fly zone was dangerous enough, but to do it in daylight raised the level of risk. The risks of doing nothing in the event of an attack on the Data Center were even more certain than a hyperactive F-16 pilot.

"Very well. Ready the aircraft, we leave immediately."

★ ★ ★

A Saudi E3A AWACS aircraft recorded the fact that three RAF helicopters blinked into existence over the southern edge of Baghdad. The computer up linked to a satellite, which down linked back to a mainframe at Central Command's headquarters. The systems talked for microseconds before sending back the identification.

The US airman called his Captain over and asked plainly, "Why are three RAF Sea King helicopters lifting off from Baghdad when their transponders say they should be Bosnia?"

"You're sure?"

The airman pointed at the confirmation on his screen. The Captain patted him on the shoulder and said, "Good work." He walked over to another screen and began to vector an F-16 to investigate.

★ ★ ★

The glass door slid open and Harper focused on the digital linear tape (DLT) drive housed on the front panel of the HP-9000 cabinet. "Sergeant, we're looking for tape cartridges. The backup tapes for anything and everything they have in this place."

"What do they look like?"

Harper kept a steady gaze on his captive audience. "About the size of a CD case only thicker. They're probably brown or black."

"Yes, Sir."

"Stillwell, I imagine the gasoline is getting heavy. Why don't you set it down over there next to the tall cabinet and find something to tie these boys up with."

"You're not going to shoot them?" he asked.

Harper sighed. The inevitable baby killer questions were coming. "I'm a soldier, not a butcher."

24

Washington DC, Sunday, November 16, 1997,
7:00 PM EST

Mister Jones drove the battered Ford through the White House Gate. Mister Smith gulped a couple more Ibuprofen and chased it down with Diet Mountain Dew. The ache from his bruised ribs and sprained wrist did not make the ride in the smashed Ford any easier. The front hood was a buckled mess. A bunge cord held it in place. They kept a jug of water nearby to fill the radiator after every drive. There was a nasty set of holes towards the top of the radiator where splinters from the wood door had penetrated.

They had a hurried dinner consisting of stale machine food in one of the company's cafeterias. Louis examined the toxicology report related to the corpse retrieved from the Persian Gulf. Smith and Jones had patched themselves up as best as they could with a medical kit they found in one of the rest rooms.

No one had bothered to watch television, but if they had, they would have seen the news footage from the television news crew replayed on CBS, ABC, NBC, MSNBC, Fox News, and CNN. By tomorrow morning, one hundred fifty million people would see the bouncing and blurred videotape from the next-door neighbor coupled with the news helicopter's aerial portrait. Of particular note would be the shattered corpse of a young woman laying face up in her driveway, a splintered fence, the ugly black top of the FBI's SWAT van, and a child's abandoned scooter.

The quiet work required for counter intelligence was noisily beamed across the nation tonight, and newspapers desperate for news on Monday morning were already writing stories that had little relationship to the facts. Nor did it help for an additional vehicle, belonging to the nearest bomb squad, to show up complete with Plexiglas shielded officers approaching a garage with a broken door.

The twenty-four news cycle jumped at the chance to report a real story. By the time Louis got out of the Ford and started towards the West Wing, stringers for the *New York Times*, the *Washington Post* and even the *Des Moines Register* were on the scene. Some were trying to piece together what really happened, others simply fabricated some *facts.* A few heard the *spy* word and ignored it. The stringer for the *New York Post* greedily gobbled up that tidbit and mistakenly attributed the Asian couple as having Japanese origins. Several of the financial networks picked up the rumor, and the Yen dropped perceptibly against the dollar in the Asian Markets that were just opening.

Most of the nation ignored such musings and settled down for Sunday Night Edition of NFL football on ESPN. The White House media machine was already gearing up to deal with the problem. Three pizza deliveries had already been made to offices in the Old Executive Office Building. It was important the White House get its own version of the story fed to whatever media outlets were listening. No one involved in this effort bothered to learn the facts either. Phone calls were made, copy was faxed, and interviews arranged in a frantic effort to deflect any negative publicity. The FBI Director remained unavailable for comment, although the rumormongers suspected he had plenty to say.

A uniformed Secret Service Officer led Louis through the West Wing corridors to the National Security Advisor's office. His chief assistant, Arthur, was pouring coffee for the three of them as the door closed behind Louis. Louis shared Jonas's visceral distaste for Arthur. He let it pass.

The NSA looked up at Edwards and waved him to a seat. He was glowering at three television screens. The broadcast was the top of the news for FOX, CNN, and MSNBC. The coifed CNN anchor said, "This afternoon, a federal raid took place in one of Washington DC's bedroom communities. An FBI SWAT team rushed this home in Odricks Corner, Virginia."

The video was from the next-door neighbor showing the van already stopped on the lawn and the muffled shouts and shots could be heard in the background. The battering ram had been abandoned and the front door looked like a yawning black hole.

"Not since the raid in Waco Texas against the Branch Davidians have we seen such dramatic footage of Federal Officers raiding a private residence. Two people were killed during the raid, and two FBI agents injured."

The scene switched to an overhead shot where the uncovered body of the woman lay amidst the broken glass and broken bones. Louis shuddered. He had watched her die.

"Eye witnesses tell us the shooting was over after a few minutes. While FBI officials would not comment at this time, sources close to the investigation claim drugs and weapons were involved.

"The Arlington bomb squad was called to remove several sticks of dynamite from inside the garage. Long time residents were as surprised as anyone that anything was amiss."

Two flak jacketed bomb squad members were hauling out a gray bomb box. The footage switched to a vacant field where the contents were detonated causing the bomb box to leap uncomfortably into the air.

The NSA snapped the broadcast off and turned threateningly towards Louis, "I understand you were present for this fiasco."

"Yes," he said quietly, "But this was the FBI's show. American soil and everything."

He grunted his disapproval.

"Arthur tells me you've been a busy boy today."

Louis let his attention drift over to Arthur. The youngster sat quietly in his own chair with a notepad propped on his knee. Arthur seemed to always be explaining something to the NSA, or providing a report, or going over some briefing materials.

"All weekend, to be truthful," replied Louis.

The NSA grunted again. "Two Chinese agents—that's what the FBI is telling me. That right?"

Louis nodded. "Resident agents, deep cover. We stumbled across them around noon today."

A scowl this time, "I suppose it was necessary to roust these two today. We couldn't let it wait for a couple days. After all, we deported two of their diplomats today handcuffed to Federal Marshals."

"Spies, Sir," corrected Louis.

"What?"

"Spies," he repeated. "The two men deported today were spies with diplomatic passports. If I had my way, they would have disappeared into a company safe house and we would have inquired of their activities," continued Louis.

"We don't do things that way. Now they're comparing this thing to Waco. We don't need a Waco right now—too close to the holidays and everything. People need to be thinking about turkey and mistletoe."

Louis wondered when it would be the right time for another Waco. The anger over doing his job and protecting the country did not disturb or surprise him. It was the way the White House worked these days. There probably was not a focus group and accompanying poll to gauge public reaction for this situation. It did not deal with Social Security or the homeless, just the trite matters surrounding national security. He wondered how anyone could lead when they waited to read the polls the next morning. After all, the polls dictated the tenor for the next twelve hours, a tenor the White House studiously manipulated overnight.

"So what brings you here tonight?" He gulped some more coffee. The NSA paused, and then demanded, "Why were you tagging along with the FBI today?"

Louis looked up from the brief case chained to his wrist. "It is my belief that this particular group has a material effect on the current operation inside Iraq."

The NSA glanced at Arthur snapping, "I thought we called it off this morning."

A shiver ran through Louis's spine. His attention shifted back to Arthur.

"We called off all military support after your morning meeting. But the team was already committed to the desert." He met Louis's gaze and said regretfully, "I'm afraid you'll have to write your team off as a loss."

Something twisted deep inside Louis. This staff member was casually explaining they had kicked the legs out from under his people. Louis cocked his head and turned back to the NSA. "Loss? What do you mean we dropped military support? That's part of the extraction plan." He did his best to keep his anger in check.

"Not anymore," snapped the NSA.

"My team will take exception to such a move."

"I don't care if they write Jesse Helms," he snarled. "They no longer exist. The mission never took place. We've already moved on the contingency plans for capture or death."

"You're assuming what?"

The NSA waved his hand. "Assume whatever you want."

"You can't just cut somebody like Harper loose. It'll come and bite you in the butt."

The NSA shook his head and pointed a pudgy finger in Louis's direction. "Your fancy super soldier is going to have to find his own ticket home Edwards. Those are the breaks," he paused and softened his tone. "Look, I know you hate to lose people, but that's the way it is. We've got to get control of events."

"Events!" exploded Louis. "You call taking down two Chinese agents events? You just sent a six man team into the desert to penetrate one of Iraq's secret bases and now you won't lift a finger to get them back out?"

The NSA leaned back in his chair. "Yeah, that's the size of it." He waved at the television. "That's something for the spin masters to deal with, let me level with you." The NSA stabbed a button on his remote control and projected a map of the Persian Gulf against a white screen. There was a red target dot in the Southern Gulf.

"One of our Los Angeles attack boats was fired on by the damaged Chinese Boomer," he paused. "You did hear me when I said boomer. Big nasty submarine capable of carrying a number of ballistic missiles."

Louis nodded.

"We sank one of their boomers inside the Gulf in the past twenty four hours. Now, no one in this administration is going to admit we did such a thing. In fact, no one in this room is going to tell the President we sank a missile boat of an emerging superpower.

"This mess gets more complicated when the Chinese Ambassador is on my door step this morning upset about his missing boat and his expelled diplomats." He stabbed another finger in Louis's direction. "Get used to the idea. Diplomats, not spies! The stinking FBI Director would not budge, so we deported them this afternoon.

"Maybe we could have gotten through this mess okay, if you and the FBI boys hadn't decide to play Rambo in Virginia this afternoon. I don't know what the final story is, but we'll see what our boys in the fourth estate come up with over night and pick something that suits our version of history.

"Whether you like it or not, China is an important partner on the Pacific Rim. No more red boogey men for this administration. We're done with that kind of nonsense. You cold warriors will just have to get used to it and write your memoirs. We need China relatively strong to hold the Russians and the Japanese in check. What I don't need is a witch-hunt for Chinese agents under every rock. The Chinese can be our partners or our adversaries. Officially, administration policy is to make them partners."

Louis looked at the map and whispered, "You sank a Chinese missile boat?"

"Not me—not on orders. Some blood and guts captain patrolling in the Southern Gulf." He shook his hand in disgust covering the lie. "Not much I can do about it. Raise a fuss and force an inquiry. Last thing we need right now.

"But what we can do, and this is where your pet project comes in, is make sure we don't make any more moves that can potentially embarrass our *little Asian buddies*—so no official incursion inside Iraq, no embarrassing accusations regarding weapon technology. It ends now, Louis. We lose six guys. They lose a boat and we all ignore history."

Louis did the calculation and completed the message, "You keep it out of the press and bury the mistake. There never was a U2 recording a clandestine weapons transfer. There never was a *Han* class sub performing the delivery, and there never was a team sent into Southern Iraq." He looked from the map to the NSA. "Have I got that about right?"

The two other men nodded.

He wondered what Harper would do when he found out. Edwards assumed Harper would go hunting for whoever left him stranded in a faraway desert. Unlike the other two men, Edwards had no doubt Harper would prevail in the desert. The question was a matter of cost, and these two had just driven the price to unacceptable levels.

He opened the locks of his briefcase and withdrew a report. "Perhaps, this will change your mind." He handed the bound and sealed report with a code level labeled ULTRA to the NSA.

The NSA took the report as if Louis had just handed him a rattlesnake. "I presume you've read this."

Louis nodded.

"So what does it say? You didn't come here for your health, and I'm not exactly sure I want to keep this little gem." He nudged it away from his side of the desk.

"What you have in your hand is a report on the corpse Jonas Benjamin pulled out of the Northern Gulf," he began. "As you know from the photographic evidence, something went wrong during the weapons transfer." He paused and said surreptitiously, "The one that never happened."

The NSA winked at him. Had he known Louis Edwards better he might have realized that the NSA had shifted on Louis's internal tally sheet from good guy to bad guy.

"Yes, well. The indications are that the Chinese delivered a concentrated form of nerve agent derived from *0-ethyl S-diisopropylaminomethyl methylphosphonothiolate* better known as VX.

"VX is persistent nerve agent first derived in 1958 and placed into full scale production around 1961. The chemical structure was published in 1972 and today any twelve-year-old can get the chemical composition off the Internet." The NSA shifted uncomfortably in his chair.

"VX is basically an oily substance that is generally absorbed through the skin," continued Louis. "That's what makes it such a powerful weapon. It will adhere to grass, trees, cars, and machinery. It can also be converted to a gas for aerosol dispersion. It is fairly stable as these things go, and can persist for several weeks.

"We suspect the Iraqis have a derivation of VX called VX-2. This would be used in a binary weapon where the chemicals mix once the shell has been fired and arrive as a lethal package on target. We are not certain that Iraq has perfected binary technology, but such a derivative makes the manipulation and storage of these types of weapons easier and safer." Arthur found a spot behind Louis and started to hum unelessly.

"For a couple of years now, we've speculated the Chinese might have developed something called VX-Beta. There have been disturbing reports coming out China that an new nerve agent, classified as a permanent toxin as opposed to persistent and non-persistent nerve agents, has been tested on prisoners condemned to death.

"We know they have cordoned areas, within a restricted zone, as completely off limits. It appears they may not know how to decontaminate VX-Beta once it's been employed. The tests they have conducted are to douse an area, and then send prisoners into the area bare foot. A prisoner lasts anywhere from three to five minutes to a couple of hours depending on the concentrations.

"After initial tests, no effort has been made to recover the bodies."

"You mean they leave them lay."

"Yes, Sir," responded Louis. "The evidence related to this is the extreme corrosiveness of the agent spilled during the weapons transfer. It appears to have eaten right through the protective gear worn by the Chinese sailors. We also have reason to believe the Iraqis knew what they were getting, and when it appeared things were getting out of hand, they started shooting hoping to keep contaminated people away."

Louis checked his audience. Not much seemed to be getting through, so he continued to his strongest argument. "A weapon purported to be a permanent nerve agent could have overwhelming effects on any population center targeted by such a weapon. We believe Saddam has the ability to mount chemical warheads on modified SCUD missiles.

"Impact on population centers such as Tel Aviv or military targets such as an aircraft carrier could have devastating consequences in terms of retaliation. There is no doubt that a chemical attack on Israel would result in an all out nuclear response.

"Primary and secondary casualties in a population center would be substantial. Casualties against a military target could be substantial enough to cripple our capabilities. This is a destabilizing weapon system, and our best bet is to determine where the depots for these weapons are located."

The NSA steepled his fingers and said quietly, "It's all very interesting, Louis. However, nothing you've reported changes the situation. We know we can't trust the Iraqi Government to be truthful and honest, and we know we can't live without the Chinese Government," he sighed. "After all, what do you think they're arguing about in the UN today?

Saddam just up and declares several sites off limits to the UN inspection team last Wednesday, and by Friday Richard Butler is pulling his teams out.

"I'll tell you what." He waved his finger in the air as if he were stirring some potion. "If your man can make it out of Iraq with the information as to where the weapon depot is for your VX-Beta, I'll go to the President with a proposal to hit it with *Nighthawk* stealth fighter-bombers. They should be able to sneak in and out without being detected by Iraqi radar."

Louis spread his hands. "Perhaps I didn't make myself clear. The Chinese have provided Saddam with the capability to severely cripple our military assets or kill a city. We don't have an effective means of dealing with this stuff. We don't even have samples—"

The NSA did not want to hear the whole sorry mess. He raised his hand cutting Louis off. "I gave you my best offer. Your guy gets back and maybe he has something, maybe he doesn't." The NSA shrugged like a Mafia Boss. "If we find out where this stuff is, we'll hit it. Now, is there anything else?"

Louis shook his head and stood up. The NSA handed him the sealed folder and said quietly, "Find a nice deep dark hole for this report Louis. It's not the sort of thing I'd like spreading around the government right now."

Louis locked the report once more in his brief case and made his way out of the West Wing. He wondered what focus group or poll they would take to determine whether or not it would be a good idea to knock out a weapon system that could kill tens of thousands of people. He weighed that bitter thought against danger posed by a Jim Harper finding himself sold out again. The consequences could be devastating.

Mister Jones looked at his boss and asked, "Tough meeting?"

"No, not after you realize you're dealing with morons. There's nothing tough after that."

25

East Of Nukhayb, Iraqi Data Center,
Monday, November 17, 1997, 2:45 PM (+3.00 GMT)

Harper sat down at the main HP-9000 console. He moved the mouse pointer down to the terminal icon on the tool bar along the bottom of the screen. It was a standard X Windows interface. A terminal window opened up on the screen and the # prompt indicated he was connected as the root user. He smiled. It was time to unravel the secrets hidden in this system. He typed a couple commands to determine the status of the database.

Stillwell finished roping his three prisoners to office chairs on wheels. He used power cords and cables from a set of monitors Harper indicated he could cannibalize. As he lifted his head and looked across the room, he was somewhat amazed at how easily this soldier and warrior maneuvered through the technological issues related to the computer system. He seemed as at ease with the mouse and terminal as with his shotgun.

Hayes walked across the computer room—his boots echoing on the raised floor. He held a fat square DLT tape cartridge in hand. He waved it before Harper asking, "Is this what you were talking about?"

Harper glanced at the tape cartridge and nodded. "Keep them together. I would assume they have some sort of labeling system. Also, there should be a bunch in the juke box."

Hayes nodded and looked around the room for a record player most often found in malt shops of the late sixties, then turned back to Harper, "Juke box, Sir?"

Harper nodded and pointed to a multi-stack tape drive mounted on one of the front panels of the HP-9000 cabinet. "Push the button that says unload and pull the stacker out. It's either a five or seven banger. There'll be some tapes inside there. Just throw the stacker into the bag and leave the tapes intact, it's probably the most recent backup. With any luck we should be able to reconstitute this database once we get back home."

Hayes nodded and said, "I'm glad you know what you're talking about."

Harper examined the UNIX prompt indicating he was logged in as the root user. He typed: **su—oracle**

The system connected to the oracle account, which owned the databases on the UNIX system. Harper was a couple commands away from owning everything. He decided it was time to ensure no one outside the computer room could access the database. He shut down the system that provided for remote communications to the databases by typing: **lsnrctl stop**

He swiveled in the chair checking his watch. They had maybe ten minutes at the outside. "Lieutenant, this computer room is protected by a HALON system."

Stillwell blinked.

Harper sighed, and explained quickly, "That red button on the wall next to the door." He pointed.

Stillwell examined the doorway, at least what was left of it. "The thing the size of a grapefruit."

"Yeah," Harper nodded to the ceiling. "Those sprayers in the ceiling are held together with lead. Once we start burning this place down, that lead is going to melt and release the HALON system. If we're still down here—we die. HALON is an inert gas designed to smother fires. Unfortunately, it also smothers people. You've got five minutes to get into the ceiling and disconnect the system from those sprayers. I don't care how you do it, just get it done." He swung back to the console.

The command to shut the database listener program had completed. No one outside the immediate UNIX network could connect to the server anymore. Harper guessed the Iraqis were running Version seven dot something of the Oracle database system. He guessed it was probably not the latest and greatest and typed: **sqldba lmode=y**

The system connected and displayed a **SQLDBA>**prompt. He wiggled his fingers over the top of the keyboard typing: **connect internal**

The screen blinked and demanded: **password:**

Harper stood up. "Sergeant, start pulling the floor panels up and dump one of the jerry cans of gas underneath the raised floor. There should be some suction cups over in the corner there."

Hayes grunted and set the canvas sack of tapes on the floor. He found a suction cup handle and started pulling the two by two foot square panels for the false floor up.

"Give particular attention to the junction and big wads of cables." If it was a typical installation, he expected to find several generations of cable beneath their feet. Once the insulators caught on fire or melted, the plastic and rubber would start to burn.

Stillwell pulled a table over. He climbed on top the table and reached up to the ceiling. Stillwell punched out the fiberboard drop down ceiling panels and stuck his head into the ceiling. He found a maze of fluorescent light fixtures, electrical conduit, and pipes running loose. He poked his head back down and asked, "If this place is burning down in a few minutes, when are we going to have time to look at the database?"

"We're not," replied Harper flatly.

"But those were the mission orders."

"Written by a jackass most likely," snarled Harper. "Get back to work on the HALON system."

Stillwell nodded. Not much respect for authority.

"How many of your bombs, you got left?" Harper asked Hayes as his fingers flew over the keyboard.

"Two."

Harper pointed back to the HP-9000 cabinet. "Pull the skins off that box. Inside you'll find the disk drives. They'll be arranged on horizontal shelves. Rig the explosives to blast up and down. I don't what anything to remain."

Hayes looked confused. "I thought our orders were—"

"Sergeant, I'm changing those orders. We're going to level this place today. In fact, we're going to blow it to kingdom come in the next fifteen minutes. I left this place intact once before, this time nothing remains."

"But, we were only suppose to retrieve data," protested Hayes.

Harper sighed. "Yes, I know. But don't you think they've caught on to the fact that we've penetrated their security?"

Hayes looked at the door, the dead soldiers beyond and the jerry can in his hand. Hayes nodded. "Yeah, I see what you mean."

"Besides, we should give our hosts the opportunity to find out how good their disaster recovery plan really is. Do you realize most Fortune 500 companies have never tested their disaster recovery plans?" Harper smiled. "I'm betting they haven't tested theirs either."

He turned to the three technicians trussed up with power cords and thin net cabling. He slid the Glock 21 out of his side holster and waved it in their direction. He said quietly in Arabic, "Gentlemen, you need to make a decision quickly. You need to decide whether you are more afraid of the your Great Leader or a crazy American with a big gun who will blow your knee cap apart if he doesn't get the passwords to the database instances."

His surprised audience looked back at him.

"You've got three seconds." He hefted the .45 ACP Glock recognizing that if he did pull the trigger, whoever he shot would never walk again. It was one of those moments that would haunt Harper for the rest of his life. He tried not to think about wives and fathers, about daughters and brothers. He focused on the task at hand. He focused on the five men he was responsible for and not the horror he was about to inflict.

No one answered. He picked the man sitting in the middle and squeezed the trigger. The .45 thundered in the small room. The man's left knee exploded in a mass of blood, bone, and cartilage. It was a horrifying sight and the resulting scream piercing, even through the earplugs. Harper's stomach tightened. It was one of those things Lynn would never understand. It was something he would never tell his girls. It was one of those horrible things about warfare that men went with to the grave.

He thought of his dad for some unknown reason. Dad had been at both battles for Tobruk in North Africa fighting as part of the resistance along side British paratroopers. The most dad had ever observed about the harshness of those days was the incredible number of empty shell casings at the end of the battle. There was no where to stand without stepping on empty cases. The rest of the story was lost to the ravages of death.

He idly noted the empty shell casing sliding across the room. "I'm waiting gentlemen."

The man on the left started to talk, and a flurry of angry words met his efforts from the right. Harper aimed and fired again. This time the man on the right screamed. Blood spewed like a fountain from the wound. Harper turned to the last man. The bile was rumbling at the back of his throat. He leveled the weapon at the man's knee and said menacingly, "You were saying."

"Please—please—" yelled the technician.

"Passwords?"

His eyes were bigger than the HALON button on the wall. He nodded quickly, "*Babylon*, *Tikrit* and *Great_Leader*, oh please, don't shoot."

Harper already turned away from the man and holstered the Glock.

Stillwell landed heavily on his feet and yelled, "What kind of butcher are you?"

Harper typed: **babylon**

The machine responded: **connected**

Harper lifted his gaze and said quietly, "Lieutenant, you've got two more minutes to make sure that HALON system doesn't work."

"You shot two men in cold blood. They were tied up like turkeys!" screamed Stillwell. His hands trembled as he pointed at the three bloodied men.

Harper narrowed his eyes fighting the self-hatred boiling inside. He said evenly, "Lieutenant, we killed a whole bunch of people getting into this place." He took a deep breath steadying himself, "And we're probably going to kill a bunch more getting out of here with our short and curlys intact. Now, you've got a job to do. I've got a job to do. If you've got time, cut the healthy one loose so he can take care of his buddies. But whatever you do Lieutenant, *don't get in my way. I'm not going to leave anyone behind today.*" Even as he said the last something whispered in the back of his brain—*death was coming and he couldn't stop it.*

He turned back to the console and sat down. He needed to destroy the ability of the system to recover. The best way to do that was to erase the SYSTEM tablespace and control files. The data dictionary, which is the repository of all information, related to the database would tell him what he needed to know. Oracle's data dictionary was amongst the best in the business. With two queries, he knew where everything was located and he shutdown the database instances.

★ ★ ★

The Saudi E3A AWACS was manned and piloted by American personnel. It had been one of the compromises made by George Bush to keep Israel from bombing Saddam back to the Stone Age during *Desert Shield.* The agreement continued with the current administration, basically due to disinterest and distaste for foreign policy.

The airman and his captain continued to watch the progression of the three RAF Sea Kings across the desert into the no-fly zone. How could three *Sea Kings* suddenly appear in a Baghdad suburb? The AWACS was fully capable of tracking hundreds of targets all the way into the Northern no-fly zone.

They displayed a satellite photo of the area, and the captain asked, "What's out there?"

The airman shrugged. "Nothing, just rocks and dirt. Based on their present heading, they'll pass into Saudi territory in about seventeen minutes."

The captain tapped the greenish display, "What's the intercept time for the F-16?"

"About three minutes."

"Call sign?"

"AJAX-3."

The last thing the captain wanted was a repeat of a particularly bad incident where a *Blackhawk* helicopter had been shot down in the Northern no-fly zone due to a lack of coordination. He closed his eyes and counted to ten.

"Patch me into the Falcon."

The airman punched some buttons saying, "AJAX-3, this EAGLE-7."

The pilot's voice crackled on the speaker.

The captain to the microphone and explained, "AJAX-3, your target is of unknown origin with valid NATO transponders, however, perform a best effort IFF. If they fumble, assume targets hostile and execute shoot down."

"Roger that, EAGLE-7," came the crackling reply. A tape was now rolling recording the radar plots, voice communications, and the computer projections. The tape would continue until the action was resolved.

☆ ☆ ☆

Duri looked out over the desert floor. The heat whipped up and broiled them in their airborne roasters. The steady beat of the rotors lulled him to lean his head back and close his eyes. They were seven minutes from the target. He had to assume Harper had not placed all his assets on the offensive. The rocket pods should dispose of any opposition from the ground. What could infantry do against an attack in force from the air?

Each helicopter carried fifteen men in full battle dress. Given the extreme heat, his men were sweating faster than they could drink. Water bottles already littered the desert floor on the angle of their flight. This was their desert, and they trained to fight in the heat. They would prevail.

The squeal of the radar detectors jolted Duri from his rest. His eyes settled on the blinking black box. The co-pilot flipped the alarm off and rattled in Arabic, "American fighter radar."

"Speak English," snapped Duri. He looked at the challenge/reply card taped to the clipboard. He feared they would soon learn how reliable the information was that they paid for every week.

The pilot said quickly over the private band to the pilots of the other two helicopters. "Prepare for evasive action."

The radio crackled, "Unidentified flight, this is the United States Air Force. Respond to challenge *Captain Crunch*."

Duri focused on the first word and cursed under his breath. The challenge word on the card read *Bugs Bunny*.

The pilot twisted around to glare at Duri who shrugged in reply.

★ ★ ★

Aboard EAGLE-7, they heard a clipped British accent respond, "*Bugs Bunny*."

The airman blinked and read the today's response: *Wiley Coyote*. The captain guessed that whoever was charged with the job of coming up with call sign/countersign had a six-year-old and cable connection to the Cartoon Network.

"Come again?" crackled AJAX-3.

"*Bugs Bunny*." There seemed to be a certain amount of stress in the reply.

The captain on the AWACS clicked the microphone, "AJAX-3, you have bandits, execute shoot down!" He released the microphone and whispered, "I hope to God I'm right."

★ ★ ★

The Iraqi helicopter pilot yelled, "Evasive action!"

The co-pilot twisted the radio band to Iraq's special military band and said quickly, "This is HARVEST flight! This is HARVEST flight. We are under attack by US fighters. Repeat we are under attack by US fighters!"

The helicopter jinxed violently and dipped even closer to the desert floor. The three *Sea Kings* broke into a blossom sliding in three directions away from their axis of flight.

☆ ☆ ☆

The *Falcon* spun sideways and dropped from its cruising altitude towards the rough terrain below. Her pilot flipped the safeties off his weapons. His radar screen identified three bandits moving at roughly one-hundred-twenty-five knots.

"Safeties off."

He was carrying six AIM-9L Sidewinders. Two on the wingtips and four more mounted on the under wing pylons. The AIM-9L is an all angle heat-seeking missile capable of targeting an airborne target from any angle within a conflict sphere. Unlike Vietnam and the old F4 *Phantoms*, when pilots had to maneuver into a rear arc of the enemy aircraft, the AIM-9L is a true 'fire and forget me' weapon.

He pushed the throttle forward snapping through the sound barrier and sending a noticeable sonic boom rippling into the still air. He accelerated from four to five to six times the speed of his targets eliminating the distance and improving kill probabilities.

☆ ☆ ☆

Captain Burns snapped his head up as the air cracked with a sonic boom. His eyes found the sky and his attention no longer centered on the entrance to the Data Center. Coalition aircraft did not break the sound barrier, because it ate up fuel and cut loiter time over enemy territory.

"Kincaid, you hear that?" he whispered.

"Ours or theirs?" asked Anderson.

"If they're fast movers we're way out of position," replied Kincaid staring at the useless Claymore mines and anti armor weapons. He shoved the clacker under a rock and stared into the northeastern horizon.

"Major, we got problems," whispered Anderson into his throat mike.

★ ★ ★

The target square centered on the nearest of the three *Sea Kings*. It blinked from red to a solid green square and a tone audible through the headphones and cockpit of the *Falcon* sounded.

"I got tone! I got tone!" he shouted and thumbed the red fire button. The rocket motor on the left wingtip mounted Sidewinder ignited and accelerated from the side of the Falcon at better than three times the speed of sound.

"Fox Two!"

★ ★ ★

Kincaid felt the explosion before he heard it. He scrambled from his position and pulled a set of binoculars up to his face. Things were definitely deteriorating.

The desert snapped into sharp focus and an angry black cloud mushroomed upwards from the desert floor. Through the shimmer, he could see a large helicopter pumping flares into the sky. They looked like angry aspirin tablets popping out the side of the helicopter and to the right of the craft.

Kincaid shifted his position and said, "I count one, two—three Jolly Green Giants incoming." He dropped the binoculars back to his chest. "Did you copy that?" he snapped.

"You say three?" asked Burns.

"Three!" Kincaid snapped.

Burns hefted the RPG-7 rocket propelled grenade. It might not take a helicopter down, but with a little luck, it might even the odds. "I got the RPG. I'm moving for position," explained Burns.

"I'm gonna find myself a hole," said Kincaid.

★ ★ ★

Harper glanced up from main console and asked, "You hear that?"

Hayes tossed the jerry can away. "We got big problems."

"Lieutenant its time to leave." Harper stood and fired a round into the console. The monitor burped back some flames and slid sideways on the table.

Stillwell glared at him. "Where we going? Its safer here than up there." He jerked a thumb upwards.

Harper shook his head. "Lieutenant, think about it. We've got three choppers inbound and a fast mover shooting at them. Those choppers have probably taken evasive action by heading for the desert floor. Its getting close to the hottest part of the day, so what kind of missile do you think their using out there?

"Radar homing?" Harper shook his head. "Too much ground clutter," he explained. "They're using heat seeking missiles, and if you get close enough to the desert floor, how is the missile going to know whether it's a hot rock or a hot engine at the terminal moment?"

Stillwell concentrated on the words. Through his anger, the common sense assessment of their situation began to register.

"The fast mover may get one of the choppers, but not all three. That's too much to hope for. Besides, they're coming to rescue these fine folks from the crazy Americans. We'd better be out of this hole by the time they land, or we'll be taking up permanent residence." Harper pulled his gas mask on and motioned Stillwell to do the same.

Hayes tripped the timer on bombs wired to the HP-9000's disk drive shelf. "Two minutes, major." He slid his mask in place.

Harper motioned to the three technicians and said through the mask, "You've got a choice, you can take you're chances with the bomb, or you can go upstairs."

They scrambled and hobbled off the raised floor and towards the stairwell. Blood dribbled down legs, and they were beginning to wheeze as the nerve gas began to wrench at their consciousness. Harper waited till they got through the upper stairwell door before abandoning them. The technicians might not pass out, but they certainly would be out of the way for the moment.

Harper, Hayes, and Stillwell started running for the air vents. The front door would just get too much attention.

★ ★ ★

The doomed *Sea King* turned to play chicken with a bullet. The Thiokol Hercules and Bermite Mk 36 Mod 11 rocket motor pushed the Sidewinder missile warhead towards a certain target at speeds approaching Mach three and with deadly certainty of infrared seeker system perfected over the last forty years. It was one hundred ninety pounds of pure death.

There was no possibility of visually sighting the missile with a five-inch diameter coming out of the sun, so the pilot guessed rather than knew. He jerked the yoke to one side sending the *Sea King* on a course sixty degrees from his axis of flight. Flares popped off the side of the helicopter as its engines attempted to drag two pilots and fifteen men from the incoming missile.

Physics, space, and time worked against their effort. AJAX-3 had launched from a distance less than three miles. The Sidewinder could cover the distance in less than fifteen seconds from a standing start, but the Sidewinder had the benefit of the *Falcon's* airspeed to send it on its way. In essence, the Sidewinder was already flying at supersonic speeds when the rocket motor ignited, and the seeker cone obtained an infrared signature.

Technically, the missile never impacted the *Sea King*. Instead, the nine-foot missile's electronic brain determined that it and the target were within lethal blast proximity. The solid-state brain ignited the twenty-one pound fragmentation warhead and sent a fatal blast into the *Sea King's* side.

The blast toppled the Sea King from a twenty degree slant to something over ninety degrees. The helicopter seemed to jump away from the blast and then turn sideways in the air. The rotors were slicing vertically in the air dragging the helicopter at an impossible angle towards the ground. Flames danced along the airframe. Some of the Republic Guard soldiers cartwheeled from the open sides of the fuselage.

After an impossibly long moment, the *Sea King* simply rolled completely over and died. It hit the hard desert floor like a broken toy. It was further flattened as gravity, speed, and mass combined to scattered broken bodies and helicopter pieces.

★ ★ ★

Duri stared at the fallen aircraft and swung himself into the cockpit. "How much longer?" he shouted.

The co-pilot spun in his seat. His eyes told Duri, the man was close to the panic level. The Iraqi Air Force had not fared well against the Americans during the Gulf War. Things had not improved since the end of the war. Lack of flight time, training, and the confidence inculcated by an *esprit d'corps* produced tentative pilots.

"How much longer?" shouted Duri.

The pilot pulled his headphones off and snapped, "One more minute, Colonel. If we're still alive."

Duri nodded. "You still need to strafe the ridges before you set us down."

The pilot pushed hard on the throttle and said bitterly, "In case it escaped your notice, one of our helicopters just got blown out of the sky. Now, we're deep inside the no-fly zone and it isn't going to take that American pilot more than twenty seconds to turn and reacquire us as targets."

"Then I suggest you get us there quickly!" spat Duri.

★ ★ ★

Burns scrambled to the top of a ridge holding the RPG-7 over his shoulder. He heard rather than saw the *Sea King*. The smoke from the fallen chopper was rising off the desert floor. All too quickly, the downdraft from the second *Sea King's* rotors found him.

He spun to see the enemy. They were the proud remnants of a humiliated army, and for the first time, they had an American soldier in their grasp. The 7.62mm rounds ripped through Burns' face and hands. The Kevlar vest and helmet absorbed multiple rounds. They slowed penetration, but the direct fusillade turned him into hamburger.

Burns screamed an agonizing, "No!" and fell backwards off the ridge.

Their victory was brief. The *Sea King* pilot never saw the HEAT round. It penetrated the Plexiglass air screen and exploded sometime after decapitating the pilot. A second round followed the first, and fire raged from the interior cockpit. The *Sea King* nosed forward skidding down the ridge before landing on its side.

The rotor blades dug into the rock and sand breaking off. The shattered blades spun into hundreds of metal shards. Captain Kincaid never felt a thing as one of the shards from the rotor sliced through his body armor. The air simply left his lungs and spun his body backwards. Kincaid never found a hole deep enough.

★ ★ ★

"EAGLE-7, EAGLE-7. I have launch warning. Repeat I have launch warning!"

The captain stared at the radar screen and murmured, "What have we stumbled on to?"

The radar detector from AJAX-3 was uplinked to an orbiting satellite and bounced back to the computer systems on EAGLE-7.

"EAGLE-7. I have launch!" The tone from the radar detector droned in the background.

"Executing counter measures."

The computer examined the wavelength of the captured radar signals, and reported AJAX-3 had come to the attention of a Russian made SA-11, known by its NATO designation of *Gadfly*.

"Where'd that come from?" asked the Captain before adding. "They're not supposed to have any of those." *Another one of Saddam's surprises.*

The airman typed in a command on his keyboard and displayed the launch point. It lay between Baghdad and the *Sea King* helicopters.

"Isn't that over the route the choppers took?"

"Yes, Sir."

"We got anything else close?"

The airman shook his head, "Everything is at least five minutes away."

"AJAX-3, this is EAGLE-7. Break off attack. Repeat. Break off attack."

"What's the speed and distance on that thing?"

The airman popped a window up and a secondary display. "According to the book, range is somewhere around thirty-five klicks. Speed is anybody's guess."

"Route him into Saudi territory and get a tanker to rendezvous with him. He'll be running on empty by the time that missile runs out of gas."

"Yes, Sir."

☆ ☆ ☆

As the Harvest Flight missile climbed into the air over the Data Center, the count down timer attached to the last two bombs inside the Data Center reached zero. Both explosive charges ignited above and below the racks of disk drives. The temperature at the explosion's epicenter exceeded two thousand degrees Fahrenheit. The plastic clamshell disk drive covers vaporized, and the harder polymer drive cases melted.

The disk drive heads slammed into the drive platters creating irreparable gouges on the media surface. The media platters, where so many secrets were kept, warped and sagged in the instant before it was ripped apart by the concussive effects of plastic explosives and petroleum vapors.

The weakest point in the computer room was the ceiling. The floor rested on solid rock and walls made of reinforced concrete. The blast naturally funneled straight up into the Data Center's office area. Cubical walls, terminals, and a great deal of paper provided the necessary fuel to complete the job.

There were secondary explosions as the desktop PC screens began to cook off. All safety systems failed to perform their missions as a catastrophic system failure engulfed the Data Center, and important people through Iraq began to wonder why their database queries were taking so long today.

A thick, greasy, black smoke began to filter throughout the upper level and find the exhaust vents. The HALON system finally activated, and flushed the oxygen from the lower level, but it was too late to save the charred and useless chassis skeletons. The damage was massive and complete.

26

Persian Gulf, Monday, November 17, 1997,
3:00 PM (+3.00 GMT)

The *Springfield* slid through the shallow depths towards the shattered *Han* class boat. Attached to the escape trunk was a forty-nine foot steel pipe that looked like a torpedo on steroids.

It was the DSRV-1 *Mystic* (Deep Sea Rescue Vehicle) newly arrived in the gulf from the United States Naval Support Facility on Diego Garcia. Diego Garcia is a horseshoe shaped archipelago located in the British Indian Ocean Territory. It serves as the last link in the logistical supply chain that stretches around the world and connects the east and west coasts of the United States.

It is the largest of fifty-two islands forming the Chagos Archipelago in the heart of the Indian Ocean. It was originally discovered and subsequently lost by the Portuguese during the early 1500's. It was claimed by France in the early 1700's, and remained a French possession until the defeat of Napoleon at Waterloo when it became a spoil of war in 1814 passing to the British Empire. Over the next one-hundred-seventy years, it remained a quiet and profitable copra oil plantation.

The pressures of the cold war, the dangers of the Indian bomb tests in the early 1970's, and the growing importance of the Gulf Oil States prompted a convenient agreement between the United States and Great Britain to use the island as a forward outpost. However, the true importance did not become obvious until the Shah fell from power in

1979. The ever so vital listening posts in Iran used to eaves drop on the message traffic in the old Soviet Empire went the way of diplomatic sovereignty and the Carter administration.

A massive effort to replace the lost intelligence assets was launched. In addition, to cold war agreement between Ronald Reagan and the Red Chinese was implemented to place listening posts in Northwest China. The Diego Garcia listening posts became the eyes and ears to keep tabs on a disintegrating Soviet Empire, an increasing hostile Indian sub continent, and the ever troublesome Gulf Region. It also proved to be an excellent staging area for search and rescue, and naval support facilities. Thus, one of two of the Navy's deep submergence Rescue Vehicles came to a permanent base in the heart of the Indian Ocean.

The DSRV was created in response to the *USS Thresher* accident. The *Thresher* was lost with all hands in 1963 due to the application of diesel submarine standards to nuclear submarine requirements. The result was a catastrophic failure and the loss of a multimillion-dollar submarine. The Navy simply had no rescue capability to dive deep enough. Hence, the *Mystic* and the *Avalon* were born.

The *Mystic* is equipped with modern electronics, microprocessors, and fiber optic links to the pressure enclosed cameras. The *Mystic* is capable of diving to five thousand feet. It is powered by electric motors using silver/zinc batteries, and can manage four knots. It was precisely the rescue tool needed to examine the wreckage on the bottom of the gulf.

With little fanfare, the *Mystic* drifted away from the larger, deadlier *Springfield.* A bank of super bright halogen lamps snapped on cutting the gloom at five hundred feet. The single shaft whirred into life pushing the thirty-eight ton super hardened submarine towards the prize. Once clear of the *Springfield's* conning tower, she banked sharply and dove towards the dead Chinese submarine.

The *Han* was broken in half. The bow showed evidence of a single blast where the forward ballast tanks were ripped angrily outwards. The entire titanium frame seemed twisted like so many threads on a screw.

The conning tower appeared to have splintered dumping pipes, wire, and antennae over the ocean floor. It looked a like a child's tinker toy set scattered after a tantrum. The silence of death still lingered on the site, and the violent gouges on the bottom were silent reminders of the *Han's* death spiral.

So far, the fish remained distant from the newly arrived feature. It still held the dull, black, rubberized sheen of a functioning warship. The bright lights danced across unscathed patches on the hull. Here and there, a hint of orange or yellow beckoned towards the open water, but the four ADCAP torpedoes had secured this gravesite to its final resting place on the bottom. There were no lights, or electronic hum, or machine noises.

Nothing penetrated the gloomy silence where the *404* came to rest on its final voyage. No letters home or final messages—the *404* had followed others under the sea, and this time the sea claimed its due. The deadly game of cat and mouse resulted in one less mouse.

Andy Hawkins brought the *Mystic* towards the open torpedo hatches on the bow. Behind him, a bank of video recorders captured everything. The cameras were enclosed in pressurized capsules and mounted above and below the halogen light rack. A passive sonar array and radar system mapped the remains of the *404*. An intelligence bonanza lay on the bottom, but speed was important. Items like codebooks, missile keys, launch systems, and electronic gear needed to be salvaged quickly.

Lucy Rabin slid back in her chair and started tapping on one of several computer keyboards located inside the *Mystic's* hull. While the DSRV was officially a Navy boat, Andy and Lucy worked directly for Louis Edwards. Diego Garcia was as much an intelligence listening post as it was a Navy Support Facility. The world had become a much more devious place with the fall of the Soviet Empire, and the proliferation of additional blue water navies made the possibility of additional naval accidents greater. Louis Edwards was a man who argued probabilities, and the *404's* unfortunate demise vindicated the expense of training Andy and Lucy.

The nuclear reactor had not ruptured. There was some additional radiation, and in the coming months, it would become a problem, but for the moment, the hardened *Mystic* would protect its crew against the hazardous atom.

"Would you look at that?"

Lucy turned to the color monitor canted down above the pilot's seat. Andy fished a fiber optic video probe through the ruptured torpedo tube causing it to slither through the outer and inner hatches. There on the racks were three Chinese torpedoes still secure to their racks. The fourth, having been fired, was missing.

"The weapon techs are going to love this. See any manuals?"

Andy wiggled the joystick on the console revealing the crushed remains of two crewmen. They must have forgotten to close the outer hatch once they fired the torpedo. It appeared the inner hatch ruptured and a pillar of seawater smashed into the cramped weapons room as solid as forged steel. "At least, it was quick," whispered Andy.

Andy pulled the probe away from the macabre scene and spooled the wire back into its housing. He pulled the mission folder they had received and reviewed en route to the site.

"Any idea where the other half of the boat is?"

Lucy examined the magnetometer, "According to the sonar tape we listened to, it sounded like they were attempting to blow ballast tanks just prior to the first explosion."

"Yeah, the sonar guy didn't think the first torpedo actually hit the boat," said Andy. It was hard to believe anything had missed considering the mess before them.

Lucy nodded agreement. "Okay, so lets think about what was happening. You are the captain of a crippled submarine. I mean the noise we heard on their sonar tapes certainly wasn't the sound of something healthy." She tapped the photograph from the U2 displaying an opening on the deck. "Now, suppose the reason you made all that noise is because you have a big hole in your deck and you have cavitation where there never used to be."

Andy nodded as he pulled the *Mystic* away from the *404's* bow. "That would mean the boat would be light in the bow relative to the stern. An emergency blow might lift the bow ahead of the rest of the boat at maybe a forty five or even sixty degree angle." He stopped imagining the deck sliding upwards beneath their feet seconds before the first of four torpedoes hit. People, charts, books, and anything else not secure would flutter in a deadly blizzard through the interior of the boat.

"The hull is already weakened by the initial problems. They probably couldn't take much more stress. So they take a desperation gamble hoping to ride out the explosion as they head for the surface," continued Lucy tapping the monitor. Her finger traced the rupture line along the forward ballast tank.

Andy snapped his finger. He rolled a second camera back towards the conning tower. "Of course, the first torpedo explodes based on proximity to the target. It figured out it was suddenly increasing the distance and triggered the first explosion."

Lucy followed his gaze to the monitor displaying the conning tower. He manipulated a second light rack and sent a blaze of several thousand candle power. "But the second torpedo hit high. It must have compensated for the movement of the *404*."

"Yeah, yeah. But the first blast took out the ballast tanks, or at least caused them to start leaking badly."

Lucy was into the mind game now. She visualized the slant of the deck and the angle of the initial two torpedoes. "But now the boat is starting to drop and the second torpedo is too close to compensate." She tapped the center of the screen. "No wonder the conning tower is gone. The torpedoe plowed right into the top and exploded due to impact."

"Blasts on top and bottom—that would account for the twisting effect on the hull. They snapped the hull in half most likely, and what we don't know is how shallow she was when she was hit. But judging from the troughs in the sea bed she must have hit pretty hard."

Lucy shook her head, "I don't think the conning tower hit was enough to break the hull." She traced a scorch mark running diagonally down the side of the hull. She tapped the video monitor screen. "This looks like it hit sideways and slid along the hull until it exploded. It could be the pressure hull was already compromised and maybe that lessened the blast damage."

Andy was quiet for a moment; "You think they were still alive after the second torpedo?"

She shrugged. "I doubt there was much that could save her by then. But this shallow, there might have been a chance to get some of the crew off alive." She manipulated the camera angle and zoomed out providing a more wide-angle view of the wreck. " I suppose the rest of the boat is over there." She cocked a finger.

Andy pushed the throttle forward and spun the agile *Mystic* in the direction Lucy indicated. However, the powerful halogen lamps did not find the rest of the *404,* nor did the powerful sonar equipment image the shape. Instead, the radioactivity detector alarm sounded. The *Mystic* stopped its forward progress and floated upwards until the alarm snapped off.

"Guess, the reactor core isn't as secure as we thought," he murmured.

Both of them were already angling the camera towards the bottom to find the hazard. The reactor vessel was producing enough heat to create steam at a depth of five hundred fifty feet. A steady stream of bubbles gurgled from a dented, spherical, blackened steel chunk. What was left of the core was dissipating radioactivity and heat into the greater ocean.

"The core dropped right through the hull," suggested Andy. "That would certainly weaken the hulls' integrity."

"Just about snap it in half, and give anyone still alive a lethal dose. That assumes they survived the blast resulting from this disaster," she sighed. Radiation burns were akin to being cooked alive from the inside out. It was not a pleasant thought to consider men still alive in stale air and a watery tomb to be finally cooked alive by their own systems.

Andy pushed the control yoke forward and steered the *Mystic* beyond the reactor core. Someone would notice the sudden release of energy on the ocean floor via satellite. He only hoped that it was American satellites that saw the blast and not a Russian or Chinese bird in orbit. Anyone who came to look would recognize obvious external blast damage and come up with aggressive action. No one would want to advertise torpedoes had been fired in anger.

"You figure its farther east?"

Lucy nodded.

They found the other half of the *404* some fifteen minutes later. Clearly, it had suffered blast damage from the final two torpedoes. It was a twisted and mangled hulk hanging over the lip of a shallow canyon. The massive screw lay shattered on the bottom several yards distant, and the massive holes created by direct hits testified to the sudden end for the *404*.

Andy brought the *Mystic* over top of the *404*. The hard radiation from the core was far enough away to not set off the alarms. He glanced at the U2 photographs and tapped the one where a square patch appeared on the deck of the boat. "Louis said the NRO people thought this was where the missile hatches should have been."

Lucy nodded as she worked the camera bank to point straight on. Andy swung the *Mystic* to point straight at the missile deck. The Halogen lamps swept up over the ocean floor to stabilize on the deck, and both stared at the digitally enhanced picture displayed on the monitors. The video recorders continued to capture every moment. The audio recorders heard their first impressions. The enormity of their discovery first came from Lucy.

"That's an elevator—like on an aircraft carrier."

Andy nodded, "Only smaller." He flipped one of the zoom lenses and fed the video to the central monitor. "You see that?" He worked a mouse cursor to point towards his interest.

"Uh huh."

"That's a cable and it's fouled in the jamb of the elevator platform." He shifted the focus displaying the shredded remains of a neoprene covering. "The cable must have slapped the side of the boat until it shredded the sound insulation." He backed off the magnification. "There, there, and there," he said spinning the pointer to different points on the screen.

"The whole compartment must be flooded." She tapped out a calculation. "No wonder she was so noisy and sluggish. If a space equal to the missile bay were flooded, it might not be possible for her to ever surface again. She might have been too heavy to make it to the surface." The remains of the *404* lay sideways tilted more than ninety degrees over the keel. Even if watertight compartments remained, there was no known method to extract men from those compartments with a vessel at such an extreme attitude.

The *Mystic* rested ten feet away from the elevator platform. Deftly a metallic arm unfolded from beneath the light and video array. The arm extended about seven feet beyond the forecastle of the *Mystic* before Andy snapped the hydraulic locks in place. He nudged the boat ahead dead slow.

"I'm going to bet this platform was held in place by some sort of hydraulic system. Now, since it never locked in place, there aren't any interlocks to prevent us from moving it. The only thing that could stop us is if the hydraulic lift is still functional." He shrugged. "My guess is that every pipe that could be ruptured was—when the reactor hit the water, or the last two ADCAP's hit this sub."

The leading edge of the *Mystic's* arm came to rest on the center of the platform. Andy started applying thrust, and somewhere above two knots, the elevator platform moved. He reversed thrust and pulled the *Mystic* away fearful that they might smash into the dead hulk and tumble into the canyon they hovered above.

The elevator platform slid about six feet before stopping. It hung with a dark frame of the broader opening below and grinned like a Jack-O-Lantern beckoning them towards tricks.

Andy was working the fiber optic video and light probe that he had used on the torpedo tube, when Lucy screamed. He snapped his head up to see a yellow suited sailor floating into their lights. His features twisted in agony and his suit perforated with acid like burns. Andy choked back the bile rising in his throat and pulled the *Mystic* from the ugly grip of death hovering outside their antiseptic world.

"Biohazard suit!" exclaimed Lucy. "He's wearing a biohazard suit," she gasped trying to regain her composure.

"Didn't do him much good," joked Andy.

She choked off a nervous laugh. "Guess not."

Andy used the arm to push the dead man out of the way. The yellow clad corpse bobbed away from the opening. The yellow was striped with angry acid like burns. The fabric flapped in the motion of the currents and flashes of dead white flesh peaked out. Most of the facemask was clouded with blood and a milky white substance. Whatever had happened to the sailor, it happened a long before the four torpedoes from the *Springfield* arrived.

They returned to the grim opening where the missile bay should have been. The probe snaked into the dark opening. Both of them ignored the monitor displaying the entrance of the probe and concentrated on the high gain display. Coupled with the fiber optic probe were two hundred-watt dime-size halogen bulbs.

The ruptured remains of a barrel lay on its side. It looked like it had bounced around on the deck. "You know, this looks like it got crunched in the elevator."

Andy grunted and moved the probe to the side of the crumpled barrel. "That looks like a bullet hole to me."

Lucy leaned over his shoulder and squinted at the ragged oblong hole. A steel jacketed 123-grain round from an AK-47 could easily punch through stainless steel. Lucy's father had learned that the hard way by shooting an MAK-90 at a half inch steel plate. Instead of causing the plate to spin, the rounds punched holes right through the steel plate. The Norinco Munitions Company produced steel jacketed ammunition for a variety of clients. Iraq was probably number one on the client list.

"I wonder if the stuff was under pressure."

"You think we found one of the barrels."

Lucy nodded. "It would be better if we had one of the barrels in tact. But that would be asking too much."

Andy twisted the joystick again to pan the rest of the storage chamber. He stopped and stared at the screen. There strapped to the deck was a stainless steel barrel with Chinese characters—an international biohazard symbol in reflective orange blinked back at them.

He pushed the probe closer examining the barrel. It appeared to be intact. "Well, we've got hard evidence. I wonder what they'll do with it?"

27

New Jersey Turnpike, Sunday, November 16, 1997, 9:00 PM EST

Trooper Margaret Daniels cruised through Sunday night traffic in one of the Crown Victoria Stealth cruisers. She was the first female trooper to be assigned one of the *super cars.* The conventional overhead lighting and siren systems had been removed to provide a sleeker silhouette for traffic enforcement on the thirty-four thousand miles of roads patrolled by the New Jersey State Police. The prominent triangular shaped state police logo was imprinted on the door panels.

The cruiser was another advance from a paper system to a fully computerized and nationwide integrated law enforcement network. It had specialized cameras, computers, and a communication array mounted in a touch screen package between the two front seats. A wire mesh cage barrier separated the driver compartment from the holding area in the rear seat. The Remington 870 shotgun was mounted vertically next to the driver and a Colt AR-15 rifle was tucked away in the trunk.

Margaret took great pride in the fact that she was the first female trooper assigned a Stealth cruiser, or that she was one of the path finders in the previous all-male domain of the State Police. She made sure her uniform was perfect every day, and worked very hard to place towards the top in weapons training and qualifications. Everyday she made sure the uncomfortable Second Chance bulletproof vest was secured beneath her clothing. The Heckler & Kock Service pistol chambered in

.40 S&W was strapped securely to her web belt along with mace, hand cuffs, two additional high capacity magazines, a spot for a telescoping baton, a spare set of keys, and a power pack to manage the remote radio clipped to her shoulder.

The nearest troopers were probably twenty-five miles down the turnpike patrolling their own sectors. The radio chatter disappeared into the background and the comfort of the Crown Victoria surrounded her like a cuddly blanket. Tomorrow would be a day off. Margaret planned to spend it painting the back bedroom. Her sister was planning to visit for Thanksgiving in a week and half. The bedroom needed a fresh coat of paint, and of course, the meal needed to be planned. She already had a department turkey in the freezer downstairs.

She thought about her niece and nephew who were growing up faster than she cared to remember. She pushed from her mind a failed marriage and the lack of her own children. After all, she had her career to keep her company. Somehow, a career was always the right kind of company she needed. Most times of the year, she could push the need from her thoughts, but the holidays from Thanksgiving to Christmas and New Years seemed to get harder each year. The holiday instituted by Abraham Lincoln to remember God for his bounty during the year past and the celebration of the Babe in Bethlehem left her cold.

The impending arrival of her sister would help her get through Thanksgiving, and she had already scheduled herself to work during the Christmas and New Year holidays. Working was a remedy—for now. She knew instinctively, it would not be a remedy forever. She could feel her biological clock ticking and the desire for her own baby and family continue to press itself closer and closer to her conscious reality. For now, she had the job and the duty. For now, it was enough.

She swung through an interchange to start back on her loop. As she accelerated back onto the turnpike, she saw the Virginia license plate out the corner of her eye. Virginia plates were not unusual. The compact nature of states in this part of the country and relative two hundred twenty mile drive along the Washington/New York corridor certainly brought all nature of travelers along the road.

It was the car, and the plate described by the federal fugitive warrant that had arrived in the thermal fax printer a couple of hours ago. She flipped to the warrant on her clipboard and checked the plate number against the car ahead of her. A charge of adrenaline sizzled through her small frame. The plate numbers matched!

She dropped the clipboard back to the seat and clicked the radio mike. "This is Sierra Tango four seven zero. I am in pursuit of Federal fugitive warrant, requesting backup."

She slid the cruiser to the fast lane and angled to the left rear quarter of the other car before hitting full lights and siren. She reached down and unsnapped the retention strap on her holster before placing both hands firmly on the wheel.

While it was never truly dark on the turnpike, this was a rural stretch of highway and the number of cars was sparse by this point on a Sunday night. The illumination of all the cruiser's lights was akin to lighting the White House Christmas Tree. The cruiser brought immediate attention to anyone driving. She punched the gas feeling the power rush up from the engine and grab the road. Within seconds, she was next to the other car and pointing towards the side of the road.

An oriental man looked at her with a confused expression, before nodding and easing the car onto the shoulder. Margaret let up on the gas and pulled in behind the Virginia car. The dashboard camera was already delivering a live feed broadcast to the nearest State Police Headquarter station. The spotlights on either side of the Crown Victoria were painting her fugitives in excess of four hundred Watts.

She killed the siren and said, "That was easy."

Getting out of the car, she put her hat on and let her right hand drift down to the grip on the H&K pistol. She stood behind the barrier of her open car door and watched as two men got out of the car in front of her—one on each side.

She stepped around the open door and said in her command voice, "Put your hands on your heads."

Her reactions were far too slow in attempting to draw the H&K. The second man on the passenger side did as he was instructed, but with one exception. His hands held a Taurus Model 669 .357 Magnum revolver. It had a blued finish making it virtually invisible in the dark. It was only the gleam off the muzzle that first drew Margaret's attention.

Time suddenly slowed down as she started to drop into a crouch and pull her service pistol. However, the Taurus muzzle continued to rise towards presentation. She knew the statistics as well as anyone. They had been drilled into her head at the Lethal Force Institute. The average person can fire four rounds from a double action weapon inside of a second. The Taurus held six rounds.

A scream erupted from her lips as the muzzle blossomed with an angry flame. The load was 125 grain Golden Saber round. The first one hit her in the left breast and pancaked to twice its size. It slammed into her at slightly less than six-hundred foot pounds of force. Enough force to lift Margaret backwards and arch her back. The second shot took her square on the solar plexus driving all wind from her lungs and shutting down her hearing and vision. The third shot walked up towards her sternum. By then, she was already turning and spinning towards the hard pavement in front of her cruiser—its lights, electronics, and marvelous gadgets useless.

The Kevlar vest saved her life, but the impact of the heavy magnum rounds at a distance slightly less than ten yards drove the air from her lungs. The impact on her solar plexus converted her world from terrible panic to mushy grayness. Light and sound retreated from her senses and her head swam. Her knees buckled, as her body's stop button had been punched mercilessly by the 125 grain round. The final round scrambled her heart's normal electrical pulse and consciousness winked out.

The driver drew his own weapon and ran towards Margaret. It was a Colt Mustang .380. He ran towards Margaret and fired twice at her head. Adrenaline was surging through his limbs and his hands quivered. It was not the practiced and smooth aim of his partner in which he delivered these last two shots, and both miraculously missed their intended target—Margaret's head.

The first shattered her collarbone and exited into the pavement. The other hit the pavement first and ricocheted into her cheekbone. However, the New Jersey Turnpike absorbed most of the bullet's energy. Margaret suffered a broken cheekbone, but she would live.

The two Chinese agents turned and ran for their car. They left the trooper for dead and continued their road trip towards the United Nations Chinese Consulate. A pool of blood was forming under Margaret's head; the live feed from the cruiser's camera caused the machinery of the New Jersey State Police to swing into action. The words, "Officer down," rolled over the State Police Net, and a response back to the FBI's Federal Fugitive Warrant indicated the men they were chasing were armed and dangerous. The hunt began in earnest.

★ ★ ★

In the basement of the Odricks Corner house, Harvey examined the growing inventory of weapons, explosives, and electronic gadgets. It looked like they had taken down a survivalist group from atop an Idaho mountain.

Harvey examined the Remington 700 chambered in .300 Winchester with an obscenely long forty-power scope. It had been packed in an aluminum foam padded case. Nestled next to the power rifle were a flash deflector and a sound suppressor. He seriously doubted they were going prairie dog hunting. It looked more like a sniper outfit modeled around a perfectly legal weapon. The owner could practice at a public or private range possibly without arousing suspicion.

A pair of Mossberg 590 shotguns with pistol grips and mounted laser sites leaned against the wall. There were several boxes of 00 buckshot, number 4 buckshot, and rifled slug. The kind of ammunition used for self-defense and not for hunting waterfowl or blasting sporting clays.

An impressive array of Colt, Glock, and Ruger handguns lay on the table—mostly in 9 mm, .40 S&W and .45 ACP for the autoloaders, and .357 magnum for the revolvers. It was a liberal assortment of weapons chambered in .22 rimfire or .32 ACP—pocket pistols for close-in work and the heavy stuff to make sure people once hit stayed down.

Harvey sat on a stool in the basement as the evidence team continued to catalog, tag, and photograph everything that was found. He drank the last of his coffee.

Larry tossed a Diet Coke can into the garbage. It had been a long day, and the various exertions were beginning to tell. "Well, what's our next move?"

Harvey let a smile grace his features and stretched. "I don't think Assistant Director Feldman wants us walking up to the White House tomorrow, do you?" Lou Feldman was the Assistant Director in charge of Domestic Terrorism, and the word had arrived the that White House was no longer on Harvey's list.

Larry shrugged, "They'll get over it. We took down an illegal intelligence operation. We have a lot of evidence, and we kicked some bad guys out of town. Not too bad for a days work if you ask me."

Harvey nodded, "Yeah, but you know how it is. Every time we come close to the Chinese thing, someone from the White House calls somebody at the JEH building and we get our butts chewed."

"Goes with the territory," replied Larry, "but we need to decide what to do about tomorrow. Do we press it and show up at the West Wing?"

"The Secret Service isn't going to like it," continued Harvey. Not that he cared very much what the Secret Service liked or disliked.

"They're supposed to be cops like us. We all work for Uncle. We are supposed to be tracking down the bad guys."

Harvey looked around the basement and said quietly, "Even when the bad guys are running the country." He raised an eyebrow. "Even when we report to the bad guys eventually. We take down one of the biggest Chinese agents in the country, and the NSA calls the Director.

The Director calls the ADIC, and someone calls CNN to watch us make a war zone out of a neighborhood."

"It happens."

Harvey nodded again. "Okay, it happens. We know something rotten has been going down between the administration and Chinese government. Every so often, something pops up on the news like Chinese fundraisers or Buddhist monks or gardeners with big contributions.

"Now, yesterday someone pops open one of their dead letter drops and it brings the man himself out into the open. He's got four body guards, at least two safe houses, and weapons." He looked at the two tables full of guns and explosives. "Lots of weapons. You ever wonder what they were going to do with forty pounds of Semtex? Or, those cute little mercury fuses?

"We wander into a middle class neighborhood and find a couple of true believers who want to shoot it out with the Hostage Rescue Team. On top of that, the Chinese Ambassador drops by for a chat at the White House and we get yelled at for doing our jobs." He shook his head. "I don't exactly like what's happening."

"Perhaps, I could suggest another alternative."

Both men looked up to find the ubiquitous Louis Edwards standing on the stair steps. The top of half of his face covered with shadows. In his hands, he held a large Domino pizza.

"Pepperoni okay?" He tossed Larry a six-pack of Diet Cokes and came down the rest of the steps.

Larry pulled one of the cans free and said, "Yeah, it sounds real good."

"How long have you been standing there?"

Louis pulled up a stool. "Long enough to understand your frustration. Really, Agent Randall, you should put a little more trust in your fellow man." He held up a hand, "Not much mind you, but a little more. For this moment, we are on the same side."

"Meaning?" growled Harvey.

Louis shrugged as he flipped open the box and grabbed a pizza slice. "Meaning we might not always have the same objectives. Please have a slice before it gets cold." He pushed the pizza box towards Harvey.

"All right, I take it you have another brainstorm."

Louis smiled, "You two are after a Chinese agent inside the White House. Let's suppose for the moment that I'm after the same fellow. At least, let's suppose that I believe there is some sort of problem coming out of the White House."

They both nodded.

"I heard you say your superiors are displeased by the progress you've made today." Louis swallowed another bite and continued, "Everywhere I turn I seem to run into a Chinese connection. You chase spies inside our government, I chase something deadly in Iraq, and we come up with a Chinese connection."

Louis pulled an envelope from his suit coat and dropped it on the counter between them.

"What's that?" asked Larry.

"A bank account number."

Harvey opened the envelope and read the bank name and address. "This is in the Cayman Islands."

Louis nodded.

"So what?" said Larry.

Louis smiled, "So—even the Chinese have accountants and pay masters. An intelligence resource sitting inside the administration is not a cheap commodity, and perhaps, this one is smarter than Aldrich Ames. This one won't be stupid enough to spend his money conspicuously."

Neither Harvey nor Larry needed to be reminded of who Aldrich Ames was—the CIA mole that sold his country out for one and half million dollars to the old KGB. How many people ended up in damp, cold cellars waiting for a bullet in the back of the head, because Ames wanted to drive a Mercedes instead of a Chevy? No one knew the count. Ames's motivating factor had been greed, not ideology. The

KGB worked off that greed to learn intelligence and cipher secrets that still haunt the halls in Langley.

It appeared greed was working again for the Chinese. However, for greed to be a motivating factor, payment needed to come with very immediate and certain results. In an era of offshore banks, wire transfers, and Internet web sites, the paymasters could handle transactions at the blink of an eye sending money around the world half a dozen times before finally landing in the correct spot.

Harvey perused the piece of paper. "I need more than a vague spook reference."

Louis smiled. "Of course, Agent Randall. I would never expect you to take my word on anything. That particular bank is used by *Goldenrod* for certain types of transactions. Payments to people." He chuckled, "You see even the brightest and most agile scoundrels slip up eventually. Well, he's slipped up now. It's a pattern we've observed over the years."

They both stared at him.

"I see you haven't quite made the connection."

"We're not as twisted as all that," replied Larry.

"Of course. Well, it really is a rather trivial thing to do. We monitored the transfer of funds from a bank in Little Rock, Arkansas to this one in the Cayman Islands. This being a weekend, the money transfers would be rather light in that direction."

"Why Little Rock, Arkansas?"

Louis smiled, "Because the Indonesians own one of the banks in Little Rock. They bought it to handle large wire transfers into the United States without having to comply with all those troublesome banking regulations. And the Indonesians are owned by Chinese Central Committee."

"You can prove this?" asked Harvey.

"It depends on what you mean by *prove.* Would this stand up in a Federal Court with jurors and defense lawyers?" He shook his head.

"No, because the means used to find this information are not—shall we say—kosher with the Bill of Rights. However, if you're asking whether this is an accurate portrayal of the facts? Well then yes, I can prove what I am saying."

"So are you saying a wire transfer came from a bank in Little Rock to a bank in the Cayman Islands?" Larry asked.

"Last night," answered Louis, "sometime after your encounter with *Goldenrod* and sometime before you found him. In fact, *Goldenrod* must have been immensely pleased with the information. They wired one hundred thousand dollars."

Louis finished his pizza. "I might add that the Chinese are not in the habit of spending one hundred thousand dollars on mediocre product. This is grade A material, which means they must be absolutely confident of the source and veracity."

"Okay. I have an account. I can't do anything with it. The Caymans aren't going to cough up information on account because the FBI says 'pretty please,'" Harvey snapped.

Louis nodded.

"And unless I have a body in hand, I can't prove anything happened in that park last night," continued Harvey.

Louis nodded again.

"But you have something else up your sleeve," suggested Larry.

Louis nodded a third time. He pulled a second envelope from his suit coat and dropped it on the table.

"More riddles?" demanded Harvey.

"Those are the phone records for this address over the last ten days. You'll notice the highlighted entry for last night."

There in pale green highlighter was a phone number.

"It connects to an ISP."

"IS what?" asked Larry.

"Internet service provider," said Harvey quickly as he stared at the phone records and the Cayman bank number.

"Precisely. They sent the information out of the country last night. It's really painfully simple to burgle the West these days. All you need is a PC, a scanner, and a web browser. After that, you connect to an ISP and send whatever you wish to wherever you need to. By the time you captured *Goldenrod*, he'd already processed and transferred the data. Granted, it may have been encrypted and that might have taken an extra minute or so, but the point is they did it from this house last night."

He pointed across the room to the PC sitting with its skins pulled off. The small IDE drive was missing. Something the size of an over sized videotape cassette could be secreted in a number of places.

"Find the hard disk and your wizards at the JEH building can tell you what was sent. If it is what I suspect, then I think I can tell you who dropped if off for *Goldenrod*."

Larry coughed on his Diet Coke, "You've got a suspect?"

"I have three. You see gentlemen, it is in my interests to figure this out before Jim Harper gets back." He kept to himself the fact that Jim Harper might have a great deal of difficulty returning from Iraq. A cancelled mission and loss of support would probably stretch young Jonas beyond certain limits. He would need to tend to that matter before the night was over.

"What do you want in return?" asked Harvey.

"Ah, Agent Randall, always the perceptive one."

Harvey grunted.

"I wish to handle this traitor out of the glare and noise of news cameras. I prefer to handle this quietly."

"How quietly?" pressed Harvey.

"I don't think you want to know," replied Louis.

"We have something called the rule of law in this country," snapped Harvey.

"Indeed we do," responded Louis, and then he leaned forward. "A rule of law and due process for ordinary criminals. But what about the due process for all those people Aldrich Ames got killed?" He spat, "Ever think about that? He turned over every network we had in Eastern Europe. People just disappeared, and not only the people working for us, they took wives and husbands, and sons and daughters, and parents and grand parents. They took them out to fields and shot them. Or, they tortured them till you couldn't recognize them from hamburger.

"I know—I watched it happen," he paused and gathered himself. "Now, I've got a team in the field, and I think you're going to find the entire classified file on the hard disk. I think you're going to find encryption software and few other goodies. I made Harper into what he is. I made the final selections on the team. I'm not going to sit here and let somebody end up in the bottom of an Iraqi torture chamber because we have the rule of law. If I'm right, then I want him. That's my objective."

"And after you're done?" asked Larry.

"Let that rest on my shoulders and not yours."

Harvey stared at the floor. It was his cell phone that interrupted his concentration. He stood up and walked to a corner. When he came back, his face was somewhat paler than before.

"What is it?" asked Larry sensing something terribly wrong.

Harvey shook his head wishing for the nightmares to go away. "You know the Federal Fugitive Warrant we issued?"

"On the two Chinese guys?"

Harvey nodded. He screwed his eyes shut and said quietly, "They shot a State Trooper on the New Jersey Turnpike."

The air seemed to whistle through Larry's lips as he said, "Oh, no."

Harvey snapped his eyes open, "Edwards."

Louis turned to contemplate the FBI agent, "Yes."

"If you're right, you get him. But on one condition."

Louis waited.

"Larry never was part of this conversation. If something goes wrong, it was between you and me."

Louis nodded.

28

East Of Nukhayb, Iraqi Data Center, Monday, November 17, 1997, 4:00 PM (+3.00 GMT)

Harper looked over his shoulder and felt the hollowness that comes after action. Instead of the smug satisfaction in the knowledge he had devastated the Iraqi asset, he felt regret for killing and maiming so many people. He found the faces of the men cut down in the firefight on the lower level lingering on his conscience. Their surprise, then shock as Harper and company had mercilessly fired into their massed bodies. The impact of bullets on flesh, metal, and bone played tunelessly in his ears. The savage wounds inflicted by the shotgun slugs, explosives, grenades, and 5.56mm military rounds churned people into human hamburger.

What stuck with him, though, were the three technicians. He had asked his questions about the computer systems and passwords. There had been no response. They were being patriots to their country, or perhaps more frightened of the soldiers coming to rescue them. Harper revealed true terror as he dispassionately blasted two men's knee caps into oblivion. It had worked. Harper had attained a result necessary to complete the mission. But they were technicians, computer geeks that he could readily identify in a hundred jobs he had worked in the civilian sector. They were noncombatants. He had crossed the line again. A line he would never reveal to Lynn or his daughters. A line where the very nature of war stomped out everything he believed.

Stillwell had expressed shock and anger at his actions. His actions were shocking. He had taken a .45 ACP Glock, held it two feet above their kneecaps and fired a 230-grain hollow point round into their flesh. The round's diameter doubled to almost an inch. Blood and bone splattered into the air covering both Harper and his victims with gore. At the time, Harper had felt nothing. Instead, he was the coldly, calculated warrior dealing with a quickly deteriorating situation.

Maybe Stillwell was right. Maybe he was a monster. The mission was coming apart with the arrival of the Iraqis. Had he placed them in harm's way? No, the Iraqis arrived via helicopter, not truck. They came by air and through the Southern no-fly zone. That took planning and preparation. The trickle of fear dripped down the back of his neck. Had they been expected? Were his worst fears true?

Behind them, the smoke from the Data Center rose like an angry fist into the air. It was still boiling black smoke, which meant the plastic and silicone parts were starting to burn hard. The fumes were probably not toxic, but they could make the toughest soldier look for his barf bag.

They were some four hundred meters on the other side of the Data Center away from the Iraqi go team. The communication links, the machines, the technicians, and power supplies were all out of commission. The data tapes were sitting in a canvas sack next to Hayes's feet. He had the information. All he needed were some HP-9000's to bring it up on.

He took a drink from his canteen. The sweat was stinging his eyes, and his uniform clung to his body. Darkness would come in about four hours. There was too much time for the bad guys to get their act together and begin a systematic search, besides, Anderson was still sitting under his camouflage blanket at ground zero.

He brought his thoughts back to the immediate problems—survival. "Hayes, ammo check."

The black sergeant brought his head up. "I've got seven magazines for the M-16, four for my M-9, a couple grenades, and your data tapes."

"Stillwell?"

Brian checked his pouches. "I got ten magazines for the M-16, four for the Beretta and six grenades," replied Brian choosing to refer to the M-9 by its more popular civilian name.

Harper had maybe fifty shotgun shells left and plenty of magazines for the Browning and Glock. He had four grenades pinned to his Alice vest. The problem would be food and water—they had only what was left in their backpacks. The majority was sitting in the HMMWV's, and the chances of that remaining secret were nonexistent.

"As I see it, we've got to take out those soldiers before they can reinforce their forces."

Hayes nodded.

Stillwell stared at the dirt between his boots. He was tired and now Harper was talking about attacking a company of Iraqi soldiers.

Harper charged his throat mike, "Anderson, I would guess you're in the middle of this mess."

Anderson responded with a single click.

"Burns and Kincaid are dead?"

Click.

Harper sighed. He would deal with those problems later. He still had four men left and he needed to bring them out alive. "Anderson, have they found the Claymores?"

Click click.

Hayes looked up from his own thoughts and said, "I know how Kincaid set them up, and I'm pretty sure I know where he has the clacker."

Harper nodded. He drew in the dirt with his fingers. "Do you think you can get back to the detonators?"

Hayes smiled.

"We're Force Recon, Sir. We own the night. I'll need somebody help me pull the ragheads in."

"Bait."

Hayes nodded. They both looked over at Stillwell.

Brian met their gaze. "Bait?"

"Yes, Sir," replied Hayes. "You run real fast, dodge a lot of bullets and hit the ground when I tell you to."

"And?"

"And I push the detonator and kill as many of the bad guys as possible."

"And if that doesn't work?"

"Then, Lieutenant, we'll probably all be dead by morning," replied Harper matter-of-factly. "We need to keep them off balance until nightfall, and try to slip away. Of course, we can't just leave Anderson there in the middle of these folks, so we're going to have to bloody them some more in order to get our man out."

Stillwell nodded. "And you sir, what will you be doing in the mean time?"

"Keeping them busy on this end," Harper replied.

Stillwell rubbed his hands together. "Which one of you has orders to ensure I don't fall into Iraqi hands?"

Harper felt his heart turn to ice. There was something else going on here. Something he had not figured out yet. Stillwell was a game player and a weapons expert. He ran simulations with the help of high-powered PC's to determine the lethality of certain weapon systems. He probably also gamed those weapon systems to determine the best scenarios to employ those same weapons.

"Those are my orders, Lieutenant," said Hayes. He spat in the dirt. "All members of the Force Recon fire team were given those orders. If it looked like this might go down badly, our orders were to make sure you did not fall into Iraqi hands. They were spelled out to us before we arrived at Andrews."

Stillwell nodded as if he understood. "So you want me to act like bait and run straight towards a bank of Claymores. I'm suppose to put my trust in a man who has standing order to kill me if things fall apart, or I can hang with a madman who shoots people's kneecaps out." His mouth was too dry to spit and his hand trembled until held it tight with his other hand. It was not much of a choice.

Harper watched Hayes and the easy manner he held the M-16. He was far enough away to bring it to cover both of them, and since his admission of his orders, his eyes never left Harper. The trigger finger on his right hand lay across the receiver just above the trigger guard. It was in the guard position and with minimal effort it could be on the trigger.

Harper shifted his weight and watched Hayes shift his hands closer to a ready position. Something was really going wrong with this mission. "Sergeant, considering our position and the fine unit cohesiveness we have achieved, who issued you these orders?" he asked sarcastically. This did not have the feel of a Louis Edwards' fiasco.

Hayes continued to watch Harper's hands. He knew Harper was too professional to speak with his eyes, but the hands would give away whatever he intended to do. "Our orders were signed by the SECDEF."

"His personal signature?" asked Stillwell.

"The SECDEF knows personally of this mission?" queried Harper. Edwards ran his missions out of Langley, not the Pentagon. The Director of Central Intelligence *might* know about their mission. The Pentagon was not supposed to be in the loop. That meant Edwards was not in the loop. If the Op were run with different players, then Carnady might be out of the loop as well. How could the SECDEF justify such an order with the Uniform Code of Military Justice*? Maybe, they just didn't care.*

"Yes, Sir."

Stillwell worked enough spit back into his mouth to croak out, "The National Security Advisor knows about this mission. They had a letter signed by the Secretary of the Army reinstating me to active duty."

Harper sighed and leaned forward rubbing his face with his hands. He shook his head and laughed slightly. Through the spaces between his fingers, he watched Hayes first tense then relax. Harper's left boot came up and smashed hard into the sergeant's gun hand pinning the rifle, his arms and his body against the sand. With his free hand, he pulled the Glock and pointed it straight at Hayes's head.

"Don't!" Hayes snapped.

Darby Hayes started to pull his hand, only to find Harper pressing the whole of his two hundred five pound frame into the Marine. "Don't make me do this, Sergeant!"

There was no dramatic cocking of a hammer with the Glock. It is a double-action-only design where the only visible safety was one on the trigger and this made it an incredibly easy gun to shoot. Harper took up the slack and said quietly, "You're four and half pounds from a really bad headache. But let me explain something Sergeant."

Hayes glared at him. "It's against the law to shoot your sergeant, Sir."

Harper nodded. "Well, Sergeant, I don't know who came up with the bright idea to send Lieutenant Stillwell on this mission. He's not a shooter. He's not a combatant. He did pretty well in the firefight, and he followed orders even when he didn't like them. But nobody sends a shooter on my team for someone else on my team—*nobody*!

"There's something really wrong with this mission. Let me explain to you the *new* rules of engagement. You copy on this Anderson?"

Click.

"If one of you Force Recon boys decide to take out Lieutenant Stillwell, you better make sure you take me out first. You better think about the ethics and honor that you were both taught. We don't *frag* our own people.

"I need both of you working together to make it home. I intend to bring the rest of us out of this hole, and I intend to finish this mission. I don't understand the orders you were given, and I certainly don't agree with them. But make no mistake, this is my command, and we are deep in Indian country with a whole lot of bad guys half a klick away.

"I don't have time to baby sit either one of you. So on your word of honor, I want you to disregard the standing order about Lieutenant Stillwell, because it is morally and ethically wrong."

Hayes looked from the Glock's black frame to the nearly half-inch muzzle staring at him rock steady. He looked to Harper, then Stillwell. "You have my word."

Immediately, Harper lowered the weapon and pulled back from Hayes.

"You're going to accept his word. Just like that. You—"

Harper looked at Hayes. Without breaking eye contact, he said, "Lieutenant, Sergeant Hayes is a United States Marine. Not just any Marine—he is a member of Force Recon. He is the best of the best. In the Corps, they still teach right from wrong and black from white. Sergeant Hayes took an oath to defend the Constitution from all enemies, both foreign and domestic. His ultimate boss is not me or the Commandant of the Corps or even the President. His ultimate boss is the people. If what we do here does not further the security of America, then what we are doing is wrong. When Sergeant Hayes gives me his word, it is his word of honor as a United States Marine and as soldier and a warrior. I accept his word, because I do not believe he will tarnish his honor or his word once given."

Hayes rubbed his bruised hand. "Thank you, sir for trusting me. I'm not sure I would have made the same decision in your place."

Harper nodded and said, "Anderson, what about you?"

Click.

"Okay gentlemen, we have a plan and a mission." He breathed a deep sigh. "As soon as we get Anderson out, I'll call for the cavalry."

Stillwell gulped and asked quietly, "Would you have shot Hayes?"

Harper leaned back against the dirt. "One of Jeff Cooper's rules—never point a weapon at something you're not willing to destroy."

Stillwell nodded more horrified than when he left the Data Center.

It took everyone a few moments to recognize what they were hearing. The vagaries of combat took a twisting path towards the intrigues called betrayal and treason. The hot, dry desert sun did nothing to warm the chill running through Harper's bones. His worst fears were revealing themselves, and the horrible sensation of having been here before raised its ugly head.

He turned towards the Data Center and the of sound the voice addressing them. “Major James Harper,” came the flat British accented English with a bouncing echo from a loud hailer. Harper turned towards Hayes and thought about the orders sending Stillwell with them. He considered all the orders and wondered briefly how many sides there were in this desert.

“Major James Harper—yes, I believe you can hear me now. Major, I see that you have lost two men so far today. A Captain Kincaid and Captain Burns I believe. Both were veterans of your country’s war of aggression in 1991.” There was a pause and then sound of a side arm popping in the distance. “But what’s a few more bullets for vermin like Kincaid and Burns.”

Harper dropped to a knee and signaled Hayes to move out.

Stillwell grabbed his arm and whispered harshly, “How does he know your name?”

Harper shook his head. He was about to reply when the voice continued. “Of course, you have three others left—four men against my fifty or so survivors. These are elite Republican Guard troops. They will find you and kill you. Maybe before the sun sets or soon after.” He chuckled quietly. “You must be wondering how I know your name. But then, I know all of your names. Captain Anderson is an accomplished sniper. He’s around here somewhere, but it would be foolish for him to make any more shots. The counter sniper actions of my men would doom him.”

Harper whispered, “Anderson, does he have fifty men?”

Click click.

“Okay, this joker’s not as strong as he thinks,” he said to Hayes. “Lieutenant, this guy is playing with our minds. He’s gaming us. We’ve got to take them out.”

Stillwell nodded. “I know about games.”

"Then I'm gonna need your help Lieutenant. I'm gonna need an edge over this guy. But to do that we've got to kill some people first."

"The Claymores?"

Harper nodded.

"Major?" asked Hayes.

Harper turned his attention back to Hayes.

"And then there's the ever resourceful Sergeant Hayes—*truly a remarkable asset*," continued the voice on the louder hailer. "Did you know, Major Harper, that Sergeant Hayes was part of an elite team in 1995? He helped spirit a woman and her children out from under our very noses in 1995 to join her traitorous husband. They did it right out of the heart of Baghdad.

"In fact, your CIA almost missed the opportunity. They didn't believe the husband was one of our atomic scientists. He was training people to build the bomb once you Americans tired of flying over our country and threatening our livelihood with your sanctions. Sergeant Hayes killed two men on that mission. Now he has returned, we will try him for murder, espionage, and maybe a few other things. Your marvelous free press will report every tidbit we give them. After all, they did such a wonderful job on the baby formula factory during the war."

Harper sat down for a second. How much did they know?

"Major?" repeated Hayes.

"Yes, Sergeant."

"Sir, they must have our Q files. I don't know how they got them, but they must have them."

Harper nodded. The Q file was classified ULTRA SECRET. It was a special personnel record complete with mission and fitness reports for anyone in Spec War Operations who had participated in a black operation. The Q files were closely guarded files maintained in a vault at Langley or the pentagon depending on where people were assigned.

"Hayes, take Stillwell and go."

"One other thing, Major."

"Yes."

"Those other orders we were given."

"Yes."

"They've got to be as bogus as the rest of this mission."

"Agreed."

Harper flipped the Mossberg upside-down and started feeding three-inch magnum rifled slugs into the magazine. He gathered the canvas bag with the data tapes and said, "Good luck."

"You also have Lieutenant Brian Stillwell," continued the voice, "kind of a surprise to have a civilian along with a soldier's uniform on. You know they had to pull the Secretary of the Army out of bed to sign your activation papers." There was the crinkling of paper. "I have a copy of your orders here. An amazing document, Lieutenant, it activates you for a mission that no longer exists. I believe you people call this a black op. Well, it certainly got a whole lot blacker.

"Now Brian, I may call you Brian?" teased the voice. Hayes and Stillwell were already moving in a large circle towards the Claymores. Harper moved in the opposite direction. He slung the Mossberg over his back and pulled the Browning from his back holster. He reached another hand into one of his leg pockets and produced a silencer.

Harper had refitted the Browning with a non-standard barrel threaded on the end. He kept a muzzle brake screwed on the end of the barrel to protect the threads, since the threaded barrel extended beyond the end of the slide when the gun was in battery. Technically, the silencer was a violation of Bureau of Alcohol, Tobacco and Firearm regulations. He did not have a proper Class 3 license for the silencer, but ten years in a Federal prison was far down the list of problems right now.

The silencer was gift from a retired Special Air Service trooper several years ago. It was the sort of thing soldiers trade with one another after the action is over. A silenced weapon could come in very handy.

"I see you're not talking yet," continued the voice. "Yes, well our plans for you are quite different. You know those alimony payments you make every month and the lousy visitation rights you never seem to get. Those are outdated. We want your brain. You know all about unconventional weapon systems. I propose to offer you your life, either with a certain level of luxury, or as a *guest* in one our lower dungeons.

"It is your choice, but I should point out. You are the only one we will let live."

Harper stopped again and took the canvas bag. He shoved it into a hole and moved a rock over the top of the bag. He wondered vaguely whether he could find the spot again. He took a grenade and yanked the pull ring. Holding the spoon tight to the side, he placed the grenade under the rock so the pressure held it in place—a small surprise for some overachiever in Saddam's Army. He started moving again checking his watch. Too many hours of daylight remained. They were fighting elite troops without the cover of darkness.

"Which brings me to you Major Harper. Oh, you have been a problem for many years. Do you know Major that we have videotape records of your attack on this facility from 1992? I compared your service photo to the ones we have on tape—a very good likeness, although, the tapes are a bit grainy.

"I really would like to take you alive. However, in reviewing your wartime service record, your peacetime missions into Iran, Iraq, Libya, the old Soviet Empire and Eastern Block, I think such a sentiment is fruitless. However, I do intend to retrieve your body and photograph it. I think your wife Lynn would be interested in seeing the blasted remains." He chuckled again.

"I will even send parts of you to your daughters Grace, and Catherine, for their birthdays. You know they'll never be safe. Someday, a car will park in your neighborhood. Maybe I'll wait until they have their own families, or maybe I'll do it a few days from now. In either case, you won't be there to save them will you?

"This car will be packed with Semtex. There is so much of it floating around these days. Everyone seems to have the formula for producing it—the North Koreans, the Red Chinese, and the Russians to name a few. Not only will I destroy your house, but I will destroy the nice little suburban community you live in.

"There will be plenty of body parts flying about, and there is nothing you can do about it. You'll be dead. All those tricky little things you've pulled off before—useless. Your exceptional IQ—worthless, your formidable skills in the martial arts—powerless, there will be no one to protect them—no one to come in at the last moment and save them. How about that, Major?"

Harper slid down another wadi and willed himself to quit grinding his teeth. Whoever was responsible for this would pay. His tormentor had just given him the motivation he needed not to fail. The tension running across the back of his neck was incredible, and the anger boiling inside his belly screamed for release.

He told himself his best weapon was between his ears. Charging like Rambo headlong into a fusillade of automatic weapon fire only worked in Hollywood, most other places it got you killed fast.

He felt the soldier before he saw him. Perhaps, it was the crunch of gravel or a shadow oddly out of place or breathing out of place with the desert wind. Harper froze and reached down with his left hand to the boot dagger. He eased the snap off feeling rather than hearing it. His fingers tightened around the hilt as he drew the black forged blade straight up.

He released his grip on the Browning and set it down against the wadi's bank. He reversed his grip on the knife and waited. No breath—no movement. He became part of the dirt and sand. He envisioned himself as nothing more than a brown patch on an endless desert. He believed he was invisible before his enemy. Time wound down to a tedious pace as he tensed.

He imagined a cat laying flat in the weeds—its tail flickering back and forth. The front paws straight ahead and the head motionless, just before the cat leaps and kills. The hindquarters rise up and down. There is a rhythm to the attack—a dance before the kill. He felt the certain knowledge and belief that nothing can stop the inevitable conclusion. Patience and focus parlayed down to the last long seconds of a soldier's life.

The Iraqi slid down the side of the embankment. His own noise expected and ignored. There was a blur of motion as Harper drove forward slamming the heel of his palm into the Iraqi's nose and obliterating his features. He spun the Iraqi around by the shoulders and locked his neck in a sleeper hold where pressure is brought to bear on the carotid artery. With his left hand, he plunged the knife under his right wrist and deep into the man's neck.

They were still descending into the wadi when the kill ended. Harper pulled the dagger and wiped it clean on the soldier's battle blouse. He replaced the dagger in his boot sheath; he grabbed the Browning and the soldier's radio before shambling away from the dead man. It was time to fight back. Three seconds had ticked by.

Harper moved quickly to a hole. He needed a few moments to compose his next move. A tremor rippled through his hands. His pulse pounded in his ears. The memories of other days, other places, and other times beckoned from his subconscious. He dare not fail. His Lynn, Catherine, and Grace had been threatened. He dare not give in to his memories and the faces of those he had killed. This had become a *last man standing* affair. *He would be that man.*

"Anderson," he whispered. "Can you see this joker?"

Click click.

"Okay, you give me a click when you do see him."

The radio check came a few minutes later. Harper turned down the gain and said slowly in Arabic, "This is the American commander, let me talk to your superior officer."

"Major, I need about ten more minutes," came Hayes in his helmet earjack.

Harper clicked his throat mike once.

The voice from the loud hailer came over the earplug from the two-way radio. It was one of the new Motorola models with a five-mile range, ten channels and thirty-eight privacy codes. Not bad equipment and easily obtainable on the world market. They sold them in outdoor catalogs for a little over two hundred dollars.

"Major Harper?"

Harper was not in the mood for polite discussion. "Whoever you are, my sniper has the base of your skull in his crosshairs right now," he lied. "Oh, you'll never see him. He's a Force Recon Marine and he could be anywhere from one hundred to one thousand meters away." He clicked off and moved away from his hole.

"Major," came Hayes's voice through his helmet earphones. "Whatever you just said must have made them a might nervous. They've stopped expanding their perimeter."

Harper clicked his throat mike again and bellied himself down behind a huge boulder.

"The only reason you're still alive is because I want to know who sold me out," continued Harper.

The Motorola earplug crackled into life. "Major Harper. I don't think your sniper is anywhere near me. What I do know is one of my men is missing, and I'll find his body and then I'll find you."

Harper scrambled away from the boulder and slid into a crevasse. He clicked the Motorola on. "I wonder what your master is going to do to you when he finds out his very expensive database is missing. Or that you shot the only person who knows where the backup tapes are—you do know what backup tapes are don't you?"

Another crunch of gravel—Harper turned on his side jerking the Browning up in a two handed grip. His sight picture came to center just below the forehead of a soldier five feet away. He squeezed the trigger twice. A 9mm round produces very little recoil and the Browning is heavy enough to absorb most of it. He rolled away before the second brass cartridge hit the dirt.

The soldier collapsed like a broken doll over the top of the boulder, his dead eyes registering surprise and his body marking Harper's location like a red flare. Harper guessed he had fifteen seconds before they realized another man was down.

Harper tucked the Browning into his tunic and unslung the Mossberg. He pushed the safety off revealing the red dot just at the base of the receiver. He whispered into his throat mike, "Sergeant, I'm running out of time."

"Yes, Sir. Kincaid must have moved the detonator. I can't find it."

Harper breathed out slowly. The back his head seemed to tighten some more. This was not getting any easier. Considering all the rock and sand, Kincaid could have hidden the clacker anywhere. He came to a spot where his back was covered by a solid piece of ground. He knelt down on one knee and sighted the Mossberg down the natural alley of the wadi he was sitting in. The ground here resembled a lunar landscape rather than a majestic Arabian Desert.

The Motorola came to life again. "A desperate man will say anything to save his life. Listen Major—we found your HMMWV's."

The earth erupted with a terrible sound less than a hundred meters from where Harper was hunkered down. The blast lifted both vehicles into the air. Twisted, spinning wrecks tumbled back towards the ground and the tortured sound of their best chance for survival crashed back to the desert floor. The orange fireball turned black then gray before the hushed crackle of flame and fire filtered on the desert breeze.

"Perhaps, Major, I will travel to Chicago myself, and kill your children. You are not good enough to get all of us."

Harper waited. Sweat dribbled down his back and sides. His battle tunic was slick and stuck to his sides. Cramps plagued his upper thighs and lower legs. His mouth felt cottony and drops of sweat slid off the end of his nose and splattered onto the shotgun's barrel. He remembered training drills when he thought his lungs would explode, and his vision narrowed due to the physical intensity. He had passed through certain physical limits where only sheer willpower kept him going. *Never give up—never quit fighting—always keep thinking.*

An excited shout in Arabic—they had found one of the two men he had killed. A warrior must have the discipline to wait for the moment in every battle—a moment when the battle turns toward victory or slides to defeat. Harper sensed the moment approaching.

He propped the end of the Mossberg on his knee and pulled the Motorola from his tunic. He pressed the transmit button and said very softly, "No one threatens my family and lives. Make your peace with your maker, I'm coming to get you." He turned the Motorola off and slid the earplug out of his ear.

Harper reached inside his tunic and found the red signal beacon. Jonas had told him the cavalry would come running if he pressed this one. His plans were collapsing and his men were scattered. Hayes could not find the detonators and Anderson was sitting in a hole where he could not move. He had an Iraqi commander who seemed to know more about the mission than he did. If ever there was a time for the good guys to come charging over the nearest hill, it was now.

He glanced at the signal beacon and pressed it. There was a part of him that believed it would send a signal, and another part of him that doubted it would be the right one. He plucked the beacon from his tunic and dropped it on the ground. It was time to see what would happen. Harper was on the move again.

29

Al Jabar Air Base, Kuwait, Monday, November 17, 1997, 5:00 PM (+3.00 GMT)

Jonas Benjamin dozed on a cot. The pace of the past few days came to a sudden halt once Harper and his team stepped off into the desert. Now Jonas waited in a small room squirreled away inside a hanger. The jet noise and airport tempo left him as sleep overtook him. All he could do was wait, and the best thing to do while he waited was to rest.

Once Harper called, he would need to get the team up and running in a hurry. He had checked on the aircraft five hours ago. They were still parked next to hanger. A crew was on stand by in the duty room. Everything seemed okay. He looked around for the commanding officers and found them missing, but assumed they were probably bunked out somewhere else. He dismissed the anomaly and went back to monitor the satellite frequency for the beacons.

There was nothing in his email account, or any encrypted faxes waiting his attention. The lack of signal traffic did not alert or alarm Jonas. After all, this was the hardest part of any operation—the waiting. The sitting next to a radio or satellite receiver for the *come get me signal* or the more urgent *come get me and bring some help!* On several other missions, it had gone this way. The flurry of activity and acquisition of supplies prior to a quick departure was the prelude to a long and silent wait.

Those things had happened. He failed to realize that this mission was not run through Langley's normal Spec Ops command structure. He did not appreciate the significant change that this operation was run through the National Security Council and out of the White House's West Wing. Louis Edwards was out of the command loop, which meant Jonas was not even considered part of the mission.

Command and military asset arrangements were managed directly through the NSC. Orders were issued from the West Wing office in the name of the President down through the National Command Authority's chain of command. Orders went to the SECDEF without question and were fed directly into the Joint Chiefs of Staff. The Pentagon's bureaucracy ignored the explanation and methodically issued instructions through out the world. It was little more than a mindless machine without a soul.

Orders were translated from paper statements to digital signals. The signals were then scrambled by sophisticated multi-thousand bit, single-use encryption ciphers. Those signals were bounced off military communication satellites in geosynchronous earth orbit and captured by the appropriate military signal transponders. The process was reversed, and the general staff officers of whatever command had been reached reissued those orders to effect the disposition and deployment of actual men and machines. With the maturing micro-processor and communication bandwidth measured in gigabits, these actions happened with incredible speed.

By the time Harper's *come get me and bring some help* signal arrived, the loop between the NSC and the *George Washington* task-force supplying the men and machines had closed. The orders never passed by Admiral Trevor Barnes. They were examined, verified, and executed by staff officers several ranks his junior. The helicopter gun ships, the fighters for over flight protection, and the men to enforce an extraction had been removed from Al Jabar Airbase. The mission never existed.

Jonas sat up in his cot staring dumbly at the satellite receiver alarm. He shook his head to clear his thinking before his fogged mind recognized the alarm's urgency. He sat forward and hit the mouse next to his laptop's screen. The signal system ran through Langley's satellite and computer system and could not be shutdown due to some order from the White House West Wing.

A map displaying the border areas between Saudi Arabia and Southern Iraq and bracketing the area with Jordan on the right and Kuwait on the left appeared on his screen. He punched the F5 key to center the blinking dot on the screen and zoom the map software to show everything within a twenty-kilometer radius. The screen blinked before repainting the map display.

He moved the mouse pointer to the printer icon and clicked. A few seconds later, the attached thermal printer hummed and a curled piece of paper showing the map location rolled off the printer. Jonas ripped the page off the end of the printer and clamped it on a clipboard. He grabbed his hat and slapped the side of his hip. The Beretta 92FS was still there. He smiled thinking about how much the Beretta bugged Harper. His only observation was, "It's not a Glock."

Harper was a Glock man, and Glock owners were fanatics who claimed their polymer-framed weapons were the best. He glanced back at the blinking screen, "See you soon." He would soon find out how very wrong he was.

Jonas ran through the hanger to the helipad and skidded to an uncertain stop. The AH-64 *Apache* gun ships were missing. He tried to suck down some air and found it too thick. Where was everybody?

He spun around looking for the Staff Sergeant assigned to the insertion team. No table, no radio, no coffee cups—nothing. Jonas stood flat-footed trying to come up with some explanation for their absence and knowing they were gone because they had been ordered to leave. He brought the map page up to his face and looked at the coordinates. Harper was in trouble; Jonas wondered if Harper knew how much.

Jonas looked around the empty hanger and the area outside the hanger. They had left without saying anything. It was probably not personal. They simple got some orders and obeyed their orders. Jonas cursed loudly, and then said abruptly, "Think!"

He pulled his satellite phone from the belt clip. He punched the ABC switch and started paging through the numbers logged in the memory. He stopped when the display showed: LOUIS EDWARDS. Jonas pulled the antenna out and stabbed the SEND button. He cursed again fuming as he stalked back to his room.

He settled down before the laptop's screen and punched the F5 key again. The screen zoomed to a two-kilometer radius. Jonas wondered why the dot had not moved. Were they hurt? Captured? He scowled as the carrier signal buzzed in his ear, then the ringing sound as he tried to find someone half way across the world.

"Hello," came the cautious voice in his ear.

"Switch to scrambler!" snapped Jonas. He waited for the two-tone beep indicating the signal encryption scrambler had engaged.

"I take it Harper has signaled."

"Yes."

"And I take it there are no helicopters to pick him up," continued Edwards.

Jonas pulled the phone from his ear and whispered, "How do you always know?"

He put the phone back to his lips and said, "Yeah."

"The White House canceled the mission. They told me tonight or rather—my is it that late—last night. I meant to call you, but as you can see things have gotten away from me."

"Yeah, well I got the come get me and bring help signal. According to the computer, he's not moving. He might be hurt or captured or—well I don't want to think about it."

He could almost see Louis nodding thoughtfully. A tired sigh hissed over the ether between Al Jabar and Washington. "We've been cut loose, Jonas. They don't want anyone coming back from this one."

"So that means going to Admiral Barnes is a waste of time."

"I hardly think getting him reprimanded would help our cause. No, I am sure our friends in the White House have shutdown all help. It's only because your signals go through Langley that you even got it."

Jonas paced across the room and looked at the sunlight. It would be dark in a few hours. "I need something now, Louis. I got a couple hundred klicks to fly."

"Yes, I know my boy." The fatigue cracked his voice. There was another pause, "Jonas you remember the fellow the SAS boys helped out during the war?"

"The one whose wife and kid they got out during the occupation?"

"Yes. I mean you're right there. I think its time to call in a chit."

"How's he going to get military clearance?"

Jonas could hear the click of a keyboard in the background. Was Louis at Langley or home or somewhere else? Something else was happening? Missions did not get canceled in a vacuum.

"Ah, here's his phone number. Where are you right now?"

"Hanger fifty-seven."

"One thing. I need to know something. You were at the briefing with the NSA and General Carnady—right?"

"Yeah, I was Langley's briefing officer. You were digging up Harper at the time." What did the briefing have to do with anything? There were men in the field calling for help—*now*! Louis knew Carnady had been there, so what was he really asking?

Louis chuckled at the thought. It seemed so long ago, and it was only Saturday afternoon when he faced down Harper at a Karate School in Roselle. "Jonas, was there someone that might not want this mission to succeed?"

"There were a lot of people there," replied Jonas.

"No, not the first meeting—the second meeting," corrected Louis.

The second meeting had been strange. "There were not many folks I'd care to be in a fox hole with," he said.

"I think one of them sold us out," explained Louis matter-of-factly.

"You mean canceled the mission?"

"No, I mean sold us out like Aldrich Ames sold us out," said Louis calmly.

"You think they were waiting for Harper."

"It's possible."

Jonas stared at the blinking dot on the screen. "I got to go get him, Louis. What are you trying to say?"

"I'm saying I don't want to lose you and Harper. I'm suggesting that if they were waiting for Harper they might be waiting for you as well," continued Louis. "Jonas, if we use the Kuwaiti, we won't have any backing from the *George Washington.* If things go down badly, how much help do you think a bunch of gung-ho Arabs who want to kill other Arabs will be?" Arabs shooting Arabs was not a new idea.

Jonas ran the possibilities through his mind. He punched the F6 key until the map showed a hundred-kilometer radius. "Louis, we'll be less than a hundred klicks from the Saudi border. We could get out that way."

"Night flying in a combat zone with Arab pilots. Kuwaiti pilots who have a hard time getting all the expensive planes we've sold them off the ground in daylight. If they panic what are you prepared to do?"

Jonas understood what Louis was driving at. "Gut check?"

He could almost see the smile under the faded blond mustache. "Yes, my boy. Gut check. If Harper is still alive and he has the information we need, he might not be very happy or understanding about seeing something other than US aircraft. In fact, I would guess he might be very upset. Have you ever seen Harper upset?"

"Well—"

"No, you've never seen him upset. Jonas, he warned me about something like this when he left. No one knows what's happening out there.

We might get a chopper in, and it may have a machine gun. You may have wounded or dead."

Jonas shook his head. "Yeah, I know—I get the picture. It's all cocked up."

"Yes."

"But it's Harper. I owe Harper."

"Most of us do, Jonas. You understand what you're up against."

"Yeah, Louis."

The carrier signals hummed with silence, "I'll make the call, Jonas. Sit tight. I'll call you back in a few minutes." The phone went dead.

It took longer than a few minutes. The sun moved to a wavering red ball kissing the top of the desert. The shadows were lengthening quickly now. The night chill, so incongruous with the daytime heat, began to render its presence.

Jonas secured the Velcro straps on his body armor. He rechecked the loads on three additional magazines for the Beretta, and slid his combat knife into its sheaf. He had collected a medical kit including some morphine, blood plasma, and pressure bandages. He glared at the stationary dot on the monitor.

Were they all dead?

He fumed in his preparations as those few promised minutes stretched into twenty then sixty and finally ninety. It was getting late. He would be over Iraq with Kuwaiti crew searching for someone who might be dead in the dark. He scooped up a half dozen flares and shoved them into the canvas bag with the medical supplies.

Finally, he dropped a six-pack of bottled water into the bag and slumped down in a chair facing the laptop on the satellite phone. Both remained silent. The clock in the lower right hand corner of the Win95 notebook computer continued to tick off minutes and the room became noticeably gloomier as each minute slid by.

With the onset of the evening chill, sweat ran down his back and chest. His combat blouse clung and seemed to freeze to his body. He played with the batteries on his night vision goggles and wondered idly who had cancelled his extraction team. Someone would pay for this. Someone probably already had, he reflected sadly. The locator dot remained ominously static.

Were they all dead?

A larger clock showed the time since the extraction signal had sounded. It was close to two hours now. They should have been there by then. They should be churning the sand with the rotor blades and blasting any Iraqi's giving resistance. He sighed. If their roles were reversed, Harper would have been airborne by now. He would have found a way to get there.

Jonas shook his head. He had failed a friend and mentor. He was sitting in a stupid hanger office with a silent satellite phone, a bag full of useless supplies and the accusing finger of the locator dot pointing out his guilt and failure. Harper would not have relied on Edwards, but Jonas did not know what else to do.

It occurred to him that he might have to face Lynn Harper and explain her husband had died for God and country. No! Harper was still alive. He had to be. He was Major James Harper—the legend. Legends do not die on foolish missions in the desert a couple hundred kilometers from the best-trained military in the world. A cold knot formed in his gut. It had to be Arthur! Unconsciously, Jonas felt the Beretta's grip. The dot continued to blink and refused to move.

Were they all dead?

The phone buzzed almost one hundred minutes since he had mashed the END button. Jonas leaped forward fumbling with the phone. He had it upside-down next to his ear, yelling, "Hello!" before he righted the phone.

"Jonas?"

"Yes, who'd expect. Do you know how long it's been?" he shouted.

"Yes—yes, I know," replied a tired Edwards. "Do you know where Hanger twenty-nine is?"

"No, but I'll find it." Jonas snapped the lip of the laptop shut and pulled the power cord from the battery pack. The batteries would power the computer for five to seven hours. He dropped it into the canvas bag and scooped the supplies up with one hand.

"All I have for you is one helicopter, a single pilot, and if you squeeze all together, it shouldn't be too bad."

"Is there a machinegun?" Jonas ambled out of the hanger and looked for the signs in English and Arabic.

"I don't know," replied Edwards.

Jonas shook his head. What was going on? "What took you so long? I could have walked there by now!"

"I had to call the Deputy Director of Operations. What we are doing is a direct violation of a Presidential Order issued sometime yesterday," explained Louis.

"Was it issued by the National Security Advisor?" snapped Jonas.

Louis was thoughtfully silent.

"Hey, Louis—you still there?" asked Jonas as he found a sign directing him to hangers twenty-five through thirty.

"How'd you know?"

"Know what?"

"How'd you know the NSA's office wrote the order?"

"Because they were the slime balls that organized this mess." Jonas stopped walking as he ran those last words back through his brain.

"An interesting assessment of the civilian command authority."

"They sold us out didn't they?" whispered Jonas.

"I don't know."

Jonas seized on the equivocation, "You don't *not* know either."

"Very good young Jonas. Now, you let me worry about this. Go fetch Harper."

"He could be dead after all this time."

"Perhaps. But people like Harper are very hard to kill. He's been in tougher spots than this. I'll talk to you when you get back," promised Louis as he clicked off.

Jonas switched the phone off and dropped it into the canvas bag next to the laptop. He looked at the sun. Only the ruby glow could be seen on the darkening desert. He arrived at the end of the row to find a Puma SA 330 J warming up. Jonas ran under the main rotor and hurriedly clamped some ear protectors over the whine of the twin Turbomeca Turmo IVC engines.

He pounded on the pilot's door, then stopped as a red headed Englishman flashed him the thumbs up. "Mister Benjamin, I presume."

Jonas nodded dumbly, and said lamely, "You're not a Kuwaiti."

The pilot flashed him a bright smile, "No dear boy, I'm certainly not. Captain Dylan Scott, Special Air Service at the ready." He stuck out a hand that looked more like paw and grabbed Jonas' hand. "Do get in. We have a long way to go."

Jonas nodded and clambered into the co-pilot's seat.

"I was expecting a Kuwaiti."

Dylan Scott bobbed his head again, punched power and pulled the *Puma* into the air. "Yes, well, as we all know, the bloody rag heads need someone to do their fighting for them. Louis thought it would be easier this way. I'm not constrained by certain niceties."

The helicopter pushed towards the west.

"You do understand we're going into hostile territory."

"You folks call it Indian country don't you?" asked Scott.

Jonas nodded. "Yeah."

"Quite aware of the fact."

"Well what are we going to do about the Iraqi Army?"

Scott jabbed a thumb into the cargo area. "It's a chain gun borrowed—somewhat permanently—from one of your *Apache* Gun ships—a marvelous weapon. The particular rag head that owns this chopper had one put in. It does trucks rather nicely. By the way, Louis mentioned you had a map of where we're going. We'll probably need it quickly."

Jonas dug the clipboard out of the canvas bag and handed it across to Dylan Scott. "Good lad. I understand we're on our way to get Jim Harper."

"Yes."

"Good man, Harper. You know we hunted SCUDs and few other things during the war. Now don't you look so worried. Harper is almost as good as our boys, and he knows this desert fairly well." Dylan Scott chuckled as night steadily settled on the desert before them.

The *Puma* roared towards the locator point at 258km/hour, passing from Kuwait into Iraq and providing the correct call signs to the ever-vigilant AWAC guardians. Jonas seriously doubted that Louis had gotten any clearance at all. It was probably cover for Jonas in case something else went wrong. He looked at Captain Scott wondering just how far they had strayed from official channels.

30

East Of Nukhayb, Iraqi Data Center, Monday, November 17, 1997, 5:15 PM (+3.00 GMT)

Harper slid over the sand until he found himself between two rocks. He set the Mossberg on the ground and hefted the Browning Hi Power. He rolled over on his back and pushed the magazine release button with his thumb. The half loaded magazine dropped into his left hand. He dropped the magazine into one of his jacket side pockets and retrieved a fully charged magazine less one round.

Technically, a Hi Power magazine can hold thirteen rounds, but the Hi Power is more reliable with twelve. There was still a round up the spout giving Harper a full thirteen. He pushed the base of the grip into the web of his hand and settled down to watch the signal beacon lying on the dirt at the end of the wadi.

He lay prone and lined up the sights up on the signal beacon. He guessed he was about fifteen yards from where he had been standing. It was time to go on the offensive; otherwise, they would all die here today.

Harper felt no surprise when two Iraqi soldiers arrived at the edge of the wadi. He should have been surprised, but he knew they would locate the signal beacon before any help arrived. One hefted his Russian Assault rifle and rolled into the wadi landing on his feet and bracing the rifle on his hip. He never even looked up to check the end of the wadi, he simply pulled back on the trigger and sent a deadly stream of bullets from a fifty round magazine.

Harper focused on the front sight allowing to the rear sights to merge into the background. The Iraqi's face loomed before Harper's vision. He adjusted his aim and fired. His first bullet caught the Iraqi below the ear; his second slammed into the temple of the falling soldier as his helmet dropped to the dirt. The noise from the Iraqi's automatic weapon masked the *pfft* from the silenced Browning. Harper remained motionless as the second soldier rose up from where he was crouched, reaching forwards with a grenade in his right hand.

In his other hand, he held some sort of electronic device. The device had a short antenna extended from a special LCD display. Harper had used direction finders in the course of his work for Louis Edwards. The direction finder was an encrypted multi frequency device that bounced off a US military satellite. To have such a device available and in the field indicated a high degree of knowledge with regard to their mission. The sell out was complete. Time slowed down, and he wondered whether the second solider had seen the shots. Harper shifted and started firing the browning. His first two shots hit center mass on the chest. He shifted his aim and placed one that creased the side of the man's neck. The direction finder tumbled from his hand.

The soldier's hands met and the pull ring slid from the grenade. Another second and the grenade would fly. Harper was uncertain where it would land. He pulled the trigger two more times. The first shot went wide. The second splattered across the soldier's face. He legs rocked and his right hand loosened on the grenade. He sighed slightly before pitching forward.

Harper rolled away and scrambled further up the dirt bank. He figured he was moving at an oblique angle to the Data Center and the second soldier. The crack from the grenade's explosion caused him to drop hard on the dirt and freeze.

"Major, you okay?" came a worried Hayes in his helmet phones.

"Yes, Sergeant. I'm having a fine time here. Any luck on the detonators?" he whispered.

"I found the wire a few minutes ago."

"Well hurry it up. It's getting a bit thick over here."

Harper rolled over and changed magazines on the Browning again. He took a deep breath and let the air slowly out through his nostrils. He wanted to slow his breathing and bring heart rate back down. The pain pounded behind his eyes and around the back of his neck. There was a long way to go before they got out of here.

"Major, I found it!" came Hayes again.

Harper rolled over on his stomach. He could see the two helicopter wrecks. The third lay nestled between two ridges, and four soldiers stood on point around the aircraft. He found a battlefield triage for the wounded. Most of them were from the helicopter crash. The Iraqi Colonel was losing too many men too fast.

The Data Center survivors were still out of action, and would stay out of action for another couple of hours. Even then, they would wake with a raging headache and nausea. There were over a dozen wounded men at the triage site, and four guarding the chopper, plus the ones he had taken out. It left the Iraqi Colonel with eight to ten men. Not enough to effectively expand the perimeter in all directions. It was time to finish this.

"Major, ready when you are."

"Anderson—when Stillwell and Hayes start their dance, take out everybody except the commanding officer. We need him alive and relatively unharmed." He paused and dug the Motorola Talkabout out. "Hayes, start your stuff in two minutes. We take as many of them down as we can. Anderson, if they take the bait, let Hayes do most of the work."

Click.

Harper shoved the earphone up and under his helmet. He turned the two-way radio on and whispered, "We're coming for you."

The mocking voice responded almost instantly, "Major Harper, you have killed a few of my men. However, there are more on the way. You are a handful, soon to be nothing. Observe Major, it is not you who is coming for me, it is I coming for you."

The rotors for the surviving helicopter began to move. The steady acceleration of the engines could be heard over the desert silence. The helicopter would be devastating if it got airborne.

Harper turned the gain down on the Talkabout. He squeezed the throat mike saying, "Anderson. Forget the ground pounders, hit the chopper!"

He turned his attention back to the Iraqi. "Think again." He flipped the Talkabout off.

It was time to draw the helicopter towards his position. Not much of a trick, since they had the basic direction. He looked across the ridges and guessed at where Anderson should still be concealed. He holstered the Browning and unslung the Mossberg. He set the dull black shotgun on the sand next to him. With his other hand, he pulled one of his last grenades free from the clips running up and down the front of his Alice vest.

He painfully noted for one last time that help would not be coming. If the Iraqi had the signal beacon frequency, then Jonas would be sand bagged as well. It meant they were being sacrificed to this desert. There had been other times when the cavalry never crested the hill. They needed to end this thing now—*before the sun set.*

Jerry never made it out of this desert, and every time Harper came to this wicked place, he had men to bury. He checked his watch. Thirty seconds before Hayes and Stillwell started a desperate charge. The chopper would probably lift off before they began their move. He closed his eyes remembering there are no atheists at a time like this. The most hardened warrior recognizes the cloaked reaper standing nearby patiently waiting.

He took a deep breath and let it out slowly through his nostrils. He willed his chest to relax, and his limbs to uncoil. He screwed his eyes shut and wished he had the certain faith Lynn had. He wanted so much to see Jesus, and find assurance he was justified in his fight.

Twenty seconds.

The chopper seemed to intensify its motion. Dust and small stones kicked up from the down draft. The avenging roar thundered on the desert floor. The Iraqis were coming for him. They were coming with their bombs, machine guns, and men. They were coming to punish him for his deeds.

Fear reached out its bony grip and clutched at his joints. He willed himself to look up and face his adversary. Through the roar, fear, and soon to be flame, he could hear Lynn's soft voice reading to him. "*For it is He who delivers you from the snare of the trapper and from the deadly pestilence.*"

He could see her walking on her treadmill quietly praying for their day, for her children, for him. He could see her with the notes and prayer journal in their home. He could see her lips moving as she spoke to God for all of them. Her visage came to him with startling clarity now. He snapped his eyes up and saw the rotors lifting the Jolly Green Giant skyward.

This animal had threatened his Lynn! This brigand for an outlaw nation who calmly talked about harming his Catherine and Grace dared to threaten his very own. Maybe his government was not the best, and maybe his actions not entirely proper. They had threatened the very lives of those he held closest to his heart.

Ten seconds.

He pushed his body up feeling power in his weary shoulders that should not have been there. He ignored the strength sapping heat. The world seemed to explode with wind and noise. He glowered at the mechanical beast coming to kill him. Thirst, hunger and exhaustion fell away and the still soft voice continued, "*No evil will befall you. Nor will any plague come near your tent.*"

Fire coursed through his being. Rage and anger welled up inside of him. In some remote part of his brain, he knew this was the final roll of the dice. It was kill or be killed. It was time to fight and perhaps die.

The world focused with sharp clarity. From his throat came the cry, "Come and get me!"

He yanked the grenade's pull ring. He reared back eyeing the open side door. His hand wrapped tightly around the smooth grenade holding the detonator spoon against the sheet metal skin. He started to run in bobbing motion towards spinning death. With a snap of his arm, the deadly ball tumbled through the air in the general direction of the helicopter. He tossed the Mossberg from his left to his right hand and took a grip on the hand and fore end grips. *"For a thousand may fall at your side...but it shall not approach you."* Someone was trying to kill him, *and he was alive*! Someone had sold them out, *and he was alive!* Someone and threatened his very flesh and blood, *and he was alive!*

Today was not the day to die!

★ ★ ★

Stillwell asked himself again, what he was doing in this forgotten desert. A friend once described the desert surrounding Interstate 80 as it comes out of Utah and cuts through Wyoming as moonscape. This place certainly could compete. It was hot, dry, and dusty. His lips were cracked from one day in the heat, and his face smeared with caked on mud as the dust turned to a gritty slime by his sweat.

According to his watch, in thirty seconds he was suppose to roll over the top of this ridge, make some noise and try not to get shot. Getting shot was hardly what he had planned for his weekend. Weekends seemed like such a ridiculous concept in this place. It was so far removed from the suburban lifestyle he maintained outside the district. He was an analyst for Uncle Sam, not a shooter trying to play soldier with a bunch Marines.

The images of blood and gore would never leave his mind: The dead men they had dropped in the firefight on the lower level; the sound of spinning copper jacketed rounds impacting soft flesh and sudden intake of breath; the coldly calculated manner Harper approached the technicians and blew their kneecaps apart; the shrunken state of death as a once breathing person takes on an unnatural stillness. He felt the cold horror as it rippled through him again, and the bile of his disgust rise up in his throat.

Death was a casual thing when examined through computer systems, statistics and drab intelligence reports. No one talked about the terror in everyone's minds, or the automatic response to keep shooting when under fire. The fine ethical discussions no longer matter when a weapon's bore is pointed towards you, and death comes with each bark and muzzle flash. The kill or be killed response is to ensure they all die before something sharp, hot, and deadly plucks the breath from your own body.

Twenty seconds.

Did any of them understand what they were doing when they sent men into harm's way? Even now, after a night and a day of prowling through the dark, planting death and visiting destruction on others, Stillwell was not sure whether he understood what was happening around him—*and more importantly to him.*

One thing he did understand, he did not like killing people. He had been the hunter and the hunted in the same time it takes to play eighteen holes of golf. Now, he tensed for another act. He was the dancing bait for a pack of hungry jackals. The task he was assigned required him to draw even more men to their doom.

Harper was the enigma he could not puzzle out. He did not seem to fit the mold for DELTA, the SEALS, or Force Recon. Was there some other service no one knew about? An agency unit used for particular nasty operations? He held the rank of major, but never attributed to a service. He used his own weapons and developed his own tactics. The briefing officer had introduced Harper as "*May I present Major James Harper. United States Special Forces Retired.*" Retired from where?

Ten seconds.

There was the other thing about the orders concerning himself. Harper had pointed a weapon at his own man. There was no compromise in his voice. The Glock 21 hung with the steadiness of a yardarm. Reflecting on the moment when Harper stood over Hayes and demanded he adhere to his oath as a soldier, he had no doubt Harper would have pulled the trigger. In this insane place, Harper demanded honor. No one discussed honor anymore. It was an anachronism from some other era, and here, less than twenty minutes ago a man's life hung on his adherence to honor.

No quake, no self doubt accompanied Harper's words: "*Nobody sends a shooter on my team for someone else on my team—nobody*!" The anger in his eyes and the passion in his words—who was this Harper they were following today? The entire horror adverted because Harper accepted Hayes's word of honor. Could it be that those who spent so much time on the edge still believed in honor?

Honor—there was so little of it left in the world he inhabited. Honor and integrity had been replaced with spin and poll numbers. It had been so long since he had met someone who truly believed in right and wrong, perhaps, even heaven and hell. Could Harper truly believe such things?

The battle yell in his helmet phones shocked Stillwell back to reality. Harper and Hayes were expecting him to crest the ridge ahead and become the bait for the Iraqis. Harper's voice filled his helmet, "Come and get me!" Stillwell recognized the drumming noise as that of a helicopter.

He scrambled to the top of the ridge and poked his head up. Half a klick distant, Harper stood defiantly waving his hands before the steadily rising chopper—one man versus a chopper and machine gun. Stillwell recognized the act not as foolishness, rather profound bravery. He was drawing the helicopter away from Stillwell and Hayes and onto himself. He was giving them a chance to live.

If Harper could scream, then so could he. He tried to ignore the weariness dragging at his limbs. When he pushed himself over the ridge holding his M-16 and half running and half falling down the ridge towards the gravel pit and the Data Center's entrance, a spurt of energy seemed to freshen his step. He pulled the trigger on the M-16 spraying a magazine of bullets randomly in the direction of the remaining Iraqi soldiers.

He stumbled towards the end of his slide down the slope. The gun flew from his grip as he made an effort to avoid smashing his face on the sharper rocks. His helmet popped off his head and spun away from his grasp. Something very hard smashed into his rib cage driving the air from his lungs and causing the world to swim.

He pushed himself up. Tears streamed down his cheeks and his breath came raggedly. He shook his head again trying to remember what he was doing. The whine of a bullet spinning passed his head cleared some confusion. He straightened himself and turned to stare dumbly at several men running towards him.

The flashes from their barrels as they fired on the run saved his life. Had they stopped to take careful aim, Stillwell would be dead. He forgot about the rifle and helmet. His bowels released as he turned and ran away from his attackers. He cared not for direction or reason; he simply wanted to get away from these people. The gunshots sounded like popcorn in a microwave. He thought they should be louder.

He jerked his eyes around wildly looking for somewhere to hide. He screamed and ran. He was alone acting like bait, and he suddenly believed he was going to be gobbled up like bait as well. A hand waved at the corner of his ever-narrowing vision. He cocked his head towards the hand and saw Hayes.

Hayes was important for some reason. Whatever the reason, he did not remember. He looked the other way and found only a steep embankment. He veered towards the bank then bounced away from it. The bullets were getting closer. He could hear their shouts and smell their sweaty bodies. He imagined their hot breath.

Television images of American soldiers being drug through the dusty streets of a forgotten Somali town made him run harder. He did not want to be drug like a fattened deer carcass across this desert. He was no great warrior. He was a guy who lived with computer models, pushed keyboards and clicked mouse buttons. This was not his world! It could only be hell!

He turned towards Hayes and ran. His legs felt like great lead weights. His arms no longer pumped at his sides like a seasoned runner. Instead, they flailed like tilting windmills. His vision swam from color to gray and back. He was running on his gut now. His body was giving out. The adrenaline surge was giving out and his system started to shutdown.

Stillwell tripped, tumbled and skidded to a crumpled shape. He pulled his head towards his chest and wondered if it would hurt to die. The ambush was set up in an open box configuration. Four M-181A Claymore mines were set on both sides of the gap in off setting blast arcs providing maximum coverage. Stillwell ran towards the Claymores and Hayes and wondered if honor really mattered anymore. He ran into the teeth of two more mines aimed at where he had come from. The open box became a three-sided shooting gallery.

Each mine was designed to spray its lethal ball bearing in a sixty-degree fan shape out to a distance of fifty yards. Slightly more than a pound of C4 plastic explosive lay in lightweight three-by-nine inch plastic case. Seven hundred ball bearings capable of punching a 9mm hole were packed in front of the explosive, and embossed on the outer casing were the words FRONT TOWARDS ENEMY—incase there was any doubt.

The gap Stillwell ran towards was less than thirty yards wide. Kincaid had arranged the Claymores with overlapping kill zones. Hayes had scribed an "X" in the dirt that Stillwell was running towards. The circuit tester still indicated a solid connection as Stillwell bobbed and weaved through the gap. Hayes was waving at him with one hand and held the PRC 25 battery detonator or clacker, as it was called, in his other hand.

Stillwell lunged like a battered running back over the goal line. He tripped and tumbled away from the Iraqi soldiers and towards Hayes. The world behind him erupted with a terrible scream and the air became a blue gray steel blizzard. Nine hundred 12-gauge shotguns firing 00 buckshot would have put the same number of pellets into the air. Hayes accomplished the same by simply squeezing the clacker.

One second there were soldiers running towards the prize—the next, a mass of bone and blood and mist. Their flesh ripped away from their bones. The terrible thunder heard so many times on battlefields descended in this place on these men. Death came instantaneously. What remained was not even recognizable as human. It was battlefield litter. The kind no one ever glorifies or talks about. The gore and stench of death visited by modern weapons.

Stillwell huddled and waited. He shouted wildly when Hayes touched his shoulder and said gently, "It's over, Lieutenant." The black Marine cradled the babbling man, rocked him gently and whispered, "It's over. It's all right. It's over."

★ ★ ★

Duri looked at the dead Motorola Talkabout. The last helicopter lifted away from the ground leaving Duri behind. Duri squeezed his eyes shut against the sand kicked up by the helicopter's downdraft. The American was playing mind games. What could they do? He had the advantage in numbers. He controlled the air. Reinforcements were driving towards the Data Center. It would be over within a couple of hours.

He walked towards the dead American soldiers lying on the hot sand. Dead Americans might be enough to soothe his great leader. He spat on the dirt next to Kincaid and Burns. It was so easy to kill these men. They had been sent to the desert and then abandoned. There were no helicopters coming to rescue them. There was no help arriving. It was over.

Harper was somewhere to the east of his position. A simple matter to deal with. The helicopter would handle a single man. They had no

Stinger missiles. At best, they had some rifles, but against an airborne machinegun, Harper's life could be measured in seconds.

They would find the backup tapes and repair the Data Center. He needed Stillwell alive. Such a man could accelerate many of their weapons programs. Of course, Stillwell needed the proper motivation applied in order to soothe an angry Saddam over the temporary loss of his computer systems. These Americans were so sentimental about their children. Stillwell's child would need to come to Iraq—a simple trade—Stillwell's cooperation for his child's life.

Harper's family could be dealt with on the same trip. These barbarians needed to understand death could visit their fine homes across the ocean. They relied on their distant land to keep them safe. They bombed others without fear of similar bombs landing on their homes. The war would be carried across the ocean. It would come to their homes, their neighborhoods, to their churches. They must come to think of this as something more than video games on their televisions. They must learn fear.

The *Sea King* lifted away from the desert. It spun dirt and pebbles in his wake. Duri felt satisfied the farce would end now. He never saw the flash of the Barrett, and by the time he heard the rifle's report, the soldier manning the machine gun on the *Sea King* was little more than bloody pulp. The next shot from the Barrett shattered the Plexiglas windscreen.

The *pop-a-pop-pop* from behind Duri drew his attention and his troop's attention to an American sliding off a ridge. The fool looked like he had slipped. Duri pulled his Makarov from his holster and waved it angrily, "Get him!"

Six soldiers started in a dead run firing their weapons. He looked down at the dead Americans saying, "You'll have company soon."

His certainty turned to horror as the hillsides burst with awesome pyrotechnics. His soldiers blazed red and orange before vanishing in the steel storm unleashed on their bodies. He turned towards his aid whose head exploded like a ripe melon hitting the pavement. Blood splattered on Duri's face and tunic.

Duri jerked away from death to see the helicopter spinning away from the sniper fire and towards Harper's springing figure—a demon racing over the sand towards the open side door. Harper flung his last grenade into the open helicopter and dove away from the Jolly Green Giant. The *Sea King* tore itself apart from the inside as the tail rotor moved away from the fuselage.

A scream pierced his concentration as he turned to see Harper flying over the ridge and into his face boot first. A flying sidekick delivered from height on an unprepared target is a devastating blow. Duri raised his hands to protect himself from the two hundred five pound human projectile. His wrist snapped catching the blow.

Harper swung the Mossberg's pistol grip baseball style smashing the left side of Duri's face. He dropped the Mossberg and grabbed the Iraqi Colonel smashing a forearm along the right side of Duri's head. His knee came next driving straight towards the groin, but Harper maintained a grip on his shoulder epaulets. Wrenching the beaten man up, he kicked his legs out from under him and slammed the secret policeman to the ground. He landed his knee hard on Duri's chest and pulled his combat knife from his belt sheathe.

Harper gripped Duri's hair and pulled his head up slamming the hilt of the knife into his nose. More blood spurted from Duri's broken face. Harper reversed the grip on the knife and set the point on Duri's throat. "No one threatens my family! No one!" he roared.

Harper shook the Iraqi awake and hauled him to his feet. He spun Duri around and smashed him against the bank they were standing next to. Somewhere in his fury, he had lost his helmet. He replaced his knife and pulled the Glock from its holster. He looked at Burns and Kincaid stretched out on the ground and punched Duri in the kidney. Duri's legs went spaghetti again, but Harper kept him standing.

"Get a shovel."

Duri stared at him and smiled, “You’re still going to die, Harper.”

Harper pistol-whipped Duri with the Glock. “I said, get a shovel!”

Anderson appeared over a ridge holding the Barrett. Harper stared at him for a moment trying to remember who he was. The raged boiled across his features. “Captain, it’s good to see you again.”

“Yes, Sir.”

“What about Stillwell and Hayes?”

“Grand slam, Major.”

“And the Iraqi wounded?”

“Sergeant Hayes has them covered.”

Harper nodded. “All right, why don’t you look for something with an engine around here that still works.”

“Already got that covered, Major.”

“Really?”

“Yes, Sir. There’s a jeep under camouflage netting a hundred meters passed the ambush site.”

“Go get it running. There’ll be five of us.”

“Yes, Sir.”

He shoved Duri forward. He noticed for the first time the discoloration along Duri’s right wrist. It looked broken. He shoved the Iraqi again keeping a wary eye for any countermove. Harper said quietly, “That’s far enough.”

Duri paused and spread his hands wide. The right hand drooped sloppily. “Do you shoot me in the back, or do I get a blindfold and cigarette?”

“That’s probably more than you’ve given others, and certainly more than you deserve,” replied Harper.

Duri turned slowly to face the Glock’s jet-black muzzle. Neither of them looked very good. “You’ve killed many people today.”

Harper waited holding the gun steady. “I may kill again.”

Duri thought about the dossier that he had read last night. “You don’t like killing, Major Harper. I’m your prisoner now—name, rank, and serial number.”

"You're my enemy, I don't mind killing you," he lied.

Duri examined the three wrecked helicopters. The still burning Data Center. He could only imagine the number of dead men inside, his wounded under the watchful gaze of the black Marine Sergeant. His remaining men were all dead. Harper had reduced his command to himself. It was better to be Harper's prisoner than to return to Baghdad. "Perhaps we can make a deal."

"Your kneecaps for answers," suggested Harper redirecting the Glock to point somewhere between his legs.

Duri continued to hold his hands wide. His wrist was beginning to hurt badly. He knew he was useless to try and attack Harper. The man was forth degree black belt, an expert marksman and obviously, every bit the warrior his dossier described. He had underestimated the skill and determination of his opponent. Harper would fire the Glock. He would not hesitate. "I see. What sort of answers do you want?"

"How do you know about me, my team, my family?"

"I received an encrypted fax yesterday. It contained your mission, your team, and a complete dossier on each of you. I knew everything about you before you even left America. I'd say you have a spy in your midst."

Harper nodded calmly. The rage seemed to pull back from the brink. "Go on!"

"Cigarette?"

Harper jerked the Glock up, "No!"

Duri nodded quietly. "We were told about Lieutenant Stillwell. Part of the mission was to hand Stillwell over to our people. You see, a weapon expert like Stillwell could advance our employment of unconventional systems beyond things we might have considered."

"It was part of the plan?" asked Harper.

"Yes. Stillwell was the prize. You were picked because we believed you could get to the Data Center. Well, if we were going to stop you here, then we needed to make sure we grabbed Stillwell. The Data Center, your backup tapes and the mess you've left. It hurts us, but not that much. There's a mirrored site. We set it up after you were here the first time.

"As far as the weapon labs are concerned nothing has happened. You degraded some assets. You—"

Harper shook his head. "You're lying." He fired once. The bullet rushed by Duri's ear rupturing the eardrum. Harper waited for the Iraqi to regain his balance. "You were running an Oracle 7.1 site. You don't have real time replication, which means you either had a standby database, or if you had a mirrored site, it was an absolute mirror. That takes a lot of bandwidth and I don't think you have the infrastructure. I think your mirror site worked off a physical hand off. So try again."

A small trickle of blood ran down Duri's cheek. "You seem to know your subject."

"You've read my file—what do you think?"

Duri shrugged.

Anderson drove up in the jeep. Stillwell sat in the passenger seat. His face a white mask plastered around a pair of glazed eyes. Anderson got out of the jeep and explained, "He didn't take to being the bait too well."

"How about the wounded Iraqis?"

"Hayes has got them wrapped up with duct tape. It'll last for a while, but nothing very permanent."

"Okay, let's get Burns and Kincaid wrapped up in a tarp or something. We're bringing them home. I'll take care of this garbage." He waved the Glock towards Duri.

Duri's eye perked up. "So now you shoot me?"

Harper shook his head. "No." They started walking away from the jeep and into the desert where Harper had hidden the tapes.

"Where are we going?"

Harper grunted, "I'll give you a choice, Colonel."

Duri doubted he would like the choices. "All right."

"I leave you here to be found by your people. I doubt they'll be very happy. One Data Center trashed, a bunch of dead soldiers, three missing helicopters and intelligence operation compromised in the United States. Not my idea of career enhancing moves, or—"

Duri stopped cocking his head to hear clearly.

"I take you with me and turn you over to the Kuwaiti authorities. I'm sure they can find a nice place to keep you safe from Saddam. Who knows, they might even let you live. Saddam is not very pleased with failures, and you, Colonel, are a failure."

"Not much of a choice, Major."

Harper shoved the Iraqi again. "A bullet in the back of the head would be too easy, and I don't want it to be easy for you."

"The Kuwaitis will kill me."

"And Saddam won't?"

"I'd rather take my chances."

Harper pulled the trigger. Duri's left knee kicked out from under him and Duri slammed to the ground howling. He leaned over the Iraqi and whispered, "Remember something."

Duri glared at him wide eyed.

"If I ever see you near my family, I won't simply cripple you. I'll kill you." He spat once and walked away to collect the backup tapes.

31

J. Edgar Hoover Building, Washington DC, Monday, November 17, 1997, 10:00 AM EST

Mary Kirsten looked up from her computer monitor and examined the two men standing at the opening of her cubicle. Harvey Randall and Larry Wheeler had not been to bed, and despite their best efforts to clean up before coming from Virginia to the JEH building, they looked bone weary and run out.

"You two are quite something."

Harvey smiled. "You got any coffee around here?" he yawned.

"Sure. Down that isle and to the left," she paused, a twinkle in her eye. "Was the party worth it?"

Larry laughed, "Don't know yet."

"Thought you might be able to tell us," Harvey said as he pulled up a paper sack and slid a bubbled wrapped IDE disk drive enclosed in a static bag and bound by large rubber binders.

"What's this?"

"A disk drive," offered Larry.

Her lips pouted, "I know that—what's this about?"

"Maybe you could show us where that coffee is," suggested Harvey.

Mary fingered the evidence card taped to the top of the static bag. She read ODRICKS CORNER on the label. After the intense news coverage yesterday, Odricks Corner had become known to half the nation—the half that watched the twenty-four hour news channels. She wrinkled her brow and asked quietly, "That was you guys on the TV last night?"

"Uh-huh," replied Larry.

She looked them up and down again. "Long night."

"Had better ones," continued Larry.

"Maybe we should get some coffee that's better than the poison they brew on this floor." She patted the disk drive and opened her desk drawer. She placed the padded package into her drawer and locked it.

"That sounds nice."

Mary had been around the Bureau for twenty years. She was one of the *civilian* employees hired for her skills in areas outside of shooting and running. Mary was a computer guru. There simply was no other way of describing her. Give her a computer system whether it is VAX/VMS, MVS, Windows NT, UNIX, or Win95 it would soon give up its secrets to Mary. She was part of the elite group of people across the country that could pry, fiddle, and unlock a system.

A mother of two and the wife of a submarine driver, Mary and Josh Kirsten chose to make their home in Virginia. Six-month sea deployments put incredible strains on a marriage, but then they did make for tearful and joyful reunions. The Bureau recognized her abilities and created a flexible schedule to accommodate the needs of her family.

Her cubicle wall had some aged crayon drawings of hillsides and daisy flowers, a photograph of a younger Josh when he had been assigned to the USS Nimitz, and their calico cat, Nicki. A big red heart was plastered on the Monday after Thanksgiving on her Thomas Kincaid calendar.

"Josh coming home soon?"

Her features brightened. "Two weeks. He'll get to see the kids' Christmas program this year," she explained.

They walked down the isle to the stairwell that led down to the cafeteria. Once the stairwell door closed behind them, she asked quickly, "What's it all about Harvey?"

Harvey glanced up the stairwell and Larry checked below. "That disk may have operational details for a black op currently in progress."

They started walking down the steps, "So?"

"The drive is from the house in Odricks Corner. They were Chinese illegals," continued Larry.

She nodded again more slowly. "And?" she prodded.

"And—" Harvey looked around again. "And if the operational detail is on the disk, then someone very important gave it to the Chinese."

"How high?"

He sighed and rubbed the back of his ear. "You know we've been trying to track down a mole inside the executive branch."

Her head bobbed up and down. "Everyone knows you two have been on the great spy hunt. From what I hear, it isn't the most appreciated assignment in Washington."

"Yeah, there's a lot of static."

"We think that what's on the disk was passed to a Chinese agent known as *Goldenrod*. Oh, he has a name—lots of them in fact. None of them are real, and we don't exactly know who he really is."

"The diplomatic thing?"

Larry snorted, "You could say we had some words with *Goldenrod*."

"But he had diplomatic immunity," added Harvey.

"So if the stuff is on the disk—what's that mean?"

"We got a list of four or five people including the National Security Advisor and a Two Star General," explained Harvey.

Her hand came to rest of the door leading out of the stairwell to the floor where the cafeteria was located. "What do you want me to do?"

Harvey leaned his hand against the door and said quietly, "I want you to tell us what's on the disk without officially entering it into evidence." He glared at Larry and said just as softly, "Larry was never here. We never had this conversation."

Larry said just as quietly, "There may be real people getting killed over this right now."

"You need to bypass the bureaucracy."

Harvey nodded.

"For how long?"

"Maybe forever."

She opened the door and walked into the corridor leading down to the cafeteria. "There's more to this than you're telling me." It was a statement of fact, no questions anymore. After all, a mother of two is a world-class expert in ferreting out the truth.

"Yes," said Harvey.

"But I don't have a need to know."

"It would be safer that way," agreed Larry.

They flanked her as they walked towards the bank of machines offering rolls, candy bars, chips, soft drinks, coffee, and fruit drinks.

"When you say people may be getting killed, what sort of people are you talking about?"

Harvey dropped three quarters into a machine and punched the button for Diet Mountain Dew. "Soldiers."

"Like Josh—those kind of soldiers?"

Larry nodded and watched as his corn chips dropped to the bottom of the machine's bin. "Yep."

"We're not at war."

"We're always at war," corrected Harvey.

"Are you saying someone sold out our people and now they may be getting killed because of it?"

It was a terrible world they lived in. "Yes." Harvey pulled the handle for a bag of Danish shortbread cookies.

"Okay," she said simply as they walked away from the machines. "What do you want me to do with the disk once we're done with it?"

"Lose it for a while," said Larry.

"And maybe forever?"

"And maybe forever," echoed Harvey.

☆ ☆ ☆

Two hours later, they had their answers. Everything was there: The original briefing papers, the U2 spy photographs, the Q files for each member of the team, satellite signal beacon frequencies, mission targets, and parameters.

Harvey, Larry, and Mary sat in a conference room on the same floor as her cubicle. They examined the printouts from the color laser printer, the contents of the Q files, which composed a massive amount of information. It piled up to almost an inch of paper before the printer finished spewing the contents.

Mary pushed a slip of paper and said, "They uploaded everything to this web site. It was encoded with these two addresses. I don't know where they sent it, but they used a commercial encryption key you can buy for a hundred bucks mail order. I have the key and everything else sitting on my hard drive.

"I also have their Netscape history file and can track where they went. This looks like something from down the road at Langley."

Harvey nodded, "Could be."

"I'd suggest you give these Internet addresses to the National Security Agency boys and see if they might want to launch an attack on these web sites."

"You can do that?"

Mary nodded, "If we get passed the firewall—assuming they have one—those boys can do some interesting things to their computer systems."

☆ ☆ ☆

Louis Edwards found Harvey standing inside the Jefferson Memorial. The FBI man had a briefcase parked next to his foot as he read the inscriptions on the wall. Behind Harvey towered the nineteen-foot statue of Thomas Jefferson presiding over excerpts from his writings engraved on the walls.

The white marble dome glittered in the whiter and harsher November sunshine. Harvey found Louis Edwards observing him with his hands clasped behind his back, and the ever-present minders hovering in the background. He wondered what Jefferson would have done, and chuckled. The man wrote the Declaration of Independence. He pledged his life, reputation, and fortune for an idea called America.

A rag tag bunch of radicals took on and chased away the greatest empire of their day. They waded through swamps and dark forests, and died on bright fields. They used weapons that failed more often than worked in an age where a flesh wound could be fatal. Then in 1812 they did it all over again when the British set fire to Washington.

Harvey found it ironic that fifty years to the day after the Declaration of independence was penned, Thomas Jefferson died at his home in Monticello. He looked up to the third president and figured Jefferson's generation would have had a pistol duel at dawn with the fog rolling in from the Potomac to settle the matters in his briefcase. They were men of action and ideas.

He pushed the briefcase towards Edwards and explained, "It's all in there."

Louis glanced down at the proffered briefcase. "And?"

"It's what you suspected, so I guess you deal with it."

Louis nodded.

"Let me know if you need to arrest anybody, but I kind of figure someone will just end up missing some morning or something like that."

"Or something," replied Edwards.

"They know all about your boys. I mean everything. We didn't have time to read it, we just printed it out, but it's not the kind of stuff you'd want showing up in the *Washington Post* anytime soon."

Louis picked up the briefcase. It was the very worst security breach.

"I was your only contact," cautioned Harvey.

Louis sighed, "Destroy the disk and get rid of the files. No publicity this time."

"You're sure."

"It's better this way."

"It's illegal you know."

"So many things are illegal these days, Agent Randall. As far as you're concerned, it never happened." He turned and walked towards his minders.

Harvey stood with his hands in his pockets alone with his thoughts. Truth and justice were not pretty words on a page. They were ideas that meant something. Harvey crossed a line today into the nether world populated with the likes of Louis Edwards. He chose to follow a risky path of uncertain destination. Finally, he looked up at Jefferson's searching eyes and asked quietly, "Were you scared when you signed your name that day in Philadelphia along with Sam Adams and Ben Franklin and the rest?"

Jefferson never answered, and Harvey shuffled towards his car. It was time to get some sleep.

32

East Of Nukhayb, Iraqi Data Center, Monday, November 17, 1997, 7:30 PM (+3.00 GMT)

Colonel Duri finally opened his eyes. The sky was changing from the light desert blue to the deeper purplish night blue. The air had chilled considerably, and the pain blazing on his right knee had retreated to a pounding blossom of pain with each heartbeat. He licked his sand blown lips and considered the disaster that today had become.

Harper would have been more merciful to aim higher. At least if he were dead, the torture meted out as punishment for his failure would be meaningless. Not that he was at all certain he would find the welcoming arms of Allah waiting for him. The certainty of Saddam's anger was ensured now. He had no Americans to parade with blindfolds and handcuffs through the streets of Baghdad. There would be no grand news conference or displays of captured American hardware. There would be no interviews with survivors from the Data Center attack with terrible wounds and rasping coughs.

This was a total failure. He would find himself in the capable hands of the scientists striving to perfect a biological weapon to unleash in Israel, London, Paris, and Washington. Perhaps, he would be one of the test subjects drugged in some bizarre fashion to determine how quickly he would die and how rapidly he could infect others. Ultimately, his demise would be brutal and barbaric, as his internal organs would begin to hemorrhage and blood dribble down his nose and out his ears. His lungs might fill with his own body fluids and drown him, or his heart could explode. It simply depended on how poorly his body dealt with the violence attached to his punishment.

He propped himself up on his elbow and examined the bloody wreck just below his knee. There were other possibilities to consider. The crusty dark splotches around his leg told him how much blood he had lost. He needed medical attention, but medical attention would place him under the *care* of Saddam's Iraq. Medical care led to death.

Using his good arm, he unbuckled his belt and fashioned a crude tourniquet above his right knee. He realized he had underestimated Jim Harper, a mistake he would not make twice. Duri tucked thoughts of revenge away for the moment. First, he had to escape his masters, and then get patched up before he could consider killing Harper and his family.

He could see the crumpled remains of a soldier killed earlier today. His rifle was laying a few inches from his outstretched fingers. Duri pulled himself over to the dead man—a veteran of the Iraq/Iran and Gulf wars according to the battle patches on his arm. The soldier had survived human wave attacks, missile, and Allied bombardment to fall to the hands of a single American commando.

Duri pulled the rifle towards him by the barrel. As soon as he could, he pushed the muzzle away from his face. The last thing he needed was another bullet hole. He dropped the magazine on the dirt and worked the bolt by jamming the rifle stock against his hip. The chambered round cart wheeled from the ejection port. He levered himself to a standing position using the AK-74 as a crude crutch. He started the awkward drag and hop movement back towards his field radio.

He considered Harper's options. Most of them were poor. He could attempt the suicidal and unexpected by heading north into the desert and attempt to place Karbala between himself and Baghdad, then skirt the Iraqi/Syrian border until reaching Southern Turkey. A very dangerous course, since he would leave the protective umbrella of the no fly zone and become vulnerable to air and ground attack.

To the west lay the twin demons Al-Hamad and Al-Harrah of the Syrian Desert—a sun blasted wasteland devoid of water and animal. So desolate is the Syrian Desert that the jackals do not hunt and the vultures do not fly. They would need food, water, and petrol before attempting to cross, and the only place to get those items was Ar-Rutbah.

The south held some promise for Harper's team. They would need to navigate to the east of the lake and travel over broken ground to get to the Saudi border. A mere line on paper. There were no markers or neat dotted lines in the hard sand and barren rocks. Somewhere further south lay the main pipeline across the Arabian peninsula and a road running east and west. The first town where Harper could find refuge was Ad-Duwayd. If necessary, Duri would kill everyone there to recapture the American.

Kuwait was over four hundred kilometers to the east. A difficult journey to accomplish over mostly Iraqi territory. It would be a simple thing to alert all the militia units between here and Kuwait to stop the Americans. Harper's best option was the Saudi route. Duri could create a wall of armored vehicles leading eastward and then drive south as fast as possible and run down the Americans. Perhaps, there was still a chance to avoid the boiling death in one of Saddam's gas chambers.

Duri realized it had become a personal war between himself and Harper. He looked down sadly at his shattered knee. He would get the American before dawn. They would meet again under the brightening stars, and this time there would be no place to hide. He would retrieve Stillwell and present Saddam with a world class weapons expert. He would batter and truss his American soldiers so that they could be dragged through the streets of Baghdad. The tame CNN reporters would gleefully play the tape over and over across their vast cable and satellite networks. It would be Somalia all over again. There was no reason to believe the American President would do much more than *feel their pain.*

He licked his lips anticipating the confrontation to come. The acrid smoke from the Data Center hung in the still desert night air. Harper was correct about a secondary site being a periodic data dump. The fail over scenario designed to ensure the survivability of the Data Center. It was supposed to prevent loss of service should a catastrophic failure occur. Fail over was one of those marvelous buzz words, but no one ever tested it for fear of failure and the implications failure held for technicians in Saddam's Iraq. Plans certainly had been drawn up and many hours spent in writing proposals and arguing technologies, but never had an attempt been made to find out if Iraq's secret weapons system network could handle the catastrophic failure of the primary site. He wondered how many irreplacable computer technicians would be shot in the next several hours.

The prowling E-3A *Sentry* AWACS and JSTAR systems would observe the increase in signal traffic. The Americans always responded to increased traffic on Iraq's radio network. Additional flights would soon sortie from air fields in Turkey, Kuwait, Saudi Arabia, and the cursed American carriers. By midnight they would be crisscrossing Iraqi airspace taking their pictures, searching for active surface to air missile sites, and dropping the occasional bomb. Flights were always coordinated by three or more AWAC command planes operating safely behind a flying shield of F-15 *Eagles*.

Duri found that some of the wounded had freed themselves from their bonds. They looked dazed. Considering his own injuries, he did not feel too good himself. He waved one of the healthier ones toward him.

The sergeant held his rifle by the receiver keeping it horizontal to the ground. He had a bandage wrapped around his thigh and it glistened with fresh blood. The sergeant did not bother to salute, he straightened his shoulders and said hoarsely, "Sir."

"Find one of the jeeps and one other solider."

The sergeant grunted and turned away to shamble towards the camouflaged bivouac. There were three secreted around the Data Center. Five additional vehicles remained at Duri's disposal. There was no need to deal with the injured, the relief column should arrive shortly from Karbala. Colonel Taha Duri needed to be gone before they arrived. Their job was to tend to the wounded and secure the Data Center. If he got tangled in the bureaucracy, Harper would escape and Duri would face the very permanent solution designed for Israel and America.

Duri shrugged and reached down for the field telephone. He started making the calls to flush Harper towards the Saudi border.

★ ★ ★

Nukhayb was not much of a town anymore. It had the distinction of being the first Tall Man radar station to be hit by allied aircraft on the first night of the air war. The Tall Man radar stations formed the early warning perimeter of Iraq's air defense system. The only warning the Iraqi command had was when those very radars went dark, and bombs began to fall on parts of Baghdad. Beyond that distinction, most of the streets are unpaved. Most of the homes go dark after the sun sets. At best, the power grid provides intermittent service due to the neglected damage inflicted during the war.

Much of Iraq had been abandoned by the Baghdad government. Those living in the periphery survived as they had for centuries. In many places, running water was replaced with a series of earthen wells. Electrical lights were basically useless fixtures, and ancient oil lamps filled the gap. The dazzling Presidential Palaces and five star hotels found in the capitol were nothing more than rumors on the periphery.

Night replaced day with a deep purple, and the Milky Way band was clearly stretching across the night sky. The billions of stars provided enough light for Hayes to drive the jeep using their only surviving pair of Night Vision Goggles. They rolled quietly down the streets finding the occasional dog examining them from folded paws or a darting cat in search of dinner.

The residents were bored with khaki colored vehicles and drab men toting automatic weapons. It was a dusty town at the edge of the real desert—a last outpost somewhat reminiscent of civilization with a mix of nineteenth and twentieth century technology. These days only nineteenth century technology worked.

Harper tapped Hayes on the shoulder and pointed to a truck parked next to a darkened barracks. Hayes slowed the jeep down as Anderson and Harper dismounted holding their weapons. Stillwell simply stared straight ahead. Hayes had pumped him full of Valium once they cleared the Data Center. It was better to have a walking zombie than someone who might start screaming.

Anderson slid up to the barracks door. Harper slung the Mossberg over his shoulder and produced the silenced Browning. He flipped the safety down and nodded to Anderson. The large man tapped with the back of his fist on the wooden door. They both heard someone grunt from inside the barracks.

The door pulled open and Harper stuck the Browning in the soldier's face. An oil lamp illuminated the room. The electricity was reserved for the radio. The Browning seemed more menacing with a thick sausage sized-silencer hanging off the end of the barrel. The soldier spread his hands wide and backed into the barracks. Harper gave him a shove and said quickly in Arabic, "Keys."

Anderson slid into the barracks behind Harper. He quietly closed the door behind him and found a second man snoring away on a cot next to the radio. His eyes snapped open when the cold muzzle from the M-16 jiggled the fatty tissue around his neck.

The soldier examining the Browning managed to point to the board where the keys were nicely tagged. Harper spun his man against the wall finding several pair of handcuffs hanging next to the keys. He turned his man around and cuffed him from behind and through the back arms of a chair. It certainly would not hold them for long, but long enough to get clear. Harper was tired of killing.

Anderson trussed his Iraqi and tossed him into a closet. The radio was of marginal value to Harper. All Allied communication was transmitted on encrypted and secure networks. The chances that someone who knew about their mission might be listening were remote.

"Captain, wreck that thing."

Anderson took his combat knife in hand. Sixty seconds later a mass of sliced and shredded cables lay on the floor beneath the radio transmitter. Harper fired a magazine worth of 9mm rounds into the case, before tapping his Iraqi with an uppercut to the chin and "lights out". Harper saw a torch and an area map on the wall. He grabbed both on the way out the door.

Hayes caught the keys to the truck. He had moved Burns and Kincaid to the bed of the truck. The rest of their gear and Stillwell kept company with the dead Marines. Anderson climbed into the rear next to his Barrett sniper rifle. Harper climbed in the cab next to Hayes.

Less than five minutes passed as the truck rolled out of Nukhayb and headed east towards Kuwait. Harper hunched over the map and Hayes drove into the night. The entire reason for the mission sat in a canvas bag on the floor between Harper's feet. Harper needed a plan, and the only ones he came up with were bad.

☆ ☆ ☆

Dylan Scott handed Jonas a spare pair of Night Vision Goggles. "It's much better than using a spot light. Doesn't give the bad guys such an obvious target if they're a mind to try their shiny new rifles."

Jonas took the pair and slipped them on. The world turned to the multi shaded green fuzziness. They were twenty klicks from the locator point. The insistent dot had remained stationary. Jonas was beginning to lose heart and considered the dreadful possibility that Harper was dead.

Dylan Scott said quite suddenly, "He's not dead, lad."

Jonas cocked an eyebrow at his pilot. "You think so?"

"We are talking about Jim Harper aren't we?" chuckled Dylan Scott.

"Yes."

"Harper's not dead. He called for help. That's what the locator beacon is for—correct?"

"Yeah," murmured Jonas dejectedly.

"Things didn't go so good did they? Someone pulled your bones didn't they?"

Jonas nodded agreement. They were seventeen klicks away. Dylan pulled the chopper from the headlong plunge towards their target and engaged the silent rotor. "Just a little extra I had added when I specified drop tanks and the chain gun. We're going silent. You see, we may not be armored, but we can be stealthy."

Jonas sighed. "I fear he's dead. The locator hasn't moved since it went off."

Dylan shook his head. "Has it even occurred to you that the Iraqis might be capable of tracking the same signal? Maybe he used it to ambush somebody. Maybe he used it because he truly needed help. We won't know for a few more minutes."

Jonas considered his words. "There's no way the Iraqis could track the signal."

Dylan held up his hand cutting Jonas off. "There's no way. Oh, I've heard that so many times. We all think these rag heads are stupid. They're not, you know, and worst thing a warrior can do is underestimate his opponent.

"We were told finding those SCUD missile launchers would be a snap. We found some of them—those that were really launchers, but we missed the trucks with hydraulic lifts, and grain silos titled sideways, and concrete culverts pointed in funny directions. We never thought our good friend and ally would turn into the evil monster he always was.

"As long as Saddam was killing Iranians, you Americans turned a blind eye to the Kurds getting slaughtered and the nuclear weapons development. You forgot Saddam was more of a Soviet client than a tame western dictator. We underestimated the threat, and then woke up one morning to find the fourth largest land army in the world was poised to roll over the Saudi Kingdom and lock up close to half of the world's known oil reserves. That wasn't supposed to happen either. So don't tell me they can't track your signal."

Dylan Scott spoke with the authority of one who had been on the sharp end of the war. An alphabet soup worth of Special Forces teams had penetrated Iraq during the Gulf War. They prowled throughout the entire country with the laser painting targeting devices, satellite phones, and a general, mischief-making bag of tricks.

Not every bridge collapsed because a *Tornado* or *Intruder* dropped enough bombs. They certainly did drop bombs, but a great deal of that ordinance was directed by the hearty souls dug into the desert buried in their steel coffins. Satellites did not always work, especially when the weather failed to cooperate and harsh storms swept over theater operations.

Targeting dozens of Saddam's underground bunkers took place because a man with a rifle was close enough to laze the correct airshaft. Launch on warning occurred many times because a soldier with gun was close enough to phone home. Dylan still believed it was the wrong decision to stop when they did. Baghdad was naked before the Allied Army, and Saddam would eventually have to surface. Instead, they had settled for a stalemate as they had in Korea and Europe at the end of Hitler's war.

The carnage suddenly swept into focus. Dylan tapped Jonas's arm pointing at the wrecked helicopter. "Looks like a *Sea King*."

Jonas peered out the windscreen. The still warm bodies quivered like ghosts in their NVG vision. Two more wrecked helicopters came into view. After the third *Sea King*, Jonas spotted the HMMWV's laying burned and broken on their backs. He tapped Dylan's arm and pointed.

"Bad news, that," muttered the SAS man.

"Those were Harper's vehicles!" shouted Jonas. "Can you pull closer?"

Dylan pulled the Puma to a mere ten feet off the deck. The wreckage was twisted and burned, but the lack of bodies struck both men odd. Elsewhere there were bodies on the ground. Some shapes still moved in a drunken way.

"If they were toast, we should see them," said Jonas explaining the obvious to the older man.

Dylan nodded. Hope is a slender reed. It takes faith to keep hope alive. "They're not here."

Dylan swung the helicopter around and flew through the smoke cloud hovering above the Data Center. "What was that?" snapped Jonas.

"Smoke—smells like some plastic melted down." He pushed the throttle towards the wadi and said, "You're locator signal must be down there."

Jonas followed the outstretched hand and saw nothing. He found the two dead Iraqi soldiers after a couple of seconds.

"It looks like war took place here."

"Right you are," replied Dylan Scott.

They flew across the quarry. Jonas recognized the land's contours from the many satellite and U2 photographs taken. The both saw the column of lights plodding southward from the north on a road that was little better than a goat track.

"Company," said Jonas.

"Fresh troops for a battle that's over," observed Dylan. "He's not here, young Jonas. He's left."

"How do you know?"

"I know Harper. I know how he thinks." They spun back over the triage finding several men milling about. "He left the wounded alive. Putting someone out of the fight was enough for Harper, unless it became personal that is. If it ever became personal, then Harper took no prisoners." He pointed to the wrecked HMMWV's.

"His transport is smashed, and probably most of his supplies. That means he's low or out of just about everything he needs to survive—ammo, food, water, medicine and petrol. Not good news."

Dylan held the *Puma* steady above the nearest wrecked *Sea King.* "So what would he do?"

"Finish his mission and get out. Obviously, someone has flattened the bad guys. And just as obvious, the plan didn't quite follow the script. Otherwise, the HMMWVs wouldn't be smashed. From the looks of this, he's probably got wounded or dead with him. He's running."

Jonas eyed the truck column approaching from the north. They would be there in less than fifteen minutes. Dylan pulled the helicopter away from the carnage below.

"He's afraid to use the other locator beacon isn't he?"

Dylan nodded. "That'd be my guess. He's been burned once. I doubt he can afford to burned twice."

"So where would he run?"

Dylan thought for moment. "I'd run south as fast as I could. Still, from here that's a long run. He'd need transport and probably medical supplies. He'll be moving fast."

"So we head south."

"It's not that easy," corrected Dylan.

"Oh?"

"There are three wrecked helicopters down there, and a bunch of casualties. Harper isn't going to trust very much. He has a couple of routes across the border. Most of those routes are more lines on a map than any recognizable landmark."

"What are you saying?"

"We're going to need help. Iraqi signal traffic might tell us something. But it's time for you to concoct some tale and get the good guys into the fight." He tossed a satellite phone into Jonas's lap.

"You're sure about him going south?"

"Closest to your own lines and this isn't the movies. Overland treks through hostile territory makes for good stories, but there's enough drama just getting home sometimes."

Jonas flipped open the laptop and punched up a list of phone numbers. Perhaps, asking Admiral Trevor Barnes to assist in securing the Saudi border was enough of a deviation from his original orders to justify a pair of Hornets.

Jonas resented being cut off from resources he had been promised. He suspected Harper downright hated the idea.

PART 3

Blackest of the Black

"Woe to those who call evil good, and good evil; Who substitute darkness for light and light for darkness; Who substitute bitter for sweet and sweet for bitter!"

Isaiah 5:20

33

Washington DC, Pentagon D-Ring, Monday, November 17, 1997, 1:00 PM EST

General George Carnady examined the photographs, the printouts, and the Q files on his people. Everything Louis pulled out of his brief case was classified above secret. For a foreign agent to have such information in his possession was a critical problem. For the information to be current, as to include a briefing he had attended on Saturday was catastrophic.

"Where did this come from again?"

Louis leaned forward in his chair, "Did you see the news last night about the FBI raid in Virginia?"

"Hard to miss it."

"Came off of a hard disk they found in the basement," explained Louis.

Carnady rubbed his brow. Not good—not good at all to have this on somebody's PC.

"Where'd they get it?"

Louis flipped open a notepad and said, "George, we've been friends for a long time." In fact, they had been friends since the Reagan years when both had proposed a plan to develop a special counter terrorist team outside all military channels. A secret team of fifty or so recruits run from the intelligence community and hidden from public view, unlike the stories regarding DELTA and the SEALS.

George Carandy had been a light colonel, and Louis a much younger man running agents inside the Indochina, Eastern Europe, and inside the still strong Soviet Empire during the turbulent seventies. The word came down early in the Reagan years; they were going to win the cold war. No one really believed such nonsense except Bill Casey and Ronald Reagan.

It was crazy to talk about defeating the evil empire. The Soviet Union was a fact of life and a permanent fixture on the world stage. So how did the new president (and former Hollywood actor) fail to understand such fundamental policies?

Today, everyone understood that the Soviet model lay on history's trash heap. The dominating post war era of mutually assured destruction, whose acronym was aptly coined MAD, was a bygone era. The mighty red army had become fragmented, impoverished, and uncertain. The bastion of Marxist revolution grew penniless, and the first faint stirrings of democratic rule sprouted through the gray rubble. Freedom attempted to find a foothold in the barren soil of people ruled for centuries by Czars and dictators.

Ronald Reagan was right. Bill Casey was perhaps one of the few men who truly understood the Great Communicator and moved like a seasoned spook to implement his president's policies. Bill Casey paged through hundreds of personnel folders to find Louis and George. Both had become refugees during the Carter Administration where force of any kind was always the last resort.

Admiral Stansfield Turner, who was Carter's Director of Central Intelligence, had a blacklist that became an honor roll for Casey. Louis had found himself prominently displaced during the Carter years due to his views on using human spies instead of relying on satellites—a concept contrary to Admiral Turner's absolute belief in satellites and machines. Louis argued that what people thought was just as important as how many tanks, planes, or missiles they might have. It was barren ground. Louis found himself banished and counting nervous looking sheep in New Zealand.

Similarly, George Carnady had written several white papers that suggested the formation of highly trained counter terrorist teams be formed to combat the increasing aggressiveness coming from the Middle East, Central America, and Southeast Asia. The right idea proffered too soon after Vietnam. This was an era of amnesty for draft dodgers. Uniforms, blood, and honor were passé. America retreated from her responsibilities and looked for ways to appease the oil producing states. Carnady found himself commanding a weather station in the Aleutian Islands.

Over warm brandy and fine cigars, Bill Casey listened to their stories and entertained their theories about what needed to be done. The times were urgent. America's armed forces had languished for lack of funding and realistic training. Should the Red Army decide to drive through the Fulda Gap with two hundred or more divisions, no one was certain the ninety or so NATO divisions could stop them short of the Ruhr Cities.

The defeat in Vietnam, Reagan's predecessor's talk of a general malaise, and the affront of the Iranian hostage taking left the world wondering if there would soon only be one superpower—a Soviet Superpower. Never should the country be faced with another embassy hostage taking. There needed to be a team ready to go and ready to fight. America's prestige and the perception of her willingness to deal with bandit states needed to be rebuilt. Words and symbols could inspire, but definite and decisive actions were needed to remove doubts regarding America's willingness to engage her enemies.

Louis still remembered the half grin on Casey's face. He reached into a drawer and pulled out a letter. It was the most extraordinary letter either George or Louis had ever seen. Signed by both Casper Weinberger—the Secretary of Defense—and William Casey—Director of Central Intelligence, the letter instructed any military commander to provide all possible assistance to the letter's bearers.

Casey puffed a cigar contentedly and explained to the stunned pair, "I've picked you two to do what you've been talking about for five years. We need a team capable of going wherever and accomplishing whatever. I don't know what the missions will be yet. Time and circumstances will dictate that. But understand this—this team is the *blackest of the black.*

"I don't want a fancy name or number or anything else that will show up in the *Washington Post* or *New York Times*. These men, and possibly women, will have to do some extraordinary things, because by the time this administration is finished in eight years, we're going to beat the Russian Bear back into its hole for good. That's the overall mission—no more containment or strained coexistence. The job before you is to give this country a weapon to break the Soviet Union into a million little pieces without lighting the nuclear fuse." He lifted his glass as a toast.

The missions required technical and martial expertise. The Soviet economy had been given several not so gentle shoves towards the brink. They had even managed to place a man inside North Korea's nuclear production facility, and helped more than one Iranian Mullah meet Allah a bit earlier than planned.

They had lost over half the people recruited. Death was not an uncommon occurrence in this silent service. The list of those who actually knew what had been done during the Reagan and Bush years never reached more than fifteen. Over time, they learned how to develop funding sources beyond the Federal treasury, and they managed to maintain a bureaucratic presence inside Langley.

In late 1992 when it became clear the tide was turning, Louis quietly turned the switch off, and this *blackest of the black* disbanded. There were times when you protected your most vital secrets from those you were pledged to work for. The 1992 election was such a time.

Carnady nodded. "Yes. What's your point Louis?"

"How did Harper's Q file leak?"

George settled back in his chair. "We *never* computerized those files. As far as I know, you have the only paper copies in a vault down at Langley. You weren't at the briefing when we discussed Harper as mission leader."

"No, I was busy convincing Harper to come back. It took some doing. He wanted an insurance policy for Jerry's wife and kids. I had to draw some funds from one of our accounts. Tricky business these days with the White House constantly looking at everything we're doing."

"Young Jonas was the briefing officer. There was a deputy Secretary of State for the Middle East—a boorish woman is the best way to describe her. The NSA and his aide attended, plus the poor fellow we sent along on this team."

"Stillwell?"

George nodded. "That's his name. I don't think he was up to stomping through the desert and getting shot at."

"So were the Q files there?" asked Louis.

George shook his head. "A briefing paper. There was a heavily edited synopsis of Harper's experience, along with the rest of the team. But the Marines were not part of our operation."

Louis nodded. Their operation no longer existed and the chances for someone with Reagan's vision in the next election were slim. "So did someone else computerize their Q files?"

"Virtually everything is these days. They scan the stuff in, compress it and store it on optical disks. WORM technology—write once read many times. With this administration and their abuse of domestic intelligence, anything is possible."

"That leaves Harper's file?"

George sighed, "Someone went into the vault at Langley and copied it."

"The only people with that kind of authority—"

"Work in the West Wing," concluded George.

"That leaves the NSA or one of his aides," replied Louis.

"Arthur somebody or other. Never did get a last name." George rubbed his hands together. "Louis, this needs to be tended to. Spitting Q files over the Internet to hostile governments exposes too many secrets."

"Agreed." Secrets cut both ways. There were secrets both wanted kept from their own government as well as China and Iraq.

"You said the mission had been cancelled."

Louis nodded. "Yeah, I went over to the White House last night to talk about the toxicology results on the body Jonas pulled out of the Gulf. A very lethal variant of VX is basically what we found.

"They told me a couple of things, George—crazy things. Evidently, one of our sub drivers sunk a Chinese boat this weekend. They were upset at the news. Then they explained that the mission was cancelled, and our men were write-offs."

George Carnady's features darkened. "Just like that—they give up on six men?"

Louis nodded.

"Harper's not going to like that," murmured George. He shook his head. "The nerve gas news—is it the *City Killer* stuff we've been hearing about?"

"I think so. The NSA didn't want the report, so I have it sitting in a safety deposit box."

"Not your agency vault?"

Louis shook his head. "I started getting squeamish about doing that after the FBI HRT hit the Chinese safe house. Now you're telling me they probably got Harper's Q file out of the Agency vault, that's not very reassuring."

"Well look at it this way. Suppose the NSA gives your boss a call." He chuckled and added cynically, "A rare event these days. Tells him he's looking for something on Jim. It's your basic Peter Principle in action. The DCI is so used to being ignored by the White House, he'll do anything for some attention. The DCI finds the Q file and rushes it over to the White House."

"You think the NSA is the leak."

George shook his head. He fished the document on the wire transfers from Little Rock to the Cayman Islands. He spun the paper around and said, "No, the NSA isn't dirty. He may be venal and stupid, but really dirty—" George shook his head.

"Arthur?"

"Yeah, that's how I see it. You put someone in place to do the day-to-day chores. Imagine what must go through their hands over there. And we both know half those people couldn't get security clearance as dogcatchers.

"The Chinese know all about their missing sub, or if they don't—they will shortly."

Louis wondered aloud, "I wonder how much money is stashed away in this account?"

"Something to find out," George suggested.

He examined the files on his desk and pulled his paper shredder close to the desk. "Louis, this stuff needs to disappear." He started feeding pages through the machine. It churned the Q files into strips going one direction then crosscut the strips again.

"Perhaps the best thing to do is let Harper meet Arthur."

"Yeah, let nature take its course."

34

The Road To Ash-Shabakah, Tuesday, November 18, 1997, 1:00 AM (+3.00 GMT)

Hayes whistled tunelessly through his chapped lips and dust caked teeth. The world was a fuzzy green moonscape as he pushed the old truck down the four-lane highway towards the Kuwaiti border. A border too far away in a vehicle too limited to make the journey. They drove without lights making fifty klicks per hour. They would probably run out of gas before they ran out of night. He felt the weight from the last forty-eight hours in his shoulders and across the back of his neck. The little white no doze pills he popped like candy kept him going. There would certainly be a price to pay. Hopefully, it would come due after they reached the good guys.

Anderson sat half-crouched in the back of the lorry. His massive hands resting on the Barrett draped across his knees. His head slumped forward. The terrible day in the desert was over. The deadly work was accomplished, and now he slumbered dreaming of tall green pines, and crystal blue lakes—a graphite rod in hands as he fished for Walleye and Northern Pike. It was a wonderful dream, because he left out the pesky mosquitoes and even larger deer flies. Waves lapped gently against the side of the boat and rocked him to sleep.

Stillwell had finally conked out. He lay on the bed of the lorry next to the bodies of Burns and Kincaid—his mouth open and slack jawed. His dreams were tortured. He relived the firefight in the Data Center's lower level. He marveled and shuddered as Hayes and Harper and he dropped into a choreographed fighting arrangement and fired without mercy into the oncoming Iraqis—punctuated by an awful silence. The only sound truly trapped in his mind was a spinning brass cartridge case ; the stench of smokeless powder, and the slight haze from their firing was still pungent in his senses.

Harper leaned against the passenger side of the cab. His face bathed in a thin sheen of sweat. Even now, when they were certainly dehydrated from the battle, he wore a sweat drenched T-shirt and BDU's. The heavy body armor was still on, and his hand never really let loose of the Mossberg. The canvas bag filled with backup tapes was plopped between his feet on the floor of the truck. Strangely, his dreams were peaceful. The horror suggested by Colonel Duri was far from his mind. Instead, he imagined himself batting tennis balls across the yard and his huge hound, *Indiana Jones,* loping to retrieve them. It was a sunny summer Friday afternoon and the various toils for the week were retreating from his mind.

The plan was to head east towards Ash-Shabakah, then turn south into Saudi Arabia. There might be a military presence on the road as it crossed the line into a safer place, but Harper felt they could deal with the issue. The alternative was to attempt to move the truck over the rough ground straight for the border.

The plan had little room for contingencies. The promised helicopters and *Apache* Gun ships never materialized. The air support and additional troops waiting just over the horizon remained over the horizon somewhere. The *come get me in a hurry* signal beacon seemed more familiar to the Iraqi troops than their own people. No fast movers appeared to turn the tide. No choppers to bring out the dead and wounded, and their transport was a twisted mass of metal.

The plan really was not much of a plan at all. It was hope and luck wadded together with sweat and blood. As Hayes crested the next ridge, he blinked a couple times. The normally deserted highway was ablaze with lights moving steadily westward. He shook his head wondering if the liberal use of no doze pills had finally begun exacting their pound of flesh.

He counted four sets of headlights moving towards them on all four lanes of the highway. He slowed the truck to a halt and tapped Harper on the shoulder.

Harper's eyes snapped open and he stared blankly through the dusty truck windscreen. It took a few more moments for the scene to register and translate what his eyes saw into some semblance of thought. Harper slowly lifted his binoculars to his eyes and counted four Mercedes Benz tractor/trailers rolling towards them not more than two klicks distant.

"We need to get off the road now," whispered Harper. His body was gearing up for a fight, perhaps the final one. Even as his breathing and heart rates increased, he was painfully aware of the many bumps and bruises protesting any sudden movement. The downtime after action had settled into cramps and twists. The fluid loss resulted in a dullness that hung heavily on his chest and upper arms.

"We won't get very far in this," commented Hayes.

"I know."

The truck rumbled over the side of the road and into the uneven terrain. The springs and shock absorbers bounced them mercilessly. Hayes muttered something about original equipment.

Harper focused on the flat beds behind the Mercedes Benz cabs. He made out the outline of armored personnel carriers. The tracks were lost in the shadows and distance, but the distinctive silhouette of a Soviet light armor vehicle was something you never forgot—especially when you have spent time half frozen in a ditch watching them pass.

"Take it as far and as fast as you can."

"Why?" asked Hayes wondering if he really wanted an answer.

"Looks like they're bringing some BTR-60's to the party," replied Harper.

"Great," snarled Hayes as he pushed the accelerator to the floor.

★ ★ ★

Colonel Duri took a few short hops on his crutches. His wrist was splinted and a pressure cast had been applied to his injured leg. He had replaced his sidearm with one from the barracks in Nukhayb. The medic had pumped him full of saline solution and painkillers—enough to get him through the next twelve hours.

Twelve hours would determine whether he would return a hero to Baghdad, or if he would slither across the border into Saudi Arabia and disappear. Those were his only choices. There was a third outcome, but Duri preferred to put thoughts of the Salman Pak's experiment stations from his mind.

He hobbled to a command vehicle, and waited as the two tractor/trailers left the Nukhayb barracks each carrying an APC. The men to run those vehicles had been scratched together from the town's militia and they had been told they were off to hunt Americans. Duri knew most had served in the war, Saddam's requirements had not been strenuous all males over fifteen and under seventy who were still breathing. Not one of them had ever fired their rifles in anger during the Gulf War. Those who did were cut down immediately by American gun ships or buried under tons of sand when US Marine engineers bull-dozed the sand berms they cowered behind..

Vehicles found in places like Nukhayb, where parts and maintenance needs are long past the end of the supply line, rely on the durability of the factory equipment. The American satellites could count the number of trucks and tanks, and American planners could assess this as capability, but the dirty secret of Saddam's army was much of it was still wrecked.

Duri had Harper in a box. It was simply a matter of time until the elements from Ash-Shabakah crushed him against the convoy moving from Nukhayb. Harper had no hope of escape; Duri had a plan with real assets and real people. Perhaps he would survive this crisis and receive the excellent medical care reserved for those select few in Saddam's Iraq. The answer would come before dawn.

★ ★ ★

Jonas and Dylan lifted off in the *Puma* from Ad-Duwayd—one of the many dusty towns on the Saudi side of the border with Iraq. It was in these towns that the ground stations for the Joint Surveillance Target Attack Radar System (JSTARS) was located. They were in contact with Air Force E-8C radar planes running a high-resolution phased array doppler radar.

The E-8C was basically a remanufactured Boeing 707 that became the eyes and ears for JSTARS. JSTARS did for ground combat (in terms of target identification and acquisition) what AWACS did for air combat. AWACS and JSTARS form a powerful information system capable of transmitting real time battlefield digital images to any number of ground stations using a surveillance and control data link.

The ground stations could bounce the signal off microwave relay towers or overhead military communication satellites to anyone with a laptop rigged with the correct encryption and imaging software. The microprocessor and fiber optics had revolutionized warfare. The old adage *if you can see it, you can kill it* took on special meaning with the advent of virtual battlefield portrayed by digital images.

The satellite phone call Jonas made to Admiral Trevor Barnes, the operational commander for the Fifth Fleet, resulted in a compromise. The heighten tensions over the expulsion of UNSCOM weapons inspectors and increased military activity by both the Iraqis and the American armada moved Iraq and America towards war's brink. The fear of stumbling into another Gulf War produced orders straight from the National Command Authority to avoid any more territorial intrusion.

"You're on you own, son," reflected Barnes, "by the way, where are you?"

"You wouldn't want to know, Admiral," replied Jonas.

"I'll tell you what I'll do. Are you close to Ad-Duwayd or Al-Qaysumah?"

"Ad-Duwayd," he said quickly, sensing there was some help coming.

"Okay, we got a JSTARS ground station there. You land and fill up your tanks. I'll call ahead and make sure someone meets you with an encrypted laptop. You'll pick them up even if they're on bicycles."

"JSTARS—yeah that would work."

"I hope so, son, it's the best I can do."

★ ★ ★

They were lifting away from Ad-Duwayd and back toward the Southern Iraqi border. The *Puma* could search until close to dawn. If they were still searching by dawn, Dylan and Jonas knew it would be too late to save Harper. He flipped up the lid on the JSTARS laptop and established secure communications with the microwave tower standing in solitude somewhere in the desert behind them.

"What's the usual search pattern with this thing?"

"On this computer about one hundred square klicks."

Dylan sighed. They needed some luck.

Jonas thought for a moment, "Let's start at Nukhayb and see if the Iraqis know anything."

Dylan nodded. "Let's get started."

★ ★ ★

The truck jolted to an abrupt stop. The front axle snapped as the wheels slammed into a large, unmoving rocky outcropping. The engine stalled and steam erupted from the ancient radiator. Great, a marker for the Iraqi soldiers to start from, thought Harper.

Harper scrambled down from the cab of the broken truck. Anderson and Stillwell hopped down from the end of the truck. Stillwell stared at him holding his M-16. The dirt and grime of the day smeared across his features. He said, "You don't have to worry about me. I'm okay."

Hayes came around the end of the truck holding his own M-16.

Stillwell looked at the highway behind them. The tractor/trailers had come to a stop. "Sergeant, whatever happens. Thanks for saving my life today."

Anderson loaded a magazine of High Explosive Anti Tank rounds into the Barrett.

"Those things work?" asked Harper.

"Sort of," replied Anderson. "It's all I got left."

They were painfully short on ammunition.

"Those are BTR-60's up there. The Soviets made a zillion of the things. We can't outrun them, and I doubt we can outfight them. Those things will do fifty miles per hour on flat ground." He waved his hand at the crevasse and craggy ground they were standing on. "They may be slowed up by this, but not enough to help."

They were about two kilometers from the highway. Four BTR-60 armored personnel carriers with four eight-man rifle squads. Thirty-two fresh troops against four exhausted Americans. Harper did not like his odds.

"Captain Anderson is going to try out his HEAT rounds on those things. If I remember correctly, the armor is thinner on the sides. I'll provide overwatch for Captain Anderson. Hayes, it's your job to get Stillwell home." He picked up the canvas bag of tapes and tossed them to the Sergeant.

Stillwell watched the exchange. "You're coming with us, aren't you?"

Harper looked up at the highway again. One of the BTR-60 APC 's was rolling off the transport flatbed. "Lieutenant, in about ten minutes four vehicles with mounted machine guns and four squads with automatic weapons are going to descend on us. Let's be realistic." He looked up at the sky. "Help isn't coming. They bugged out on us." He pulled the other signal beacon from around his neck and punched the ON button.

"This signal beacon is as useful as the truck here," he said bitterly and tossed the beacon into the darkness. "Brian, this wasn't your fight. You were set up like the rest of us. You're not a warrior. Hayes and Anderson are." He nodded to the truck again. "Burns and Kincaid knew the score when they signed up. You didn't. Okay, I think there's something on those tapes. I mean there better be something on those tapes.

"In the next hour someone has to live and someone has to die." He pointed a finger at Stillwell. "You live. You get those tapes back home and make someone listen. I'm going to give you a fighting chance." He looked around to Hayes and Anderson. "It should have gone differently, I regret it is ending this way." He paused. "You have your orders."

Hayes and Anderson came to parade attention and saluted Harper smartly, Harper half grinned and returned the salute.

"Harper, we can all run now! You don't need to stay," exclaimed Stillwell.

"Lieutenant. It's over. Get going—have a good life.' He paused and said, "Sergeant—you two need to get home."

Hayes grabbed the bag, tapped Stillwell and started south.

"All right Captain, where do we go?" asked Harper.

★ ★ ★

Duri listened with satisfaction. They first group had found the Americans and forced them from the road. It was a matter of minutes now. They were thirty kilometers from the point on the map. Duri tapped the driver and indicated he should drive faster. Next, he checked his Makarov ensuring one 9x18mm round was loaded in the breach.

★ ★ ★

The insistent beeping from the other laptop finally got Dylan's attention. He tapped Jonas and pointed to the other computer sitting at his feet. Jonas stared dumbly for a few moments concentrating on the dark gray colored lid before he heard the alarm beep.

Jonas set the JSTARS laptop to one side and picked up his original machine. Flipping up the screen, he gasped. The second beacon had gone off. He punched up the commands to show him the coordinates according to the army sector maps being used by JSTARS. He keyed the displayed information into the JSTARS laptop and waited for a few moments as the image loaded off the relay tower.

Jonas ran the mouse up to eight targets that appeared to be stopped on the highway. He clicked one and a box emerged on the screen identifying it as a BTR-60. He clicked the others and said quickly through the radio headphones, "Dylan, we've got to get here," he said pointing to the screen.

"Fifteen minutes," replied the former SAS man.

"They don't have fifteen minutes," whispered Jonas. The blips on his screen were moving off the highway and to the south.

★ ★ ★

Harper loaded the last of his shotgun shells into the Mossberg. It had been a long day, he reflected. Somehow, he never imagined he would die in a nameless patch of desert. He pushed the thought from his mind. He was still alive, and while alive he could use the best weapon he had—his mind.

Anderson set up the Barrett on a ledge a few feet from him. They were a couple hundred meters from the truck. Not much use in getting too far away. It was Stillwell and Hayes who had to escape. Their chances of making it to Saudi territory were extraordinary low.

He settled down behind a rock and felt Lynn's Bible one last time. It was too dark to see their pictures or read anything. It was enough to feel her Bible. To know it was something she treasured. To understand that even in this terribly lonely place she was still with him. "I did my best," he whispered.

★ ★ ★

Dylan was following the road from Nukhayb towards Ash-Shabakah. He tapped Jonas on the shoulder and pointed at the truck convoy ahead. "You said they had BTR-60's?"

"Yeah." He glanced back at the screen in horror. The wheeled vehicles were racing away from the highway and spreading out into coverage.

"Those are BTR-60's down there."

Jonas thought for a moment. "More friends to the party?"

"You're learning. Right now we can take them out of the fight by smashing the tractor/trailer rigs." He pointed back to the custom-made chain gun belt system.

"Do it."

"You realize it's an act of war," commented Dylan.

"What would Harper do?"

Dylan chuckled, "He had this saying that he picked up at one of your gun shows—*Peace through superior firepower*."

"So lets be peaceful."

The *Puma* ran ahead of the convoy and spun violently. Dylan pulled the targeting lens over his right eye and engaged the shoot-and-see fire control system. The chain gun unlatched itself from its mount and trained itself on the picture displayed on Dylan's targeting lens.

He brought the *Puma* to hover twenty feet off the ground and pressed the trigger stud on his control stick. The chain gun ripped the darkness apart with 30 mm shells. The first tractor/trailer radiator and engine exploded pulling the rig sideways across the path of the other tractor/trailer. The second truck collided with an angry screech of metal on metal.

Dylan focused on the diesel tanks and pressed the stud a second time. Sparks, petroleum, and metal rolled over the highway pavement, eventually something caught fire, but Dylan did not wait to examine his handiwork. He turned the *Puma* away from the carnage and continued along the highway ribbon towards the location identified by Jonas.

★ ★ ★

The heavy machine guns mounted on the BTR-60's tore the truck apart. Two vehicles riddled the truck with mounted fire as they approached at a leisurely twenty klicks per hour. The other two vehicles ran quickly down the flanks forming up some five kilometers from the road before turning inwards on the box they had formed.

Unfortunately, someone knew what he was doing. Harper prepared for the inevitable as the two APC's came to a halt next to the truck. The side hatches pointing away from the truck body opened up. Incredibly, they thought someone could still be alive as they were using the APC as a shield between themselves and the truck.

Anderson needed no prompting to take advantage of the situation. He acquired the black opening through his night vision scope and gentle squeezed the trigger. The effectiveness of a HEAT round penetrating light armor when fired from a Barrett was questionable. However, the effectiveness of a HEAT round sailing through an open hatch was an entirely different situation.

The HEAT round first hit a soldier exiting the BTR-60. It punched him back through the hatch opening before a fireball erupted from inside the APC. Two other hatches blasted away from the front of the APC as ammunition and fuel exploded in a violent cook off.

The APC on the other side of the truck responded with a full barrage of automatic and machine gun fire. The rifle fire was panic driven and wild. Usually, this results in a waste of ammunition and a great deal of noise. Rarely is anyone hit unless they are stupid enough to fire their weapons straight up into the air. Tonight was the exception.

The ground around Harper and Anderson was pelted with rifle rounds. A burst of shells found Anderson lying prone. He never felt the impact of the bullets as the first one drove through the top of his skull and out the brain stem.

Harper hunkered down behind the rock as bullets walked across his position and then stopped. The frantic Arabic drifted over the desert night. The men from the second BTR-60 were checking on their comrades whom they had just shot through. Harper shrugged, the tactical commander might know what was suppose to happen, his troops were lacking in any fire discipline.

He turned to Anderson and whispered, "Let's move captain."

Anderson just lay there. Harper crawled across to the sniper and shook his shoulder only to smell the coppery blood scent and feel the stickiness on his fingers. "Oh no," whispered Harper with remorse.

★ ★ ★

Duri lifted his head from the dashboard he slammed into. He looked around for his driver only to find him with a broken neck on the seat beside him. He shook his head to clear his vision and found the crackling flames from the two tractor/trailers and BTR-60s. They were a mass of twisted, jagged metal burning on the roadway.

He spat the blood from between his teeth before pushing his dead driver on to the ground. He was unsure as to what had happened on the road to Ash-Shabakah, but it was obvious one component of the trap was gone. It could not have been Harper, but then who and what? The road simply exploded into a sheet of flame and metal.

He revved the jeep's engine and pulled along side the burning wreck. It was time to leave Iraq. The chances of cornering Harper were too iffy for his comfort. He would simply proceed to Ash-Shabakah and then head south across the Saudi border. It was his operation; he certainly could maintain control—at least until dawn.

★ ★ ★

Hayes peaked around a clump of dirt when he heard the heavy machine gun fire. The night was alive with red and orange fireballs. He looked back at the flanking BTR-60s. They were stationary while searching for them with night vision and infrared scopes. It was what he would do if their positions were reversed.

Stillwell moved even with Hayes and whispered, "Did they start World War Three?"

"Not sure, Lieutenant." He eyed the BTR-60s.

"If they come forward to respond to this, we move. Harper's making a big noise back there. He's trying to draw the flankers back," he explained referring to the two BTR-60's that had run long to form up the outer corners of the box.

Stillwell nodded. "Do you think he'll get out?"

Hayes shook his head. "Lieutenant, I'm not real sure *we're* going to get out."

☆ ☆ ☆

Harper grabbed the Barrett's muzzle and pulled it towards him. It was thirty pounds of weapon compared to the Mossberg's six and half pounds. He slung the Mossberg over his shoulder and rolled away from Anderson. The Barrett felt clumsy and unfamiliar in his hands.

Still, it was a weapon. He figured there would be a round chambered—fed from the magazine by the recoil. He had no time for safeties and hoped they had not reset themselves. He needed to convince the other BTR-60s to come back for him—to do that he needed to appear like a small army. He had nine HEAT rounds left in the Barrett.

He sidled down the slope and leaned the heavy weapon over a rock as a rest. He pulled the stock tight to his shoulder and found the gray green night vision world through the scope. He brought the cross hairs to rest on the forward hatch of the second BTR-60.

Harper figured Anderson had adjusted the elevation and drift for the distance. He grabbed the forend grip and held it tightly as he tightened pressure on the trigger. There was *whump* as the recoil bounced him back against the hillside. The barrel lifted upwards and then settled back down. Harper wondered briefly if his shoulder was still in one piece, then said to himself, "I need to get one of these."

The round pulled to one side finding the engine block of the truck rather than the center of the hatch. The truck exploded and flipped over on its side catching a couple of soldiers in its wake. Always the shooter, Harper looked at the cart wheeling truck and back to the Barrett, "Cool," he muttered. He picked up the heavy weapon and started moving again.

☆ ☆ ☆

Hayes tapped Stillwell and started moving south as the flanking BTR-60s reversed their course and turned towards the burning BTR-60.

Stillwell stared back at night where Harper was and said, "We can't leave him."

"Lieutenant, those are our orders. We follow orders in this army. Don't let him die for nothing!" snapped Hayes.

Stillwell nodded and started running behind Hayes.

★ ★ ★

Dylan Scott looked at the burning vehicles on the desert floor. Tracer fire was coming from the two flanking BTR-60s as they raced back to aid their fallen comrades. Dylan pulled the *Puma* around the burning wrecks. In the light scattered by the flames, some men were still crawling, but they were out of the fight.

"Where's Harper?"

Dylan shook his head sadly, "It looks like he shot his wad."

"What'd you mean?"

Dylan pointed to the two icons on the map screen representing the flanking BTR-60s. "He made a big noise to pull these fellows back to this point. It's got to be a diversion someone else can get away," explained Dylan. "It's working too. These boys look like their coming in a hurry. But for it to work, someone has to stay behind and keep their attention."

"So who's running?"

"Haven't the faintest idea. It's your team," replied Dylan.

★ ★ ★

Harper tossed the empty Barrett away. He crept down towards the burning vehicles and rolled a dead soldier over. There was a string of four grenades and AK-47 in his hands. Grenades would do nothing to the APC, but a big noise might keep their attention. The shotgun was pretty much useless, unless he intended to get inside the APC—an unlikely scenario.

He looked around the burning wrecks. There were people still alive, but they were moving in a stunned and feeble manner. Both APCs were burning, and half the enemy force was out of the action. Four grenades, an AK-47 and a few rounds left in a shotgun do not make good odds against two fully armed APCs.

He backed away from the fire hearing the mounted machine gun popping as they drew closer. There was no time to get several hundred meters away this time. He found a hole less than fifty meters away from the wrecks. It would be over soon, he concluded.

★ ★ ★

Dylan flipped the targeting lens back over his eye and said, "So we simply change the equation. Whoever did that has found himself a hidey-hole for the moment. It won't do him much good if the bad guys dismount, and they will."

The *Puma* reared up for a strafing run. It dove straight at the western flanking APC. The *Puma's* blades beat at the thinning air as a hint of dawn began to grace the horizon. Dylan found his target and pressed the firing stud. The BTR-60 was put in service in 1961 and retired in 1982. It was never designed to handle modern armor piercing ammunition.

The chain gun punched through the APC's top armor, and in some cases, exited through the floor. The first pass stitched a line of shells diagonally across the rectangular shape of the APC. The second pass sent a fusillade through the thinnest armor on the rear hatches. The APC spun sideways and stopped.

★ ★ ★

Hayes looked up at the odd sound on the battlefield. The pop of the automatic weapons and the bark of the machine guns had become commonplace, but something new was happening. It sounded like the chain gun from an *Apache*. There were no *Apache* Gun Ships. They never showed up at the Data Center.

He came to a stop. It was still too dark to see anything. The only machine gun fire he heard came from the east. The western flanker was silent.

"What is it?" asked Stillwell.

"I don't know. Something else is out here." He dropped to a knee.

"Good or bad?"

"Not sure." Even a drowning man clings to hope. Hayes wondered if they dare start hoping again.

★ ★ ★

Where were the flankers? Harper wondered impatiently. He poked his head up and cursed savagely. The flankers had stopped coming, and that could only mean they had another target. He was in no hurry to die, but the mission was to get Stillwell out of here.

He pulled a grenade off the belt he had acquired from the Iraqi. He pulled the pin, and hurtled the fragmentation grenade towards the dazed men next to their burning vehicles. He figured it would land short enough make a big noise, but really do little damage. He grabbed a second grenade and threw it at a thirty-degree angle from the first.

"Come on!" he yelled. What did it take to get someone to shoot at you these days?

After the third grenade exploded, the last BTR-60 roared over a ridge blasting away with its mounted machine gun. Harper barely had time to drop behind a rock. The heavy machinegun fire found the rocks he was behind. The Iraqi gunner never let up on the trigger. A green tracer round broke the darkness every tenth round as steady fire turned the rocks into powder. The gun barrel was starting to glow a dull red as the heat generated from continuous fire started to burn out the barrels.

Did death have to be so loud? he asked himself.

★ ★ ★

"There, did you see that?" asked Jonas pointing through the windscreen.

"Grenade flash," explained Dylan.

"It has to be Harper."

"He's drawing the other BTR-60 toward his position," observed Dylan.

"If he's tossing grenades, he must not have much left."

"He thinks they found his people!" snapped Dylan. "He's making himself a great big target."

The *Puma* leaped forward a final time. The chain gun exploded with a heavy burst ripping a jagged scar along the right side hatches. Brass was strewn around the inside of the passenger area. It was close to over.

☆ ☆ ☆

Duri drove past the battle. From the road, he could see the fireballs and smell the death. He had dispatched the transport drivers to the wreckage between here and Nukhayb. His time was over. Best not linger over a failure and find the chambers in Salman Pak. The last thing he wanted was to become one of Doctor Germ's subjects.

He continued towards Ash-Shabakah. Dawn was approaching too fast for his comfort.

☆ ☆ ☆

The terrible clatter of guns ceased. The crackling of flames broke the hollow silence, but after the thundering sounds of battle, Harper heard nothing but a painful drumming in his ears. He had nowhere to run. He half lay in a ditch behind a rock that was considerably smaller than when the BTR-60 started shooting at it.

He pulled the AK-47 to his chest and rolled to one side. The BTR-60 was stopped. Smoke drifted from the right side hatches. How did that happen? He crab crawled sideways to another ditch and looked towards the burning wrecks. A ragged line of soldiers was staggering towards the last BTR-60. Their weapons held at ready.

Where was the last BTR-60? And, what killed this one? He took the last grenade and tossed it towards the center of their line. These soldiers could not have much more fight in them.

A bullet *zinged* by his head. Harper dropped again to the dirt wondering where this one came from. He felt the scream before he heard it. Twisting around on his back and pulling the trigger on the AK-47 he cut the soldier diving towards him in two. Blood, bone, and gore splattered everywhere. The dead man landed heavily next to him—not much of a secret where he was now.

He dropped the empty AK-47 and pulled his Glock from its holster. Save the shotgun for a little more distance, he figured, or maybe he just wanted to feel the Glock in his hand one last time.

He steadied his hands on a rock. They were trembling badly now. The day had caught the last of his strength reserves. The sight picture continued to quiver in and out of focus. A bullet slammed into the Kevlar helmet and sent it spinning into the night.

He pulled the trigger on the Glock. Then the night exploded in thunder and fire for a final time. The heavy downdraft from the *Puma* spun sand and gravel about in a sweeping vortex. His thoughts muddy now as he kept firing the Glock to no effect. The chain gun pulverized the line of soldiers coming toward him, just before the *Puma* landed.

★ ★ ★

Jonas dropped out of the *Puma* and ran across the uneven ground towards Harper. He knelt next to the older man and saw blood running down the side of his face. There was blood everywhere, but Jonas was not sure if it all belonged to Harper.

A muddy, bloody hand grabbed Jonas by the side of his shirt and pulled him close. The strength of his grip was surprisingly strong. "You're not a dream are you?"

Jonas shook his head.

"Where you been?" he asked. His lips cracked. The last of his strength ebbed away.

"Problems Jim—we had problems."

"Find Hayes and Stillwell—they're out there."

"Is that what this is about?" asked Jonas looking at feast for vultures and jackals.

"Yes. They've got the tapes."

"Tapes?"

"Data Center tapes. We got everything." Then he slipped to unconsciousness.

Jonas grabbed the Glock and pulled Harper over his shoulder. He half carried and half dragged the larger man to the *Puma*.

"Anyone else?" asked Dylan.

"Hayes and Stillwell," replied Jonas.

"Okay, we'll find them." Dylan looked at the limp form. "Is he dead?"

Jonas shook his head. "He's out of gas."

☆ ☆ ☆

Dawn broke across the desert. Colonel Taha Duri drove across the border bouncing every other second and feeling his battered body scream in protest. He left the highway before reaching Rafha on the Iraqi side of the border and pointed the jeep towards Lawqah on the Saudi side. He would tell them that he was a prisoner who had just escaped a terrible place where nightmares were hatched.

He had thought for many hours what kind of lies he would tell the Saudi officials once he left Iraq. It would be best to be gone from the area before Valentine's Day. The Great Leader still expected his missiles to fly.

35

Dulles International Airport, Wednesday, November 19, 1997, 10:00 AM

Jonas Benjamin looked out the window of the *Gulfstream IV* jet as she pulled around the familiar fields and landmarks near Dulles International Airport. He muffled a yawn with his hand and looked at what he had: sets of computer backup tapes and a technical list from Harper explaining how they should be restored. A three-hour videotape debriefing session with Hayes and Stillwell describing what had happened and what went wrong. An additional two hours of tape with Harper explaining his decisions, secret orders, and evidence of an outright sellout.

A Navy Medic had taped his head up. Scalp wounds do not have to be deep to bleed copiously. When Harper lost his helmet the bullet had been deflected enough to tear a three-inch long gash over his left ear. Until his hair grew back, he would look like an extra from *The Last of the Mohicans*.

Jonas also had a report of three American Marines killed in action, bodies not retrieved, a fifty percent casualty rate. Jonas shook his head. Last Saturday the mission seemed so antiseptic. The orders were printed on white bonded paper, the men assembled, and equipment procured. Satellite photographs showed the target's location, a simple bunker surround by rock and sand. There was no evidence of a reaction force, yet according to the survivors, they showed up in helicopters with RAF markings.

A reaction force based on deception and only crippled because the Iraqis were a day behind on their passwords. *A day behind*—it would certainly get the attention of those responsible for secure communications. He wondered who else might be listening in on encrypted systems.

The world press had dutifully reported the incident involving the American fighter and ground targets earlier this week. No one reported the helicopters were British *Sea Kings*, or the missile fired at the *Hornet* was of a type previously unknown to exist in Saddam's arsenal. The three rifle platoons ferried on those helicopters remained unknown to the Western press, and the fact that half of them had perished during the brief air battle.

Unrelated reports indicated an unusual fish kill in the Southern Gulf region. No one had associated this with the missing *Han* class submarine, and besides a limited number of American Officers, enlisted men, and those in the information loop—that underwater battle remained a secret. The possible pollution from the shattered nuclear core would be watched carefully, and probably two additional submarines would be tasked to clean up the mess before anyone investigated the problem.

A much smaller group knew about the intact cask retrieved from the hold of the submarine. The cask was already in a level four biohazard lab at Fort Dietrick, Maryland. The suspicion was that this was an intact sample of the *City Killer* VX variation. At present, there are no known protocols to deal with VX Beta.

Sergeant Darby Hayes had spent his time asleep while crossing the desert and ocean. A shower, some chow, and a new set of fatigues gave Darby a new outlook on life. He ate two more meals between naps and drank a great deal of water. He lay with his hands crossed and his head against a folded pillow. The change in engine whine caused his eyes to flutter open and check his surroundings.

Brian Stillwell, the civilian analyst, sudden soldier, and civilian again, gave up trying to stay awake shortly after they left England behind. He slept a troubled and fitful sleep. Twice he had cried out and mumbled to himself. There were things he had seen and done that he found difficult to explain during the debriefing. The one thing that was obvious, he never should have been sent along on the mission.

Jim Harper spent the first part of the trip working on his weapons. He had requested some Shooter's Choice solvent, cleaning patches, brass brushes, jags, and cleaning rods. He worked the finished metal of the handguns mercilessly until the stainless steel barrel from the Browning gleamed in the subdued light. He seemed to be attempting to eradicate all traces of the desert from anything he held precious. He pulled the Mossberg apart and blasted compressed air in the cracks driving sand particles out onto the carpet. Next he cleaned his dagger and combat knives. Jonas could not help but notice the flakes of dried blood as he dropped the used cotton patches into a barf bag.

Harper was dressed in a new pair of denim slacks and a dark blue tee shirt with the *George Washington's* insignia embroidered on his left breast. The Glock was still holstered along his right hip, and Jonas knew the Browning Hi Power was cocked and locked in a second holster located on the small of his back. The Mossberg lay in a case at his feet. The combat dagger slung inside the upper lip of his new boots.

Jonas felt the wheels touchdown on the tarmac. The long ride home was almost over. He flipped the seat belt loose and gathered his videotapes, camera equipment, laptop, and data tapes together. The *Gulfstream* did not aim for the normal customs area; instead, it followed a ground cart towards a restricted hanger.

Hayes snapped his eyes open and looked across the aisle to Harper. The older man nodded slightly. They stood up one after the other and Darby retrieved his Beretta M9, racking the slide as he slid it into the oversized leg pocket. Harper followed Stillwell and Jonas down the steps and into larger hanger. The doors were already closing. Harper focused on Louis Edwards.

Louis stood with his feet spread shoulder width and his hands folded at his waist. Mister Smith and Mister Jones were flankers on either side of Louis. There was no pretense here. Each held a Glock 19 with silencers screwed on a threaded barrel in their hands. They wore mirrored glasses effectively hiding their eyes and denying anyone from knowing where they were focused for the moment.

Stillwell noted the weapons as well and stopped. He turned back to Harper as if to ask a question, only to get a shake of the head. Stillwell turned back to Edwards who smiled, "Welcome back, Mister Stillwell." He glanced at Jonas, "Jonas, I hope all is well with you."

Jonas nodded and stepped sideways.

Harper came to a halt twenty paces from Louis. A twenty-yard shot from a standing crouch with the Glock 21 was about a one and a half inch group. Hayes stepped away from Harper and to a steady aim point on Mister Jones who was standing across from him. A twenty-five yard shot with a 9mm. Not as accurate as .45 ACP, but certainly doable.

Louis looked to Harper. The two men measured each other. Harper waited.

"Jim," Edwards sighed. "It's good to see you alive."

Harper remained silent wondering if he would kill again today.

Edwards nodded and folded his top lip over his bottom. "Your fight is not with me or my men, Jim." He pulled a bulky envelope from his suit coat. "The man you want is described in here."

"It looks like you've taken up body armor as a fashion statement, Louis."

"Jim, I know you lost three men in the desert."

Harper let his hand come to rest on the Glock's grip. Smith and Jones tensed. They failed to see Hayes slip his hand inside his pants pockets and get a grip on his Beretta.

"Three men died. Louis, did you know their names? Captains Burns, Kincaid, and Anderson got shot up, because the Iraqis knew more about our mission orders than we did," he snarled examining the concrete. "How's that possible that an Iraqi Colonel would know the name of my wife and daughters? They knew everything about us. They had to have the orders almost faster than we got them. How's that possible?" Harper growled.

Louis motioned Jonas to come and get the envelope. "The man detailed in this envelope had access to all information related to this operation and additional information not directly related to your mission." He handed the envelope to Jonas, before continuing. "He is an aide to the National Security Advisor, and quite likely this mission was compromised before you even left Andrews on Saturday.

"You are correct. They knew everything, Jim. This is the first time this administration used our organization to perform any mission. In one shot, they managed to compromise this operation and our existence to hostile governments. This is not the sort of thing we'd like appearing in the *Washington Post*."

"Meaning?" snapped Harper.

"I'd like you to take care of it."

Jonas walked across the hanger floor and handed the envelope to Harper. Harper popped the wax seal and pulled out a set of papers. He rifled through them quickly. "Isn't somebody going to miss this Arthur fellow?"

"There's a phone number."

Harper nodded, "An FBI agent?"

"A tame one, Jim. He'll take care of any messiness left behind. You have to trust me."

Harper snapped an angry look back to Louis. "*Trust*?" He pointed the envelope at his bodyguards. "Do you think your two goons can stop me? Three men died and you hand me the answer wrapped up in this tidy little envelope."

"It was hardly tidy," explained Louis. "The keys, you will note, are for the Ford Explorer over there."

"Complete with a homing device?" snarled Harper.

"There's no need to follow you. I know where you're going and I know what you're going to do." He pointed to the bag of tapes on the floor next to Jonas. "Those tapes hold the answer. I'll find it. You've done your job."

Harper let the envelope slide back to his side. "If you've lied to me this time, Louis—you'd better find a hole and pull it in after you."

"I understand, Jim."

Harper turned and gathered his cased shotgun to his hands. Stillwell said quickly, "Was that the same guy that briefed me?"

"Indeed it was, Mister Stillwell," replied Louis.

"I want to come along," he said quickly.

Harper stopped and turned, "No, you don't."

"I came this far."

Hayes laid a hand on Stillwell's shoulder. "Let it go Lieutenant," he said softly.

Stillwell turned to Hayes. "But I want—"

Hayes shook his head. "Go back to your world Lieutenant. This isn't your world. The major here, the reason he did what he did in the desert was because he knew his world was not your world. You're a civilian, Sir. The major is something else. Something we need to protect this country, but it isn't always pretty."

Stillwell turned back to Harper who smiled. "Brian, this is not something you want to do."

Stillwell relaxed as the two men walked away. He turned back to Louis. "Mister Stillwell, can we drop you somewhere?"

Stillwell nodded dumbly.

Louis snapped his fingers and Mister Smith came to guide Brian Stillwell away from *Gulfstream*. Jonas followed them out holding the canvas bag with the dried blood soaked into its side. He hoped the bag held the answer; the cost had been very high.

★ ★ ★

It was dark by the time Arthur reached his condominium. It had been another long day of guiding an inept administration through a foreign policy morass as they traded barbs with Saddam Hussein. It accomplished nothing positive to elevate the stature of a tinhorn dictator to the same level as the Presidency. However, this President and the sycophant advisors thought nothing of peddling the Presidency away.

The prestige and power of the Oval Office went to the biggest campaign contribution no matter where it came from and no matter what the cost. As long as they did not seem to care about what was happening to the country, then why should Arthur care? He would need to move some funds around tonight. The Chinese would pay big money for the details on the sinking of their submarine.

He would set up a drop using the new email account they had established since last week. The details were in his brief case. *Two hundred thousand dollars in less than a week!* He would check his totals and figure out if there was enough to retire on yet. The Cayman Islands were lovely this time of year.

He whistled as the elevator doors opened on his floor. The UNSCOM problem should be cleaned up by the end of the week. Of course, UNSCOM was a sham. The UN threatened to inspect weapon facilities, and Saddam promised to let them inspect. It had become a huge shell game and the Iraqis were winning. Everyone knew the truth except the American public. The White House media machine would ensure they remained ignorant.

He walked through his door and flipped on the light as he let the door close behind him. The light was burned out. No problem, he could find his way to the living room. It was then he sensed he was not alone. A second later he felt the muzzle of a gun jam into his neck.

A light flipped on and he stared into the familiar face. His eyes focused more closely on the seven-inch combat knife in the man's hand.

Harper nodded to Hayes who arm barred Arthur over to a couch and set him down roughly. A pair of zip cuffs materialized and he felt his hands roughly pulled behind his back. The thin plastic strip cut into the flesh around his wrists.

"Recognize me?" asked Harper.

Arthur squinted. He looked to the other man, but the lights were wrong. He could not make out the features.

A grayish white raincoat landed on the floor between them. A photograph was shoved in Arthur's face. "Looks like the same coat to me. See the way the stitching works along the back of the collar?" It was the photograph from Harvey Randall's surveillance films. All they had was a raincoat, not a face.

"That's not me!" he whispered.

Harper nodded.

"I spent some time on your computer this afternoon. I suppose these accounts in the Cayman Islands, Switzerland, and Brazil aren't yours either." Harper waved an Quicken account report in his face.

"You've got an interesting set of emails on your system too."

Arthur eyes grew wider. "But I deleted those files," he blurted.

"Yeah, but you never emptied your recycle bin. Besides, you have a well-written email program. It keeps back ups of everything you've ever written. That's because computer jocks like me don't trust the blasted things to work right, so we protect ourselves by making archive logs. You bought good software and someone wrote archives out there. All you have to do is bring them back at the click of a button—works real good," explained Harper.

Arthur stared at the denim-clad man and noticed the holster on his belt. What did they want? Why had they not read him his rights? Who were they?

"Figure it out yet?" asked Harper.

Arthur knew the face, but where had he seen it? He would remember an imposing man like this. It had been recent, but where?

"He's not so smart is he, Major?" said the man behind him.

"They're never very smart when their string runs out," replied Harper. He pulled the briefcase across the couch and popped the latches.

"You're the guy we sent to Iraq," he spluttered as if he had been underwater for a long time.

Harper smiled, "Very good."

"And you're the guy who told the Iraqis all about us," said Hayes.

Harper pulled a slim folder from the briefcase and flipped it open. He looked at the maps and read the FLASH messages from the *Springfield* to the *George Washington*. He shook his head not believing his eyes.

"Sergeant?"

"Sir."

"Did you know we sank a Chinese submarine?"

Hayes narrowed his eyes, "No, Sir."

Harper waved the file under Arthur's nose. "Sending notes home tonight?"

"Ah, I can explain that."

Harper dropped the file back into the briefcase and closed the top. "I doubt it."

"Look I have plenty of money. Maybe we could make a deal," Arthur said quickly.

"You want his money, Sergeant?"

Hayes back fisted Arthur on the ear and shook his head, "I don't want any blood money, Sir."

Harper nodded and said, "Blood money. Do you know what that means?"

Arthur saw the knife had become prominent again. He shook his head slowly.

"Aren't you going to read me my rights?" he asked hurriedly.

"No," replied Harper.

"But I'm an American citizen—I'm entitled—"

Harper leaped forward and palm healed Arthur in his nose. There was a red splat as the bridge of his nose collapsed. Hayes clamped a strong hand over Arthur's mouth and the scream became muffled moan.

Blood, mucus, and tears streamed down his cheeks and lips. Harper waited until his breathing returned to normal.

"You broke my nose," whined Arthur.

Harper nodded, "Yeah, I did."

Arthur reassessed the menace sitting calmly on the other living room chair. Something else was going on here. Something he did not quite connect.

"You don't have any more rights. You're not going to prison," explained Harper.

"Then where am I going?" he asked.

Harper stood up and walked around the room. "Do you even know what you did?"

Arthur stared at Harper and shook his head.

"You got a hold of our Q files. You remember that?" Harper asked, then added, "Don't lie to me."

Arthur nodded.

Harper walked around the room and pulled out a CamCorder on a tripod. He flipped it on and made sure the automatic focus was working.

"I want you to tell this machine everything you've done."

"Or what?" demanded Arthur.

"Or I'll hurt you." He played with the black bladed knife. Harper reached down and flipped on the RECORD button.

What followed was a rambling explanation and sometime defense of Arthur's actions over the last ten years. He hit the big time about three years ago when he was promoted to aid status on the National Security Council. The vetting of staff was so pathetic after three years of obfuscation and obstruction, no one bothered with a career researcher.

Once inside the NSC, Arthur gained access to several secret memos, faxes, and orders. As the quality of his product increased, so did his compensation. Eventually, he was handed off from one case officer to another, until his control was the senior Chinese spook. Arthur was getting a cool hundred thousand dollars for each item now.

From offshore accounts, Arthur turned around and invested the money in mutual fund accounts to take advantage of the booming American stock market. Arthur was a very wealthy young man.

Harper flipped off the recorder. "So when were you going to retire?"

"Soon," he admitted.

"I suppose it doesn't mean anything that your little message to Beijing got three men killed and nearly got the Sergeant and myself permanent residency in Iraq?"

Arthur shook his head.

Hayes smacked Arthur along the back of the head, "The Major's talking to you."

Arthur cringed and looked up, "I didn't understand that aspect of it."

"You think selling secrets to the Chinese and whoever they shared the information with is just okay?"

"They're all doing it!" he protested in defense.

"That makes it right?" snapped Harper.

Arthur struggled at his bonds. "Look I didn't want anyone to get hurt, I just—"

"You just wanted the extra cash?" asked Harper. He felt the silencer in his left hand and held it tightly.

"I wanted to hurt the fools running this country," he said limply.

"Six of us went to Iraq. Three of us came home. The other three became food for the vultures. Not even a decent burial," explained Harper.

"It was an accident," he said quickly.

"Accident?' Harper asked cocking an eyebrow. "What was the accident? You giving the Chinese the information, or the Chinese passing it along, or the forty five guys who showed up to kill us?"

"I didn't do that—someone else—" he blubbered.

"No, you did it. You dishonored the oath you took as an intelligence officer. You betrayed the people who hired you. Now you want honor. You want the rights and privileges afforded an honorable man?"

He nodded.

Harper pulled the silencer from his pocket and sheathed his knife. He reached behind his back and pulled the Browning from its holster.

"No, no we can work this out."

Harper shook his head. "You're no better than a mass murderer. The only difference is you don't do the dirty work. Others do it for you. You don't have the stomach to see what happens after you pass along your information. I could have done my job, and I didn't have to kill so many people in the field. You made that impossible. You see, I really hate killing people. But people like you sit in your fancy offices and play little word games with real life people."

"I never meant—" His words choked off as Hayes drove his Kabar combat knife through the back of Arthur's neck and out the front of his throat. Hayes jerked the knife back and forth, then stepped back as Arthur flopped to the floor and twitched a couple of times.

Hayes looked across the room and said quietly, "They were my Captains, Sir."

Harper looked down at the dead man on the floor. "Yes, they were Sergeant." He felt the blackness of his life swallow him up again. He shivered involuntarily, and said slowly, "I'll fix the answering machine."

Hayes hit the rewind button on the CamCorder and wiped his knife on the beige couch.

★ ★ ★

Harvey Randall's pager buzzed in his pocket. He shook his head and flipped off David Letterman with the remote control. He pulled the Motorola pager to his face and stared at the number. It was not one he was familiar with, but he stretched and padded across the apartment to his cordless phone.

He punched in the number and heard the line ring three times, before it picked up with a recording machine. The phone machine announced, "Agent Randall, a mutual acquaintance suggested I contact you regarding the contents of a certain hard disk. I'm certain you can figure out the location of this address from the phone number, caller ID is such a wonderful feature these days. Oh, and the briefcase should be returned to our mutual acquaintance." The shrill beep from the machine sounded and Harvey fumbled hanging up the phone.

He was wide-awake now.

✯ ✯ ✯

Harper stepped out of the phone booth and got back into the Explorer. He looked across to Hayes and asked, "Can I drop you somewhere?"

Hayes shrugged, "I think I'll just get out and walk. It's been a long night."

Harper nodded understanding. He stuck out a hand and said, "If you're ever in Chicago, look me up."

"Yes, Sir. I think I will." He shook Harper's hand and stepped out on the curb.

Harper started the long drive home. He felt the hollowness inside that came at the end of a mission. There would be some nightmares, regrets, and guilt. He checked the rear view mirror and saw Darby Hayes standing solitary on the curbside. Hands in his pockets, Hayes stepped off into the darkness and vanished into the night's black pool.

Harper hoped it was worth the price. A price measured in blood and honor.

EPILOGUE

White House

Louis Edwards watched the National Security Advisor read the report. This time there was no aide to observe the conversation. His former aide vanished a couple of weeks ago. No resignation letter, and really no trace. Not that anyone would ever find Arthur. He was feeding the fish several hundred miles off shore.

They had learned a great deal from what Harvey found at the condominium, bank records, email accounts, a pattern of deceit stretching back ten years. A video taped confession waited for the FBI when they arrived, and a complete run down on the sinking of the Chinese submarine—evidence of a crime, but nothing that would stand up in court.

Mister Smith and Mister Jones had handled the clean up duties. Within a week, Arthur ceased to exist. They recovered over three million dollars in stocks, mutual funds and other assets. The wonders of electronic bank transfers and the correct numbers and passwords deposited everything into accounts control by Louis Edwards and George Carnady.

The National Security Advisor closed the report and pushed it away. It was something filthy and evil. Something no one wanted to face.

"This came off the database tapes?"

"Yes, Sir." Louis pointed to the red folder marked ULTRA and said quietly, "You see the report from Fort Dietrick. They're quite concerned about the permanent effects of VX Beta. We have satellite imagery over China showing it to still be fatal to unprotected personnel five years after the initial application.

"There is the target list we found on the system. They're targeting most major cities within range of the missiles and our carriers."

"You're recommending a strike on the Salman Pak Weapons Lab."

Louis nodded. "We have the exact location and we have slaved two satellites plus an additional U2 flight to the area. It is obvious from the Data Center tapes there is a series of hidden bunkers in this area. Now that we know where to look for some of this stuff."

"I'll need to think about this. The timing and everything," the NSA said dismissing Louis with a wave.

Louis remained seated.

"Is there something else?" he asked irritated by the spook.

"I really must insist on an immediate military strike."

A frown turned to a scowl and blossomed into a murderous glare. "Do you know who you're talking to?"

Louis pulled a second folder from his briefcase and set it on the NSA's desk.

The NSA stared at the folder like it was a venomous snake. He pointed at the folder and demanded, "What's this?"

"A transcript of Arthur's confession," replied Louis.

The blood seemed to drain from his face, "A what?"

"Arthur—you remember the nosey fellow who worked for you up to a few weeks ago and then disappeared," explained Louis.

The NSA nodded.

"That's his confession to espionage. I don't think it would go along with the Christmas spirit to report in the *Washington Post* a story where six men went into Iraq and three of them never came back, because an improperly vetted NSC staff member leaked to the Chinese who sent it to the Iraqis. Taking illegal campaign contributions is one thing—and you folks have learned how to spin those stories. However, abandoning American soldiers in the desert might be a little harder to explain, especially when I produce family and friends."

"You wouldn't," whispered the NSA.

Louis leaned forward and pulled the yellow folder back. He produced a blue folder and flipped it open. "These are mission orders for the six F-117A *Nighthawk* fighter-bombers based in Al Jabar Air Base in Kuwait. You simply need to get the right signatures. The crews have been briefed and have run the simulators for the mission. They just need presidential authorization," explained Louis.

"I can't just go and get—"

Louis shook his head and replied evenly, "Sir, you didn't have any trouble cutting off extraction orders for my team when it went to Iraq. You didn't have any trouble covering up the mess with the Chinese sub. You have twenty-four hours to get this mission off the ground, otherwise, this story will hit the wires."

Louis gathered his things and stood.

"I won't forget this Edwards."

Louis examined the NSA as if he were so much refuse to be avoided and said, "I should think not."

★ ★ ★

Some fifteen hours later six *Nighthawks* delivered their ordinance of SMART weapons. The bombs glided down airshafts, ran along tunnels and punched through steel doors. Bomb damage assessment indicated Saddam's known stores of VX Beta had burned up in the raid. Perhaps the raid was successful, for no missiles flew next February.

Afterword

I want to thank Sharon and Randy Mueller, Brian St. George, Sharon Baer, my mom Lu De Bono, and my lovely wife, Cathy, all of who gave me comments and encouragement on *Point Of Honor*, and special thanks to my relentless editor, Gail Abel. All inaccuracies with regard to historical and technical data are mine alone.

Point Of Honor was the first book written in the Jim Harper series, however, it was not the first book published. By the time this manuscript makes it to publication, I have had two additional projects to understand and develop the characters. Therefore, before bringing this book to market, I went back and examined the characters to make sure they reflected the people they have become in the later manuscripts of *Blood Covenant* and *Reap the Whirlwind*. As always, my first goal is to entertain; my second goal is to make you think.

Point Of Honor is based on real world events that took place in November 1997. Doctor Rihab Rashida al-Awazi, called *Dr. Germ* by western intelligence agencies, is one of Iraq's chief chemical weapons designers. Salmon Pak is an actual location somewhere south of Baghdad where chemical and biological agents are administered to prisoners. VX gas is a chemical weapon found in several arsenals around the world including Iraq. Much has been made of the Anthrax threat, of which Iraq has a plentiful supply, however, VX is a far deadlier chemical agent. Iraq did expel the UNSCOM weapon' inspectors during the week *Point Of Honor* covers.

The *George Washington* and *Nimitz* carrier task forces were present in the Persian Gulf during November 1997, although I may have fudged slightly on the *George Washington's* deployment. The deployment of the *Springfield* and other attack boats is fictional. However, American carriers never leave home without one or two attack boats somewhere in the neighborhood.

The PLAN has five *Han* Class boats numbered *401* to *405*. The 1994 incident between the *Kitty Hawk* and the Chinese Navy took place. The *401* was retired due to radiation problems. The concept of turning the *404* into a delivery truck is fictional. China is attempting to build a blue water navy to challenge American interests in the Pacific. It is folly to ignore this burgeoning threat.

Aldrich Ames was one of the most devastating KGB agents ever uncovered. His treachery certainly sent several hundred people to their deaths. The espionage envisioned between China and the United States is fictionalized. In my opinion, China will continue to be a threat.

There is a karate school more or less, where it was placed in Chapter 2. While I do not train there, those folks know their stuff. Finally, there is a big, black dog named *Indiana Jones*.

I want to thank the many people who have encouraged me with their letters and comments. You will never know how much a writer needs to hear these things.

Minnetonka, Minnesota October 1998
www.pointofhonor.com

About the Author

Douglas De Bono is a database administrator and designer in the Minneapolis/St Paul area. He runs his own consulting company called Systems Consulting, Inc. Doug makes his home with his wife Cathy and their three children Amanda, Ben and Amy. His writing stems from a lifelong interest in military and political affairs, and his goal is to make the reader wonder where the facts leave off and the fiction begins. Doug is a graduate of Carleton College (1978). He currently holds a second degree black belt, and he is an avid shooter.

His previous novel is *Blood Covenant*, and he is currently working on *Reap the Whirlwind*

9 780595 097241